The Disengagement Ring

Clodagh Murphy was born in Dublin. She moved to London in the 1980s and lived there for several years. She currently lives in Dublin with her beloved laptop. She is an aunt to five nephews and one niece. *The Disengagement Ring* is her first novel.

CLODAGH MURPHY

THE

DISENGAGEMENT

RING

HACHETTE
BOOKS
IRELAND

First published in 2009 by Hachette Books Ireland
A division of Hachette UK Ltd

1

A CIP catalogue record for this title is available from the British Library.

ISBN 978 0 340 91902 6

Typeset in Sabon and Garamond by Hachette Books Ireland
Printed and bound in Great Britain by Mackays, Chatham ME5 8TD

Hachette Books Ireland policy is to use papers that are natural, renewable and
recyclable products and made from wood grown in sustainable forests. The
logging and manufacturing processes are expected to conform to the
environmental regulations of the country of origin.

Hachette Books Ireland
8 Castlecourt Centre
Castleknock
Dublin 15, Ireland

www.hbgi.ie

A division of Hachette UK Ltd.
338 Euston Road,
London NW1 3BH

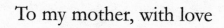

To my mother, with love

Chapter 1

The sun poured in through the high stained-glass windows of St Jude's, throwing multicoloured patterns on the polished wooden floor and on Kate O'Neill's dress as she floated down the aisle on a cloud of silk to the strains of 'The Bridal March'. She felt weightless, as though she were floating above the ground, her father's arm the only thing anchoring her to the earth and preventing her flying up to the ceiling like a helium balloon. On both sides heads spun to watch her pass, and she exulted in the admiring looks and the gasps of delight as she wafted by. She had never felt so beautiful or powerful in her whole life.

It's true what they say, she thought, this really is the happiest day of your life.

She acknowledged the smiles and good wishes of her family and friends as she moved towards the broad shoulders and bent dark head of the tall figure waiting for her at the altar. She was touched to see Johnny Depp among the guests, smiling bravely at her while he received consoling pats on the shoulder from her relations – poor darling Johnny, whose heart she had so cruelly broken. She felt the spark between them as his dark eyes met hers, and she experienced a moment of panic. Was she mad to have thrown him over for—

Just then, when she was within a foot of the altar, the dark head lifted and turned towards her. She felt Will's smile like a physical caress – a smile of such tenderness and warmth that it banished all doubt. As he took her hand, gazing adoringly into her eyes, she knew everything was exactly as it should be. She had never been so sure of anything in her life . . .

BEEP! BEEP! BEEP!

'Holy shit!' Kate shot upright in bed and hit the button on the alarm clock. She checked the time – eight o'clock – and collapsed back against the pillows. Still disoriented from her dream, she struggled to remember where she was and what day it was. The sun was pouring through the window, and she took in the posters of Brad Pitt, Johnny Depp and Leonardo DiCaprio that papered the walls, the dressing table covered with cheap make-up and perfume, the wardrobes bulging with teenage clothes. It was her old bedroom in her parents' house. And, looming over it, the dreaded dress was hanging on the cheval mirror. The big day had arrived, and at two o'clock she would have to walk down the aisle of St Jude's in it to the strains of 'The Bridal March', just like in her dream – except that now she was awake it felt more like a nightmare.

She smiled at the image of Johnny Depp, smouldering enigmatically at her from the wall, oozing cool. No prizes for guessing why *you* turned up in my dream, she thought. But why on earth had she been dreaming about Will Sargent? Okay, so she would be walking down the aisle today while the organist played 'The Bridal March' and Will would be standing at the altar rail – but she wouldn't be the bride, and he wouldn't be the groom. She didn't even think about him that way any more . . . did she? She'd got over her stupid teenage crush on him years ago, so why was she suddenly dreaming about marrying him? It was very unsettling.

Hearing signs of life downstairs, she knew she couldn't put off getting up any longer. Rachel's big day was kicking off with a family breakfast, and she was under strict instructions to attend.

2

'In real life I would have picked you,' she told Johnny Depp, as she threw back the covers and got out of bed.

The evidence of last night's down-to-the-wire arrival from the airport was all over the room, and a rucksack full of dirty clothes spewed its contents onto the floor where she had raked through it last night to find her toothbrush. She hopped around the room, avoiding duty-free bags and tripping over carved Masai warriors as she gathered up shampoo, conditioner, soap and deodorant, then headed for the shower.

Oh Christ! she suddenly thought. Knickers! She didn't have a single clean pair, or a bra for that matter. Rather than ask Rachel to lend her some, she rummaged through her bags for her mobile phone and dialled her flatmate Freddie.

Feeling more human after breakfast and a shower, Kate stood in front of her bedroom mirror and examined her naked body. It had taken two rounds of conditioner to get the knots out of her hair, but she was scrubbing up like a regular Eliza Doolittle. She had a fantastic tan, and, best of all, the trip had done wonders for her figure. She had spent the past three months working as a cook on an overland expedition in Africa, travelling from Kampala to Cape Town. It had been hard work, physically demanding and often exhausting to the point of tears, but she had loved every minute of it. And it had certainly paid off, she thought, looking over her shoulder at her bum and thighs, which she reckoned were about half the size they used to be. And she had a waist!

She caught sight of the dress again, and her spirits sank. It seemed such a waste – she had lost all this weight and now she had to cover herself up in that great balloon. Well, she thought, pulling it off its hanger, might as well know the worst.

As she slipped it on, the raw silk felt cold and deliciously sexy against her skin. She felt her nipples harden as she pulled it over her shoulders. She stood back and surveyed herself in the mirror, pulling a face. How was she supposed to face her teenage crush looking like this?

'Freddie's on his way up, love,' her father shouted, from the bottom of the stairs.

A second later, there was a rap on the bedroom door. 'Are you decent?' he called, bouncing in without waiting for an answer.

'Freddie!' Kate squealed, spinning around from the mirror and rushing across the room to throw herself into his arms. 'I missed you,' she said as he hugged her. He gave the best bear-hug of anyone she knew.

'Me too.' He smiled down at her. 'So, how was Africa?'

'Brilliant – I'll tell you all about it later. Sorry I couldn't get home last night. My flight was delayed, and I had to come straight here from the airport.'

'You were cutting it a bit fine, weren't you?'

'I know, and I'm in terrible trouble around here, but the trip ran way over schedule. For a while I wasn't sure I'd even get back in time. Rachel was going mental, and I still haven't been forgiven for missing the rehearsal.'

'Still,' she pulled away from Freddie and tugged at the voluminous skirts, 'she's got her revenge.'

Freddie waved the plastic bag he was carrying. 'I brought your knickers and bra. Couldn't find anything very glamorous, I'm afraid, but rootling through women's drawers isn't exactly my forte.'

'It doesn't matter. Thanks, Freddie, you're a lifesaver.' She turned back to the mirror. 'Zip me up, will you?'

Freddie obliged, and Kate pulled a face as she surveyed the full horror. She turned to face him, kicking yards of raw silk out of her way.

'I love weddings.' Freddie threw himself belly-down on the bed and regarded her admiringly. 'They're so romantic.'

'You wouldn't think it was romantic if you had to wear this. Look at me – I look like a hot-air balloon!'

'Well,' Freddie said mischievously, 'it does look as though there's room for a few more on top – not to mention what you could hide under that skirt.'

'I can't hide *anything* under this skirt because Rachel will have a scout around under it to make sure I'm not wearing my trainers.'

'Trainers!' Freddie rolled his eyes.

'I guess she didn't count on me losing so much weight.' Kate bunched up the material behind her so that the dress clung to her curves. It was a definite improvement.

4

'You *have* lost a lot of weight, haven't you? You look amazing – terrific tan too.'

'Thanks – but I still look like a two-ton Tessie in this dress.'

'Come on, cheer up. Bit of slap, you'll look fabulous. It's just wedding jitters.'

'I wouldn't mind so much if bloody Will Sargent wasn't going to be there when I walk down the aisle,' Kate fretted. 'Why did the best man have to be my worst nightmare?'

'Oh dear.' Freddie winced. 'Still carrying a torch, are we?'

'No. He's like a brother to me, really.'

'But wasn't he your first?'

'Yes.'

'Well, that wasn't very brotherly of him, was it? Didn't he shag you after some Trinity Ball?'

'Yes, but don't *ever* mention that around anyone else. No one else knows about it – not even Will, I think.'

'What do you mean?'

'He was so pissed that night, I don't think he even remembers it happened. He's certainly never given any indication that he does.'

'God! No wonder you were so screwed up about him.'

'I just have a sort of revenge fantasy about him now. You know, I want him to see me looking absolutely stunning with the most beautiful, prestigious boyfriend.'

'Ah, yes, *that* fantasy! But you *do* look stunning – and you have a boyfriend. You *do* still have a boyfriend, don't you?'

'Yes but he's not going to be there.'

'Brian isn't coming?' Freddie tried to keep the hope out of his voice.

'No. Apparently he finds my family "overwhelming" *en masse*. Anyway, he's doing a workshop thing, screaming to release your inner child or something.'

Freddie giggled. 'Good at screaming, is he? I mean, you know – good enough to teach it?'

'Shut up, Freddie, I'm not listening.'

'Never mind,' Freddie said. 'You've still got me. Look, I'll find a needle and thread and see what I can do about your dress.'

Kate smiled. 'Thanks, Freddie, you're an angel.'

'But first things first. We could both do with a drink.'

'There's a whole kitchen full of champagne downstairs. And if there's any grub left, grab it. I'm starving again. Maybe if I can eat enough sausage sandwiches between now and two o'clock this dress will actually fit me.'

'Hello, Mrs O.' Freddie greeted Kate's mother as he met her on the stairs.

'Freddie,' Grace O'Neill said breathlessly. 'What's Kate doing? I was just on my way up to tell her the hairdresser will be here any minute. Rachel's in a state and Kate should be calming her down, smoothing things along. That's the bridesmaid's *job*.'

'I'll tell her about the hairdresser, Mrs O. I was just going down to get her a cup of tea.'

'There's some champagne in the fridge – help yourself. And call me Grace.' She hated the way Freddie addressed her as 'Mrs O.' – it sounded so working class, like something off *EastEnders*.

'Hi Rachel,' Freddie called as he passed the sitting room, where Rachel was enthroned in an armchair, wearing a silky robe open over some very sexy underwear and having her nails painted by a beautician. 'How's the blushing bride?'

'Hi Freddie – where the hell is Kate? Tell her she's to come and have her nails done – the hairdresser will be here any minute. Orla is just finishing mine and then she'll be ready for Kate. And Kate has to help me get into my dress. And tell her—'

'You look sensational,' Freddie purred, cutting into the stream of demands.

'Thanks.' Rachel gave him a sugary smile.

'Kate's just getting into her dress, actually,' he said.

'What?' Rachel exploded. 'She can't get into it before she has her make-up and hair done. Tell her to get out of it again and come down here in her dressing gown.'

'She was just trying it on for size.'

'Should have done that a month ago,' Rachel huffed. 'How does it fit?'

'Frightfully. Could I borrow a needle and thread?'

'You'll find some in a box in that cabinet,' Rachel replied, indicating it with her foot. 'It's her own fault,' she went on, as Freddie rummaged for the sewing box. 'She shouldn't have agreed to be a bridesmaid if she wasn't going to take it seriously. She missed the fit-tings for her dress and then she goes and loses weight after all the trouble we'd gone to, modelling it on one of her old tents. She missed the hen party. She even missed the rehearsal, after swearing blind she'd be home by then. Then, to top it all, she turned up here last night looking like Worzel Gummidge on crack.'

Freddie nodded non-committally and backed out of the room to avoid any further onslaught. 'Tea?' he offered hopefully.

'G and.' Rachel giggled. 'Would you be an angel and get me a drink, Freddie? There's some champagne in the fridge – have some yourself.'

'You had enough champagne at breakfast, Rachel,' Grace shrilled, suddenly appearing and flapping about in the doorway. 'You don't want to be staggering up the aisle.' As Freddie wandered off towards the kitchen to get the drinks, she added, 'And you shouldn't be sitting there talking to Freddie in your knickers.'

'Oh Freddie doesn't mind. He's gay.'

'I know he's gay. What's that got to do with it? He's gay – he's not a woman.'

'Well, the point is he might as well be, for all the excitement he's going to get out of seeing me in my bra and knickers.'

'What's he doing here so early anyway? He's not in the wedding party.'

'He's sort of Kate's date.'

'You mean the Tree-hugger isn't coming?'

'No, and don't mention it to Kate. I don't want her walking up the aisle with her eyes all red and puffy, looking like the bridesmaid of Dracula.'

In the kitchen, Freddie found the remains of a vast champagne break-fast. He was just hoovering up some congealing cocktail sausages and helping himself from the fridge when Kate's father walked in.

'I'll have a triple whiskey please, son.'

'Wedding nerves, Mr O?'

'I need something to numb the pain. These bleedin' shoes they're making me wear are pinching the bejaysus out of me.' He winced graphically.

Freddie loved Kate's father. He was the most easy-going member of the family, and Kate very much took after him. He popped the cork on a bottle of champagne and began to pour it into glasses. 'Champagne instead, Mr O?'

'Better not.' Jack patted his stomach. 'That fizzy stuff gives me wind and I had enough of it at breakfast. Don't want to be farting like a buffalo when I'm walking up the aisle.'

'Rachel would never forgive you.'

'What do you think of this business of the Tree-shagger not turning up?' Jack asked.

'It's a bad business, Mr O.' Despite his misuse of the family's favourite epithet for him, Freddie knew that he was referring to Kate's boyfriend, universally loathed by her entire family. 'Apparently he's working.'

'Huh! That lad wouldn't know work if it jumped up and bit him. Some day I'd like someone to sit me down and explain to me exactly what he does.'

'Well, apparently today he's teaching people to scream.'

'Jaysus!' Jack raised his eyes to heaven. 'Mind you, they've got the right man for the job. He'll have them all tearing their hair out in no time flat. Can't stand the little git, with his recycled jumpers and his tofu cigarettes.'

'And his holier-than-thou attitude,' Freddie joined in. 'He lords it over anyone who has a real job, but he's always scrounging money from Kate.'

'I know. Still, she seems to like him. We just have to hope she eventually sees sense.'

Freddie was buttering bread and dividing the remaining sausages and bacon between two slices. 'If she's on her own at the wedding maybe she'll meet someone nice.' He slapped the sandwiches together and cut them in half, then piled them onto a plate.

'You'll look after her anyway, won't you, Freddie?'

'Course I will, Mr O. She'll always have me.' Freddie finished filling the glasses and sailed out.

After he had distributed drinks to Rachel and her mother, he returned to Kate's room and kicked open the door. He was laden down with the sandwiches, sewing box, champagne bottle and glasses.

'How are things downstairs?' Kate asked.

'Well, it's safe to say you've pissed off Rachel. And your mother's wigging out big-time.'

'What's new?' The O'Neill children often joked that their mother, a former actress, had retired from the stage but had never given up drama.

'Rachel says you're to take the dress off again and come down in your dressing gown to have your hair and nails done.' He deposited his booty by the bed and began rummaging through the sewing box. 'But keep it on for moment while I pin it. And tell me about Africa,' he said, through a mouthful of pins.

'Oh, it was fantastic! Bloody hard work, but worth it.'

'There, done,' he said, a few moments later.

Kate took off the dress, got into her dressing gown and flopped on to the bed. 'Oh God, I just want to sleep for three days.'

'Tired?' Freddie ruffled her hair.

'Absolutely knackered.'

'That reminds me – I've got an extras job for us Monday. D'you mind?'

'No. I could do with the cash. I'm flat broke. What is it?'

'*Northsiders*.' Freddie supplemented his income as a costume designer with occasional work as an extra, and Kate sometimes joined him when she was between jobs, which was often. *Northsiders* was the latest home-grown soap opera.

'I told them I'd bring you along too, but you don't have to do it if you don't want to.'

'No, that's great. Financially Africa was a disaster. I barely managed to scrape the money together for the flight home – thought I'd be stuck there for life at one stage, unless I sold myself to a camel trader. So I'll have to start hauling my arse around looking for a job – at least now I can put it off until Tuesday.' She heaved herself up. 'I suppose I'd better go down and get tarted up.'

'First things first,' Freddie said, pouring champagne.

Kate joined him on the floor and they sat leaning against the bed. 'Brilliant breakfast sandwich,' she said, through a huge bite.

'Did you meet anyone nice on your travels?'

'Oh please, Freddie, don't start that – I'll get enough of it later from my relations.'

'Oh come on, you must have *some* gossip – you've been gone three months. No bed-hopping on the road?'

'No beds, remember? It was a camping trip.'

'Well, sleeping-bag hopping, then? You really expect me to believe you kept to your own little tent the whole time?'

'Of course I did,' Kate replied, grinning guiltily.

'You didn't open your flap to *anyone*?'

'Well,' she said, 'there *was* this Australian guy who joined the trip in Nairobi.'

'That's more like it.' Freddie refilled their glasses. 'Tell me more – fit or flabby?'

'Oh fit. Definitely fit.'

'Smooth or hairy?'

'Smooth.'

'Mmm – I like him already. Circumcised or un?'

'Un.' Kate wrinkled her nose.

'Oh well, can't have everything, I suppose. Big or puny?'

Kate smiled smugly. 'Not so much *big* as— '

'Humungous?!'

'Like if the Grand Canyon needed a shag, he'd be the man to fill it.'

'Oh my God!'

Tom McAuley was waking up, or coming round from a coma – he wasn't sure which. Sensation was creeping back into his body. His mouth felt numb and furry, and everything hurt. Everything he could feel, that was. He concentrated hard, trying to figure out where he was, what day it was, and what was wrong with him. Perhaps he'd been in an accident. Maybe he was in hospital. He opened his eyes a fraction and the sharp stab of pain from the blinding light seemed to confirm his suspicions.

Something nudged his leg. 'Do you suppose he's still alive?' a voice said from very far away.

'Dunno . . . try giving him a kick,' said another voice.

If these were doctors, Tom thought, their bedside manner left a lot to be desired. He struggled to open his eyes, thinking he'd better show signs of life in case he was about to be consigned to the morgue. He almost passed out again from the pain but managed to keep his eyes open long enough to see his best friends, Will Sargent and Lorcan O'Neill, towering over him.

Well, if I'm dead I'm definitely not in heaven, he thought. Those two would never make it there.

He closed his eyes again, trying to regain oblivion. Consciousness wasn't all it was cracked up to be. But something in the back of his mind wouldn't quite let go, something he felt was important . . . something he needed to remember.

'Hey, Tom!' Will clapped his hands close to Tom's ear. 'Come on, wake up – it's D Day.'

D Day? Tom thought fuzzily. He concentrated hard. The last thing he could remember was rolling up to Will's sprawling Dalkey mansion for his . . . STAG NIGHT!

'Jesus!' He shot up, eyes open wide now. His head spun and he thought he was going to throw up.

'I think he's awake.' Will's deep voice was tinged with amusement.

'Wh-what day is it? What time is it? What happened?'

'Today is Saturday, the first of July.' Will spoke slowly and carefully, as though he were talking to a child. 'Your wedding day, sunshine. The time is nine o'clock – T minus five hours. As for what happened, well, where would you like me to start?'

Tom looked around the room for clues, but there were none. He was lying on the couch in Will's living room, but there were no signs of a party. It seemed everything had been cleared up but him.

'I remember coming to the stag party . . .'

'Yes?'

'Well . . .' Tom thought hard. 'Well, that's it.'

'Oh dear. We *have* got a lot of catching up to do.' Will turned to Lorcan. 'Better get started,' he said.

They bent over him, took his arms and hauled him to his feet. In return, he threw up over their shoes.

'Jesus, my head.' Tom groaned, kneeling back in front of the loo. 'My head feels weird.'

'Hardly surprising,' Will drawled.

'No, I don't mean that. I mean it feels sort of . . . *cold.*'

Lorcan and Will exchanged a meaningful glance, which Tom

intercepted. What did it mean? He moved his hands gingerly over his scalp.

'Jesus!' he shrieked. 'What's happened to my hair? It's gone!'

'Try not to panic, Tom.' Lorcan patted his shoulder.

Tom stood up, pushed Lorcan out of the way and lurched over to the bathroom mirror. 'I'm *bald*,' he whispered in disbelief. 'I'm fucking bald.' He turned to his two friends, who were looking very sheepish. 'I'm fucking bald on my wedding day!' he wailed, with mounting panic in his voice.

'You're not bald.' Will came over to join him at the mirror. 'You've got a good quarter-centimetre of hair there, and I'm told the military look is really big this season.'

'Rachel will kill me! The military look isn't the theme of our wedding.'

'Look on the bright side.' Lorcan grinned. 'It'll make you more aerodynamic.'

'I'm getting married, not entering the fucking Olympics!'

'You're getting hysterical, Tom. Hang on.' Lorcan raced out of the room and came back, moments later, clutching a paper bag. 'Here, try this,' he said, thrusting it at him.

Tom looked at him uncertainly but took the bag. He placed it on his head, pulled it down over his ears and surveyed himself in the mirror.

'Well, I suppose it's an improvement . . .' he said, turning his head to look at it from different angles.

'You're not supposed to wear it, you twat!' Lorcan snatched it off. 'You're supposed to breathe into it.'

'What bloody good will that do?'

'It might calm you down.'

'I'd still be bald!' Tom shrieked.

'Well, I think it really suits you. And it feels gorgeous.' Will rubbed the crown of Tom's head. 'Rachel will love it.'

Tom touched it again. It felt lovely – so soft. Despite himself, a little smile tugged at the corners of his mouth, and he saw Will and Lorcan brightening. 'I'm still a dead man,' he warned them. 'How did it happen anyway?'

'Phoenix did it.'

'And you *let* him?'

'You asked him to, actually – begged him, in fact.'

'But you must have known I was out of my head. You should have stopped him.'

'We would have, but by the time we found out what was going on he was already halfway through. It would have looked worse if we hadn't let him finish it.'

'What on earth possessed me?'

'Apparently you wanted him to do your hair like his.'

'But Phoenix isn't a skinhead.'

Lorcan shook his head. 'He is now – he's a Hare Krishna or a Buddhist or something.'

'Since when?'

'Tuesday, I think.' Will said. 'Anyway, he had his head shaved, and apparently you kept saying how great it looked and wouldn't leave him alone until he shaved yours. You really don't remember *any* of this?'

Tom thought hard. 'No, nothing.'

'Well, that doesn't matter now anyway,' Will said. 'We've got to concentrate on getting you in shape for the big day.'

'That's another thing I don't understand,' Tom said. 'How can it be my wedding day today? The stag party was on Wednesday. If today's my wedding day, that was three days ago.'

'It was a good party.' Lorcan said.

'Wish I could remember it,' Tom said.

'You'll remember today,' Will said breezily. 'That's the important thing.'

Tom looked at Will as though he were mad. 'You don't think I'm going to go through with it, do you?'

'What are you talking about? Of course you're going through with it. It's just a haircut, not the end of the world.'

'That's what *you* think! *You* don't have to face Rachel.'

'You have to face Rachel either way,' Lorcan pointed out.

'Not if I run away,' Tom said, a mad gleam in his eyes. 'I could go to South America. I've always wanted to see Machu Picchu.'

'Don't be daft, Tom,' Will said firmly. 'You're not going to Machu Picchu, you're going to St Jude's, and you're going to marry Rachel.'

13

'Come on, Lorcan,' Tom pleaded. 'You know how scary your sister can be. I can't face her like this.'

'Only one thing for it,' Will said, appearing behind Tom in the mirror. He grabbed an electric razor from the shelf, plugged it in and turned it on. Then he began to run it through his hair, huge chunks falling to the floor.

'What the hell are you doing?' Lorcan gasped.

'It's called solidarity, mate. And you're next.'

'Could you put the phone down, darling?' Tony, Freddie's very camp make-up artist friend, said to Rachel. 'I can't do your face with that thing clapped to your ear.'

'Wait a minute.' Rachel waved him away. 'I just have to make one call.' She hit redial. Tom's mobile rang and rang, then went to voice-mail again.

'Shit!' She hung up and called Lorcan's mobile. It was picked up on the second ring.

'Lorcan, where are you?' she demanded. 'Is Tom with you?' she continued, before he had time to answer.

'Yes, of course he is. We – er – we stayed with him last night. At least he stayed with us at Will's.'

'At Will's?' Rachel squawked. 'Why did you stay there?'

'Well, he *is* the best man – and I'm the second-best man or what-ever you call it.'

'Groomsman.' Rachel gritted her teeth.

'Yes, well, it's sort of traditional, isn't it?'

'No, it's traditional to stay at the groom's place, where all his clothes and stuff are.'

'Oh.'

'Look, just put Tom on, will you?'

'Well, do you have to speak to him now? You're going to see him soon enough, aren't you?'

Her brother sounded like Basil Fawlty trying to hoodwink Sybil, she thought. 'He is there with you, isn't he?'

'Well, yes,' Lorcan prevaricated.

'Let me speak to him, then.'

'It's just that he's sort of . . . busy.'

'Where are you now? At Will's?'

'No . . . no, we're somewhere else.'

'*Lorcan*,' Rachel growled, 'put Tom on the phone.'

'All right, all right.'

Rachel heard him yelling Tom's name very loudly. He was obviously holding the phone away from him now and she could hear other sounds – a lot of voices and what sounded like water splashing. 'He's just coming,' Lorcan told her.

'Where are you, Lorcan?'

'We're actually, um,' he laughed nervously, 'you're not going to believe this but . . . we're at the Forty Foot.'

'*What?*' Rachel exploded. 'What the hell is Tom doing at the Forty Foot on the morning of our wedding?'

Lorcan looked across at Tom, who at this very moment appeared to be chatting up a very nubile young Spanish woman. The Forty Foot, formerly a men-only nude bathing pool in Sandycove, now required that swimming costumes be worn and was open to anyone mad enough to plunge into the Irish Sea. Or in Tom's case, hungover enough to let themselves be pushed in. However, Lorcan mused, he seemed to be enjoying it now.

'It was Will's idea, actually.' Lorcan said. 'He thought it would sob— er, freshen him up for the big day.'

'Is Tom hungover?' Rachel asked suspiciously. 'I specifically asked Will to arrange the stag party early in the week and to make sure Tom wasn't out on the piss the night before the wedding.'

'Well, the party was on Wednesday. It just sort of went on longer than planned.'

'How much longer?'

'Um . . . two days.' Lorcan winced, waiting for the onslaught. But he was saved from having to explain any further by the emergence of a very flaccid, dripping Tom from the water.

Now Tom was on the line. 'Hello, darling.'

She could hear his teeth chattering. 'Tom! What the hell are you doing at the Forty Foot? You should be starting to get ready by now. Honestly, do I have to do everything? Will and Lorcan should be organising you, not leading you astray and leaving me to pick up the pieces. I hope you managed to get your hair cut. And don't forget . . .'

*

Tom half listened as Rachel issued orders and watched wistfully as
Lorcan plunged into the water and swam straight up to that Spanish
girl with the honey-coloured skin. Even from this distance he could
feel the heat of their flirting. Then they disappeared behind a rock
together. If Tom hadn't felt sober before, he did now, as the enormity
of what he was about to do hit him.

Behind the rock, Lorcan gazed into a pair of dark eyes. 'By the way,'
he asked, 'what's your name?'

'Carmen.'

'Short for Carmencita, I suppose,' he said, feeling very clever.

'No – Maria del Carmen.'

God, her accent was delicious. She had a deep, gruff voice, which,
mixed with her guttural Spanish accent, sent shivers down his spine.

'I'm Lorcan.'

She repeated his name, making it sound new and exotic.

'I'm going to a wedding later today. Would you like to come?'

'I always like to come.'

Lorcan laughed. 'Where did you learn to speak English like that?'

'From Irish men.'

God, she's amazing, Lorcan thought, longing to pull her out of
the water, peel off her swimsuit and make love to her wet, slippery
body. It was a long time since he had felt such stomach-churning
excitement about a woman. Between the cold of the water and the
heat of desire, he was fighting for breath.

'Whose wedding is it?' Carmen asked. 'Not yours, I hope.'

'God, no! My friend, Tom – the one you were talking to earlier.
He's marrying my sister.'

She glanced over to where Tom and Will stood, drying themselves.
'I thought you were a group of Buddhist monks.' She nodded at
Lorcan's shaved head.

'Oh no, we're not monks – definitely not.'

'You don't have anyone else to take?' she asked.

'No, I was going alone, as a matter of fact. I split up with my girlfriend last week.'

'You don't seem very upset about it.'

16

'I'm not.' Lorcan grinned, 'She was a pain in the arse.'

Carmen laughed.

'So, will you come – to the wedding, I mean? There'll be champagne,' he said, 'and cake.'

'Well, I do love champagne,' Carmen said. 'Okay, I'll go with you.'

Out of the corner of his eye Lorcan saw Will and Tom starting to get dressed.

'Look, I have to go with my friends. Why don't you come back with us and have some breakfast?'

'Sure.'

'Good. I can run you home after, if you want to change before the wedding.'

'I live just over there.' She tossed her head towards the row of houses facing the sea. 'If you can wait here a few minutes, I'll pick up my stuff and come with you. Okay?'

'Okay.'

I must be in a dream, Lorcan thought. Women aren't this easy. Most of the ones he knew prided themselves on being bloody hard work – his sister Rachel, Will's girlfriend Tina – and Sarah, the girlfriend he had just split up with.

They pulled themselves out of the water, and Lorcan followed Carmen to where she'd left her clothes. He couldn't help staring as she put them on over her swimsuit without drying herself. She pulled her thick dark hair up behind her head and let it fall again, shaking it vigorously and showering Lorcan with water. Then she shuffled into her shoes. 'I'll see you in a few minutes,' she said, picking up her bag and turning towards the road.

'See you soon, Maria del Carmen,' Lorcan called. Walking back to join the others, he realised he was sporting an enormous erection.

Back at his house, Will looked around the table with satisfaction as everyone tucked into an enormous fried breakfast that he had cooked. Even though he no longer drank, he was an expert at managing hangovers, thanks to the hell-raising antics of Walking Wounded, the band he had managed since leaving college. He could draw on years of experience of coping with the morning-after fallout from its members' nights of debauchery. It was one of the reasons he was such a popular choice for best man. After all, compared to getting those four hooligans on to a stage on time and sober night after night – especially a loose cannon like Owen Cassidy – having a groom at the altar rail on time and in reasonable shape was a piece of piss.

'Where are you from, Carmen?' Will asked.

'Galicia. And you? You're not Irish, I think?'

'Well, no, not really. I grew up in England. My mother was Irish, though, and I've lived here since I was fifteen.'

'An adopted son of Ireland, eh?' Carmen's eyes twinkled.

'An adopted son of my mother, actually.' Lorcan laughed.

'She seems nice.' Will said to Lorcan when Carmen left to go to the bathroom. 'Are you bringing her to the wedding?'

'Yes, I am,' Lorcan said, looking ridiculously pleased with himself.

'Might take a bit of the heat off me and my hair,' Tom said.

'What do you mean?'

'Well, she's not on the seating plan, is she?' he pointed out. 'And I don't think Rachel's going to be too impressed that you're bringing someone you found this morning in the Irish Sea.'

'Sarah was on the seating plan,' Lorcan reminded him, 'so I'm sure there'll be room for Carmen. If not, she can sit on my knee.'

'Sit on your knob, you mean.'

'Is Tina coming to the wedding?' Lorcan asked Will.

'Yeah, I'm meeting her there. She's been staying with friends.'

Tina hadn't been at all happy to be banished from his house for the duration of the stag party – but, then, she wasn't happy about much these days, Will thought wearily, unless it involved having her photo in a magazine. They hadn't been getting on lately and he had felt guiltily relieved of an excuse not to see her for a few days. Part of the problem was that Tina, seeing her modelling career coming to an end, wanted to branch out into other things and was on a mission to raise her public profile. Will had found himself sucked into her vortex. When she was in town she filled his house with a constant parade of hangers-on and wannabes. She made sure that paparazzi followed them wherever they went, and, to his intense mortification, they were becoming quite a celebrity couple. She had even tried to persuade him to throw open his doors to *MTV Cribs*, so they could find her lurking decorously in one of the rooms, no doubt.

'What's all this about the two of you getting engaged?' Tom asked.

'It's just a vicious rumour,' Will said, 'started by that bloody gossip-columnist friend of Tina's. I'm sure Tina put her up to it.'

'Crikey! I'll get Rachel to fire the bouquet well away from her then.'

'Thanks.' Will grinned. 'Much appreciated.'

The conversation stopped as Carmen drifted back into the kitchen. 'This house is amazing,' she said, sitting down at the table. 'I got lost on my way back from the loo. Do you all live here?'

'No, just Will,' Lorcan told her.

'Is it your parents' house?' she asked Will.

'No, it's mine.'

'And you live here alone? But it's so huge!'

Will shrugged apologetically.

'And you own it?' Carmen persisted, as Lorcan and Tom shifted uncomfortably, darting surreptitious glances at Will.

'Yes.'

'Wow! You must be really rich!' She exclaimed.

Will merely smiled.

Suddenly Tom thumped the table, causing everyone to jump. 'Did Tessa dance topless on the table?' he thundered.

'What?'

'It's suddenly coming back to me – last night, or the night before, or whenever it was. Did Tessa strip off and dance topless on the table?'

Lorcan laughed. 'In your dreams!'

'You mean she didn't? I could swear I remember—'

'I'm telling you it was a dream.'

Will knew Tom and Lorcan were deliberately changing the conversation because they knew he found it embarrassing when people made a fuss about his money. But he hadn't been offended by Carmen's completely artless curiosity and, touched though he was by his friends' solicitude, it was mortifying to witness them dancing around his sensibilities like this.

19

'You could have humoured me,' Tom moaned, 'left me my illusions.'

'Come to think of it, someone did dance topless on the table. It wasn't Tessa, though.'

'Will, you were sober,' Tom appealed to him. 'Did someone dance topless on the table at my stag party?'

Will smiled. 'Yes – but Lorcan's right. It wasn't Tessa.'

'Who was it, then?'

'Owen.'

'Ugh!'

Everyone laughed.

'We should hit the showers,' Will said, getting up to clear the plates. 'The good thing about a house this size is that we can have a bathroom each.'

Later, Will and Lorcan stood in front of the mirror knotting each other's bowties.

'God, we do look weird, don't we?' Will said, when they'd finished. 'Shaved heads and DJs – like bouncers.'

'*You* look weird,' Lorcan assumed a cocky expression. 'I look cool.'

In fact, the bald look suited Lorcan better than it did Will, accentuating the baby-faced features that made women swoon – the big spaniel eyes framed by ridiculously long sooty lashes, the sensuous mouth. The O'Neills were a good-looking family, all olive-skinned and dark-haired. Rachel was acknowledged as the beauty, but everyone knew Lorcan was the real knockout.

'Be extra nice to Kate today,' Lorcan said. 'She's on her own.'

Easier said than done, Will thought. He had the impression that Lorcan's fat little sister didn't like him very much any more – probably with good reason, he reflected guiltily. Although he was practically a member of the family, he and Kate hadn't seen much of each other in the past few years, mainly, Will suspected, because Kate was avoiding him. On the few occasions they had met, she had spoken in monosyllables if he tried to talk to her. It was a pity because they'd been good friends. Still, he had only himself to blame. 'Has she split up with that boyfriend of hers, then?' he asked Lorcan.

'Sadly, no. But he's not coming. Apparently he finds us "overwhelming". He's afraid we'll swallow him up or something.'

Will laughed. 'He should be so lucky.' He had been 'swallowed up' by the O'Neills years ago and considered it the best thing that had ever happened to him.

'Indeed,' Lorcan said drily, 'if we swallowed *him* up we'd spit him out again pretty sharpish.'

'Still, you must admit, your family can be a bit . . . Greek.'

'*Greek?*' Lorcan was bewildered.

Will smiled. 'You know what I mean.'

'You mean histrionic.'

'No – though your mother would make a mean Medea.'

'Incestuous then?'

'No, I was thinking more in terms of doing good to your friends and harm to your enemies. I can vouch for the doing-good-to-your-friends bit.'

Will had benefited from the O'Neills' Greek qualities – their fierce, unswerving loyalty to family and friends, their boundless hospitality – but, much as he adored them, he understood why someone might find them overwhelming. Clannish, talented, decadent and hospitable to a fault, they were not for the faint-hearted. The worst sins as far as the O'Neills were concerned were being boring and crimes against hospitality. Will got the impression that Kate's boyfriend had been found guilty of both.

'I suppose Mum *would* make a pretty scary enemy,' Lorcan admitted. 'Not to mention Rachel. I hate to think what would have happened to us if Tom had done a runner.'

'Rachel doesn't take any prisoners.'

'Speaking of which, I'll go and chivvy Tom along. See you downstairs in a mo.' Lorcan went to the door, but paused. 'You really think we're Greek?'

'In a good way,' Will reassured him.

In a very good way, Will thought, as he finished knotting his tie. The O'Neills had saved his life and stopped him becoming a hopeless drifter. There had always been money in his own family, so there had never been any pressure on him to achieve academically or to work hard. That he had done both was as a result of his connection with the O'Neills and, most of all, his friendship with Lorcan. They had been best friends at school, and when Lorcan had gone on to university, Will had followed him because he would have followed him anywhere. Once there, he had discovered a capacity for hard work and self-discipline that surprised no one more than himself.

His childhood had been at once deprived and privileged, arbitrarily indulged and neglected by his wealthy, talented parents. His mother, Helen Kilgannon, a beautiful but mentally unstable artist, was an Irish aristocrat and heiress to a large fortune. His father was a brilliant, acclaimed (and recently knighted) playwright, as well as a notorious hell-raiser and womaniser. Helen had supported the young Philip Sargent in the early days of their marriage before he had made a name for himself as a playwright. By the time Will came along, Philip had won a BAFTA and was beginning to earning serious money in his own right.

Will seemed to have everything. Then, when he was fifteen, his world fell apart. His father left his mother for the glamorous star of his latest West End play. The betrayal shattered his mother's fragile sanity and she sank into a deep depression, broken only by episodes of mania that were even more difficult to cope with. During one such phase she uprooted herself with Will and moved back to Ireland to start a new life among her 'own people'. At first Will bitterly resented the upheaval, constantly mocked for his 'posh' accent and resented for having been born with the proverbial silver spoon in his mouth.

Things had improved considerably when he became friends with Lorcan, who was hugely popular. Through him, Will gained access to a wide circle of friends and acquired a surrogate family. But his home life had continued to deteriorate. His mother sank deeper and deeper into depression, and Will felt helpless in the face of her despair.

One Sunday morning, after they had been living in Ireland for a year, Will found her dead in her bed: she had swallowed a bottle of sleeping pills. His father had flown over for the funeral (thankfully without his new wife), and Will, wild with grief, had cold-shouldered him throughout, determined to let him know that he held him responsible for his mother's death. His father had insisted that he move back to England with him to finish his schooling. Will had agreed, reluctantly, dreading leaving the one place he'd been happy but secretly pleased that his father wanted him, and that he hadn't been abandoned by both his parents. In fact, part of him longed to be with his clever, witty father. Moreover, he was looking forward to being a thorn in the side of the woman who had wrecked his mother's life.

When he got to England, though, his father promptly packed him off to boarding school. His new wife had had a baby and the last thing she wanted was a sulky, resentful teenager around the house. Besides, Philip was a firm exponent of the public-school system, having been through it himself, and this was one of the finest schools in the country. He had never approved of the move to Ireland or of Helen's ridiculous obsession with keeping Will at home with her. Now that he was overseeing Will's education, he would see that it was done properly.

So Will was dispatched to boarding school, while his father devoted his attention to his new family. It was the last straw for Will. If he was going to be alone in the world, he decided, he might as well be alone in a place where he was happy. One stormy November day he walked out of his school gates and kept going, not stopping until he turned up on the O'Neills' doorstep two days later. It was part of O'Neill family legend that they had answered the door one night to find Will standing there in his school uniform, soaked to the skin and shaking like a puppy. He had run out of money and had had to walk all the way from Dun Laoghaire.

When he had left, Will hadn't thought beyond getting away from school and going to see Lorcan. He was appalled, as realisation dawned, that by turning up on their doorstep he had made himself the O'Neills' problem. The last thing he wanted was to be a burden to his friends. However, to his enormous relief, it soon became obvious that the O'Neills didn't see it like that. As he had dripped onto their kitchen floor, the whole family had rallied around to boss, cajole and fuss over him.

'You should have rung – we'd have picked you up,' Grace had said as she rubbed his hair with a towel.

'I didn't have any money left for the phone,' Will replied, meekly succumbing to her ministrations.

He was mentally and physically exhausted, but, as the O'Neill family machine swung into action around him, he felt all the uncertainty of the past two days seep away and began to relax. He felt safe and secure in a way he had never experienced before. His parents had been so haphazard and chaotic that he had had to fend for himself most of the time, and since his father had left he had had to look after his mother too. It was a relief to let someone else take over. Under cover of the towel, Will grinned, enjoying the novel experience of being mollycoddled.

Lorcan brought him up to his bedroom and provided him with dry clothes. When he returned to the kitchen, Kate fed him soup and bread, followed by chocolate cake and copious amounts of hot, sweet tea – she had decided he was in shock. Conor, the eldest, cleared out the spare room, and Rachel made up the bed for him. Jack just kept patting him on the shoulder and telling him everything would be all right, while Grace tried to get information out of him.

'I'm not going back,' was all Will would say. He tried to sound tough, but everyone could see he was on the verge of tears.

'Ah, come on, son, everything'll be all right,' Jack said gruffly. 'How about a drop of whiskey in that tea?'

Jack's gruff kindness was the final straw, and Will broke down. He covered his face with his fists, but a fat tear sploshed into his soup.

Grace had finally coaxed his father's phone number out of him.

'I'm not going back,' Will warned her as she dialled.

'Of course not,' Grace soothed him. 'We're not going to make you.' She had an Irish mother's horror of public schools.

It was Grace's finest hour. She went into maternal overdrive and spent more than an hour on the phone to Philip Sargent, cajoling him into letting Will stay in Ireland. It wasn't easy. Philip had begun by insisting that Will return to England and finish his schooling. There was the matter of money too. Will stood to inherit a fortune from his mother, but not until he reached the age of twenty-one. Until then, Philip insisted, he was Will's guardian, and he would not support him if he stayed in Ireland.

'Tell him I'll get a job,' Will said stonily when this was relayed to him. 'I don't need to finish school.'

'He's only sixteen,' Philip argued. 'He can't live on his own and do as he likes.'

'He wouldn't have to live on his own,' Grace told Philip. 'He can stay with us and go to school with Lorcan like before. It's no bother. We're all terribly fond of Will and we'd love to have him here.'

'He can't just wander off and move in with another family, like a bloody cat!' Philip fumed.

'I'm very fond of cats,' Grace said defensively.

'Look, put him on.' Philip sighed.

Finally Will was persuaded to speak to his father. He was cold and unyielding. He wasn't going back. If he was sent back he would run away again.

Finally, after a good deal of wrangling, Philip had to admit defeat. Faced with the choice of Will staying in Ireland with his friends and finishing school or getting some menial job while he waited to become a hopeless dilettante, he opted for the lesser of two evils.

But Will had never forgiven his father and that night in the O'Neills' kitchen was the last time he had spoken to him.

Chapter 2

'Okay, showtime!' Kate announced. She had spent the past five minutes on her hunkers behind Rachel, fluffing up her skirts. She wasn't too sure what she was supposed to be doing, but she had a vague idea that, as bridesmaid, she was expected to fiddle with Rachel's dress for a decent interval before they could go into the church. She gave the skirt one last hefty tug so that Rachel would think she meant serious business, then pronounced her 'ready to roll'.

'My veil! Don't forget my veil!' Rachel trilled.

Boy, that red carpet's really gone to her head, Kate thought, but she dutifully draped the veil around Rachel's face. Rachel had gone for the whole traditional thing: the O'Neills were a theatrical family, both by profession and in spirit, and this was her big production.

At last they were ready. Rachel took her father's arm as they went inside and the organist started to play 'The Bridal March'. Everyone stood as they began the walk down the long aisle amid a riot of flash-bulbs as guests ducked out of the pews to take photographs.

This must be what it's like being famous, Kate thought, enjoying it more than she had expected. She caught Freddie's eye as she passed him and gave him a broad grin. She noticed he was beside her disreputable aunt Iris.

Halfway down the aisle, Rachel stopped dead. Kate, not paying attention, crashed into her. 'Dad, stop!' Rachel hissed from beneath her veil. '*Stop!*'

'Sorry, love, am I going too fast?' Jack slowed his pace but continued to move forward.

Rachel dug her heels in. '*Stop*, Dad.' She leaned closer to her father. 'I've made a dreadful mistake!' she whispered urgently.

'Not at all.' Her father smiled nervously. 'Don't worry – Tom's a lovely fella.' He patted Rachel's hand reassuringly and continued down the aisle.

Rachel yanked him back. 'No, Dad, *stop*! This is all wrong!'

'Well, isn't it a bit late to be thinking about that now?' Jack pleaded, beaming wildly at the guests.

'I don't mean I'm having second thoughts,' Rachel hissed through clenched teeth. 'I mean I've made a *mistake*. Look,' she pointed to the altar, 'this is some kind of skinhead wedding. We're at the *wrong one*!' She sounded like a bad ventriloquist.

Jack glanced around him. All the guests, who were staring at them in bewilderment, were familiar. He winked at a couple of acquaintances. But Rachel was right: there did seem to be a bunch of skinheads at the altar. Could they have invited everyone to the wrong church? Or for the wrong time?

Kate peered at the altar rail. 'God, you're right,' she whispered. How could this have happened? she wondered. And to Rachel of all people – *Bride* magazine's poster girl, for God's sake!

'Of course I'm right,' Rachel snapped. 'I think I'd recognise my own fiancé. What are we going to do?'

As the three stood in the middle of the aisle, trying frantically to think of the least undignified way of legging it, the wedding guests began to mumble. Kate kept glancing over her shoulder, half expecting some jackbooted bride to come goose-stepping along the aisle and mow them down.

'Ooh, it's just like that film, *Runaway Bride*,' Aunt Iris whispered

27

excitedly to Freddie, who was shocked to see her punch the air, while she whispered encouragement to Rachel to bolt. It was as if she was cheering a horse she had backed in the Grand National over the finish line.

At the top of the church, Tom stared fixedly at the altar rail, afraid to turn around. I knew it, he thought, I should never have let Lorcan and Will persuade me into going ahead with it. Rachel had obviously seen his hair – or lack of it – and decided to do a runner.

As the organist launched staunchly into the third round of 'The Bridal March', Tom summoned the courage to turn and face the music. What he saw was not encouraging. Rachel, Kate and Jack were huddled together in the middle of the aisle, having what looked like a fairly heated argument. Jack appeared to be trying to reason with Rachel, probably persuading her to go the extra mile and marry him, even if he *was* a slaphead, Tom thought despondently.

But then something miraculous happened. Rachel saw him, and her face lit up. 'It's Tom!' he heard her gasp to her father and sister. She seemed surprised to see him, but pleasantly so. In fact, she appeared overjoyed.

'Look! It's Tom,' she squealed again. Then she picked up her skirts and practically ran the rest of the way to the altar, Kate water-skiing after her, hanging onto her train.

Rachel flung back her veil, threw herself into Tom's arms and covered his face in kisses. 'Oh, I'm so glad to see you,' she babbled. 'I didn't recognise you. We thought we'd come to the wrong church.'

'My hair.' Tom rubbed his head. 'I can explain.'

'It looks brilliant.' Rachel pulled back to examine him. Her brush with disaster had put Tom's radical haircut into perspective. 'What made you do it?'

'I just thought it'd make our wedding more rock'n'roll.' He was giddy with relief.

'And it feels gorgeous.' She laughed. 'So sexy.'

'That's what they said.' Tom nodded to Will and Lorcan. Rachel had been too preoccupied with Tom to notice them, but now they smiled at her.

Kate gave a hoot of laughter when she saw them, but Rachel

narrowed her eyes beadily. She might have known this had had something to do with them. 'Oh, you've all done it,' she said, 'What a brilliant idea!' She knew there was more to this than Tom was letting on, but she didn't care. She was too happy that Tom was there and everything was going according to plan after all. Besides, the photographs would look really cool.

Finally the priest got tired of wringing his hands, pointedly clearing his throat and looking at his watch. 'Good afternoon, everyone!' he boomed into the microphone, bringing the congregation to attention.

'Oh, we're off,' Tom said, taking Rachel's hand and leading her to the altar.

The entire congregation heaved a collective sigh of relief as the ceremony got under way – everyone except Auntie Iris.

'Same ol', same ol',' she muttered dejectedly to Freddie, as she settled down for a nap. 'Give me a poke when it's over, would you?'

By the time the wedding party got to the hotel, the guests had already been taking advantage of the free bar for more than an hour.

'Where the hell have you been?' Freddie asked Kate, when she had pushed her way through to him. He handed her two enormous gin and tonics. 'Here, get these down you – you're way behind.'

'Mmm, thanks.' Kate knocked back half of one, then came up for air. 'We had to go to the park for a bloody photo shoot, so now I'm immortalised for all time in this get-up.'

'God, I wish *I* could have been posing in the park. I got nobbled by some woman with enormous boobs. I think she was scheming to get off with me.'

'Well, you clocked her boobs, she must have thought you were interested.'

'I couldn't help it! She kept slipping her cup size casually into the conversation. I had to check them out.'

'God, I hate women like that.'

'I must say, I like the look of your Will – very tasty.'

'You should see him with hair,' Kate said.

'Straight or curly?'

'Curly.'

'Oh dear.' Freddie pulled a face. 'We prefer straight, don't we –
when it comes to hair, that is? Actually, I usually prefer straight right
down the line. That's my tragedy.'

'I usually hate curly, but Will's is different.'

'I'll take your word for it,' Freddie said. 'Oh, look, something
wicked this way comes.' Lorcan was pushing through the crush with
Carmen in tow. 'Being bald hasn't marred your gorgeous brother's
beauty one jot. Who's the sultry piece he's with?'

'No one seems to know much about her, so they can't have been
together long.'

'This is Carmen,' Lorcan announced, as he led her forward.
'Carmen, this is my sister Kate.'

'Nice to meet you, Kate.' Carmen shook her hand.

Kate took to her instantly. There was something very appealing
about her direct gaze and warm smile.

'I love what you're wearing,' she said. Carmen was wearing a
short raspberry-coloured shift dress that complemented her skin
tone. It had a wide slash neck, which meant it was always falling off
one shoulder or the other, but elsewhere the soft jersey material clung
to every curve of her whippet-thin body. Combined with the
espadrilles on her feet and the soft dark ringlets falling loosely
around her shoulders, the effect was of a casual, effortless glamour
that made Kate feel like a drag queen with her over-made-up face,
complicated hair arrangement and over-the-top dress.

'Thanks. It was the first thing I found.'

'This is Freddie, Kate's flatmate,' Lorcan continued. 'We work
together from time to time.'

'Oh? What sort of work do you do?' Carmen asked.

Kate and Freddie raised their eyebrows. Either the pair hadn't
been together very long or they didn't waste much time talking.

'I'm a director,' Lorcan told her, adding 'in the theatre'. He
was used to women's faces falling when they realised he wasn't in
films. 'Freddie's a costume designer. I've been meaning to call
you, actually,' he said to Freddie. 'I'm trying to get a touring company together – you know, travelling around Ireland bringing cul-
ture to the great unwashed. Would you be interested in tagging
along?'

'Would I!' Freddie was thrilled at the prospect of following Kate's gorgeous brother up hill and down dale.

'What do you do, Kate?' Carmen asked.

'I'm a chef, but – *oof*!' Kate was hit hard from behind. She turned to discover her six-year-old nephew, Jake, struggling to free himself from her skirt, which had engulfed him like a parachute. 'Hi Jake! Here, let me help.' She freed him.

'Jake! Say sorry to Kate – you nearly knocked her over.' Helen, Kate's sister-in-law, came trotting up after him.

'Don't worry, Helen. No chance of that in this dress – too much ballast!'

'Sorry, Kate,' Jake panted. 'Spiderman's after me. I'm the bad guy.' His four-year-old brother Sam was storming through the crowd towards them, while her brother Conor tried to field him. They sent a kind of Mexican wave through the crowd as drinks were hoisted aloft to save them from spilling.

'Well, there goes my reputation as Supermum!' Helen smiled wryly. A former actress, she was now at the centre of a growing industry built around her cult status as an Olympic-standard home-maker. A tall, strikingly attractive blonde, she seemed effortlessly elegant, her precision-cut bob gleaming as if it had been newly polished, her tailored oyster suit showing off her figure, which was still girlishly slim even after two children.

Sam thundered up to Jake on his chubby little legs, with Conor, red-faced, in the rear.

'Sam!' Kate grinned. 'You wore your Spiderman costume!'

'He wouldn't put on his new clothes,' Jake explained importantly, with all the superiority of an elder brother.

'It was the only way we could get him out of the house,' Helen said. 'Rachel's furious.' She giggled.

'Huh! I'd like to see *her* wrestle Sam into something he doesn't want to wear.'

Sam and Jake tore off again.

'No more running, you two!' Conor roared futilely.

He greeted Kate with a kiss. 'Hi Lorcan,' he called to his brother. 'Saw your show last week – complete bollocks!' he roared cheerily.

'Uh, thanks Conor.'

31

'I'll call you during the week, give you a few pointers where you went wrong.'

'Great!' Lorcan grimaced. To create a diversion he introduced Conor and Helen to Carmen. 'Helen's quite famous, actually,' he told her. She's kind of a Jane Asher on speed – Ireland's answer to Martha Stewart.' When Carmen looked blank, he explained, 'She's a sort of housewife guru. She has her own TV show.'

'Oh really? I've never seen it.'

'Oh, no one ever *sees* it,' Lorcan said airily. 'It's on during the day when real people are at work.'

'I do have my adoring public, Lorcan,' Helen protested mildly.

'It's kind of *Blue Peter* for grown-ups. She shows you how to make a dinner service out of pastry and knit your own Christmas tree, stuff like that.'

'Don't mind him.' Helen laughed. 'It's a lifestyle show,' she explained to Carmen. 'We do cookery slots, features on entertaining and home decor, stuff like that. It's not going to set the world on fire but—'

'Don't sell yourself short, Helen,' Lorcan said. 'You're setting the world on fire one homemade scented candle at a time.'

Meanwhile, Conor was badgering Kate about her career plans. 'So, what's next?' he asked.

Kate hesitated to tell him that she didn't have any plans. 'Freddie and I are doing *Northsiders* on Monday,' she said brightly.

'Right.' Conor sounded unconvinced. 'That's, what, half a day's work?'

She should have known he wouldn't be that easily fobbed off. 'It might be a whole day,' she mumbled. She knew Conor meant well, but he always made her feel like such an idiot.

'I meant what are your plans long-term?'

'I'm going to sign up with a temp agency while I look around for something.'

'Give the poor girl a break,' Helen butted in. 'She's only just got back.'

The truth was, career-wise, Kate was the failure of the family. Since qualifying as a chef she had worked her way steadily down the ladder of success, drifting through a series of short-term, dead-end jobs that allowed her to cook without the pressure of a restaurant. Food was her passion, but she found most professional kitchens terrifying – huge, frenetic places lorded over by megalomaniacal bullies. Between cooking jobs she kept body and soul together by waitressing, catering the odd dinner party and occasionally being a TV extra.

'Helen could put in a word for you with her producer,' Conor was saying now. 'They're always looking for people to develop new cooking shows – they're so popular now.'

'Oh yes,' Helen chipped in, 'and I could get you in for a cookery slot on my show any time you want.'

'There you go,' Conor said, in his another-problem-solved tone. 'You could do the odd cookery slot on Helen's show and build up an audience from there.'

Why, Kate wondered, did everyone in her family assume that she wanted an *audience*? 'I don't want to build up an audience, Conor. I'm a chef, not an entertainer.'

'Same thing nowadays, isn't it? Get known on the box and the world's your oyster. You could do whatever you want after that – write books, open your own restaurant, whatever.'

Any minute now he'd have her launching a range of cookware or ready meals, Kate thought.

'And you look terrific – slim but voluptuous. You've lost just the right amount of weight but not so much that you look like you don't enjoy your own cooking. They say you should never trust a skinny chef.'

Kate was aware that Conor was schmoozing her, but she had to admit he was good. She was almost starting to believe she was the next Nigella Lawson, bending over her pots in a low-cut top while she licked sauce off her fingers and made come-hither eyes at the camera. But that was Conor's talent, bringing out the best in people, making them believe in themselves and getting others to believe in them. His bullying charm had made him the hugely successful theatrical producer that he was.

Unexpectedly, Carmen got Kate off the hook, saving her from any further onslaught. 'My God! Is that *Phoenix*?'

They followed her gaze to the door through which Phoenix, the biggest rock star in Ireland, was entering, accompanied by his stunning Egyptian wife, Summer, an edgy looking, snake-hipped supermodel. A frisson of excitement went around the reception as everyone clocked them. As the singer with Walking Wounded, Phoenix was the most visible member of the band and probably the most famous Irishman in the world, although the legendary excesses of his bandmates, Rory and Owen Cassidy, had earned them more column inches of late. He was swiftly followed by the least visible member of the band, his little sister Georgie, who played drums. They took up position in a corner, while the rest of the guests acted cool, pretending they weren't there.

'You *know* them?' Carmen asked.

'Will is Walking Wounded's manager,' Lorcan told her.

All the guests were acting like bad extras, feigning absorption in their conversations and studiously ignoring the stars while their eyes drifted surreptitiously towards them. Nobody missed it when, moments later, Rory and Owen Cassidy came in together with their girlfriends and joined the private party in the corner. They were all dressed down but still managed to look more glamorous than anyone else. Beside them, all the other guests appeared clownishly overdone and frumpy.

'I don't know why they were invited to the wedding,' Conor said. 'Tom's partied with them a few times, but they're not that close.'

'Rachel wanted to up the ante,' Helen said drily. 'They'll add cool to the proceedings and give her a much better chance of getting the wedding written up on the society pages.'

'The real question is, why did they come?' Kate said.

'Free grub and booze, according to Will,' Lorcan told her.

'But they're loaded – they don't need free booze.'

'Ah, you can take the boy out of the tenement, but you can't take the tenement out of the boy. Will reckons they can't shake off the ligger mentality.'

'Phoenix seems to have copied your hairdo.' Kate grinned slyly at Lorcan. 'What's the real story on that? I don't buy for a minute that it was Tom's idea.'

'I could tell you, but then I'd have to kill you.' Lorcan laughed, and proceeded to tell her anyway.

*

As there was no sign of dinner and everyone was mingling, Kate armed herself with another pair of gin and tonics and dutifully did the round of her relations, who all asked jovially when she would be giving them a day out. With a pain in her face from pretending to take this in good part, she decided she wasn't quite pissed enough yet to deal with them and drifted towards the bar in search of rein-forcements.

She was seething at the unfairness of it all. For once she had a boyfriend she could parade in front of them and now when she mentioned him they looked at her as though she'd made him up. What was the use of having a boyfriend if you couldn't pull him out on occasions like this, like a trump card?

'Hello Kate.' A familiar baritone shook her out of her private strop.

'Will, hi!' She turned, smiling at him.

He bent to kiss her cheek.

'I haven't seen you in ages,' she said, immediately realising how idotic that sounded. They had just spent the afternoon in each other's company at the wedding and posing for photographs. 'I mean, you know, before this afternoon,' she babbled. 'I hadn't seen you for ages.'

God, what the hell was she saying? She'd had too much to drink. Still, she thought, maybe it was just as well – the booze might loosen her up. She was ridiculously shy with him. It was ludicrous that after more than ten years she still felt that night after the Trinity Ball hanging in the air between them whenever they met. She wondered yet again if Will had any recollection of it. She'd probably never know.

'You look fantastic,' he said.

'Thanks.'

'You've lost weight, haven't you?'

'I'm surprised you noticed!'

'It suits you.'

'You should see me without this dress on.'

'What?' Will spluttered.

Kate blushed to the roots of her hair. 'I didn't mean, you know, the full monty or anything. I just meant this dress is so massive I'm amazed you can tell I'm a bit thinner,' she explained, in a desperate attempt to save face. Too late – Will was already smiling at her like the idiot she was.

God, she's cute, Will thought. I wouldn't half *mind* seeing her without that dress on. Immediately, he gave himself a mental slap, appalled at where his mind was straying. He had been down that road once before – how far he didn't know – but he should have learnt his lesson. The O'Neills had taken him in when his life was falling apart, and he was repaying them by lusting after the baby of the family.

'I heard what happened with Tom's hair,' Kate was saying. 'It was really nice of you to get yours done in sympathy.'

'Well, we couldn't hang the poor sod out to dry, could we?'

'It looks cool.' She gestured at his shaved head. 'It suits you.'

Will smiled wryly. 'It doesn't look so cool now Phoenix has turned up. We look like wannabes.'

'Well, it looks cooler than this.' Kate pointed to her shining mahogany hair, which had been scraped back from her face and piled on top of her head, complete with flowers. 'It actually hurts. I wish I could take it down.'

'I'm sure it'd be okay now that the photographs are done.'

'Oh, I think I'd be *allowed* to, I just don't think it's possible. Even if I took out all the pins and stuff, it'd stay exactly where it is. I think the hairdresser sprayed some kind of all-weather woodstain on it. It'd withstand a hurricane.'

'It does look sort of . . . sturdy.'

'Just what every girl wants – sturdy hair.'

'Well, I'd better go over and say hi to Phoenix and the guys. Why don't you come and meet them?'

'Oh, I'm sure they don't want to be bothered by a load of plebs.'

'They're not exactly surrounded by adoring fans,' Will said. 'Everyone's so concerned about not bothering them that no one talks to them.'

'Still . . . '

'Come on,' Will coaxed, holding out a hand to her. 'I'll tell them that's not your real hair,' he teased when she hesitated.

Will started pulling her in their direction and she allowed herself to be persuaded. After all, she'd be the envy of everyone in the room. Better still, Brian was a huge Walking Wounded fan and he'd be sick when Kate told him she'd got to meet them. It would serve him right for being so unsupportive and not coming to the wedding.

It felt surreal to be in the midst of so many famous faces – especially to see such an iconic figure as Phoenix in the flesh. The closest she had seen these people in real life up to now was from the front row at their concerts when Will had got her and Lorcan VIP tickets.

'Everyone, this is Kate,' Will announced adding, as promised, 'The hair isn't hers – it's an impostor from another planet.'

'Hi, Kate.' Phoenix smiled and shook her hand. His wife's smile was tense but there was warmth in her eyes.

Up close, Phoenix's piercing blue eyes were more penetrating than ever, especially now he'd had his head shaved. Summer towered over him, and he spoke so quietly that Kate had to lean in close to hear him, but he had charisma you could almost touch. 'And what happened to you?' He gestured at Will's head. 'Did your hair get abducted by aliens?'

'Long story,' Will said ruefully, then continued the introductions, 'This is Rory, Tessa, Georgie . . .'

Owen was as stunning up close as he was in all his pictures. He had a wild mop of thick black hair and eyes so dark you couldn't see the pupils, framed by long, spiky lashes. His pale washed-out face bore a permanent five o'clock shadow, but there was something boyishly innocent about his face, which was at odds with the excess baggage under his eyes.

His elder brother, Rory, had a craggy, prematurely lined face and weary eyes that made him look old beyond his years. Kate had already recognised the petite blonde draped over him as Tessa Bond, an English television presenter and *Heat*-seeking missile with a fluffy, bubbly persona. They seemed an unlikely pairing.

Georgie nodded at Kate, her eyes quickly slanting away shyly. A tiny, sullen-looking girl with a cloud of soft dark hair and huge green eyes, she was ravishingly pretty but did her best to disguise it with ugly clothes and confrontational body art in the form of multiple piercings and tattoos. She was dressed in baggy sports clothes, a jewelled belly-button ring her only concession to wedding attire.

Will was stumped when he came to Owen's girlfriend, a pretty blonde whom he had not met before and didn't expect to meet again. Owen was sweet to his girlfriends, but he had the attention span of a four-year-old with ADHD. At least he had better taste than his brother, Will reflected.

'This is Fiona.' Owen did the honours. 'And I'm Owen,' he said, flashing Kate a smile that made her feel like Angelina Jolie. He was alternately swigging Jack Daniel's from a bottle and sucking at a cigarette.

'Oh yes, I know.' Kate giggled.

'For God's sake, put out that cigarette, Owen,' Will ordered. 'You know it's illegal to smoke in here.'

'Oh, it's okay,' Owen said, taking another puff. 'It's not nicotine.'

'Well, *that's* illegal everywhere,' Will told him, exasperated. 'Always has been.'

'Oh, right.' Owen stubbed it out dutifully.

Tessa peered at Kate's hair and smiled smugly.

'Don't worry about your hair, Kate,' Owen said, 'Tessa's lips aren't hers either. She got them off a duck-billed platypus at the zoo.'

Tessa shot him a murderous look, but Kate was the only person unwise enough to laugh, and Tessa rewarded her with an even more homicidal stare.

'So, what are you up to at the moment, Tessa?' Will asked, to distract her.

'I have a book coming out next week, believe it or not.' She gave him a dazzling smile, the frothy persona back in place now that the attention was on her. 'Imagine, me – a book! And it's not just pictures, it's got words and everything.' She giggled flirtatiously.

'What sort of book is it?'

'Well, it's sort of about the journey I've been making over the past year and what I've discovered about—'

'It's a diet book,' Rory said flatly, before she could get into her stride.

'It's not a diet,' Tessa corrected him sharply. 'It's an eating plan for life.'

'Oh, that's . . . er . . . such a new concept,' Will said.

Kate stifled a snort.

'Yes, and it's sort of my personal story too, the journey I made and what I discovered about myself along the way.'

'Right,' Will nodded politely. 'Sounds great!'

'Oh yeah, a real page-turner,' Owen muttered.

Phoenix slunk off, mumbling something about seating. As Tessa and Rory drifted off to find more drinks, Owen made trout lips behind Tessa's back. 'You've made an enemy for life there, Kate,' he smiled at her conspiratorially. 'And what about you, you slut?' he mocked Will. 'I thought there'd only be your big toe left to pull you out by, you were so far up her jacksie.'

'I was not!' Will protested. 'I was just being polite.'

'Don't know what Rory's doing with her,' Owen went on.

'I don't imagine it'll last long.' Tessa's relationships weren't renowned for their longevity.

'Don't be so sure,' Owen said darkly. 'I think Rory's looking for a father figure.'

'A father figure? *Tessa?*'

'Yeah. You know – someone to tell you you're shite and beat the crap out of you.'

Tom and Rachel had spent so long posing for photographs that all the guests were sozzled by the time they were summoned to dinner. As everyone piled into the ballroom and took their seats, Helen noticed to her extreme annoyance that Walking Wounded had commandeered a table for themselves, scuppering the seating plan she and Rachel had spent weeks arranging.

She wasn't the only one put out by their piracy.

'Phoenix was supposed to be sitting beside *me*,' Tina was complaining to Will. 'I can't believe he's abandoning me to go and do the gang thing with the band. First you and now him. I don't know why I bothered coming!'

'I'm not abandoning you. I'm the best man. I have to sit at the top table.'

'Now I'll get stuck with some bloody randomer!' Tina huffed.

Just then Helen came bustling up and overheard her. 'Sorry, Tina,' she said, 'but there's nothing I can do. Your lot have rather landed us in it, I'm afraid, Will.'

'Should have known better than to try and separate the inseparable,' Will said coolly. 'And *please* tell me you weren't trying to fix Georgie up with someone.'

Helen smiled guiltily – she was an enthuastic matchmaker. She ran a singles club purely as a hobby, inspired by her sincere desire to help others achieve the state of wedded bliss that she enjoyed. 'And another thing,' she leaned closer to whisper in his ear, 'I think she and Owen are doing coke.'

'Probably,' Will agreed. 'And I'm sure they're not the only ones.'

'Yes, but I mean out on the table, in front of everybody.'

'*What?*' Will groaned. He wished people wouldn't invite the band to their parties and then expect him to nursemaid them. He had warned Rachel that if she insisted on asking them to her wedding he wouldn't be responsible for policing their behaviour. Still, there was more at stake here than the smooth running of Rachel's wedding. 'Right, I'll have a word with them.'

'Thanks.' Helen turned to Tina. 'I've put Kate's friend Freddie beside you, Tina,' she said, then placed a firm hand on Tina's back to propel her to her seat.

Will went over to the band. Sure enough, Owen had all his gear out and he and Georgie were chopping out lines of coke in view of everybody. 'For God's sake, Owen, put that stuff away,' he said impatiently. 'If you must do it, at least go into the bog.'

'Hey, don't sweat it, Will,' Owen said. 'It's a private party.'

'So what? Surely even *you* know that stuff's illegal!'

'Yeah, but we're among friends, aren't we? Who's going to shop us?'

'So, you know every waiter and waitress here personally, do you?' Will countered.

'No, but—'

'Because you can be damn sure they know you. And they aren't paid so much they wouldn't be tempted by the nice fat bonus they'd get from a newspaper for a story about you and your Class-A nosebag.'

'Oh . . . right. Sorry.' He cleared everything away and shoved it into his pocket. 'Love the lollipop look, by the way. Very cool.'

'Thanks.' Will chuckled. It was impossible to stay angry with Owen for long.

As he was about to head for the top table, Owen got up, took Georgie's hand and made for the door.

'Owen,' Will pulled him back, 'the *gents'* loo.'

Owen turned and smiled ruefully at Georgie. 'Sorry, babes, won't be long.'

Fiona was watching the proceedings sadly, looking as if she wished *she* was the one being invited to join Owen in the loo. Will felt like telling her she had no reason to be jealous, but he knew that wasn't true. Any girlfriend of Owen's would have to get used to playing second fiddle to Georgie Holland. She and Owen had a connection that went way deeper than sex.

As Owen left the room, Will stood in front of Georgie with his arms folded, glaring down at her. 'Don't even *think* about following him,' he warned her.

Georgie looked mutinous.

'Come on, give me a break.'

'Sorry, Will.' Georgie sagged, relenting.

'You know that stuff's no good for you anyway. I thought you'd stopped.'

'I have – more or less.' She evaded his eyes.

Will glanced at Summer, who spread her hands and raised an eyebrow helplessly. He sat down beside Georgie.

'How are you doing?' he asked.

'Okay,' she said, drawing patterns on the tablecloth with a finger.

'Really?'

'Yeah, I'm fine.' She looked at him this time, smiling shakily. 'I just miss the tour, you know?'

'I know.'

Georgie was the only one in the band – possibly the only person in *any* band – who was happiest on tour. She loved the way they all lived in each other's ears on tour buses, in hotel rooms, on flights. She loved the fact that there was always someone around if you got the night horrors. But, then, she rarely got the night horrors in the topsy-turvy days of touring because they stayed up all night and slept in the day. It was easier sleeping when it was bright.

'Well, we'll be going to Tuscany soon.'

'I'm really looking forward to that.' She beamed. 'It's a brilliant idea.'

Fiona was looking rather lost, Will observed. He didn't envy any-one trying to infiltrate the tight-knit gang of four that was Walking Wounded. It wasn't that they were hostile to outsiders; they simply didn't need them. They were a self-contained unit, never more relaxed and happy than in each other's company where nothing needed to be explained or justified.

Both sets of siblings were the product of one-parent families, Georgie and Phoenix (neé Peter) having been raised by their father after their mother had died, Owen and Rory by their mother after their father had walked out. They had grown up next door to each other, united by poverty and a blistering hatred of their respective fathers. The Cassidy brothers hated theirs for having walked out, leaving their mother to fend for herself and two small children, while Phoenix and Georgie hated theirs for sticking around to inflict his drunken violence on them – and worse, Will suspected, in Georgie's case.

When the three boys decided to start a band, they hadn't given Georgie any choice about being part of it. She was presented with a set of drumsticks and a teach-yourself-drumming book and ordered to learn. Then they had plonked her in the band where they could keep an eye on her and stymie any chance she might have of a love life. All three were fiercely protective of her. Will often thought the way they stood on stage was symbolic of their relationship, Georgie perched on her drum-riser, locked away behind her huge kit, with Owen and Rory ranged in front of her, wielding their guitars menac-ingly, and Phoenix in front, staring everyone out defiantly.

Musically, Georgie was the weakest link in the band. In the early days, her drumming had been decidedly ropey and several record-com-pany executives had suggested replacing her. Instead, they had found themselves replaced, while Georgie was sent for more drumming les-sons. She would never be one of the greatest drummers in rock, but anyone who knew the people involved was aware that Walking Wounded was about a lot more than music. It was a lifeboat for all of them, and they weren't about to throw one of the family overboard.

'Go on, do your best-man thing.' Georgie smiled at him now. 'Don't worry about me.'

'Knock 'em dead, Baldy,' Owen said, as he passed Will on his way back from the loo.

*

Grace's sister, Iris, no respecter of cool, had planted herself in the empty seat at the Walking Wounded table, showing the same blithe disregard as they had for the seating plan. She hadn't bothered to consult it. She knew exactly the sort of boring old fart Helen would have considered a suitable dinner companion for a sixty-something widow such as herself. Helen meant well, but these boys looked much more fun and more her kind of people.

Tessa was gawping at her now as though Iris was a bug she had found in her salad.

Owen seemed amused, though. 'Hi, I'm Owen.' He extended his hand, eyes twinkling.

Such a beautiful boy! Iris thought. If only I was forty years younger.

'You look familiar, dear,' she told Tessa. 'Have I seen you on TV?'

Tessa brightened, deciding the old bag wasn't so bad after all. 'Yes, you probably have. I'm Tessa Bond.'

Iris smiled vacantly at her. 'Oh, you're not who I thought you were,' she said.

'Who did you think she was?' Owen asked. He had clocked the mischief in the old dear's eyes.

'What do you call that woman who does the topless gardening – you know, with all that frizzy hair?'

Georgie blew bubbles into her beer, while Owen roared laughing.

'She has some man's name – Jim or Fred or something,' Iris continued.

'Charlie Dimmock.' Tessa was puce with rage.

'Oh yes, that's the one!'

Owen thought he might be in love.

'I don't look anything *like* Charlie bloody Dimmock!' Tessa fumed.

'Tessa doesn't do topless gardening,' Owen explained helpfully. 'She presents a game show on TV. And she has a diet book coming out next week.'

'It's not a *diet*,' Tessa explained, with a rictus smile. 'It's more of a healthy-eating plan for life. Dieting is such a negative concept – all about depriving yourself. My plan is about making positive permanent changes to your eating habits.'

'That's interesting.' Iris yawned. 'Do you follow this diet yourself, dear?'

'I don't diet. It's a healthy-eating plan. And, yes, I do follow it.'

'Poor you,' Iris said, as she slathered an inch of butter onto her bread roll. 'I'm lucky – I've always been able to eat whatever I want without putting on an ounce.'

'Fair play to you, missus.' Owen grinned at her.

'I've always felt sorry for chubby girls who have to diet all the time – it must be such a bore. And it makes you a boring person too, doesn't it?' She was addressing the whole table now.

Tessa was literally lost for words, her mouth flapping open like a fish's, her face a mask of unbridled fury – a lesser woman than Iris would have cringed.

'I am *not* chubby.' In fact, Tessa's weight-loss credentials amounted to nothing more than a brush with bulimia and a couple of fad diets that had seen her go from a slim size twelve to an almost anorexic size six.

'No, of course not,' Iris agreed. 'Your diet has obviously worked wonders – you're a great advertisement for it.' She smiled condescendingly at Tessa. 'I'm sure you'll sell tons of books.'

Owen was roaring with laughter. The daft old bat was priceless!

Undaunted by Tessa's dagger looks, Iris proceeded to introduce herself to everyone. 'I'm Rachel's aunt, on her mother's side,' she explained grandly.

'Who's Rachel?' Owen whispered to Rory.

'Fuck knows!'

'This is Rachel's wedding we're at,' Tessa spat. 'That *binge* you were all on for the past three days was the stag party.'

Owen fixed her with a cold stare. 'It wasn't a binge. I do not *binge*. This,' he said, raising the bottle of Jack Daniel's to Tessa, 'is a drinking plan for life.'

With the endless speeches, toasts, presentations and cake-cutting out of the way, the bopping and table-hopping began in earnest.

'Ugh, that was interminable,' Kate groaned, when she found Freddie. 'If I don't get to bed soon I'll go insane from sleep deprivation.' Alcohol and adrenalin had carried her through so far, but now she was starting to crash. 'D'you think anyone noticed I fell asleep during the speeches?'

'You're joking, right?'

'No . . . What are you getting at?' Kate didn't like the way he was looking at her. 'Freddie – what?'

'Oh, nothing. It's just that when Will was talking about the beautiful bridesmaid, everyone turned to you and you were sort of . . .' he hesitated, grinning.

'*What?*'

'Well . . . face down in your dinner.'

'Oh, my God, Freddie!' Kate covered her face with her hands.

'You looked cute! Didn't you notice everyone laughing when you woke up?'

'Yes, but I thought Will had just said something funny.'

'He said some very nice things about you.'

'Oh, he had to,' Kate said dismissively. 'It's in the best man's book of rules to say the bridesmaid's beautiful even if she's like the back end of a bus. And don't get excited when he comes for a duty dance either, because that's all it is. I wish he wouldn't – it's so humiliating.'

'At least you got to sit at the top table with him – the divine creature,' Freddie waved at Will. 'I had Tina, who was sulking because I wasn't Phoenix, and some woman who went on interminably about her yeast infection.' He shuddered extravagantly.

'That'll be Rachel's friend, Karen. She's allergic to every edible substance known to man, apparently.'

'Didn't stop her scoffing her dinner and hoovering up everyone else's leftovers. She kept referring to "down there". I pretended I thought she was talking about Australia.'

'Good save!'

'Until I went too far and said I'd spent some of the happiest times of my life "down there". Let's just say she looked at me with renewed interest.'

Kate giggled.

'Your dotty aunt got the best seat in the house.' Iris was now engaged in a fiercely competitive drinking contest with Owen.

'I wouldn't like to put money on who'll win that one,' Kate said.

'And there's our boy.' Freddie nodded to where Will was emerging from the dance floor. 'If you really don't want him, do you mind if I have a go?'

'I really think the lad's not for turning, but feel free to try – he's all yours.'

'Ooh, if only!'

Kate watched anxiously as Freddie bounded over to Will like an overgrown puppy. Straight men could find him a bit intimidating, especially if he obviously fancied them. However, she experienced a pang of jealousy as Will rested a hand casually on his shoulder and they were soon guaffawing together like old chums.

'Well, of course he'd like Freddie,' she told herself crossly. 'Who wouldn't? He's adorable.'

'Hello, Kate.' Mary, one of her gin-soaked Cork aunts, wove up to her. 'What have you been doing with yourself lately?'

'Working in Africa for the past three months.'

'Oh, how lovely.' Mary beamed. 'Did you meet anyone nice?'

Kate recalled all the people she had met on the trip – the cheerful, capable drivers; the passengers of all ages and nationalities, some of whom had become good friends; the tantalisingly fleeting encounters with friendly locals in the towns and villages – but she knew that none of these were what Mary meant by 'anyone nice'. In her book, 'anyone nice' was code for 'any eligible young man who might be interested in marrying you'. 'No, Mary. I didn't meet anyone nice.'

'Oh dear,' Mary said, not sounding in the least surprised. 'What a pity.'

'My bloody relatives,' Kate fumed to Freddie when he returned to her. 'I could scale Mount Everest and they'd only want to know if I'd "met anyone nice" up there!' She was beginning to find the wedding seriously depressing. As the DJ launched into another slow set, couples melted into each other's arms all around her, swaying slowly to the music, snogging for Ireland.

'That Will of yours is a seriously good bloke,' Freddie told her.

'So I hear.' Kate watched miserably as he pulled Tina onto the floor and into his arms. Seconds later they were devouring each other.

'Kate, are you okay?'

She was aware that her eyes were full of tears. 'I'm just so sick of being a wallflower, Freddie. Always the bridesmaid, never the bride. Everyone says a wedding's a good place to meet men, but it's not.'

'All the romance getting to you, is it?'

'Don't mind me, I've just had too much to drink and too little sleep.' She sniffed. 'I need my bed and my own clothes.'

'Anyway, do you *want* to meet men?' Freddie asked cautiously. 'What about Brian?'

'Yes, what *about* Brian? Where the fuck is he when I need him? I mean he hasn't seen me in *three months* and instead of racing over at the first opportunity, he's made a bloody *date*.'

'So, when are you seeing him?'

'Tomorrow evening.' She sighed heavily.

'You don't sound too happy about it.'

'I am, it's just—'

'Feeling guilty about the long dong from Down Under, are you?'

'No, not at all. I'm totally off the hook on that one. Before I went away, Brian and I agreed we were on a break and we could see other people.'

'His idea, I suppose?'

'Of course. I think he had someone in mind when he said it. Probably one of his *groupies*.'

'He's got groupies?'

'Oh yes, lots. You'd be surprised.'

'I'd be absolutely gobsmacked.' At least it had backfired on the little toerag, Freddie thought gleefully. 'So, if it's not that, what's bothering you about seeing him?'

'It's just that I know he'll start a serious discussion about "the relationship" – where we are, where we're going, blah, blah, blah – but I just want a nice dinner, a bottle of wine and a welcome-back shag. I was supposed to be giving some thought to "the relationship" while I was away. I just wish he didn't make me feel like tomorrow's the exam and I haven't done any revision.'

'Never mind. Monday we'll have a quiet night in on the sofa. I can't offer the shag, I'm afraid, but I could stretch to a bottle of wine and a pizza. And we can have a Dr McDreamy marathon – I've got three months' worth of *Grey's Anatomy* on tape for you.'

'God, Freddie, if you could just give me that shag I'd dump Brian in a second.'

Just then, the DJ started playing 'Dancing Queen'. Freddie jumped up, extending a hand to Kate. 'Come on,' he said, 'they're playing my song.'

'And I thought we could move that painting of your mother's from the hall.' On the dance floor, Tina was outlining to Will her plans for inviting *Hello!* magazine to interview her in his 'gracious home'.

'I *love* that painting.'

'It's so dark and gloomy!'

'Well, she did it not long before she died.'

'Oh.' Tina made a sympathetic face. 'Well, we can discuss it later,' she said soothingly. 'Anyway, in the living room, I thought I could pose in front of the fireplace, and we could hang your mother's drawing of you over it – that little pencil sketch. I love that. And since you refuse to be in any of the pictures, I thought it would be nice if you were present in some way.'

Will looked down at her. 'I don't refuse to be in any of the pictures.'

'You don't?' Tina's face lit up in delight.

'No. You can put my urn on top of the mantelpiece and get a picture of that. Or you can scatter my ashes in the living room and they can get a shot of me sprinkled over the carpet.'

'*What?*'

'You can even invite them to my wake, if you like,' he said cheerfully, 'and you could pose with my corpse.'

'What the hell are you—'

'Because that's the only way *Hello!* is getting into my house,' he said. 'Over my dead body.'

'God, you're so bloody selfish!' Tina's eyes sparked fury.

'You don't *need* that,' he said.

'It's what I *want*. I can't believe you won't help me move on in my career!'

'You don't need my help. You can do your own thing.'

'Well, it's just as well I have *some* friends. Tessa's put me in touch with her publicist – Dev Tennant, no less – and he's agreed to take me on.'

Oh, great! Will thought. With the notorious Dev Tennant on the case, he'd never know another moment's privacy.

When Will turned up for his duty dance, Kate was grateful the DJ was starting another slow set. She and Freddie regularly burned up the floors of the hottest clubs in town, but if years of school debs' dances had taught her anything it was that no one looked cool shaking their booty in a ballgown and, besides, right now she didn't have the energy for anything more than a desultory shuffle around the floor propped up by her partner.

When she stood up she realised she was seriously drunk. The room was spinning sickeningly and she closed her eyes, putting her head on Will's chest as they swayed to the throbbing music. The warmth from his body and the steady beat of his heart were comforting.

'Kate, are you all right?' Will frowned.

'I'm fine. Just knackered. I was travelling all day yesterday.' She shivered.

'You're shaking.'

'I'm a bit cold – it's just sleep deprivation.'

'Here.' Will whisked off his jacket and put it around her shoulders, then took her in his arms again.

Next she felt his fingers in her hair. He was slowly and gently removing the pins. What about the woodstain? she thought, panicked. I'll look like a scarecrow. It took an enormous effort to lift her head to protest.

'It's okay.' Will soothed her. 'I'll fluff it out – you won't look weird, I promise.'

'Mmm.' Kate settled back happily. As the pins came out, he massaged her scalp and she felt the tension seeping away. God, this is sexy, she thought, if only I was properly awake to enjoy it.

The next thing she knew, Will was shaking her gently. 'Kate?'

'Hmm?' She opened her eyes lazily, then realised she'd been asleep, and the only thing keeping her upright was Will's arms, vice-like around her. 'God, sorry.'

'You poor thing, you're completely exhausted.' He peered down at her in concern. 'Come on.' He pulled her off the dance-floor, 'I'm taking you home.'

'There's no need. I can get a taxi.'

'Don't be silly. It's no trouble. Anyway, we can't have you taking a taxi on your own in this state. And I don't think anyone else is quite ready to leave yet,' he added drily, as Grace hopped past, leading a long, snaking conga.

'But what about you?'

'I wouldn't mind getting out of here for a while. When you don't drink, these things pall after the first ten hours or so.' Tina was happily holed up in a corner with Summer and Phoenix and he'd be back before she missed him.

'Well, thanks, it's really nice of you. I'd love to get to bed. I'm staying with Mum and Dad tonight.' Kate was almost tearful with gratitude.

'I'll go and tell your father I'm driving you home.'

When he was gone, Kate sank into a chair and laid her head on the table. A moment later, she felt a hand on the back of her neck. 'Okay, I'm ready.' She sat up with effort and turned around. 'Oh! It's *you*.'

While Kate had been dancing with Will, Freddie had lost no time in bounding off in search of Jack O'Neill.

'Mr O., I bring glad tidings of great joy,' he announced gleefully and proceeded to regale Jack with what Kate had said about Brian. 'I think his character might be getting written out of the series,' he concluded triumphantly.

Just then, Will came up to them. 'Jack, I'm going to drive Kate home. She's completely played out.'

Way to go, Kate, Freddie thought, delighted.

'Okay, Will, thanks.' Suddenly Jack's face froze with horror.

'Oh, my God!' Freddie had followed his gaze.

'Trust him to turn up just in time to save his skin.'

A tall, fair-haired man was pulling Kate into his arms.

'Who's that?' Will asked – he was rather put out, Freddie thought.

'It's the bloody Tree-shagger,' Jack snarled.

'Who?'

Freddie rested a hand on Will's shoulder. 'That, my dear William,' he said, 'is Kate's boyfriend – the dreaded Tree-hugger.'

*

'Quick – now!' Kate laughed, gathering up as much of her skirt as she could while Will hastily slammed the car door before it escaped again. 'I come with my own air-bag,' she joked, as Will sat in.

'Sorry about the delay,' he said, as he started the car. 'I just thought when your boyfriend turned up that you'd want to go home with him.' He had hung back and Kate had eventually come in search of him, asking for her lift.

'Oh no, Brian wanted to stay for a while. Besides,' she added, 'he was on his bike.'

'Ah, right.' He swung the car into the road. 'You're not exactly dressed for riding pillion.'

'Crossbar,' Kate corrected him.

'Sorry?'

'Crossbar, not pillion. Pushbike, not motor.'

'Oh! Oh, right.'

Kate suppressed a giggle at the comical expression on Will's face.

'I wanted to come on my bike,' he said apologetically, 'but it had a puncture, so I had to make do with the Jag.'

'I'm very glad you did.' She didn't want Will to think she was one of those awful inverted snobs who looked down on people for driving big fuck-off cars.

She yawned contentedly, snuggling into the plush upholstery, lulled by the gentle purr of the engine. The day had turned out well after all, she thought. Brian hadn't been able to wait until tomorrow to see her. He had told her how much he had missed her and had given her the most gorgeous kiss in front of everyone. She just hoped her bloody aunts had been watching. She had been reassured to find how glad she was to see him and how much she fancied him still. He really was devastatingly attractive – and so sexy. She hadn't even minded that he'd wanted to stay on at the wedding without her. He'd had a tiring day at his workshop and he wanted to unwind with a few drinks and a dance. Besides, it would give him the chance to get to know her family better. She felt sure that once they got to know him, they'd love him almost as much as she did.

'Do you think one of us should tell him his invisibility's wearing off?'

Lorcan said, staring stonily at Brian, who was giving it loads on the dance floor, engaged in some extremely dirty dancing with a very buxom girl.

Freddie, also glaring at Brian, felt unaccountably miffed that the Tree-shagger was with *his* buxom girl – Ms F Cup no less. Fickle tart! he thought huffily.

'Doesn't he realise,' Lorcan ranted, 'that all Kate's family and friends can *see* him?'

'He doesn't think he has anything to feel guilty about. He fancies himself a free spirit.'

'Huh!' Jack grunted. 'Anything as long as it's free, that's him. Free spirits, free beer, free wine.'

'Free lurve and all,' Freddie whispered to Lorcan so that only he would hear. He didn't want to upset Jack.

'You reckon?' Lorcan asked worriedly.

'Wouldn't be surprised.' Freddie sighed. 'Like your father said, anything as long as it's free.'

Lorcan watched Brian's partner gyrating maniacally before him, her comedy boobs spilling out over her skimpy top, and thought longingly of Carmen. He knew that, as a bloke, his stance on boobs was supposed to be the bigger the better, but he found the kind of industrial rigging they required extremely unsexy. That and the way their owners were always shoving them in your face, he thought, watching Brian's partner arch her back and thrust out her chest to give Brian a better view of her undulating cleavage.

Still, Brian seemed to be enjoying it, Lorcan thought morosely, and turned to scan the room for Carmen. She was taking an unconscionably long time in the loo. Just as he was wondering if she had left, he saw her coming through the room towards him and relaxed again, a slow smile spreading across his face as their eyes met. All he wanted to do was take her upstairs and spend the rest of the night making love to her. But, at the same time, he really liked her: he didn't want to rush things and risk scaring her off. When she reached him, he pressed a chaste kiss to her forehead.

Carmen smiled. 'You promised me three things if I came to this wedding with you today,' she reminded him, eyes twinkling. 'I've had the cake and the champagne . . .' She let the rest of the sentence hang in the air suggestively.

Lorcan could hardly believe they were both so much on the same wavelength. 'I'll get us a room,' he said, tense with excitement, but hoping he hadn't misunderstood.

Carmen put his fears to rest. She held up her hand. A room key dangled from one finger.

Lorcan's face lit up like a child's on Christmas Day. 'Never let it be said I don't deliver on my promises.' His heart was pounding as he took Carmen's hand and practically ran out of the ballroom with her.

Chapter 3

'Home sweet home.' It was the next morning and Kate sighed with
relief as she kicked open the door of the top-floor apartment she
shared with Freddie in the trendy Temple Bar area of Dublin. She was
in a lather having hauled her bags up the four flights of stairs but was
greeted ecstatically by Didi and Gogo (formally Vladimir and
Estragon), their two cats, who wound in and out of her legs, purring.
'Hi guys.' She bent to stroke them. 'I missed you too.'

They were really Freddie's cats ('The only kind of pussy I'll ever
have,' as he was fond of introducing them). He had found them as stray
kittens and brought them home, naming them after the two tramps
from *Waiting for Godot*, which he had been working on at the time.

'Freddie!' Kate called. 'Are you home?'

'We're in here,' Freddie called from the sitting room.

'*Who's we?*' Kate wondered.

Before she had time to investigate, Freddie bounded out to her.

'Your sister-in-law's a genius!' he whispered excitedly, casting his eyes towards the sitting room.

'Helen?' She looked askance at him, but he merely nodded. She glanced warily in the direction of the sitting room. 'Is she giving you a master class in napkin-folding or something?' Admittedly, Helen's swan napkin was pretty impressive, but it was hardly the sort of thing that would have Freddie wetting his kecks.

'No.' Freddie laughed, then mouthed, 'She fixed me up.'

'Oh! Well done you!' Kate clapped him on the shoulder.

'Well done Helen!'

'So when did this happen?'

'Well, you know I was supposed to be on the table that was taken over by Walking Wounded?'

'Yes.'

'Well, Helen mentioned there was supposed to be another gay bloke on it, so, knowing Helen, I guessed he was a set-up for me. I found out who he was and went to check him out surreptitiously. When I discovered he was drop-dead gorgeous, I introduced myself. The rest, as they say, is pornography.' He licked his lips lasciviously.

'Wow! Helen must be really good at this matchmaking stuff. I wouldn't have credited her with being able to pick your type.'

'Me neither. But that's the best thing about him – he's not my usual type at all. He's actually *nice*.'

Kate hadn't seen Freddie so excited about someone for ages.

'His name's Ken,' he babbled. 'And get this – he's a *solicitor*!'

'A *solicitor*!' Kate mimicked Freddie's awestruck tone.

'Well, I *mean*, it's so grown-up! It's like a real job – he wears *suits* to work and everything.'

'Imagine!' Kate mocked.

'And he's got a briefcase!' Freddie continued, unabashed.

'Are you sure he wasn't just saying that to get you into bed?'

'If he was, it worked.' Freddie picked up Kate's bags and carted them to her bedroom. 'When you've sorted yourself out, come and meet him,' he said, dropping her luggage. 'Then we're all going for a long, boozy brunch and a post-mortem.'

'Oh Freddie, I can't.' Kate grimaced. 'I literally haven't a bean, and all my plastic's maxed out.'

'Don't worry about that.' Freddie dismissed her objections. 'It's not as if I don't owe you one. Besides, I'm sure you could use a few champagne cocktails to shake off the post-wedding anticlimax.'

'True,' Kate conceded.

'And we can't let the wedding of the year pass without a thorough autopsy, can we? So, when you're sorted, two gorgeous men are waiting to take you out.'

In the sitting room, Kate found Freddie sharing the couch with a handsome, rugged, square-jawed type. He was wearing a soft denim shirt of Freddie's that brought out the intense blue of his eyes. He certainly seemed a more likely prospect than the parade of deadbeats Freddie usually dragged home.

'Ken, this is Kate, my flatmate. Kate, Ken.'

'Hi.' As they shook hands, Ken's eyes lit up with recognition. 'You were the bridesmaid,' he said.

'Oh, and I thought my disguise was perfect.'

'Almost.' It was like Cinderella in reverse, Ken thought. She was infinitely prettier today and seemed about ten years younger, dressed casually in jeans and a T-shirt, her long dark hair falling loose down her back. With her face devoid of makeup, her clear green eyes sparkled and her skin was glowing and flawless. 'You played a blinder,' he said. 'Snoring through the speeches was a nice touch.'

'Thanks. I thought the whole smiling-graciously-looking-dignified thing had been done to death.'

'Well, you certainly avoided that pitfall,' Ken remarked. 'It was a novel approach.'

'Okay, let's go,' Freddie said, having glanced at his watch. 'We'll be late if we don't get a move on.'

'That shirt suits you,' Kate commented to Ken, as they went out.

'You should keep it,' Freddie said. 'I've never worn it. Can't think why I bought it – must have been having a lumberjack moment.'

It's good to be back, Kate thought, as they strolled along the winding, cobbled streets, with the peaceful sound of the Christchurch bells ringing in the background. She loved living in this part of the city. It was always busy at night, with its proliferation of clubs, bars and restaurants, but she liked it most of all on quiet Sunday mornings like this, when it had a lazy, muted feel. Tourists spilled out of hotels and clubbers drifted home or sat at outdoor cafés eating breakfast, still in their party clothes, slowly coming down from the highs of the night before. The quiet was broken by the high-spirited laughter of a few young girls in veils, obviously refugees from a hen party, who burst onto the street with a clatter of shrieks, and were gone, disappearing into the morning like wraiths.

She had missed this morning-after life – the late Sunday breakfasts that she and Freddie spent woozily picking apart the depredations of the previous night, piecing together hazy details, or swapping stories of disastrous dates. Kate had always secretly enjoyed these post-mortems more than the dates and the clubbing, though there had been less of either for her since she had been going out with Brian. Now she listened to Freddie's stories with a mixture of relief that she was no longer putting herself out there and envy that he was still having adventures.

The restaurant was packed, buzzing with animated chatter and the clatter of plates as white-aproned waiters slid between the tables bearing huge plates of food or colourful jugs of Bloody Marys and Bellinis.

'So, tell all,' Freddie said, when the waitress had taken their order. He propped his arms on the table and fixed Kate with an expectant stare.

'There's nothing to tell,' she said. 'Sounds like you two are the ones with the tale to spill. I had an uneventful night.'

'Oh come on! Last I saw you, you were about to cop off with Will but Brian turned up – and then you copped off with him anyway,' Freddie said.

'I wasn't copping off with Will,' Kate protested, glancing warily at Ken.

'You don't have to be discreet,' Freddie said. 'Ken knows everything. I've filled him in – so to speak.' He wiggled his eyebrows like Groucho Marx.

'He knows everything about what?'

'About you and Will.'

Oh great! Kate thought.

'Don't look so worried! You can trust Ken,' Freddie assured her. 'He's a solicitor.'

Ken hooted at this. 'It's the first time I've heard that one!'

'Will was just giving me a lift home,' Kate insisted.

'I was so afraid you were going to say that.' Freddie sounded disappointed

'Well, it's true.'

'Never mind,' Freddie perked up, 'here are the drinks. It'll all come out over a few cocktails.'

'Honestly, Freddie, there's nothing *to* come out,' Kate sucked her Cosmopolitan through a straw, relaxing as the zingy-fresh sharpness of the vodka surged through her veins, at once soothing and invigorating. 'Will really just gave me a lift home. I was too comatose to do anything. Besides,' she added sadly, 'I fell asleep while we were dancing and I drooled on his shoulder – not exactly sexy, is it?'

'I guess not,' Freddie conceded.

They were interrupted by the waitress arriving with their food. Kate ploughed into smoked haddock and poached egg on a bed of creamy mashed potato. 'God, this is divine.'

'Better leave some room,' Freddie advised. 'Aren't you going out to eat with Brian tonight?'

'Oh, it'll be one of his bran-mash places,' she said. 'You know, cheap and cheerless, not a Cosmopolitan in sight.'

'Well, last night proved one thing,' Freddie said, bolstered by the food. 'You're still hung up on Will.'

'I am not!' Kate objected, somewhat half-heartedly.

'Oh come on! You've just admitted you couldn't even have a dance with the bloke without drooling all over him.'

'It wasn't that kind of drooling. I'm over him,' she asserted, unconvincingly.

'Liar!' Freddie scoffed. 'She's not over him, you know,' he said conversationally, to Ken.

'Okay.' Kate felt defeated. 'Maybe I'm not. Maybe I never will be, but so what?'

'*So what!*' Freddie was aghast.

'Yes. Okay, if Will asked me to marry him tomorrow and have his ten kids, I'd say yes.'

'I knew it!' Freddie crowed.

'But the same is true of George Clooney, and, guess what – *it's not going to happen!*'

'Well, not with George,' Freddie agreed. 'He seems to be untame-able,' he added wistfully.

'Not with George, and not with Will either,' Kate said firmly.

'So you and him are history?' Ken asked.

'Not even that, since we never *were* in the first place.'

'What about the time you shagged him?' Freddie enquired.

Kate shook her head. 'One drunken shag doth not a Summer of Lurve make. Anyway,' she added, more brightly, 'none of that matters now. I love Brian.'

'Well, I think you're settling.'

'I'm not. You just don't like Brian.'

'I don't *dis*like him,' Freddie prevaricated.

'Yeah you do.'

'Okay, I admit I'm not his biggest fan, but it's not that. You may love Brian, but Will is the *one*.'

'Like Keanu Reeves in *The Matrix*,' Ken put in.

'Mmm.' Freddie was momentarily distracted by the thought of Keanu Reeves. 'Will is the love of your life,' he continued, returning to the subject at hand. 'He's Neo, he's Mr Big, he's Heathcliff. Life's too short to settle for less. You've got to go after what you want.'

'I am. I'm going after Brian.'

Freddie sighed in exasperation.

'Maybe I can resolve this,' Ken suggested. 'I have a system for working out who's the better prospect when you have to choose between two people.'

'Sounds great!' Freddie said. 'Let's do it.'

'But I'm not choosing between them,' Kate said. 'Will isn't a possibility.'

'Well, nine times out of ten the one you're choosing anyway comes out on top, so it reassures you that you're making the right decision.'

Kate was dubious.

'Come on,' Ken coaxed her. 'At least you can prove to Freddie that you're not settling.'

*

Of course, Kate thought dejectedly twenty minutes later, this *would* turn out to be the tenth time out of ten.

Ken had claimed it was a simple mathematical calculation. His 'system' consisted of dividing a sheet of paper in half, allocating one side to Will and the other to Brian. He then made each a 'pro' and a 'con' column, arbitrarily awarding points from one to ten for positive attributes and deducting them for negative ones. 'Add up the scores at the end and you have your answer,' he had concluded.

'For example, a cool job gets ten points. Will has about the coolest job in the world, short of actually being in a band. Plus he's loaded, so that's another ten points. Now, what does your boyfriend do?'

'He's a psychotherapist.'

'Not as cool as manager of a band, but pretty lucrative,' Ken decided.

'Not the way *he* does it,' Freddie cut in, as Ken's pen was poised over Brian's 'pro' column.

'How does he do it?'

'With Tibetan singing bowls and dancing.'

'Ah!' Ken promptly crossed out 'psychotherapist' in the pro column and wrote 'space cadet' on the con side. 'Band manager, *dix points*,' he said, in a fake Eurovision accent, 'professional hippie, *nul points*.'

'This is fun, isn't it?' Freddie grinned, wrinkling his nose at Kate. He was evidently enjoying himself.

'Brilliant!' Kate said drily.

And so it had gone on, with Will outscoring Brian consistently. Ken and Freddie had become so engrossed in their little game that Kate wondered if they'd forgotten she was there.

'I've got another! I've got another!' Freddie shrieked, bouncing around in his seat like a schoolboy begging the teacher to let him answer a question.

'For Brian or Will?'

'Will. He's got a cleft in his chin. A really deep one,' he added, as this announcement was greeted with bemused silence from Ken. Then Ken remembered the cleft in his own chin and smilingly awarded Will five points.

'I take it the boyfriend is bereft of cleft?' he asked, describing another big fat zero on Brian's side, as Freddie nodded happily. 'Don't worry, Kate,' he said sympathetically. 'It's anyone's game yet. Your chap can still catch up.'

Studying the sheet of paper, Kate doubted it. Brian had been awarded eight points for his good looks, but that was still less than Will's ten. The only point on which he had outscored Will was his straight hair (ten points) versus Will's curly (minus five). In an effort to bump up Brian's score, Kate had made no defence of Will's hair.

'And Kate's family all hate Brian, but they love Will,' Freddie piped up again.

Ken considered. 'That can go either way,' he said. 'Are you close to your family, Kate?'

'Well, fairly . . .' Kate saw an opening for Brian.

'Are you kidding?' Freddie looked at her scathingly. 'They live up each other's arses!' he told Ken.

'That's a biggie, then,' Ken decided, giving Will ten and Brian minus ten, cancelling out his straight hair at a stroke.

'Isn't there *anything* against Will?' he asked, trying to be fair.

'Well . . . ' Freddie hesitated, 'there is one thing . . .'

'Yes?'

Freddie was silent for a moment, seemingly reluctant to say whatever it was. 'He's an alcoholic,' he said finally.

'He is *not*!' Kate gasped.

'Okay, retired,' Freddie allowed.

'Still,' Ken sucked his breath through his teeth, 'he'll have to have minus twenty for that. What if he decides to come out of retirement? Most alcos make at least one big comeback before they retire for good.'

'Twenty points is a bit harsh.'

'Any kind of substance abuse, addiction or violence is minus twenty,' Ken said firmly. 'It's not negotiable.'

Freddie was thrilled. 'He's very strict, isn't he?' he remarked to Kate.

'But Will *isn't* an alcoholic,' Kate demurred, 'and he never has been.' She couldn't let this go by, even in the interest of bumping up Brian's score. 'What on earth gave you the idea that he was?'

'Well, he was out of his tree when he shagged you that time.

And it was all fizzy water and coke at the wedding yesterday. Quite sweet, really.' Freddie smiled fondly.

'So?'

Freddie shrugged. 'Doesn't drink, used to be a pisshead – you do the math, as the Americans say.'

'Freddie, your "math" is completely skewed. You're adding two and two and making twenty-two.'

'You mean he really isn't an alco?'

'No.'

'So why the about-face on the drinking front?'

Ken and Freddie looked at her intently, waiting expectantly for her answer like members of an interview panel.

'He can't tolerate alcohol. He'd get plastered after half an alcopop, and he was always having blackouts. Lorcan says he stopped because it was freaking him out, not knowing what he'd done or where he'd been – or who with,' Kate added.

'Wow! So he's never been an alcoholic?'

'Nope.'

'And he gave up drink because he's basically allergic to it?'

'Yep.'

'You know what this means?'

'What?'

'He's perfect.'

Ken was adding up the final scores. 'Freddie's right, Kate,' he said matter-of-factly. 'It's no contest. You simply can't choose an impoverished vegetarian cyclist over a billionaire carnivorous motorist. It just doesn't compute.'

Freddie had been right about one thing, Kate thought later, as she got ready for her date with Brian. Life was too short, and you had to go after what you wanted – which was why she had decided to lay her cards on the table tonight and give Brian an ultimatum. There were certain things she wanted in life – marriage, children – and she knew she wasn't going to get them drifting along with him. She was almost thirty and felt ready to settle down. She was also pretty sure that settling down was not on Brian's agenda. He was too much of a free spirit – a fancy way of saying he was a commitment-phobe, according to Freddie. But it was better she should find out now so she that could move on and find someone else.

She was going all out to vamp Brian tonight. She had decided to wear her new favourite new dress, a flirty poppy print with a fitted bodice and full, almost fifties-style skirt that flattered her figure to perfection. She had acquired it from one of the passengers on the African trip, who had lent it to her when she had nothing pretty to wear to the farewell dinner and later insisted she keep it. She would never have picked it out for herself – it was ridiculously girly, and she suspected it was also very expensive and way out of her price range – but she loved it, and it really suited her.

This was confirmed by Freddie, who came in a few moments later for the 'dress rehearsal', a pre-date ritual. 'Killer dress!' he said, his eyes popping gratifyingly. 'You look stunning!'

'Thanks,' Kate smiled. 'Okay, which shoes? There's these . . .' She held up a pair of flat cream pumps, which Freddie dismissed.

'What about these?' She held up a pair of flat red ballet shoes.

Freddie sighed in despair. He was always trying to cure Kate of her flat-shoe fetish.

Kate's shoulders sagged despondently. 'What then?'

'What look are we going for?'

'Marry-me-or-else,' Kate replied unhesitatingly.

'Okay, stand back.' Freddie knelt down to rummage in her wardrobe. 'I seem to remember . . . yes!' He emerged with a pair of red kitten heel mules with bows.

'Aren't they a bit over the top?'

'With that dress?' Freddie squealed. 'Besides, they just scream, "Snap me up quick before someone else does."'

Kate slipped her feet into them and inspected herself in the mirror. Freddie was spot-on: they matched the poppies on the dress perfectly, and the increased height they gave her showed off her slim, tanned legs.

'Perfect!' he said contentedly, admiring her reflection in the mirror. 'You'll knock him dead.'

'That's the general idea.'

'And they won't know what hit them at Lentils R Us.'

*

As she applied her make-up so that it looked like she wasn't wearing any (Brian liked the natural look), Kate suddenly felt defeated. She flung her blusher brush on to the dressing table. Why was it always like this with Brian? Why did she always feel as if she was on a winning-back mission, pulling out all the stops to attract him anew?

The trouble was, she knew there were always plenty of women hovering around Brian, vying for his attention, while he was the only proper boyfriend she'd ever had. Confidence had never been Kate's strong point, and when she had met Brian she had been at a particularly low ebb, dented by a series of encounters with increasingly hopeless men, who always seemed primed to run if someone better came along – and someone always did. She was beginning to rival even Freddie in her ability to attract the most awful men.

Then Brian appeared and changed all that. She had met him when she was working for a couple of months as a vegetarian cook at a retreat centre in Galway. He had come to do a weekend workshop and Kate had been instantly smitten. He was so attractive, so gregarious and charismatic. Amazingly, the attraction was mutual, and they had started going out together. Kate had expected it to follow the familiar pattern of her previous relationships and spent the first few weeks waiting for the other shoe to drop. Only when they had been together for about six months did it dawn on her that Brian was her boyfriend and she was finally in a proper relationship.

But they had been together for almost two years now, and she didn't want to drift any longer. She loved Brian, but the three months in Africa, as well as doing wonders for her figure, had given her new self-confidence. Being away from her family had helped. She had always felt like the runt of the litter, never quite measuring up to her dazzling siblings. In Africa, she had felt powerful, sexy and confident, among people who knew her in her own right rather than as the youngest and least significant of the O'Neills.

She wasn't at all confident about how Brian would react to her ultimatum. He strongly disapproved of possessiveness, but Kate was tired of trying to be cool and detached and wasn't prepared to do it any longer. In reality, she was fiercely possessive of Brian and gut-wrenchingly jealous of the other women who were always hanging around him – his little coven of workshop junkies with their serene smiles, their homespun jumpers and their vegetarian shoes, who looked down on her because she worked for a living while they made a virtue of living off the State while pursuing their hobbies – writing poetry, throwing pots or making incomprehensible art. Their scrubbed-clean faces always wore an air of self-righteous superiority, as if they were somehow saving the world by not wearing make-up or nice clothes.

Well, she could give them a run for their money, Kate thought defiantly, applying a slick of deep red lipstick to her full mouth. Despite his principles, Brian was not averse to a bit of glamour. She surveyed herself in the mirror, twirling to inspect every angle. She looked fantastic. Luckily she had commandeered one of Rachel's army of beauticians to wax her legs yesterday, and they were wonderfully smooth and brown. Brian's acolytes would never dream of waxing – they preserved their leg hair with the same zeal they applied to saving the rainforest, as though the entire ecosystem of the planet depended on it.

She was just putting on the big bead earrings she'd bought in Africa when she heard the buzzer.

Seconds later, Freddie rapped on the door. 'Three minutes to curtain,' he called.

It was one of the advantages, Kate thought, of living on the fourth floor of a building with no lift that you were never caught unawares – or perhaps the only advantage, she amended.

There was just one problem, she thought, looking at herself in the mirror. The sleeveless dress was far too light for an Irish summer's evening. Scanning the room for inspiration, she spotted Will's dinner jacket hanging with her bridesmaid dress on a hook over the door – the only things she had managed to unpack so far. She pulled it on, checked it in the mirror and was pleased with the effect. Rather than detracting from the glamour of the outfit, it lent it a slightly decadent, morning-after look, as if she was on the way home from a dinner dance. She took it off, so that Brian would get the full effect of the dress, and settled down to tweaking her hair and make-up for the final few minutes.

Brian was ensconced on the sofa, with Freddie grilling him mercilessly about yesterday's workshop. 'So, how do you teach people to scream?' he was asking eagerly. 'Do you do a course or something?'

'I wasn't teaching so much as *facilitating*,' Brian explained, always happy to talk about his work to anyone who would listen. 'I was giving people permission to scream and providing a safe space where they could feel free to let go. It's very cathartic.'

'I'm sure.' Freddie nodded vaguely.

'As children we express our emotions so directly,' Brian continued expansively, on a roll now. 'When we're angry or scared or outraged, we just come right out and scream. Then we grow up, become socialised and lose that spontaneity.'

'Right,' Freddie concurred. 'So it was sort of temper tantrums for the over-twenty-fives.'

'It was actually very moving,' Brian continued, refusing to rise to Freddie's bait. 'Some people really opened up.'

'Deafening too, I imagine,' Freddie said. 'Your ears must be ringing.'

'You'd be surprised at how little screaming there actually was. We're all so inhibited. People find it incredibly difficult to make that noise, often for the first time since they were children – in some cases, the first time ever.'

'Like this, you mean?' Freddie opened his mouth wide and let out a bloodcurdling shriek that wouldn't have been out of place in a schlock horror movie.

At that moment Kate emerged from her bedroom and glanced worriedly towards the door, expecting the neighbours to be pounding on it at any minute.

'Okay.' Brian laughed. 'Obviously you're the exception.'

'Oh, I'm just a screaming queen,' Freddie quipped.

As Kate joined them, the look in Brian's eyes was flatteringly appreciative and lustful. 'Wow, you look amazing!' he gasped. Kate rarely went in for such full-on glamour, which made the effect all the more stunning when she did.

'Thanks.' She smiled into his eyes. 'Were you giving Freddie a crash course in screaming?'

'He doesn't need any help in that department. I was just telling him about my workshop yesterday.'

'Was it good?'

'It was very powerful. There was one woman who couldn't make a sound all day, but in the last five minutes she screamed for about a minute solid. It was a real breakthrough for her.'

'Amazing!' Freddie breathed.

'Suzanne, I suppose?' Kate said caustically.

'As a matter of fact it was.'

'Who's Suzanne?' Freddie asked, sensing tension.

'She's Brian's shill,' Kate told him.

'You have a shill?' Freddie asked Brian, regarding him with new respect. Maybe the guy had hidden shallows, after all.

'No, I do *not* have a shill.'

'So who is she then?'

'She goes to all Brian's workshops and groups, and she *always* has a breakthrough. No matter what the theme is – co-dependency, childhood trauma, buried memories, survivor guilt, you name it – Suzanne always has a breakthrough and bursts into tears, and Brian is guaranteed at least one big success.'

'Sounds like a shill to me.' Freddie nodded.

'She's not a shill,' Brian said. 'She's a very courageous woman who's embarked on a difficult journey.'

Kate blushed. She hated it when Brian talked like this.

'Wow, where's she going?' Freddie asked disingenuously.

'You know what I mean, Freddie.'

'The journey within,' Freddie intoned portentously. 'The most difficult journey of all.'

'You should try it yourself some time,' Brian said, apparently needled by Freddie's tone. 'You should come to one of my men's groups.'

'Oh, I don't think I'd really fit in, do you?'

'Come on, you're not the only gay guy in the world.'

'Sometimes it just feels that way,' Freddie said tragically.

'Seriously, I think you could make a valuable contribution,' Brian said, looking at Freddie with interest now. 'We explore all aspects of the male journey. You're so open and in touch with your feminine side – the group could learn a lot from you.'

It was the source of Brian's charisma that he could make anyone he was talking to feel like the most fascinating person on the planet. He had a way of focusing on whoever he was with that made them feel really special and interesting.

'Do you have a shill in the men's group?' Freddie asked eagerly.

'Oh, I'm sure Suzanne's got it covered,' Kate said. 'No doubt she'd be there exploring her masculine side or getting in touch with her penis envy or something . . . Well, I guess we should be off,' she said, standing up and putting on Will's jacket.

'Whose is that?' Brian frowned.

'Will's,' Kate told him absently, pulling her hair free of the collar and shaking it loose. 'I forgot to give it back to him last night – luckily as it turned out. I really like it – I'm considering nicking it.'

'I'm sure he won't miss it,' Brian said. 'I expect he's got dozens.'

This constituted severe criticism from Brian, who considered it immoral to own more than one jacket at a time – especially if none of them came from a charity shop. Kate made a mental note to keep the designer label hidden – if he saw it he'd think Will was beyond redemption.

'It looks better on you anyway,' Freddie chipped in. 'So, where are you two off to?'

'It'll have to be somewhere cheap,' Kate warned Brian. 'I'm broke and I don't have any job lined up.'

'Oh, I forgot to tell you,' Freddie said. 'Will gave you a great plug in his speech, so you might get some work out of that. He said you were available and gave your cooking an absolute rave review.'

'Oh,' Kate said, pleased, 'that was nice of him. I don't know how he could rave about my cooking, though. He hasn't had anything I've made in yonks.'

'I suppose he remembers what a brilliant cook you are from when he lived with you.'

'I guess so,' Kate said. 'Okay, let's go.'

'You *lived* with Will Sargent?' Brian asked accusingly. 'You never told me that.'

'What? Oh no!' Kate gasped, realising his mistake. 'I didn't live with him – I mean, not in *that* way. He stayed with my family for a year. It was a long time ago,' she added. Will had impinged on her consciousness quite enough for one weekend. She didn't want to think about him any more.

But Brian wasn't going to let it go. 'How did that come about?'

'His parents had split up and he was living here with his mother but she committed suicide. His father brought him back to England and packed him off to boarding school. He absolutely hated it, so one day he ran away and came to our house.'

'Oh, you're not telling it right,' Freddie said crossly. 'He walked all the way from some godforsaken hole in the north of England,' he told Brian, 'turned up at the O'Neills in the middle of a storm and practically collapsed on their doorstep. It's a wonderful story, isn't it?' he said wistfully. 'So *David Copperfield*.'

'It must have been really traumatic for him,' Brian said. 'He should come to my abandoned-children group. He might find it helpful.'

'Will is thirty-two,' Kate said dryly.

'It's not for children, as you well know,' Brian said patiently.

'Anyway, he's English,' Kate said, with an air of finality.

'What's that supposed to mean? English people have feelings.'

'He has that kind of English reserve. Sitting around moaning about his childhood with a bunch of strangers wouldn't be his scene.'

'It's not about "sitting around moaning about your childhood",' Brian said huffily.

'Well, whatever it is – drumming your pain or dancing the abandoned child within – I don't think it's him. Besides, it was a long time ago. He's got over it.'

Brian looked at her pityingly. 'You don't "get over" being abandoned by your parents just like that,' he said, clicking his fingers. 'Feelings of abandonment run very deep, Kate. I have people in my group well into their fifties who are still dealing with abandonment issues.'

'Really?'

'Believe me, deep down Will is still that abandoned child, crying out for love and security.'

'God, do you really think so?' Kate was horrified. She had two abiding images of Will: one of him standing alone by the grave at his mother's funeral, his pallor emphasised by his dark suit and black mop of hair, the other of him sitting in their kitchen, soaked and shaking like a puppy when he'd run away from boarding school. It broke her heart to think that, deep down, Will could still be the lost, unhappy boy who arrived on their doorstep all those years ago.

'Well, maybe not,' Brian said, watching the play of emotion on Kate's face.

Kate raised her eyebrows at his sudden about-face. 'But you just said—'

'You know him better than I do. Lack of sensitivity and self-awareness has its advantages.'

'Will is not insensitive or lacking in self-awareness,' Kate protested, 'just because he's not constantly navel-gazing and having breakthroughs. Suzanne isn't self-aware, she's self-absorbed. There's a difference.' Kate was aware that she sounded catty, but she couldn't help it. Suzanne was the person she'd figured Brian had in mind when he'd suggested they see other people. 'I suppose Suzanne is in the abandoned-children group?' she asked.

'Actually, she is. She was adopted.'

'I'm not surprised. If she was *my* child, I'd abandon her.'

'She *is* a bit intense,' Brian admitted, to Kate's surprise. The fact was, the break with Kate had allowed him to explore his relationship with Suzanne and he had found her neediness very trying. It had proved to him that Kate was the person he wanted to be with. She was the least neurotic person he knew, which was relaxing and restorative when he spent his working life dealing with other people's pain. 'I thought we'd go for a pizza,' he said breezily. 'I know it's your favourite – and don't worry about money. It's my treat, to celebrate your first night back.'

'Vegetarian deluxe,' the waitress announced cheerfully. Kate made a strenuous effort to hide her distress as a twelve-inch pizza was plonked in the middle of the table. Early on in their relationship Kate had discovered, to her dismay, that when Brian suggested going for 'a pizza' that was exactly what he meant – a pizza, singular, which he had proceeded ceremoniously to carve down the middle. That first time Kate had said nothing. Brian had already been faintly shocked to discover she wasn't a vegetarian and she hadn't wanted to compound it by having him watch her wolf down a pizza big enough to feed a small African nation for a month. One of Brian's favourite themes was the shortage of food on the planet, and she didn't want him to think she was partly responsible for it. Besides, she hadn't expected the relationship to last long, so it hadn't seemed worth making a fuss – which meant that now she was stuck with hiding her irritation and anxiety as Brian cut the pizza in half. It also meant she was always limited to having the vegetarian, while she longed for pepperoni, leaching its oily spiciness into the tomato sauce.

Still, she mustn't be ungrateful. Brian had come here to please her. It wasn't his fault she had never come clean with him about her pizza habit. Determined to cheer up, she tucked into the pizza, which was delicious.

'I've really missed you,' he said, smiling across at her.

Kate wished he hadn't sounded so surprised about it. 'I've missed you too,' she said. Sometimes she still couldn't believe he was her boyfriend. His thin, angular face was so handsome, and he had a fantastic body, honed from years of strenuous yoga and in peak condition from always eating the right stuff in moderation and getting enough sleep. And he was so caring and considerate. It was all very well for her family to be derisive about him, but they didn't know how sweet he was to her. Freddie could rant all he wanted about Will being 'the one', but the reality was that he hadn't been very nice to her – and it was screwed up to keep hankering for someone who wasn't interested in you. She had adored Will, but what she had with Brian was real, grown-up and, best of all, mutual.

The sex was fantastic too. She looked at his long, thin fingers playing with his wine glass and thought with longing of the pleasure they could give her. Suddenly overcome with lust, she considered abandoning the pizza and dragging him home to bed.

Brian smiled at her intimately, catching the look in her eyes.

'Did you enjoy yourself at the wedding last night?' Kate asked, shaking herself out of her stupor.

'Oh, I didn't stay long, but, yes, it was fun.' Brian felt a momentary pang of guilt as he thought of the rather desperately eager girl he had slunk off with. 'It was interesting seeing you there with all your family,' he said. 'You're different when you're with them. You become an O'Neill.'

'I *am* an O'Neill. What else would I be?' Kate said.

'That's exactly what I mean. When you're with them you're an O'Neill. With me, you're just Kate.'

'God, you must be the only person in your line of work who'd consider it a problem that I'm close to my family.'

'I don't. I just think you're a bit . . . enmeshed.'

'*Enmeshed?*' Kate scowled.

'Yes. Your identity is submerged in the family. You need to differentiate yourself more from them. You need to be Kate, not just one of the O'Neills.'

It was pretty much what Kate had been thinking earlier about how she had felt in Africa. But it was one thing for her to think it and quite another for Brian to say it. He was like the psychological equivalent of a plastic surgeon, believing everyone could be improved with a little work. Why couldn't he accept her as she was?

'Your being away the past few months has made me think,' he said now.

Here we go, Kate thought, sighing inwardly. The relationship discussion.

'I've been giving our relationship a lot of thought while you were away,' he continued. 'It's made me realise how much I care about you and want you in my life.'

Kate had hoped to put off the ultimatum for a bit longer, but now that the subject had come up, she was determined to stick to her guns and tell him she wanted marriage, kids, the whole bit, or they would have to call it a day and go their separate ways. She would also, she decided, have to let him know where she stood on the subject of pizza. A lifetime of shared pizza was too horrific to contemplate.

She was so anxious, building herself up to present Brian with her ultimatum, that she couldn't concentrate on what he was saying. Still, it wasn't really necessary, she thought wearily, as she caught the word 'commitment' floating by. It wouldn't be anything she hadn't heard from him a million times already – that he wasn't ready to make a commitment, that you didn't need a piece of paper to love someone, that he lived 'in the now' and you couldn't legislate for what might happen twenty years down the line, etc., etc.

'What are you thinking?' Brian cut into her reverie. He was giving her one of his deep, intense looks. Kate sometimes wondered if he practised them in the mirror.

Marriage, kids, pizza, Kate thought, drilling herself in her head, pumping herself up to say her piece. God, she wasn't cut out for this – she wasn't the ultimatum type. Marriage, kids, pizza, marriage, kids, pizza.

'I still don't know how you feel,' Brian persisted.

'About what?'

'About what I've been saying.'

'Oh, um, about commitment and all that?' Kate prevaricated, not having heard a word.

'Yes, about commitment and all that,' Brian said mockingly. 'I mean, I've told you what *I* want. I don't know what *you* want.'

It was now or never. She wasn't going to get a better opening. Marriage, kids, pizza, she rehearsed one last time, and took a deep breath.

'I want my own pizza,' she heard herself say.

'What?' Brian burst out laughing.

Shit! She hadn't meant to start with the pizza thing – but he'd taken her by surprise. How could she go from pizza to marriage? It wasn't exactly a natural segue.

'That's what I love about you, Kate,' Brian said through fits of mirth, 'you're so basic. I'm here pouring my heart out, and you're talking about pizza!'

Kate smiled weakly. 'I'm sorry, it's just that I don't share pizzas. I'm a big girl, and I can handle a twelve-inch all on my own. How do you think I came to *be* a big girl?'

'You're not such a big girl any more.'

'I was beginning to think you hadn't noticed.' She had felt a bit irked that everyone else was telling her how fantastic she looked but Brian had remained silent.

'Of course I did,' he said. 'You look great. But to me you always did.'

Kate felt chastened. In fairness, Brian had loved her when she was fat and had made her feel beautiful and desirable. He had never once suggested she ought to lose weight.

'Why didn't you say something before,' he asked, 'about the pizza thing?'

'I didn't want to scare you off,' Kate said meekly. She had misjudged him.

'So if I agree to separate pizzas, do you think we should get married?'

'What?' Kate asked, confused now. 'What are you talking about?' If this was a joke, it wasn't very funny.

'Well, I suggested we get married, and when I asked how you felt about it you said you'd have to have your own pizza. So I take it that's the only bar to our union, as you see it. Maybe we could draw up a pre-nup,' he joked, 'though I doubt there's a standard clause guaranteeing the woman her own pizza.'

'You suggested we get *married*?' Kate felt as if she had strayed into the twilight zone.

'Didn't you hear anything I said?' Brian was regarding her as though he feared for her sanity.

'Sorry.' Kate shook her head. 'I was in a bit of a daze. Tell me what you said. I promise I'm listening this time.'

'Well, I said that I'm ready to make a commitment, and as you're the person I care about most, I want to commit to you.'

'Oh!' Kate regretted asking him to repeat himself – she had imagined something much more romantic. He made it sound like she was this week's lucky winner in some sort of lottery. She appreciated that Brian was quite a cerebral person and tried to cultivate detachment, but sometimes he could be so lukewarm.

'You're the person I want to share my life with,' he continued. 'I was hoping you felt the same way.'

Hardly an impassioned declaration of undying love, Kate thought. Nevertheless, Brian wanted to get married and he had been the one to suggest it. She hadn't even had to issue her ultimatum.

'Oh, I do,' she assured him, smiling now. 'I really do. It's exactly what I want.'

'Good.'

'You really want to get married?' Kate checked.

'Yes, I really do.'

In fact, Brian had only come to this conclusion the previous night when he had gone to meet Kate at the wedding. It was true he had missed her while she was away and he had decided he wanted to make some sort of commitment to her, but he had been thinking more along the lines of moving in together. However, seeing Kate in her own milieu, he had realised she was quite a conventional person at heart and had come to the conclusion that only marriage would do. He'd have to go the whole hog if he didn't want to lose her.

Last night, for the first time, he had felt unsure of her, and it had given him a jolt. Everyone was knocked out by how much weight she had lost and how fantastic she was looking. If he was honest, he had liked Kate being overweight. Paradoxically, it seemed that the bigger a woman was, the less people noticed her, and he had never had to feel jealous of Kate. But he had been aware of the admiring glances and flirtatious smiles she had been getting last night and he had begun to feel quite proprietorial.

But what had really shaken him was the way her face had lit up like a Christmas tree when she had first looked at him. Her eyes had sparkled and she had positively glowed – which would have been great, he thought huffily, if it hadn't been that she'd expected to see someone else.

'Oh, it's you!' she had said, smiling at him sleepily, surprise evident in her voice. It wasn't that she had seemed disappointed when she'd realised it was him, just that she'd looked like that because she'd thought he was someone else – and that someone else was bloody Will Sargent. To make matters worse, he had discovered tonight that Will had come into her life in rather romantic circumstances when she was at an impressionable age. He was a good-looking guy, and it was almost inevitable that Kate would have had a crush on him at some stage. And then she had become almost tearful when he had suggested Will might still be suffering from the effects of his disrupted childhood.

Bastard, Brian thought, feeling uncharacteristically jealous. He loved the fact that Kate was such a soft-hearted, affectionate person – but he wanted all that affection focused on himself. He had had several flings while they had been together, and a few more while she was away (last night counted as one of those, he told himself, because their relationship was only officially back on tonight), but most of the girls he had been with were so hard and selfish, so oblivious to his needs. Kate could give him all the love he required. He also felt she'd be the perfect partner in the retreat centre he planned to open. She'd make a great cook and house-mother.

'So we're engaged, then?' Kate asked incredulously.

'Well, it doesn't have to be a formal engagement, does it?'

In other words, no ring, Kate thought glumly. Still, she was getting what she wanted, she reminded herself. She mustn't be greedy. 'No, of course not,' she said brightly.

'There's no reason why a simple decision to make a commitment to each other has to turn into a circus, is there?'

'When are we going to do it?' Kate asked excitedly.

'There's no rush, is there?' Now that it was settled, Brian was beginning to feel there was no need for the wedding. He didn't want to marry Kate so much as to secure her. 'You wouldn't want a big bash like your sister's, would you?'

'God, no!' Kate was genuinely with him on that one. 'But nothing too outlandish either,' she added hastily, suddenly envisaging them being married by a druid or new-age shaman in a fairy fort.

'No, your family would never approve.' Brian laughed.

Cripes, the family! In her excitement, Kate had forgotten she'd have to tell them – and they wouldn't exactly be overjoyed at the prospect of Brian as an in-law. 'The thing is, once I tell my family it'll be hard to rein them in and stop them taking over.'

'Well, I'm pretty busy all summer. Why don't we keep it to ourselves for the moment and spring it on them nearer the time?' Brian was feeling claustrophobic now with all this talk of weddings. He needed breathing space.

'Good idea,' Kate agreed. She was relieved at not having to break the news to her family straight away. They'd have time to get to know Brian better and warm to him.

'Well, we should celebrate, shouldn't we? They don't do champagne here, but we could have another pizza – start as we mean to go on.'

Kate grinned. 'I'll have pepperoni on mine.'

Chapter 4

Kate managed to keep her engagement secret for the next fortnight, even though she was bursting to tell someone. She had told Freddie, of course, but that didn't count. 'It isn't a formal engagement,' she had said, swearing him to secrecy.

'In other words, no ring.'

But that was it. She had been feeling remarkably flat about the whole thing, but she put it down to the fact that she couldn't talk about it. There were no congratulations, no wedding plans. It made the whole thing seem unreal. Still, she had promised Brian, and she felt quite proud of herself for holding it in.

Then her mother called. 'Darling, Helen's having one of her singles things tonight. You should go.'

Kate groaned. 'But I'm not single, Mum,' She said.

'Oh? Did I miss the wedding?' her mother replied.

'You know what I mean. I'm with someone. I'm not looking for a man because I already have one.'

'Hmm.' Her mother sounded unconvinced. 'If you're not married, you're single,' she said firmly. 'Anyway, it'd be no harm to meet some new people. You shouldn't put all your eggs in one basket, you know.'

'Mum, Brian and I are serious about each other.' Kate longed to say more, to impress on her mother just how serious they were, but she clenched her teeth and said nothing.

'You're wasting your time with him, Kate. I don't think he's marriage material – and you're not getting any younger.'

Kate sighed. She was only twenty-eight and her mother was consigning her to the scrapheap!

'I mean, do you honestly see him marrying you, Kate?' Grace persisted.

'Actually, Mum, I've got news – but I don't want you to tell anyone else just yet, okay?'

'Of course not, if that's what you want,' Grace assured her. 'What is it, darling?'

'I'm not going to be single for much longer,' she said, pleased to be able to take the wind out of her mother's sails. 'I'm engaged!'

Silence.

'Mum? Are you there?'

'Oh yes, darling. I'm still here.'

'Well?'

'Well, what?'

'Aren't you pleased?'

'Is it the Tree-hugger?'

Kate sighed. 'I wish you wouldn't call him that. He has a name, you know.'

'Next you'll be telling me that, no less than the trees and the stars, he has a right to be here,' Grace sniffed. 'So it is him?'

'Yes, of course it's Brian – who else would it be?'

'I just thought . . .' Grace said faintly.

'*What* did you think?'

'Well, you could have met someone new for all I know. I thought in Africa perhaps . . .'

Hoped, you mean, Kate thought, her heart sinking. She hadn't expected her mother to be ecstatic, but this was downright depressing. 'Well, I didn't, Mum. It's Brian. I thought you'd be happy for me.'

'Of course I'm happy for you, darling,' Grace said uncertainly, 'if you're sure it's what you want.'

'Don't sound so bloody enthusiastic!' Kate sulked.

'I'm your mother, Kate. Naturally I want you to be happy.'

'Look, I know you don't like Brian—'

'I wouldn't say that,' her mother butted in defensively.

'It's true, Mum. Be honest. But it's just that you don't know him very well.'

'Well, whose fault is that? We've gone out of our way to include him, to get to know him better – you can't say we haven't tried, sweetheart. But he spurns us at every turn.'

Spurns! thought Kate. Her mother was entering melodramatic airspace.

'You can't deny it, Kate. He makes no secret of the way he avoids having anything to do with us. He didn't even bother turning up for your sister's wedding until it was almost over.'

'I know, I know,' Kate said placatingly. 'But you can be a bit—'

'*Overwhelming?*'

Shit! Kate kicked the wall. Why the hell had she told Lorcan that? She should have known he'd declaim it from the rooftops. 'Well that's just because he doesn't know you very well,' she said soothingly. 'Mum, if you *really* knew him like I do—'

'That's all very well, Kate,' Grace snapped. 'I'm sure his mother adores him and his granny thinks he's the dog's bollocks – but don't you think there's something to be said for how one appears to the world at large? I mean, do you really have to go on one of these love-in weekends with someone before you can tell what they're really like? There's a lot to be said for first impressions, you know.'

'If we just went on first impressions, Elizabeth would never have ended up with Mr Darcy,' Kate pointed out.

'I rest my case,' her mother replied tartly. 'Mr Darcy was exactly what he appeared to be to anyone who met him – an insufferable snob and an anal retentive that would make Mr Anal from Uranus look like a slacker.'

Tell me what you really think, Kate thought bitterly, on the verge of tears now. 'It's not fair!' she wailed. 'You weren't mean to Rachel when she got engaged to Tom.'

'But we all adore Tom – you know that. He's an absolute pet.'

'So you *don't* like Brian,' Kate pounced. 'I knew it!'

'When's the wedding?' Grace asked stiffly.

Damn, she thought. Why had she let her mother goad her into spilling the beans about the engagement? Grace would have a field day when she discovered there were no concrete wedding plans.

'Oh, we haven't set a date yet,' she said, trying to sound casual. 'It's not a formal engagement.'

'In other words, no ring,' Grace said.

Kate decided to ignore that. 'We don't want a lot of fuss. That's why we're not telling anyone until nearer the time. Mum, you have to promise you won't tell anyone.'

'Of course.'

'Promise, Mum.'

'Honestly, darling!' Grace huffed, as if mortally wounded not to be trusted.

'Promise, Mum.' Kate knew what her mother was like.

'Okay, okay,' Grace said. 'I promise.'

Grace tapped a long red talon against the phone. Who to call first? That was the question. Normally she would have rung Rachel, but she was just back from her honeymoon and still wrapped up in her own newly-wed status. Lorcan would be hopeless and, no doubt, extremely disapproving and uncooperative. Helen, she decided. She'd know what to do.

'Helen?'

'Grace! How lovely. Just hang on a sec – I've got something on the stove.'

Grace felt calmer already. There was something so comforting about Helen's domestic proficiency. It made her feel that everything was going to be all right. All she had to do was tell Helen and it would be taken care of.

'Okay, I'm all yours,' Helen said, returning.

'Helen, I've got some news,' Grace began.

'Not good, by the sound of it. What is it?' Helen sounded concerned.

'It's about Kate,' Grace hedged, feeling a little guilty now to be betraying her daughter's confidence so soon.

'What's she done?' Helen hooted. 'Run off to the Himalayas with a circus?'

'Nothing so sensible, I'm afraid.' Grace paused for effect before dropping her bombshell. 'She's gone and got herself engaged to the dreaded Tree-hugger.'

'Gosh!' Gratifyingly, Helen gasped at this.

Good old Helen, Grace thought. Trust her to grasp the full horror of the situation straight away.

'It's supposed to be a secret. I shouldn't even be telling you. But I needed to talk to someone – and you'll know what to do.'

'Do? What's the problem?'

'I've just told you the problem,' Grace replied, a little impatiently. It wasn't like Helen to be obtuse. 'Kate's got engaged to the Tree-hugger.'

'Oh, you mean the engagement itself?' Helen asked, a little disconcerted.

'Yes!'

'The fact that you can't stand the Tree-hugger?'

'Exactly.'

'I see. Well, I know it's difficult, Grace, but—'

'We've got to stop it, Helen!' Grace interrupted. 'We can't let her go ahead with it.'

'I don't see how we can stop it.'

'Don't you?' Grace wavered. Surely Helen wasn't going to fail her.

'Well, what did you have in mind?' Helen asked.

Grace sighed. 'I don't know,' she admitted. 'I thought you'd have some ideas.'

'For breaking it up?' Helen clarified.

'Yes, of course.'

'Do you really think that's best?' Helen asked. 'Couldn't you give him a chance, try to get to know him better?'

'Have you ever met Brian, Helen?' Grace asked.

'No, I don't think I have. Apparently he turned up at Rachel's wedding at the eleventh hour, but I didn't get to meet him. What's he like, anyway?'

'A turd in a woolly jumper.'

'I think you mean nerd.'

'No,' Grace replied, 'I don't. Honestly, Helen, if it was just that I didn't like him, I wouldn't mind. If I really thought he'd make Kate happy, I'd go out of my way to try and get to like him. But it'd be the biggest mistake of her life. He'll make her miserable.'

Helen thought quickly. 'Look, how about a family meeting to discuss it?' she suggested. 'The rest of the family feel the same way as you about him, don't they?'

'Oh, yes!'

'So let's all meet, put our heads together and see what we can come up with.'

'But how can we organise a family meeting without Kate getting wind of it?' Grace fretted.

'We could do it on Sunday and I'll ask her to take Sam and Jake out for the day – I'll say we're having people over.'

'Tell her you're having one of your singles things,' Grace said bitterly. 'That'll keep her away.'

The following Sunday, Grace stood at the mantelpiece in Helen's spacious sitting room before the assembled O'Neills. Helen had rustled up drinks and a few nibbles, and everyone was tucking in and looking at Grace expectantly.

'You're probably wondering why we called you all here today,' she began, her actress's voice easily commanding everyone's attention.

'She's going to reveal which of us murdered the vicar,' Lorcan whispered to Tom.

Tom snickered and got a disapproving frown from Rachel.

Aloud, Lorcan said, 'I'm wondering why we're having a family meeting without Kate.' She had been dispatched to the cinema with Sam and Jake, followed by a trip to McDonald's, and they had all been under strict instructions not to let her know about the meeting.

'There's a good reason for that,' Grace answered, getting into her chairwoman stride. 'The meeting is *about* Kate.'

'It's not her birthday yet, is it?' Conor asked. 'Are we planning a surprise party or something?'

'No, darling, nothing like that,' Helen said to him.

'I doubt we're planning anything so pleasant,' Lorcan said darkly. He was getting a bad vibe about this meeting.

'Oh, stop carrying on like you're the only person here who cares about Kate,' Grace snapped. 'We all care about her – which is why we're here.' She paused – she knew how to capture and hold an audience's attention. 'None of you is supposed to know this yet, but Kate is engaged to Brian.'

'Oh, well done, Kate!' Tom exclaimed cheerily. He was met with a stony silence and much eye-rolling from Rachel. 'Oh, aren't we pleased about it? Sorry. Some objection to the bloke, is there?'

'Only the fact that he's the biggest knob on the planet,' Rachel snarled. '*Engaged*? I can't believe Kate would be so stupid.'

'I couldn't either. She only told me on Friday.' Grace was relieved to be able to bitch about it with someone who was on the same wavelength. Rachel was such a comfort.

'God,' Rachel fumed, even more incensed than Grace. 'I thought we could at least rely on that creep to avoid marriage at all costs.'

'Yes, it's a bit conventional for him, isn't it?' Helen commented.

'It's not a conventional engagement, though,' Grace said, pursing her lips.

'Which lets him out of buying her a ring, the shagger,' Jack growled.

Grace was touched by Jack's support. She knew he didn't approve of what she was doing, but he approved of the Tree-hugger even less and had reluctantly agreed to be party to the plot.

'And none of us is supposed to know about this?' Lorcan asked.

'No.'

'So you thought it would be a good idea to call a family meeting to tell us.'

'We need all the time we can get,' Grace said defensively.

'This isn't about deciding what to get them for a wedding present, is it?' Tom asked. He was entertaining serious doubts about the kind of family he had married into.

'No, Tom, I'm afraid not,' Lorcan answered dolefully. 'I think my mother has something much more Machiavellian up her sleeve.'

'So what exactly *are* we here for?' Conor asked, impatient to get down to the business at hand, whatever it was. If someone would spit it out, he could get it sorted and everyone out of the house. He had important calls to make.

'We're here,' Grace said, 'to decide what we're going to do about it. We can't just let it happen and do nothing. We're going to have a brainstorming session, and I want us to put our heads together and come up with some ideas.'

'Ideas for what?' Tom asked.

'For breaking it up, of course,' Lorcan told him.

'Oh, come on, Lorcan,' his mother chided. 'You hate him as much as the rest of us. And you know he's wrong for Kate.'

'Yes, but don't you think maybe we should respect Kate's decision?' he asked tentatively. 'She's old enough to know what she's doing.'

'Oh, don't be ridiculous.' His mother dismissed his qualms, as though she were swatting a fly. 'Where would we be if we all minded our own business and let everyone run their own lives? Look at your Auntie Sheila.'

Auntie Sheila was always trotted out at times like this, a cautionary tale to anyone who advocated a non-invasive approach to family affairs.

'What happened to Auntie Sheila?' Tom asked.

'She married a transsexual,' Lorcan told him.

'I've never heard about this before!'

'He's a skeleton in our closet,' Lorcan said.

Sheila's husband may have been a skeleton in the O'Neills' closet, but Grace had no compunction about dragging him out and giving his bones a good rattle in the interests of bringing the family into line.

'Her husband was a pervert, Tom,' Grace embellished. 'My whole family knew there was something not right about him. But we said nothing. We didn't *interfere*,' she said, 'and he made poor Sheila's life a misery – took all their money and ran off to South America to have a sex-change operation.'

'Golly!'

'Yes, it was quite a shock.'

'Uncle Geraldine now lives in Rio with a barber called Carlos,' Lorcan informed him. 'They're poor but happy.'

'And you *knew*?' Tom asked Grace incredulously.

'Well, we didn't *know*, of course. We knew something wasn't quite right about him, but it was hard to put your finger on it.'

'Especially after the operation!' Lorcan quipped.

Grace fixed him with a quelling look. 'There were little signs,' she continued nostalgically, gazing melancholically into the middle distance. 'He started wearing a poncho.'

'A what?' Tom thought he must have misheard.

'A poncho, Tom,' Lorcan prompted him. 'Try to keep up.'

'Ah, right,' Tom nodded, as if this was a universally recognised sign of gender confusion.

'In hindsight, of course, it was obvious. But it was the seventies,' Grace said. 'Everyone was wearing them. And Clint Eastwood wore a poncho in those cowboy films, and there's nothing wrong with him, is there?'

'Well,' Tom said uncertainly, 'wasn't he hanging around with that monkey for a while?'

'It was more of an orang-utan,' Lorcan corrected him, clearly struggling to keep a straight face.

'Still, doesn't make it right,' Tom said staunchly.

'Anyway, I don't think there was really anything going on between them,' Lorcan whispered, as Grace shot him a furious look.

'Ah! One of those trumped-up romances to promote their film?'

Grace was sorry she had ever mentioned Clint Eastwood now. So was Conor – Tom and Lorcan could go off on a riff like this for hours on end.

'The point,' Grace said firmly, bringing them back on track, 'is that we knew something was wrong but we kept making allowances, turning a blind eye.'

'To the poncho?'

'To everything, Tom. Until it was too late.' She sighed heavily. 'We could have saved poor Sheila from a lifetime of misery, but we didn't. Well, that's not going to happen again in my family.'

'So what happened to Auntie Sheila?' Tom asked. 'She wasn't at our wedding, was she?' He looked to Rachel.

'She hooked up with a Greek billionaire and they spend all their time sailing around the world. They're in the Caribbean at the moment,' Rachel told him.

'Oh!' Tom was surprised. He had expected to hear that she had died of a broken heart. 'Not exactly a *lifetime* of misery, then, was it?' he said cheerfully. He was surprised that Grace didn't seem more pleased that things had turned out so well for her sister.

'That's not the point, Tom,' Grace corrected him. 'The point is that we could have saved Sheila from a disastrous marriage, but we stood back and did nothing. Well, I'm not going to stand idly by and watch Kate ruin her life. We're her family. It's our duty to interfere.'

'So, any ideas, anyone?' Helen asked, aware that Conor was getting antsy and was anxious for everyone to leave.

'She needs to find someone else,' Rachel said.

'Not much chance of that happening,' Grace said. 'She considers herself off the market.'

'We could tell her about the floozy he was with at the wedding,' Jack suggested.

Grace considered this. 'No, we don't want to be seen to be interfering. We have to make her see for herself what he's like.'

'She needs to find someone else,' Rachel said again, more insistently.

'There isn't time for that,' Grace said impatiently. 'We don't even know how much time we've got – they're planning to spring the wedding on us at the last minute!'

'We need to show him up, make her see him in a bad light,' Conor mused, thinking aloud. This meeting was going on far too long and he wanted to wrap it up.

'And how do we do that?' Grace asked.

'We invite him for a family weekend in the Cork house,' Conor suggested, as if he was presenting them with the definitive solution.

Grace was surprised he could be so dense. This wasn't about making friends with the twerp.

Lorcan voiced her concerns. 'What will that achieve,' he asked, 'apart from ruining a perfectly good weekend?'

'Well, it's obvious, isn't it?' Conor said to the room at large, meeting a lot of blank faces. Apparently it wasn't obvious so he'd have to spell it out.

'When we've got him there, we do what we do best, apparently.'

Everyone gazed at him questioningly.

'We overwhelm him,' he said, as if stating the blindingly obvious. Everyone digested this.

'Kill him with kindness sort of thing?' Helen clarified. 'It might work.' She looked hopefully at Grace.

'It's worth a try, I suppose.' Grace wasn't convinced.

'Of course it'll work,' Conor said. 'Kate's an O'Neill. He can just about pass muster when she has him on her own, one on one. Once she sees him in the family context, she'll realise what a tosser he is.'

'We could all go to work on him,' Grace mused. 'Everyone could do their bit.'

'Well, I'm afraid I won't be able to join in the fun,' Lorcan said. 'I'll be in America.' He had been invited to direct *A Streetcar Named Desire* in a Tennessee Williams festival on Broadway and would be gone for most of the summer.

'Well, we'd hate you to do anything against your principles,' his mother said waspishly. 'Just don't come crying to me if you end up with the Tree-hugger as a brother-in-law. At least the rest of us will have the satisfaction of knowing we did all we could to prevent it.'

Shortly after that, the meeting broke up. As Rachel was leaving, she darted a glance at her mother. 'I'll call you later, Mum,' she said.

'Mum?'

'Rachel, hi!' Grace was a little alarmed that Rachel was calling her so soon. She'd only just got home.

'Look, I have an idea about this Tree-hugger thing, but I couldn't say it with everyone there – especially Lorcan. He'd never agree. But desperate situations call for desperate measures.'

Grace's heart leaped. She liked the sound of 'desperate measures'. She didn't feel the family had grasped the enormity of the situation, and, despite Conor's assurances, she wasn't convinced that they could scare off the Tree-hugger with a weekend en famille. 'What is it?' she asked excitedly.

'Well, like I said, the only way to get Kate away from the Tree-hugger is to get her interested in someone else. You know she's never had much luck with men. I think she believes he's the best she'll ever get.'

Grace's heart sank. 'You're probably right, darling, but there's no chance of that happening. She refuses to go to any of Helen's singles things – she won't entertain the idea of meeting anyone new.'

'I'm not talking about her meeting anyone new,' Rachel said mysteriously. 'I'm thinking of someone she already knows.'

'You have someone in mind?'

'Yes – someone she's crazy about.'

Grace thought. There was only one person who fitted this description.

'Oh, Rachel,' she said, 'I don't think there's any chance of Freddie going back into the wardrobe.'

'What?' Rachel screeched. 'I'm not talking about Freddie, Mum,' she said crossly, 'and it's the closet, not the wardrobe.'

'I thought only Americans said "closet"?'

'Not in that context. Besides, you just come out of it, you don't go back in.'

'Oh! Well, if you're not talking about Freddie, who are you talking about?'

'Will.'

'*Will?*'

'Will.'

'Will,' Grace heaved a great sigh of contentment.

A few days later, Grace and Rachel sashayed into Will's plush offices, both dressed to the nines. Rachel had never been an enthusiastic member of the workforce. She had done a little modelling in her teens and early twenties but lacked the self-discipline and commitment to make a career of it. Since then she had dabbled in this and that, working in fashionable boutiques, doing a little PR work for well-connected friends, occasionally fronting a smart restaurant or nightclub but mainly just biding her time until she got married. Now she had given up all pretence of having a job and devoted herself full-time to being a barrister's wife and a lady who lunched.

Grace waved airily at Louise, Will's PA then sailed past her and into Will's office before the young woman had a chance to stop her.

Will was at his desk, talking into a tape-recorder. He looked startled when Grace burst in, followed swiftly by Rachel. 'Chase Tony for the contracts,' he finished, looking up and nodding hello, 'and get Claire to contact the people from MTV.'

'Grace, Rachel.' He greeted them with a smile, leaning back in his chair and tossing the microphone onto his desk. 'This is a surprise.' He gestured them to seats. 'To what do I owe the pleasure?'

'Sorry for bursting in on you like this, Will,' Grace began, 'but we needed to talk to you rather urgently – and in private,' she mouthed confidentially.

Grace was a sort of method actress in reverse, using former stage roles to inspire her performance in real-life situations. For today's meeting with Will she was borrowing from her critically acclaimed turn as Mrs Bennet in *Pride and Prejudice*, all fluttering helplessness and breathless distress.

'Is everything all right?' Will asked, clearly concerned.

'Things have been better,' Grace told him.

'What's wrong?'

'We need your help, Will, with a family matter,' Grace said, breathing from the top of her chest to achieve just the right note of imminent hysteria.

Will looked alarmed now.

'You're getting him all wound up, Mum,' Rachel said. To Will she said, 'Don't look so worried – it's not that serious. Mum's just being dramatic, as usual.'

'Not that serious?' Grace exclaimed. 'It's only your sister's life!'

'Is Kate in some sort of trouble? Will one of you *please* tell me what's going on?' Will begged.

'Yes, it's Kate.' Grace had finally collected herself enough to speak plainly. 'She's got engaged.'

'Oh! To the so-called Woodcutter?' Will asked chirpily – too chirpily: he received a withering look from Grace.

'Tree-hugger,' Rachel muttered.

'Sorry?'

'The so-called Tree-hugger, not Woodcutter.'

'Oh, right.' Will waited expectantly for more. 'And?' he asked, when nothing else was forthcoming.

'Well, none of us likes him,' Grace said. 'He's wrong for Kate – he'll make her miserable.'

'I know Lorcan doesn't think much of him.'

'None of us does.'

'Except Kate.' Will winced as his piquant observation was met with another glare from Grace.

'We need your help, Will.' Grace was trying to impress the seriousness of the situation on him. 'You're our only hope.'

'Well, I can see you're upset about it,' he smiled sympathetically, 'but I don't see what it's got to do with me.'

'Don't you?' Grace asked. 'No.' She sighed. 'I suppose you wouldn't.'

'So?' Will raised his eyebrows enquiringly.

'We have to put a stop to it and save Kate from a lifetime of unhappiness. The whole family are united on this. Everyone's doing their bit.'

'I see,' Will said cautiously, not really seeing at all but rather dreading the moment when all would become clear. He sensed he was going to be asked to do something deeply unpleasant.

'We want Kate to break it off of her own accord,' Grace explained, 'so we're going to do everything we can to make her change her mind about the Tree-hugger.'

'And where do I come into all this?'

'Kate has a crush on you,' Rachel said, matter-of-factly. 'Always has had.'

'Oh, I don't think—'

'Don't be so modest, Will.' Grace was cheering up now. 'Of course she does. What young girl wouldn't?'

'We thought you could lure her away from the Tree-hugger,' Rachel said.

'Yes,' Grace continued, more breezily now, 'we thought you might – you know – encourage her a bit.'

Will was aghast. 'You mean . . .' He didn't quite know how to say what he thought she meant.

'Flirt with her a bit, show an interest,' Grace said cosily.

'You want me to *seduce* Kate?' Will asked bluntly, hoping he would shame them into backing off. No such luck.

'Oh, don't make it sound so *Tess of the d'Urbervilles*,' Grace said. 'You don't have to go that far.'

'We don't expect you to make the ultimate sacrifice,' Rachel added sarcastically.

'It's just that we feel the best way – the only way – to get Kate away from the Tree-hugger is to get her thinking about someone else,' Grace went on. 'If she thought you were interested in her, she'd drop him like a hot potato.'

'Yes, but I'm *not* interested in her,' Will said. 'Well, you know, not in *that* way.'

'Of course you're not. We know that,' Rachel said, earning herself a hard look from Will. He'd never had much time for Rachel, whom he considered vain, spoilt and self-centred. He thought Kate was worth ten of her. 'What about Tina?' he said, clutching at straws. 'How do you think she'll feel if I start hitting on Kate?'

Grace restrained herself from telling Will that she didn't care how Tina would feel – in fact, she hoped it would put the spoilt, sulky little madam's nose very firmly out of joint. Anyway, if Tina got the hump about Kate and broke up with Will, it would be killing two birds with one stone. Tina was nowhere near good enough for Will, and she spent too much time away from him, constantly jet-setting around the world in pursuit of her career. Will needed more stability in his life, she thought, and a damn sight more affection and good humour than could be found in that bag of bones.

Still, now wasn't the time to be telling him what she thought about his girlfriend. 'It doesn't have to be anything too blatant,' she assured him, 'just flirting and subtle hints that she can think she's misinterpreted.'

'But isn't this a bit . . . ' Will bit his lip.

'I know what you're thinking, Will,' Grace reassured him, 'but sometimes we have to be cruel to be kind. We're just thinking of Kate's long-term happiness. Believe me, if we thought there was any other way, we wouldn't ask you this.'

'But I hardly even see Kate any more,' Will protested.

'Well, we can soon fix that,' Grace said, 'starting with next weekend. We want you to come to Cork with the family. We'll gang up on the Tree-hugger and you can go to work on Kate.'

'Well, of course I'll come, but it sounds like a long-term project and I'll be away for most of the summer. I'm taking the band to Tuscany to work on the next album.'

'I know – perfect!' Grace trilled.

'How is that perfect?' Will asked warily.

'We want you to take Kate with you,' Grace announced triumphantly.

'I'm not the Foreign Legion, Grace.'

'We don't need the Foreign Legion. Kate isn't suffering from a broken heart.'

'Not yet,' Will said, lip curling. 'I gather that's where I come in. Anyway, it's a working holiday, not a house party,' he said. 'I want to get the band isolated in a villa in the middle of nowhere where they can get some work done. I really can't have any hangers-on. Besides, Kate isn't likely to hare off to Tuscany with me out of the blue when she's just got engaged.'

'I'm not suggesting you take Kate as a guest. You could bring her as your cook. You will need one, won't you?'

'Well . . . yes.'

'And Kate is a fantastic cook, as you know.'

'And she needs a job, so she's bound to go for it,' Rachel added.

'See? Perfect!' Grace trilled.

Will felt cornered. Grace was a hard woman to say no to, especially when he owed her so much. 'Look,' he said, 'Kate may have had a crush on me when she was a teenager, but that was a long time ago.'

'Well, give it a try anyway,' Grace said briskly, 'and if she doesn't go for you, don't worry too much about it.'

Will stopped himself saying he hadn't planned to.

'There's more than one way to skin a cat, you know,' Grace added.

Will grimaced. What the O'Neills wanted him to do to Kate was sounding more alarming by the minute.

'I just mean that if you take her to Tuscany, you can show her a different lifestyle, turn her head a little. Once she's had a taste of the high life there's no way she'll want to go back to Mr Brown Rice and Pushbikes. Besides,' Grace pointed out brightly, 'maybe one of the boys in your band will fall for her.'

Christ! Will thought. Kate's boyfriend must be some piece of work if Grace thinks one of "the boys" was a more suitable prospect.

'It's not that I don't want to help, Grace. You know I'd do anything for you and yours. It just seems a bit . . . extreme.'

'If you don't feel you can help us, Will, we understand,' Grace told him, smiling at him sharkishly. Then she went in for the kill. 'It's not as if you owe us anything.'

'How does Lorcan feel about this?' he asked, suddenly seeing a way out. He felt sure his friend would never be party to something like this. Kate was his favourite sibling.

'Oh, Lorcan's behind it all the way.' Grace waved away his reservations. With Lorcan in America, she felt on safe ground. 'We had a family meeting just before he left for New York,' she continued, 'and everyone agreed this was the best course of action.'

'I just can't imagine him agreeing to it.'

'Are you accusing me of lying, William?'

Will groaned inwardly. Grace only called him 'William' when she was displeased with him. 'No, of course not, Grace,' he said. 'It's just that I couldn't agree to anything Lorcan wouldn't approve of.'

'I understand that, but Lorcan is behind this one hundred per cent.'

'Ask him yourself,' Rachel piped up. Grace scowled at her daughter.

Rachel ignored her. 'I'll tell him we've discussed it with you and you can ask him if he agrees the next time you call him,' she continued smoothly.

'I'll do that,' Will said firmly, giving her a hard look. She held his gaze. If she was bluffing, she was good.

'Good.' Rachel smiled complacently. She was enjoying watching Will squirm. When he had come to live with them, she had expected him to join her band of slavishly devoted admirers and had been more than a little put out when he remained impervious to her charms. She had found it bewildering and annoying that he seemed to prefer Kate, not only tolerating her ridiculous schoolgirl crush but positively indulging it. He was always helping her with her homework, flirting outrageously with her while hearing her lines of Shakespeare, playing a very enthusiastic Romeo to her Juliet.

93

He frequently included her in trips to the cinema or theatre with him and Lorcan. He had even taken her to that Trinity Ball when she was way too young and Rachel should have been the one to go. Rachel liked to think she had broken a few hearts when she married Tom, and she resented the fact that Will's wasn't one of them.

'Now,' Grace said, 'how about taking us to lunch?'

'Sure. I have a few things to finish up here and I'll be with you.'

'Right. We'll go to the loo to freshen up.'

As he watched them leave his office, Will sank back into his chair. He was beginning to sympathise with Kate's boyfriend. He, too, felt decidedly overwhelmed.

'Well, that went well,' Rachel said to her mother, as they touched up their make-up in front of the mirror. 'I think we've got him on board.'

'It was going fine until you got carried away,' Grace hissed. 'What were you thinking of, telling him to ring Lorcan and see what he thinks? You went too far. He *will* ask him, you know – and when he does, we're sunk.'

'Oh, don't be such a fusspot, Mum,' Rachel said, calmly applying more lipstick. 'I've got Lorcan covered. In fact, he'll be our trump card in getting Will on side.' She smiled knowingly at herself in the mirror.

'But how—'

Rachel tossed her lipstick back into her bag and turned to her mother. 'Okay, listen.'

As Rachel explained her plan, Grace's smile grew wider and ever more serene.

'I'll be right with you,' Will said, as Grace and Rachel returned to his office in a cloud of expensive perfume. He stood up, taking the tape out of the machine, and was putting on his jacket when the phone rang. He picked up the receiver. 'Yes?' he said, glancing at Grace and Rachel apologetically. 'Bollocks!' he swore, after a few moments. 'Who the hell let him out of his cage?' He was silent, listening. 'Right, I'll take care of it.' He slammed the phone into its cradle angrily. 'Sorry, Grace, I'll have to forgo lunch,' he said. 'Bloody Owen's escaped and is holed up somewhere in Temple Bar with an

American journalist – no doubt regaling her with tales of drugs and sex with underage groupies.'

'Oh, do you have to go?'

'Yes,' Will said, fishing in his drawer for his keys. 'Damage limitation.'

'Oh well, some other time,' Grace said. 'We'll leave you to it. I'll be in touch about next weekend.'

Great, Will thought. He pocketed his keys, picked up the tape and went out, stopping at Louise's desk. 'I've made a list of a few things we need to take care of,' he said, handing her the tape. 'I'm not sure how far I got before I was interrupted.'

'Sorry,' Louise said. 'I couldn't stop them.'

'Oh, don't worry about it. I wouldn't expect anyone to stop Grace O'Neill in full sail – not even you.' This was saying something as Louise was the most capable person Will had ever met. She was the sort of girl who could conjure a helicopter in the middle of the desert at a moment's notice. Her efficiency would have been terrifying if it weren't for the fact that she was so kind and down to earth, adored by everyone from Phoenix to the roadies, who regularly fell in love with her when they were on tour.

'Well, I'm going to root out Owen. Any leads?'

'I was just talking to Rory,' Louise told him. 'He thinks he might be in Bar One.'

'Okay. I don't know when I'll be back.'

'Good luck!' Louise called after him.

Stuck in traffic on the way to Temple Bar, Will had time to brood over the meeting with Grace and Rachel. The more he thought about it, the more incensed he became. Damn it, he thought crossly. Since when was it up to him to be everyone's Mr Fix-It? As if he didn't have enough to do chasing around after Owen! Now he was expected to save Kate from a fate worse than death. Picking up the pieces after Owen and the rest could be trying, but it was his job, and he had chosen it. He had never signed up for putting the kybosh on Kate's love life.

He suspected he wouldn't have felt so bad about the request if he hadn't already had a guilty conscience about Kate. To make matters worse, he wasn't even sure how guilty he should feel. He knew something had happened between them after that Trinity Ball, but not how far it had gone – what base they'd got to, as the Americans would say. That was when he had still been drinking, and he had been absolutely legless by the end of the evening. He had woken the next morning, as he had on so many mornings in those days, with virtually no memory of the previous night. The only reason he knew anything at all had happened was because of the bollocking Tom had given him the next day. He had bumped into Will and Kate during the evening and told Will he had been coming on pretty strong to Kate. Later he had seen them disappearing in the direction of Will's room in the college.

Will couldn't remember the details of Tom's lecture, but he knew it had revolved around the basic theme of not shitting where you live and that Lorcan would 'go apeshit' if he found out that Will had been messing his sister around.

Later, he had flashbacks, and a hazy memory of kissing Kate on the lawn and then waking in the early hours to find her sleeping beside him, still in her dress. When he woke up properly – which wasn't until late the following afternoon – she was gone.

Kate had never said anything, but she had changed towards him. She had started avoiding him, and when they did meet up, the old camaraderie between them was gone. Will suspected he had hurt her, but he couldn't apologise when he didn't know what had happened, and it would be too humiliating to her to ask. He had been aware that she had a girlish crush on him and, in his cups, he had probably taken advantage of it, he thought. And now Grace wanted him to romance Kate and scupper her marriage plans.

Finally making it through the lunchtime traffic, he parked the car and walked to Bar One. Sure enough, Owen was lounging on a sofa in a dark corner at the end of the room.

'So, do you enjoy being famous?' the pretty blonde opposite him was asking flirtatiously in a Californian accent.

'Well, you never have to wonder where your next shag's coming from.' Owen grinned. 'That's pretty great.'

Will noticed the tape-recorder on the table. They hadn't seen him come in and he hung back, deciding how to play it. Then he strode purposefully up to the table. 'You,' he said, eyeballing Owen, 'out-side!' He jerked his head towards the door.

'What?'

'You heard me.' He put a firm hand on Owen's shoulder. 'Out!'

'Okay, man, no problem.' Owen raised his hands as if Will was holding a gun to his head. He got up and left.

Will slid into the seat opposite the blonde.

'You're Will Sargent,' she said.

'I know who I am,' Will said coldly. 'Who are you?'

'Janice Carter.' She switched off the tape-recorder and put it into her pocket.

'What have you got there?' Will asked.

'It's an interview with Owen.'

'You think that was Owen Cassidy?'

'Of course it was.'

Will shook his head. 'It wasn't.'

Janice seemed at a loss for words.

'He's a lookalike,' Will told her.

'Oh come on!'

'I know.' Will nodded sympathetically. 'He's good, isn't he? Makes a damn fine living out of it, I believe.'

He had flustered her, he could see. 'Okay,' she said finally, regaining her composure. 'If he's just a lookalike, what are *you* doing here?'

'I have my client's reputation to protect,' Will said smoothly.

Janice snorted, probably at the idea of Owen having any reputation worthy of protection.

'Look,' Will continued reasonably, 'I have no problem with the bloke making a living impersonating Owen. Everyone has to pay the rent. But when he tries to pass himself off as the real deal, that's another story. And when he poses as Owen to give interviews to gullible journalists,' he said, 'I have to put a stop to it.'

The girl eyed him warily. 'What do you want?' she asked, eyes narrowed to slits.

'The tape.' Will gestured at her pocket.

'No way!'

Will eyed her, sizing up the situation. He was relieved that there was no photographer, and no evidence of a camera. He reckoned she was just an opportunist who had happened to get lucky – or so she thought. 'That tape is no earthly use to you,' he told her, 'so you might as well hand it over. You're freelance, right?'

'Actually, I'm on the staff of *Rolling Stone*,' she said defiantly, with a toss of her head.

'No, you're not.'

'How would you know?'

'Because if you worked for *Rolling Stone* – or any other reputable music paper, for that matter – you'd have gone through our press officer.'

The girl shrugged, but she was obviously spitting teeth at having her bluff called.

'Won't stop me selling it,' she said sulkily.

'Maybe not. Some rag might buy it, but if you're hoping to build up any sort of reputation for yourself as a serious music journalist, I wouldn't advise it. Who do you think is going to be interested in an interview with some wanker pretending to be Owen Cassidy?'

'It was Owen,' she said. 'You know it and I know it.'

'Prove it.'

Janice's eyes sparked, but she said nothing.

'It's your word against mine,' Will said coolly, 'and Owen's. Believe me, the real Owen Cassidy doesn't take any more kindly to this sort of thing than I do.'

Janice was pink with rage and her mouth had disappeared into a thin line. 'I could write about this,' she threatened. 'I could write a story about how I was strong-armed by Walking Wounded's manager into suppressing a damaging story about Owen.'

'There *is* no story about Owen, remember? Anyway, I'm not strong-arming you,' Will reminded her. 'I'm just trying to stop you making a damaging career move.'

'Yeah, right,' the girl drawled, but Will could tell from her eyes that she was defeated. He could see her weighing up her options.

'What will you give me if I give you the tape?' she asked.

'I don't have to give you anything. But I'll tell our press officer to be accommodating if you contact her. Her name's Martina.'

'You'll give me an official interview? With Owen?'

'Owen doesn't do interviews – as you'd know if you were legit. With Phoenix, or maybe Rory.'

'Phoenix,' Janice said quickly. She had read 'interviews' with the notoriously taciturn Rory: the hapless reporters had struggled in vain to get more than a few monosyllabic grunts out of him.

'I'm not promising anything. You'll have to discuss the details with Martina. All I'm promising is that I'll tell her not to hang up on you when you call.'

'Okay,' she said, reluctantly handing the tape to Will.

'Good girl.' Will pocketed it and got up. 'Be in touch.'

Will found Owen waiting for him outside the bar, head hanging.

'Sorry, man, I got a bit carried away.'

'It's okay.'

'I gave her an interview, you know,' Owen admitted.

'No, you didn't.' Will pulled the tape from his pocket and showed it to him.

'Actually, I gave her some pretty good stuff,' he said. 'I was showing her my feminine side – chicks love that.'

'Right,' Will said, 'and then you planned to have lesbian sex with her, I suppose?'

'Stop it, mate. You're turning me on.'

They had reached Will's car. 'Christ, Owen, you look like shit,' he said. 'Come on, I'm taking you home.'

Unshaven, bug-eyed and reeking of alcohol, Owen looked like he hadn't slept for a week.

Will bundled him into the passenger seat. 'When was the last time you ate?' he asked, as they pulled out into the traffic.

'Uh, dunno,' Owen said vaguely.

Will sighed. 'What have you had today?'

'Nothing.'

'Let me rephrase that,' Will said stonily. 'What have you *ingested* today?'

'Uh?'

'Tell me everything that's passed your lips, or whatever other orifice you're shoving stuff into these days.'

'Well, I had a few hits of E in the early hours. Then I did a few lines of coke this morning, sort of for breakfast. And Janice gave me some more.'

The hell she did, Will thought furiously. Owen could make enough trouble for himself without that bitch feeding him drugs to get him to mouth off. It was a good thing for her he hadn't known about this when he was with her – he'd have wrung her neck instead of making a deal with her. He was sorely tempted to head back to the bar and do just that. He would cheerfully have her busted if it weren't for the fact that she'd bring Owen down with her. Well, if she came looking for an interview he'd make sure it was with Rory – and he'd warn him beforehand to be wary of her. Rory was guarded at the best of times. It would be like trying to get blood from a stone.

'What else?' he asked Owen. 'A few dozen bottles of Jack Daniels, I suppose?'

'Well, a few scoops, yeah,' Owen confessed.

'I'll buy you lunch, then take you home. When we get there I want you to go to bed – alone.'

'You'll make someone a lovely mum one day, Will.'

Will felt tired. The sooner he got the band to Tuscany, the better. He needed them out of Dublin, away from their dealers and all the hangers-on. They'd worked bloody hard to get to where they were, but lately they'd allowed themselves to become distracted by the trappings of fame and wealth. Italy would be good for them. They could relax, recharge their batteries and focus on the work.

Rachel had lost no time in calling Lorcan. She had to make sure she got to him before Will did. 'Lorcan! It's Rachel.'

'Hi, Rachel. How's tricks? How's married life?'

'Great. How's America?'

'God, don't ask! My Blanche is the bloody producer's wife and she's ancient. I know Blanche was supposed to be going off a bit, but this woman would have to do a lot more than avoid standing under forty-watt bulbs to hide the fact that she's on the turn.'

Rachel stared into space while Lorcan prattled on, waiting for him to finish. She should have known better than to ask him a simple question about his work. 'Look,' she said, breaking in eventually, 'I'm calling you about Will.'

'Will?'

'Yeah. I had this really odd conversation with him the other day. He kept going on about Kate. He was humming and hawing, being very English about it, but basically he kept asking me about her and he seemed pretty upset when I told him she'd got engaged.'

'*Really?*' There was no mistaking the delight in Lorcan's voice.

'Yeah. It turns out he really took a shine to her at my wedding and he was planning to ask her out.'

'Gosh! I'd never have guessed. As far as I could see, he was pretty involved with Tina.'

'I was surprised too. Anyway, he was pretty shocked when I told him she was spoken for. But I told him that, as far as the family were concerned, he was welcome to lure her away from the Tree-hugger.'

'Do you think she could be lured?' Lorcan sounded hopeful.

'I don't know, but she always did have a bit of a thing for Will. If anyone can lure her, he can. It'd be pretty great, don't you think?'

'Bloody fantastic! It'd be the answer to our prayers.'

God, Rachel thought, Lorcan's such a prat – can't he see that Will's way out of Kate's league?

In fact, Lorcan had hoped for a long time that Kate and Will would get together. They were his two favourite people in the world, and he'd always thought they'd be perfect for each other.

'Anyway, I'm calling you because Will's afraid you wouldn't approve so he's holding back. So if he asks, will you give him the green light?'

'Absolutely!'

When he got back to the office after force-feeding Owen a huge lunch and dropping him home, Will rang Lorcan. After they'd discussed Lorcan's problems with *Streetcar*, he braced himself to ask his friend what he thought about Grace's scheme. He was pretty sure he knew what the answer would be, but he had to ask before he went back to Grace with a firm refusal.

'Lorcan, the reason I called . . .' he began hesitantly, 'has Rachel mentioned this Kate business to you at all?'

This Kate business, Lorcan thought, smiling. Will really was coming over all English. He was tempted to make him spell out exactly what he was talking about, but his better nature prevailed and he decided to put his friend out of his misery. 'Yes, she's told me about it,' he said.

'Well . . . what do you think?'

'It's a fantastic idea!'

'*Really*?' Will sounded surprised – shocked, even – and not at all as pleased as Lorcan had expected.

'Absolutely,' Lorcan hastened to reassure him. 'You have my blessing, my son.'

'Are you sure? I mean, I wouldn't go ahead if you didn't think—'

'Go for it, mate. Anyone who took Kate away from the tosser she's with would be doing her – and the family – a huge favour.'

'Well, if you say so.'

'He was with someone else, you know, at the wedding.'

'At the wedding? But Kate was there!'

'It was after she left, when you were dropping her home.'

'Christ!'

'Yeah, the minute her back was turned. So . . .'

'Right, yeah. I see,' Will said.

Shit! he thought, hanging up. There goes my out-clause!

In the outer office, Louise was listening to the tape Will had given her earlier. 'Chase Tony for the contracts,' he was saying.

Done, Louise thought. They were already sitting on her desk.

'And get Clare to contact the people from MTV.' Louise sighed. Sometimes she missed the old days when it had been just her and Will, and she'd never known what she might be called on to do from one day to the next. She had been press officer, tour manager, PA and publicist all rolled into one. On occasion, she'd even been pressed into service as a driver and roadie. Now she delegated. Still, it was a mark of how successful the band had become, and she felt proud to have been part of that.

She missed the immediacy of those days, though, and the closeness with the band. She missed Rory – she didn't see nearly enough of him now. Still, maybe it was just as well: she couldn't bear him being with Tessa. She wouldn't have minded so much if she'd thought Tessa really loved Rory – but she didn't believe it for a minute. She was convinced that if Rory hadn't been in the band Tessa would never have given him the time of day.

Will's last instruction was followed by a clunk. The microphone had obviously been thrown onto the desk, and Louise heard Grace and Rachel coming in. Will hadn't switched off the machine, and she knew she shouldn't eavesdrop, but she couldn't help herself.

As she listened, Louise could hardly believe what she was hearing. Grace O'Neill was reputed to be a formidable woman, but this was unbelievable – asking Will to seduce her own daughter away from her fiancé! She couldn't wait to hear Will telling her where to get off.

'You want me to *seduce* Kate?' Will said, but as she waited expectantly for more, the tape whirred to the end and clicked off.

Chapter 5

The following Friday Kate and Brian caught the bus to Cork city, where Will was to pick them up to drive the rest of the way to the O'Neills' house in West Cork. Kate sank back in her seat and made a conscious effort to relax. She was exhausted already, and it was only mid-morning. She had been up till the small hours the previous night catering a charity dinner and had made the mistake of partying till dawn with some of the kitchen staff – old friends whom she hadn't seen since getting back from Africa. She was paying for it now with a hangover of epic proportions. When she had finally got to bed she had hardly slept a wink, tossing and turning in nervous anticipation of the weekend. She kept telling herself she was being ridiculous, but she couldn't escape the feeling that that this weekend was crucial and she was filled with anxiety about Brian's performance. She so wanted the family to like him, and vice versa, but she was afraid that they would bring out the worst in each other.

To add to her anxiety, Grace had insisted they would have to drive down with Will: everyone else would be leaving at dawn to avoid the traffic, she had claimed, whereas Will couldn't get away until the afternoon, and Kate could have a nice lie-in if she went with him. When Kate had protested she wasn't bothered about a lie-in, Grace had told her there wouldn't be room in any of the other cars.

'Conor and Helen's will be packed with the kids' paraphernalia,' she had said, 'and, of course, they'll have Josie. You know how much room she takes up.'

Josie was their nanny, a cheerful, strapping girl from the wilds of Galway.

'And your father and I will be bringing the food and booze,' Grace continued.

'Just how much food and booze are you bringing?' Kate asked, envisaging giant kegs taking up the entire back seat.

'Oh, loads,' Grace said airily. 'And we have to bring a bit of furniture down too – some chairs,' she improvised vaguely.

'But what about Tom and Rachel?' Kate had asked, desperate to avoid having to start the weekend in a state of nervous tension on a four-hour car journey with Will. It was too much of a strain trying to act cool around him, especially in front of Brian.

'Tom and Rachel are newly-weds,' her mother had argued with typical irrationality. 'You don't want to be a gooseberry, do you?'

Kate hadn't bothered to say that, with Tom driving, he and Rachel wouldn't be able to perform the entire Kama Sutra. Her mother had decided that she and Brian should drive down with Will, and once Grace got an idea into her head it was futile to argue.

But when Kate rang Will to make the arrangements, she was mortified to discover that this was the first he had heard of it. As it happened, he was going to be in Cork city on Thursday attending a charity function with Walking Wounded where they were to be the guests of the Lady Mayoress. He offered to pick Kate and Brian up the next day and they would drive the rest of the way together.

Grace was bitterly disappointed when she learned that her plan to throw Kate and Will together for the drive down had been scuppered. However, she cheered up when Rachel pointed out to her that this would be better for their cause as it would provide what she called 'maximum lifestyle contrast'. Brian would be too cheap to spring for the train so Kate would have a nightmare journey down by bus, surrounded by smelly students going home for the weekend. Then Will would roll up in his classic car, a knight in a shining Jaguar, to whisk them the rest of the way in speed and comfort.

True to form, Brian hadn't let them down. Kate's relief at not driving the whole way with Will turned quickly to regret when Brian insisted that they take the bus, complaining that the train was too expensive. Besides, he said, the bus was 'friendlier'. Kate longed to override him by paying the difference, but she was too broke to make the gesture.

So, the bus it was, and now, apart from being knackered, she was in a foul humour. The bus was indeed half the price of the train but it took twice as long. Her mood wasn't helped by Brian wittering on about the wonderful 'characters' you got on buses. Kate wondered if he was referring to the backpacker behind them, whose surreptitious weed-smoking was making her nauseous, or the red-faced pensioner across the aisle who was leering at her.

'Are you cold?' Brian asked, amazed, as she took a big black cardigan out of her bag.

'Just tired of being the floor show,' she said, pulling it tightly over her breasts and folding her arms over it.

Four hours later, the bus pulled into the station in Cork city. They found Will waiting for them outside, leaning against his car, the sun bouncing off the gleaming paintwork and his snowy white shirt. 'Hi, Kate,' he said and bent to kiss her.

Kate noticed that his hair was beginning to grow out. 'This is Brian – Brian, Will,' she said, introducing them.

'Hi, Brian, nice to meet you.' The two men shook hands.

'Isn't Tina with you?' Kate asked.

'She's off doing a photo shoot for *Vogue* in the Caribbean.' Will took their bags and opened the boot of his car.

Kate was relieved. She always felt uncomfortable around Tina. Out of the corner of her eye, she caught Brian glowering at Will's car, no doubt mentally calculating his carbon footprint.

'Crikey, what have you got in here?' Will asked, as he hefted Kate's bag. He wouldn't have batted an eyelid if it had been Tina's – she never went anywhere without her own weight in cosmetics and enough shoes to sink the Titanic. But Kate had never struck him as the high-maintenance type.

'Oh, you know,' Kate shrugged evasively, 'just a few bottles.' She had spent half of yesterday running around buying gifts for Brian to give her parents, not trusting him to do the right thing.

It was such bliss to stretch out in the front of Will's car with the window open and the wind in her hair that Kate forgot to be self-conscious.

'This is lovely. It's a lot nicer than the bus, isn't it?' she said to Brian.

'Afraid I can't enjoy it,' he said. 'I feel too guilty about travelling in such a gas-guzzler.'

Why couldn't he resist the chance to have a go, Kate thought irritably. It was so rude when Will had been kind enough to give them a lift. If this was the way he was going to behave all weekend, acting superior, making snide remarks and getting in digs at people, it was going to be a total disaster.

Will eyed Brian coldly in the rear-view mirror. It was on the tip of his tongue to say he could get out and walk if his conscience was bothering him but, for Kate's sake, he let it go. 'I'd better warn you,' he said to Kate, 'that Rachel's bringing the wedding DVD and she's going to make us watch it at some stage over the weekend.'

Kate groaned. 'But we were *there*. We lived through the whole thing in real time.'

Will laughed. 'I knew you'd be pleased.'

'How did your charity ball go?' Kate asked.

'Oh, great – until Owen tried to shag the Lady Mayoress.'

Kate giggled. 'He didn't.'

'Oh yes, he did.'

A doughty matron with a twinkle in her eye, Will suspected that the Lady Mayoress had in fact been hugely flattered to be propositioned by someone so young.

'But she's old enough to be his mum!'

'Owen doesn't discriminate on grounds of age, race, creed – or species. He doesn't discriminate much at all, actually. Luckily for us, she was a very good sport about it. Her husband wasn't so pleased, though.

I just hope we never get invited to Buckingham Palace. I doubt the Queen would be amused.'

'And Prince Philip would beat him to a pulp!'

It wasn't long before they were winding up the steep, twisting road that led to the O'Neills' rambling country house.

'Wow! What an amazing place,' Brian gasped, as the ocean fell away beneath them. Kate turned to smile at him. She had known Brian would love it and he was seeing it at its best today. The house was set in a stunning location on the side of a hill, overlooking the broad expanse of the bay. The sun was shining in a cloudless blue sky, and below them the water sparkled and danced.

Kate felt a familiar bubble of happiness, like the first sip of champagne, when she caught her first glimpse of the house, its creamy yellow walls half covered with a riot of fuchsia. They had been coming here for as long as she could remember, and it was full of happy memories. As children, they had spent endless summer days running wild outside, practically living on the beach, learning to swim in the tidal pools, catching fish from the rocks, collecting shells and pebbles and making friends with the local children, only wandering home when they were hungry. In winter it had a different kind of charm, with huge waves crashing dramatically on the shore. Bracing walks along the beach in the stingingly cold sea breeze were followed by warming up around the fire with hot chocolate.

· As she got out of the car, Kate breathed in deeply. The salty tang of the sea air was instantly invigorating, sharpening her appetite and bringing her senses alive.

'You go on in,' Will said, opening the boot. 'I'll unpack the stuff.'

Taking Brian's hand, Kate led him to the house. When she pushed open the door, she was immediately accosted by Sam and Jake, almost tripping her up.

'Hi Kate!' they chorused in unison. 'Where's Freddie?'

'Oh, he isn't coming. But this is Brian.'

'Aw-awww!' Sam let out a multisyllabic groan.

Jake was a little more diplomatic. 'We thought you were bringing Freddie.' He smiled valiantly. They adored Freddie, who would spend hours playing the most mind-numbingly boring games with them.

'Well, I brought Brian instead. Brian, this is Jake, and this is Sam.'

'Hi!' Brian grinned down at them.

'Hi Brian,' Jake said, rallying quickly. 'D'you want to play Twister – or Hide and Seek? Whichever you like.'

'Hide and Seek, Hide and Seek!' Sam begged, jumping up and down.

Just then Helen appeared from the kitchen. 'Come on, you two,' she chided, 'let Kate and Brian get in the door. You have the whole weekend to play with them. Hi, I'm Helen.' She extended a hand to Brian over the children's heads.

'And I'm Brian, as you obviously already know.'

'Yes, it's nice to meet you at last. I've heard a lot about you.'

She was surprised by Brian. Tall, good-looking and well-built, he was almost the complete opposite of the pale, weedy hippie she had imagined from Grace and Rachel's descriptions – and he seemed perfectly nice too. In typical O'Neill fashion, they'd probably never given him a chance. Once they get to know him, she thought hopefully, they'll probably realise they've been wrong about him, and we'll all have a thoroughly enjoyable weekend.

'You're the last to arrive,' she told Kate, as she led the way down the hall, herding the children in front of her. 'We're in the garden – come on out when you've got settled. We'll eat outside – make the most of this weather.'

'*Will!*' Jake roared, eyes lighting up as Will pushed open the door and nudged inside, laden with luggage. The boys wriggled beneath Helen's arms and charged back down the hall to throw themselves at him, almost knocking him over.

'I'd better go and rescue Will.' Helen smiled wryly, as the children could be heard importuning him to play with them.

Kate was about to take Brian up to her room when her mother rushed in from the garden to greet them. 'Hello, Brian, you're very welcome.' She threw her arms around him and enveloped him in an enthusiastic embrace. 'It's lovely to see you again, and it's wonderful to have you here.'

'Oh, thanks, great to be here,' Brian stuttered, looking a little overwhelmed already.

'I can't tell you how happy we are that you decided to accept one of our invitations at last,' Grace continued, her gracious smile belying the barbed comment.

'It's good of you to have me.' Brian smiled.

'Once you get to know us, I'm sure you'll find we're not that bad,' she said gaily. 'You might find we have more in common than you'd think. I bet you'd be surprised to hear that I was a bit of a hippie in my youth.'

Not as surprised as I'd be, Kate thought. She appreciated that her mother was trying to make Brian feel at ease, but this was just the sort of behaviour that sent him scarpering in the other direction. He already had that cornered-rabbit look.

'Really?' Brian seemed surprised to hear that *he* was a bit of a hippie.

'Oh, yes!' Grace trilled. 'Always protesting about this, that and the other, world peace, civil liberties, the Pill – you name it, I was there with my placard. Nowadays it's all about the environment and animal rights,' she added regretfully. 'Human beings don't get a look in. Still, it's good to know there are still people willing to fight the good fight.'

Kate rolled her eyes. 'Mum, it was the sixties. You did drugs and shagged everyone in sight, and the only place *you* ever marched was down the King's Road.'

'We didn't "do drugs",' Grace protested. 'No one "did drugs" in those days – it hadn't even been invented.'

'Oh, I forgot,' Kate said, 'you didn't "do drugs", you *experimented.*'

'Exactly.' Grace was oblivious to her youngest child's sarcasm. 'Honestly, she'll have you thinking I was some kind of debauched commune-dweller,' she told Brian. 'Anyway, why don't you two go and get settled? Kate, you're not in your old room. I've given you two the guest room – it's bigger and it has the en-suite. I'm putting Will in your room.'

'Oh!' Kate experienced a moment of panic. She hoped to God there weren't any of her old diaries lying around in there. Maybe she could sneak in later and turn the room over. As a teenager she had filled whole notebooks pouring out her unrequited love for Will, faithfully recording every word he had spoken to her and forensically analysing his every glance. 'Why didn't you put him in Lorcan's room?'

'Carmen's in there,' Grace told her.

'I didn't know she was coming.' Kate was taken aback.

'Lorcan's afraid someone will run off with her while he's away. She came down with your father and me.'

'Oh, I see.' Kate was a little hurt that they had managed to find room in the car for Carmen, while she and Brian had been reduced to travelling by bus. It also threw the family's attitude to Brian into sharp contrast. Despite her mother's effusive welcome, she couldn't see her family spending time with him for his own sake.

'You do like Carmen, don't you, Kate?'

'Oh, yes. She's great. I just didn't know she was coming.'

Each of the O'Neill children had his or her own bedroom in the house, which they had been allowed to paint whatever colour they liked. The result was a diverse range of idiosyncratic colour schemes that would make the house an estate agent's nightmare if they ever chose to sell. Kate had painted hers a beautiful burnt orange, the colour of the evening sun just before it sank into the sea.

The room she and Brian had been allocated was perhaps the most beautiful in the house, never having been subjected to a makeover at the hands of a whimsical teenager. It was also uncluttered by the confusion of shell and pebble collections, bodyboards, books and inflatable toys that filled the others to bursting point. The walls were painted a calming cornflower blue, and the muslin curtains blowing in the breeze added to the Zen-like atmosphere. The shelves contained only a few artfully placed knick-knacks, and the wardrobes and drawers were empty. As she kicked off her shoes, Kate noticed that the wooden floorboards didn't have a trace of the sand that, despite rigorous sweeping and hoovering by the housekeeper, had insinuated itself into every nook and crevice of the rest of the house.

Kate dumped her bag on the floor and threw herself onto the big double bed, sinking into the fat duvet and breathing in the smell of crisp, clean linen. Brian wandered over to the window, which overlooked the garden and, beyond, the sea. The sounds of the children playing drifted up to them.

'Sorry about Mum,' Kate yawned. 'She gets a bit carried away.'

'It's kind of cool that she was a hippie.'

'Oh, don't listen to her. She was *not* a hippie. The closest she ever came to it was being groped by John Lennon at a party – or was it Mick Jagger?'

'Who's Carmen?' Brian asked.

'Lorcan's latest girlfriend. He only met her the day of Rachel's wedding,' Kate confessed, aware that this was an example of the way her family took people over. If only Brian knew he had nothing to worry about on that score.

She pushed herself up from the bed. 'Ready to face the music?' she asked.

'Not quite.' He came to join her on the bed. 'The sea air has given me an appetite,' he mumbled, pulling her into his arms and kissing her.

'I'm not sure we have time.' Kate gasped as she felt the soft warmth of Brian's lips on her neck. 'Everyone will be wondering where we are,' she protested half-heartedly, raising her arms so that he could pull off her T-shirt and tugging at his. She moaned softly as he caressed her breasts, his thumbs rubbing her nipples until they were as hard as he was.

'I think we're eating soon,' she muttered ineffectually, as he pushed her back on to the bed and unzipped her jeans.

He lifted his head momentarily, eyes dark with desire. 'I'm eating now,' he murmured, running his tongue from her belly button to the edge of her knickers.

Some time later, showered and changed, Kate and Brian made their way to the garden. It was a perfect summer's evening, the sun still warm, the only background noise the peaceful rustling of the trees and the soporific hum of bees as they plundered the overstuffed flowerbeds. The quiet sounds of nature seemed at once to magnify and soften the low buzz of conversation, the clink of ice in glasses and the occasional shouts of the children as they kicked a ball with Will and Josie at the far end of the lawn. The evocative summery smells of suntan lotion and barbecuing food mingled in the air.

Conor and Tom were standing, drinks in hand, discussing their respective journeys down, swapping notes about snarl-ups and short-cuts, while Conor idly manned the barbecue. 'Your big mistake was not taking that turn-off where I told you,' he was telling Tom, as he shuffled things around on the coals.

'Hi, Kate, Brian.' He smiled fondly at his sister. 'How was your journey? Kate and Brian came on the bus,' he told Tom, without having waited for an answer, 'the only way slower than the one you took.'

'Brian came on the bus because he's committed to the environment,' Grace informed Conor reprovingly, as she swept past with a tray of glasses and cutlery and began to set the long wooden table under the magnolias.

'Should be committed to a mental institution,' Conor murmured to Tom.

'You'll be glad to hear we came in only three cars, Brian,' Grace said. 'The whole family!'

'Oh, good for you!' Brian said politely. He thought balefully of the fleet of Mercs and BMWs that had been parked in the drive when they'd arrived and wondered how the O'Neills could possibly have come in more, unless they'd got the children to drive down by themselves. Still, he supposed Kate's weird mother was trying to be nice and to find common ground between them, however tenuous.

'Well, everyone has to do their bit for the environment, don't they?' Grace said, patting Brian's shoulder.

Jack waved to Kate from where he was sitting in the shade of a tree at the end of the garden, reading the paper. Carmen was on the grass, babbling into her mobile, no doubt to Lorcan.

Rachel was pegged out on a sunbed wearing a skimpy lime-green bikini, topping up her honeymoon tan, her newly polished toenails glistening in the evening sun. She sat up as they came out, raising an arm to shield her eyes. On seeing Brian, she leaped up, threw her arms around him and kissed him lightly on the cheek. 'Hello, Brian, it's lovely to see you again.' She beamed, keeping an arm around him and throwing back her shoulders to show off her golden breasts to full advantage. Rachel was an egalitarian flirt and felt everyone had an equal right to fancy her, even her little sister's horrible boyfriend. 'You know most people here, don't you,' she said, 'except Josie and Carmen? Come on and I'll introduce you. Here, have a drink first – Helen's made a big jug of Pimm's.' She poured some into a huge glass and thrust it into his hand. Then, taking his other hand, she bore him off around the garden.

Conor handed Kate a glass of Pimm's. 'So, which way did the bus go?' he asked.

'Oh, it goes via Timbuktu, just in case anyone wanted to get on. It's very democratic,' Kate replied.

'Darling, what on earth are you wearing?' Grace hissed, coming over to join them.

Kate had hoped no one would notice her clothes, but she should have known better. She had been aware of her mother eyeing her askance since she had come down. 'They're trousers I bought in Africa,' she mumbled.

'Was a circus having a closing-down sale?' her mother said.

'Very colourful!' Tom said. 'They sold some great stuff on the beach in Thailand, but I couldn't get Rachel to buy any of it – and it was so cheap!'

'Well, that's probably why,' Conor said sardonically.

'These trousers only cost about a euro,' Kate told Tom.

Grace's expression clearly implied that Kate had been robbed.

'They look very cool,' Tom said.

'Well, I wouldn't go that far,' Kate said, grateful for his support.

'Oh, I didn't mean cool as in trendy. I meant, you know, light and summery.'

The problem was, Kate's fat clothes didn't fit her any more and the stuff she had bought in Africa had been fine when she was there, in the dazzling light and surrounded by people who dressed as if every day was carnival, but now that she was home they seemed garish and outré. She was all too aware that today she looked like a clown.

'I thought maybe you were thinking of entering the Notting Hill Carnival this year,' Conor teased.

Kate widened her mouth in a mock smile, but she had to admit that all she needed was a big feathery headdress and she wouldn't be out of place sambaing down the Portobello Road to the beat of a steel band and the shriek of a thousand whistles.

'Kate, I hope you're not going to start dressing like a hippie, just because you're – you know . . .' Grace pushed her mouth close to her daughter's ear, '. . . engaged to Brian.'

'It's just that my old clothes don't fit me any more, and I don't have any money for new ones.'

'Oh, don't worry about that,' her mother said. 'Rachel and I will bring you on a shopping spree when we get back to Dublin and get you kitted out with a whole new wardrobe.'

'But I can't afford it,' Kate protested – especially the sort of places where Rachel and her mother shopped.

Grace waved away her objections. 'My treat. You have such a fantastic figure now, Kate, you need to make the most of it with some decent clothes.'

Kate could see her mother was already excited at the prospect – she liked nothing better than the chance to overhaul someone's wardrobe. Kate, however, wasn't sure how happy she was to be the subject of one of her mother's makeovers, but she was grateful for the offer. 'Thanks.' She smiled. 'That's really generous.'

Suddenly Carmen jumped up from the grass and made a beeline for the house, rather pink in the face.

'Hi, Kate.' She stopped briefly to give Kate a kiss. 'So nice to see you again.' She rushed away as her mobile rang again.

'Off to her room to have phone sex with Lorcan,' Tom said.

When Brian had finished his tour, he rejoined Kate. Jake bounded up to them. 'D'you two want to play football?' he asked eagerly. 'Rachel won't, but Will and Josie are playing, so it'll be three against three.'

'Well, I don't know . . .' Kate realised she had no idea how Brian was with kids.

'*Please*,' Jake begged, putting his hands together in a prayer position. 'We'll let you have Will on your side,' he added.

'Is he good, then?' Brian asked him.

'He's from England, same as Beckham,' Jake explained, with irrefutable logic. 'Or you can have Josie, if you like. Josie's good in goal because she's built like a big shithouse – that's a kind of toilet,' he explained, plainly delighted with the expression.

Kate tried to look disapproving but couldn't help laughing. 'Jake,' she admonished him, 'you shouldn't say things like that.'

'Josie said it first.'

'Well, you shouldn't repeat it. And, anyway, it's a *brick* shithouse, not a *big* shithouse.'

'So, will you play?' Jake persisted.

'Okay,' Brian agreed. 'We'll take Josie.'

Kate just hoped she wouldn't be required to tackle Will too vigorously.

After they had allowed the children to trounce them at football, dinner was ready. Everyone crowded around the long wooden table as Helen and Carmen carried huge dishes from the kitchen. 'You'll have to put up with my cooking tonight,' Helen said to Brian. 'I'm not quite up to Kate's standards, I'm afraid.'

'Oh, don't mind her, Helen's a brilliant cook,' Kate told him, smiling at her sister-in-law. 'What are we having?'

'Fish,' Helen announced, lifting the lid on a platter of glistening barbecued sea bass, their skin scored and blackened. 'Fresh out of the sea this morning. It's the only thing to have down here really, isn't it?'

'Oh!' Kate said, dismayed.

'Yes, and Conor's done a really good job of barbecuing it,' Helen continued as she arranged the side dishes on the table.

'Is there anything else?' Kate asked.

'Well, there are potatoes *boulangére*, peperonata, salad, bread.' Helen indicated the various dishes. 'Help yourselves, everyone.'

'It's just that Brian's a vegetarian,' Kate said, hating to make a fuss when Helen had gone to so much trouble. 'I thought you knew.'

'Oh!' Helen looked from Grace to Rachel. 'I knew he didn't eat meat, but I thought he ate fish.'

'I thought all vegetarians ate fish,' Grace said.

'I'm sorry, Brian, I could have sworn someone told me you ate fish,' Helen said.

'No, nothing with a face,' Brian said.

'Oh, it's okay,' Jake piped up from the far end of the table. 'My mum cuts the face off, don't you, Mum?'

'I don't think that's quite what Brian means, Jake,' Helen told him.

But Jake thought he had found a kindred spirit and was keen to reassure him. After all, it wasn't every day you found an adult who was so sensible about food. Most of them were always boasting that they'd eat any old rubbish. 'I don't eat faces either,' he continued chummily. 'Imagine eating the eyes,' he said, screwing up his face in disgust. 'They'd be all squelchy and yukky.'

'Yes, okay, Jake, we get the picture.'

But Jake was just getting into his stride. 'And the nose!' He was relishing the opportunity to gross everyone out. 'Imagine if you ate the nose and it was full of snot. Yeugh!'

'Jake, it's not just the face that Brian doesn't eat,' Helen said wearily.

'I just feel that animals with faces are so like us, aren't they? They're our friends,' Brian explained. 'You wouldn't eat one of your friends, would you?'

'I wouldn't eat their nose anyway,' Jake said, 'in case it was full of snot.'

'Jake, stop talking about snot and eat your dinner,' Conor snapped. 'Sam, what's wrong?'

No one had noticed that Sam had gone very quiet and was looking morosely down at his plate. 'I don't want my dinner,' he wailed, his face crumpling.

'What's wrong with it?' Conor asked.

'It's all got a face!' Sam sobbed, as his smiley-face potato waffles and fish nuggets with fishy faces beamed up at him. He had been going through a phase of only eating novelty food.

'If Brian's not eating his fish,' Jake piped up, 'can I not eat my vegetables?'

'No,' Helen said firmly. 'You have to eat your vegetables.'

'It's not fair!' Jake said. 'Why is Brian allowed be picky and I'm not?'

'Because guests can be as fussy as they like and you just have to put up with it,' Helen answered tetchily.

'You're lucky,' Jake told Brian. 'We're not allowed be finicky about food, aren't we not, Sam?' His younger brother shook his head glumly.

As everyone passed dishes around and Jack poured wine, Kate heard her mother still trying to persuade Brian to try the fish. 'Go on,' she was saying. 'We won't report you to the Vegetarian Society.'

'No, really. I'll just have the salad and vegetables,' Brian said politely. 'It looks great.'

Soon everyone was tucking in hungrily, complimenting Helen extravagantly on the food.

'These vegetables are wonderful,' Brian enthused, aware that he was responsible for all the disruption. 'Are they organic?'

'Yes,' Helen admitted resentfully, suddenly wishing they'd come out of a can.

'This is a great house,' he said to Grace.

'Yes, isn't it? I suppose it's very decadent of us to have two such beautiful homes when some people haven't even one,' she said.

'"All property is theft" and all that,' Brian said jauntily.

Jack bristled visibly. 'Not this property, son,' he said, glowering owlishly at Brian from the far end of the table. 'I'll dig out the deeds later and show them to you.'

'Oh no, I didn't mean . . .'

'Dad built this house himself,' Rachel said to Brian reprovingly.

'You know that's not what he meant,' Kate said crossly. 'It's just an expression.'

She looked at Will, who was opposite her. 'Thanks for giving me a plug at the wedding, by the way.'

'Oh, no problem. Did you get any work out of it?'

'Yes – a couple of dinner parties and the charity bash I catered last night.'

'Brilliant! So you're pretty busy, then?' Will said cheerfully, hoping she'd be unable to accept the job in Tuscany.

'Well, nothing long-term, but at least I won't have to bonk the landlord.'

Hearing this, Brian said, 'The Haven has an opening for a cook over the summer – it'd be three months' steady work.' The Haven was the centre where Kate had met Brian.

'They don't pay much, though,' she said. 'I can't afford to work there.'

'But you'd get your accommodation and meals thrown in,' Brian pointed out, 'and a free workshop.'

'I don't need accommodation,' Kate protested. 'I have my flat.' *And I don't need a bloody workshop*, she thought. 'Besides, it's in Galway.'

Will was aware that Grace was gazing at him expectantly. This was his cue to ask Kate to work for him in Tuscany. 'If you don't want to go to Galway for a job,' he began hesitantly, 'I don't suppose you'd consider Tuscany?'

'Tuscany?'

'They're hardly the same thing,' Grace put in.

'Yes,' Will answered Kate. 'I'm taking the band to Tuscany for the summer to work on the new album. We'll be staying in a villa just outside Florence. It'll be a chance for the guys to chill out and get some work done at the same time.

'Anyway, we'll need a cook,' he continued, 'and I was wondering if you'd be interested. It'll be pretty relaxed, just me and the guys most of the time. There'll be a few house guests in the last couple of weeks, but, up until then, it's strictly a working holiday.'

'Wow!' Kate was unable to contain her excitement, her eyes sparkling. 'It's an amazing offer. How long are you going to be away?'

'A couple of months. I'd understand if you don't want to be away from Dublin for that long.'

'Well, I *have* just got back,' Kate said, glancing at Brian and trying to stop herself automatically jumping at the chance to spend the summer in a villa in Tuscany cooking for one of the most famous bands in the world . . . and Will. She was engaged now, she reminded herself. She had to consider Brian's feelings.

'Nonsense, Kate,' Grace said briskly. 'You can't miss out on an opportunity like this.'

'They don't come along every day,' Conor advised her. 'It would open lots of doors for you.'

'I don't know . . . ' Kate procrastinated. Brian seemed rather put out.

'Well, think about it,' Will told her.

'What is there to think about?' Grace said imperiously. 'It's the chance of a lifetime, Kate.'

'I'd pay well over the odds,' Will added, sensing the power struggle that was going on between Kate and her boyfriend and suddenly wanting her to say yes.

'That's settled, then,' Grace said.

'Nothing's settled, Mum,' Kate said. 'I'll have to discuss it with Brian.'

'And there's the job at the Haven,' Brian reminded her.

'Kate, you can't work for food like some . . . hobo!' her mother declared. 'Especially when Will has offered you this fantastic job – well paid and working for really important people.'

119

'I'll *think* about it,' Kate said firmly.

With Kate's next career move sorted out to his satisfaction, Conor was haranguing Brian about his work. 'What you do really taps into the *Zeitgeist* right now,' he was saying. 'The whole new-age thing is huge. Look at Deepak Chopra or Louise Hay – they do sell-out gigs at big venues. But you want to strike now while the iron's hot, before the bottom falls out of the whole thing.'

'I hope there'll always be people willing to grow,' Brian countered.

'Well, hoping's not enough,' Conor said bossily. 'You want to get yourself firmly established before people have moved on to the next big thing and you find yourself left behind. How do you do in terms of bums on seats?'

'Well, I don't really . . .'

'You've got to quantify,' Conor told him sternly. 'Got any merchandise?'

'*Merchandise*?'

'Self-help books, inspirational CDs, stuff like that?'

'Oh, um, no,' Brian stuttered, knocked off balance by Conor's rapid-fire interrogation.

'Well, you'd want to get cracking,' Conor advised him. 'Don't let the grass grow under your feet. Do you have an agent?'

'An agent?' Brian looked confused.

'Yes, someone to help you get your message out there, book you onto talk shows, that sort of thing. You can bet Louise Hay has an agent.'

'Well, I'm sure she has, but—'

'And Deepak Chopra.'

'Probably,' Brian said sourly. 'Wherever there's talent, you'll usually find a whole rake of people leeching off it, usually ripping people off. The music industry is rife with it, isn't it?' he said conversationally to Will. 'Every other week some musician's suing their manager for embezzlement.'

Will looked at him with a mixture of hostility and amusement.

'I hope you're not suggesting that Will—' Grace was outraged.

'Oh, no, I was just speaking generally,' Brian said innocently. 'No offence,' he said to Will.

'None taken.' Will smiled pleasantly. No offence my arse, you little shit.

Grace continued to glower at him. 'Will takes extremely good care of those boys. God knows where they'd be without him.'

'In jail, probably, in Owen's case,' Conor said.

'Or up the Lady Mayoress of Cork,' Kate muttered, and Will laughed.

'You need to focus on something that'll capture the public imagination,' Conor continued. 'Doesn't matter what it is – yogic flying, finding yourself through pole-dancing, whatever. The madder the better. If you could get a few big stars interested, you'd be laughing. Will might be able to help you with that – he knows lots of people.'

'I really don't think—'

'Is there any way you could tie in a diet?' Conor asked.

'Well, not really. I follow a wholefood vegetarian regime but—'

'Have you lost any weight since you started?' Conor pounced on this enthusiastically. 'Have you got any "before" pictures of yourself as a fatso?'

'Er . . . no, I've always been pretty much the same weight.'

'Ah, pity! The number-one way to sell anything, these days, is to connect it to weight loss. Look at Tessa Bond – lost a few pounds and now she's reinvented herself as a diet and fitness guru.'

'Is Tessa as much of a pain in the hole in real life as she always seems?' Josie asked Will, in her thick Galway accent.

'Oh, God, no, not at all,' Will said.

'Really?'

'She's twice as awful in real life,' Will drawled.

Josie giggled. Sam and Jake were giggling too, thrilled that Josie had said 'pain in the hole'. She was always using forbidden expressions.

'You've got to admit, she does look amazing now,' Rachel conceded. She had just been reading a magazine interview in which Tessa had talked up her new book.

'Do you think so?' Will asked. 'I think she's too thin.'

'Oh, we all know how you feel about curvy girls, don't we, Will?' Grace winked at him.

'You'd hardly call Tina curvy,' Rachel scoffed.

'Not without risking a black eye,' Will said.

'Don't you think Kate's looking wonderful?' Grace asked him.

'Yes, I think she looks great,' Will said.

Kate blushed, wishing her mother wouldn't draw attention to her.

Grace sat back contentedly, surveying the table.

'It's so lovely to have all my family around me.' She twinkled at each member in turn.

'Except Lorcan,' Kate said.

'Yes, it's a shame he couldn't make it,' Grace said, with an edge to her voice, as if she was annoyed with him. 'And, of course, it's lovely to have Brian and Carmen here too. And Will.' She turned to him. 'You know we regard you as one of the family. In fact, there was a time when I thought—' She broke off, with a wistful smile. 'Well, a mother can dream.'

Oh God, who's she being, Kate thought, throwing a panicked look at her mother. Please not the mad old bint from *Long Day's Journey into Night*. Or one of Tennessee Williams's nutjobs. If only Lorcan was there. He knew Grace's repertoire better than anyone and always won when they played 'Name That Character'.

'You thought what?' Helen asked innocently.

'Well,' Grace smiled coyly, 'there was a time I thought Will might actually *be* family,' she said, throwing significant looks at Will and Kate.

'You mean you thought . . . Kate and Will?'

'Well, they *were* sort of childhood sweethearts, Helen.'

'Really?' Brian said.

'We were *not*, Mum!' *What the hell had gotten into her?*

'Well, no,' Grace conceded. 'I mean you weren't exactly *children*.'

'I never knew!' Helen beamed.

'That's because it's not true. Mum—'

'Oh, I'm sure Brian won't mind me saying this, darling. No doubt he has a past himself, haven't you Brian?' She smiled at him encouragingly.

A past!

'They were inseparable,' she said to Helen. 'When we came down here I wouldn't see them from one end of the day to the other. They'd be off cavorting on the beach together . . .'

Cavorting! Kate didn't dare look at Will but she glanced at Brian: he was scowling at her.

122

'Have you been speaking to Lorcan, Grace?' Will interrupted. 'This production of *Streetcar* seems to be causing him problems.'

'Yes,' Grace said, apparently a little startled by the sudden change of topic. 'I can't understand why these producers will insist on casting their wives, no matter how unsuitable they are.'

'Oh, I've spoken to him about it,' Conor said. 'I told him what to do to nobble the old biddy . . .'

The conversation drifted on to Lorcan's production and Kate was grateful to Will for the diversion. But what her mother had said was hovering in the air, and when Helen announced that she was going to make some fruit salad for dessert, she offered to do it instead. 'You've done enough, Helen,' she said, and scurried off to the kitchen.

She began to relax as she peeled and chopped mangoes, hulled strawberries and spooned the seeds out of passion fruit. The familiar rhythm of chopping and slicing soothed her and gave her space to think.

'Can I help?'

It was Brian, seeking refuge from her family, no doubt.

'You can cut this up,' she said, handing him a pineapple. 'Sorry about Conor,' she said, as Brian set to work. 'He tends to see the megastar in everyone. I think he reckons with a bit of effort you could be the next Tessa Bond.'

'Actually, he was comparing my work to Deepak Chopra's,' Brian said, sounding affronted.

Kate winced. She couldn't believe Brian had let Conor get to him with his grandiose plans for taking the world by storm. 'You shouldn't mind him,' she said quietly. 'It's just his way of being kind.'

'Is that *your* way of saying you don't think I could be Deepak Chopra?' he asked.

'You don't want to be him, do you?'

'No – I don't think he has a diet, does he?' He grinned. 'I wouldn't mind being Louise Hay, though,' he added.

'Nah,' Kate chuckled, 'you don't have the tits for it.'

Just then, Josie came into the kitchen. 'Kate,' she hissed in a conspiratorial stage whisper, 'as soon as dinner's over, I say we make a bolt for the pub. Are you in?'

'Sure.' Kate couldn't see the necessity for the cloak-and-dagger routine.

'We've got to make a break for it before Rachel gets out the wedding video,' Josie said urgently.

'Oh, right!' Kate said. 'But it's only putting off the misery until tomorrow night,' she warned.

'It's every man for himself then,' Josie rejoined. 'But tonight's my night off, and I'm fucked if I'm spending it watching the rerun of her bloody wedding. More to the point, I *won't* be fucked if I spend the night watching it.'

'Well, I wouldn't count on it either way, if I were you. This village isn't exactly bursting at the seams with talent.'

'I'll take my chances,' Josie said.

There was a magnificent sunset by the time they set out for the pub. Now the sky was streaked with pink and shot through with gold, promising another glorious day tomorrow. Grace and Jack had opted to stay at home with Helen and Conor, and Carmen was holed up in her room again, sending Lorcan dirty text messages. So, Will, Kate, Brian, Josie, Tom and Rachel sauntered down the hill in the still evening and along the beach road.

Inside the little whitewashed pub they found a hot mass of bodies and the whole place was jumping with chatter and laughter. People were packed ten deep at the bar, and in one corner a local four-piece band was playing, the jangle of electric guitars adding to the din.

Tom and Rachel were soon borne off by old friends who hadn't made it to the wedding, congratulating them and vying with each other to buy them drinks and tell Tom what a lucky man he was. Rachel was in her element, surrounded by admirers: she liked to think that some of the local boys had spent the year ticking the days off on their calendars until the next time she brought a splash of unattainable glamour to the sleepy fishing village.

Kate knew the pub was fraught with danger for Brian, so she was pleased when he insisted on getting the first round. To her intense relief, he didn't even have to ask her for money to go up to the bar. It wasn't that she minded giving him money, but not when her family were watching.

She settled on a stool opposite Will, wedged in by Josie, who was avidly scanning the room.

The four-piece that had been playing rock standards when they came in suddenly went into full-on rock-star mode, thrashing their instruments with gusto, the drummer going into a showy impromptu solo that evidently took his fellow band members by surprise. The singer and lead guitarist were leaping about so much that they ended up banging heads in mid-air with a sickening crunch.

'Jesus!' Will laughed.

'I imagine this is for your benefit,' Kate said.

Brian returned, holding a clutch of drinks to his chest and distributed them. Kate caught surprise on Will's face as Brian placed a glass tumbler in front of him. 'Is that *tap water?*' she asked.

'Yes,' Brian said defiantly. 'What's wrong with that?'

Kate raised her eyes to heaven. 'Sorry Will,' she said. She snatched up the glass and stormed off to the bar.

'It's fine, Kate . . . ' he began, but she pretended not to hear him.

She stood, fuming, in the crush. She thought it would take her another half-hour to get served, but the barman must have seen the sparks flying off her, because he pointed at her over the crowd, tilting his head as an invitation to shout her order.

When she got back to the table, Josie had disappeared and Brian was giving Will his bottled-water speech. '. . . people aren't happy unless they're paying for it,' he was saying. 'You're just paying for the designer label and the corporate advertising to make you think you need bottled water in the first place. And don't even get me started on the plastic bottles—'

'Okay, I won't,' Will said. 'Thanks for the heads-up.'

'Sorry about that, Will,' Kate said, placing a glass of sparkling mineral water in front of him, complete with ice and a slice of lemon.

'Thanks, but there was really no need—'

'I don't think anyone should have to pay for water,' Brian persisted.

'Well, you *didn't* pay for it,' Kate reminded him, 'so forget it.'

'That's not the point. It's not about the money.'

'Of course it's about the money.'

'How much was it anyway?' Brian asked, looking at the till receipt Kate had tossed on the table. 'Four euro!' he exclaimed indignantly. '*Four euro* for a glass of water.'

What an unbelievable shit, Will thought. It wasn't that he gave a damn about the water but he could have wrung Brian's neck because he had embarrassed Kate. It was no mystery why the O'Neills were so keen to be rid of him, but all Grace's scheming seemed unnecessary. As far as he could see, Brian was doing a bang-up job of digging his own grave.

'Nice pub,' Brian said, clearly anxious to change direction now.

'Yeah, we've been coming here for years,' Kate said.

'Lorcan and I bought you your first drink here,' Will reminded her.

'And then I helped him carry you home.'

'You spend a lot of time with Kate's family, don't you?' Brian said, almost accusingly.

'Will is like the third brother I never had.'

'Ouch! I'm not sure I like that! Brothers don't perform acts of devotion like I did.'

'When?' Kate asked mockingly.

'Remember that time you had a really bad fall off a horse and I stayed home with you all the next day when everyone else went into Cork?'

'Only because you knew I'd make you brownies.'

'True,' Will laughed. 'Kate makes the best brownies in the world,' he told Brian.

'Yes, I know,' Brian said tightly, peeved. Will might have known Kate longer than he had, but he needn't think he knew her better.

'Remember that Christmas we spent here?' Will said. 'We all got plastered on Christmas Eve and went into the sea.'

'Yes!'

'Was that the year you lived with the O'Neills?' Brian asked.

'No, it was another year.'

'Will always spends Christmas with us,' Kate explained to Brian.

'You never go home at Christmas?'

'This *is* home,' Will said. 'I live in Ireland now.'

'But I mean to your family.'

Kate glanced at Will. 'Like Mum said, we're sort of Will's family.'

'How does your father feel about that?' Brian asked.

'I wouldn't know.'

'Will doesn't speak to his father,' Kate said quickly.

'What – never?'

Brian was eyeing Will like a vulture that had spotted a hobbled lion – no doubt measuring him up for one of his therapy groups, Kate thought.

Will fixed him with a cold stare. 'Never,' he said, raising his eyebrows challengingly at Brian, daring him to have a problem with it.

'That must be difficult for you,' Brian said.

'It's very easy, actually.'

In fact, it had been anything but easy, but he had succeeded through sheer steely determination to make his father suffer. In Will's teenage fantasies, the full impact of what he had done would hit Philip one day and render him catatonic, impotent, unable to work, eat, sleep or love. He had stopped believing such a devastating road to Damascus possible, but he still persisted in punishing his father. It was the only real bone of contention between him and the blood-is-thicker-than-water O'Neills. It was the one thing about him that they all disapproved of – Lorcan, his best friend in the world, sweet, soft-hearted Kate, even Jack, the gentlest, most forgiving man on earth. And he knew Grace disapproved because she invariably addressed him as 'William' when she was talking about his father.

'I spoke to Philip today, William,' she would inform him, in a tone of reproof. When Will showed no interest, she would proceed to relay the entire conversation to him, while Will remained stubbornly aloof.

But deep down Will feared it wasn't in his power to make his father suffer by withdrawing his love. After all, what was his love worth? It hadn't been enough to make his father stay. It hadn't been enough to make his mother want to go on living.

'There's a guy not far from here who does wonderful work on healing the past,' Brian was saying. 'He's doing a workshop tomorrow that sounds really interesting, based on dealing with fear.'

As far as Will was concerned, Brian was speaking in a foreign language.

'He uses a mixture of experiential role play and dynamic bodywork,' Brian continued, oblivious.

'Sounds like a nightmare,' Will said and, out of the corner of his eye, saw Kate giggle.

When last orders were called, Rachel and Tom joined them. They were finishing their drinks and preparing to go when Josie came thundering towards them from the depths of the bar. 'There's going to be a lock-in,' she announced, eyes dancing. 'Are you going to stay?'

'God, no. I can't keep my eyes open another minute.' Rachel yawned. 'Must be all this fresh air.'

One by one, everyone declined, saying they were knackered.

She grabbed Kate's hands. 'Kate, you'll stay, won't you?'

'Well, I am pretty tired,' Kate began.

'Please!' Josie begged. 'I'm chatting up a guy at the bar and I'd like to stay, but not on my own.'

'Which one is he?' Kate peered towards the bar.

'Him,' Josie nodded at an astonishingly tall African, who stood head and shoulders above everyone else in the bar and looked rather lost. 'He's called Michael – it's not his real name, but it's what he goes by over here. He's from Nigeria and he's fierce lonely.'

'Well . . .' Kate longed for her bed, but she didn't have it in her heart to refuse Josie. Besides, 'Michael' seemed in need of company, and she'd feel guilty if she deprived him of Josie's.

'Go on,' Josie pleaded. 'He's a refugee, and they've stuck him here in the arsehole of nowhere, poor aul' sausage. You've just been to Africa – you could have a chat with him about it.'

'I suppose I could stay for a while.'

'Good girl, yourself!' Josie clapped her heartily on the back. 'You'll stay too, then, won't you, Brian?'

'Sorry, Josie.' Brian shook his head. 'I need my eight hours.'

Chivalrous too, Will thought, disgusted. Kate was only staying because she was too kind-hearted to let Josie down, and the bastard wasn't even willing to keep her company.

'I'll stay too, if you like, Kate,' he offered.

'Oh no, I'll be fine. Josie'll look after me, won't you? Besides, there's only so much listening to people talking shite that a sober man can take.'

'I'm perfectly happy. I could listen to you talk shite all night.'

'Really, there's no need.'

'If you're sure?'

'Yes, go.'

'Don't worry about her,' Josie told him, squeezing Kate to her side. 'If anyone looks crooked at her I'll punch their lights out.'

'I believe you.' Will liked her more by the minute.

'No better woman!' Josie assured him.

As Will got up to go, the singer from the band was standing at his elbow rather diffidently, waiting to be noticed – or, perhaps, discovered.

'Mr Sargent,' he said deferentially, 'we'd appreciate any advice you could give us.'

'I'd put an ice pack on that, if I were you,' Will said mischievously, gesturing to the bump on his forehead from where he had clashed with the guitarist.

'Oh, yeah, thanks.' The boy looked down at his shoes. He seemed about to run, but he screwed up his courage and met Will's eye. 'Um, I meant about the music,' he said shyly.

Will was torn between saying something meaningless and telling him what he really thought. 'Ditch the drummer,' he said and turned to go.

'He's shite, isn't he?' the boy nodded comprehendingly.

'No more shite than the rest of you,' Will told him brutally, 'but he doesn't give a bollocks about anyone else so he has no business being in a band.'

With that Will was gone, leaving the boy dumbfounded.

'I didn't want to say anything while Brian was here,' Josie whispered to Kate, as she led her into the depths of the pub, 'but Michael isn't the only Nigerian posted here. He's got a friend.'

God, Josie sure could knock them back, Kate thought woozily, as she staggered home in the small hours. She had left Josie in the pub, with Michael trying to match her pint for pint. Kate had got a reprieve when she conked out on the table. Josie had offered to escort her home, but Kate knew she wanted to stay with her Nigerian and had assured her she would be fine walking back by herself. Now she was regretting not having taken Josie up on her offer.

The countryside was pitch black and she was a little spooked, walking as fast as her floppy legs would carry her. She couldn't see a thing, couldn't walk straight and, several times, almost ended up in the ditch. She imagined the re-enactment of her last known movements on *Crimecall*. As she puffed up the hill, her heart was pounding, and it wasn't only because of the steep climb. She was relieved to see the house with its welcoming lights and all but ran the last few yards to the door.

Thankful to be home, she went straight upstairs. She had to lie down quickly to stop everything spinning or she'd throw up. Very quietly, so as not to disturb Brian, she opened the door and crept into the room. He was sleeping soundly. She couldn't find anything in the dark so she stripped off her jeans and got into bed beside him in her T-shirt. Grateful to feel safe again, she decided to forgive him for the tap-water episode. He stirred in his sleep and she snuggled up to his back, then went out like a light.

Chapter 6

When Kate woke the next morning, it took her a while to remember where she was. Since she had come back from Africa, where she had moved to a new place almost every day, it had been taking her a while to get her bearings. She was pretty sure she wasn't still on the trip, but she had a feeling she wasn't at her flat either. She opened her eyes and looked for clues. The first thing she saw was a huge inflatable shark, leering at her. The sun was streaming in through the window, illuminating burnished orange walls and polished wooden floorboards. It was her bedroom in West Cork. She sank back into the pillow. She remembered now. She and Brian had come down for the weekend. They'd had a nightmare journey on the bus, and then Will had picked them up. Grace had given them the guest bedroom . . .

Kate's blood froze and her eyes flew open in horror as the events of the previous day slammed to the front of her brain. Grace had given her and Brian the guest room, and had put Will in Kate's.

Which would make the arm thrown across her and the warm breath on the back of her neck . . . *Will's.*

Shit, shit, shit! The rest of it came back now – Josie's Nigerian, the lock-in at the pub, staggering home alone and crashing into bed. It had always amazed her how effectively you could operate on autopilot when you were completely smashed: your internal GPS somehow got you home unscathed – except when it didn't. This time her automatic pilot had failed her and had landed her firmly in the poo.

She looked dolefully at the shark.

Gotcha, it seemed to say, grinning evilly. Even the orange walls mocked her as she recalled a friend of Brian's, a *feng shui* aficionado, telling her that orange was not an auspicious colour for a bedroom. She had always dismissed *feng shui* as a lot of hocus-pocus, but now she wondered if perhaps there wasn't something in it, after all.

At least Will was still asleep. If she was very careful, she might just manage to wriggle out of bed without waking him. Flattening herself into the mattress, she attempted to slide out smoothly from under his arm without disturbing him. She had almost made it to the edge of the bed when she felt him stir and knew that he had woken up. 'Kate?' he asked groggily, his voice husky with sleep.

She felt the mattress give as he propped himself up on an elbow, and turned to face him.

'Hi.'

'Hi,' he echoed, a little dazed. 'This is a nice surprise.'

'For me too,' she said hastily, terrified that he would think she had somehow engineered this. 'I mean it's a *surprise* for me too,' she added, 'not that it's nice.' She didn't want him to think she was some kind of mad stalker who had sneaked into bed with him when he wasn't looking. 'Not that it's *not* nice,' she added, realising she'd sounded rude.

Oh, shut up, Kate, shut up!

Will was smiling at her indulgently. 'How did you get here?'

'I was led astray last night,' Kate said, edging away from him so that he wouldn't smell her morning-after breath.

'You're not accusing me, I hope?'

'Oh, no – Josie. I was pretty smashed when I came in last night, and I guess I just crashed in here automatically. It *is* my room.'

'I know – perfectly understandable.' Will seemed hugely amused. He was grinning at her like a Cheshire cat.

'Sorry.'

'Good Lord, don't apologise!' Will laughed. 'I have no objection to finding a beautiful girl in my bed in the morning.'

He had called her beautiful! And the way he was looking at her made her feel he meant it. Kate's heart was pounding so hard she was surprised that the duvet wasn't lifting a foot in the air with every beat. She edged further away, terrified Will might hear it.

'You're going to fall off the edge if you're not careful,' Will told her.

God! How could he be so relaxed about it? She really ought to jump out of bed as quickly as possible, she thought. She didn't want to give the wrong impression by lingering. But, at the same time, she didn't want to risk flashing him – that would definitely give the wrong impression. She did a mental check of what she was wearing: last night's T-shirt and – phew! – knickers. It could have been worse. Relieved, she wondered if Will was wearing anything. His broad, tanned shoulders and chest were all she could see over the duvet. God, he was gorgeous, and it was so amazing to be in bed with him – if only she could enjoy it. He was so close that she could feel the heat of his body. It was all she could do not to reach out and touch that taut chest or to run her fingers over the rough stubble of his chin.

'Are you afraid your boyfriend will think this is Freudian?' he asked teasingly.

Oh Christ, Brian! Kate panicked. She hadn't even been thinking of him. 'What time is it?' she asked. 'Maybe he won't have noticed I'm missing.'

Will consulted the bedside clock. 'Ten past nine,' he told her.

'*Shit*! He usually rises with the sun and does yoga.'

'You're fucked then,' he said casually, eyes/dancing. 'Want to canoodle?'

'No thanks!' Kate backed away until she was clinging to the bed by one bum cheek. She knew he didn't mean it, but there was nothing she would have liked more, and she was terrified he'd see the longing in her eyes.

'If you're going to do the time, you might as well do the crime,' he said, seductively. His blue eyes sent her an X-rated message that hit her right in the groin. Then he leaned almost imperceptibly closer. Kate thought he was about to kiss her.

'Brian isn't a Freudian,' she babbled. 'I'm sure he'll understand it was just a silly mistake.'

'Fair enough.' Will threw back the duvet. To Kate's relief he was wearing boxer shorts. He went to stand by the window and she admired the bunched muscles in his broad, tanned back.

God, Michelangelo would be so pissed he missed this, she thought dreamily, momentarily forgetting her troubles as she imagined Will gracing an Italian piazza. She watched as he grabbed a pair of jeans and pulled them on.

He whispered something to himself that sounded like 'Down, boy,' as he pulled up the zip. 'What?' she asked.

'Nothing.'

He turned back to the window, resting an arm above the casement, looking down into the garden.

'Wow! Brian's bendy, isn't he?'

'Is he out there? What's he doing?'

'Playing Twister with the kids – and I think he's winning.'

No doubt he was using Twister as an excuse to show off his yoga moves, Kate thought.

Suddenly Will was laughing.

'What happened?'

'Helen just nobbled him – knocked him over as she went past.'

'I'm sure she didn't do it on purpose.'

'It looked very accidentally-on-purpose to me.'

Kate screwed up her courage and got out of bed, tugging her T-shirt down as she joined Will at the window. Brian was now sprawled on the Twister mat. She ducked as he looked up.

'D'you think he saw me?' she whispered to Will.

'No. But he must have noticed you weren't in bed this morning.'

'Maybe I could say I got up early and went for a walk.'

'Before sunrise?'

'Good point.' Kate chewed her lip anxiously. 'I know! I'll say I didn't want to disturb him and spent the night in Josie's room.'

'It's exciting having an affair, isn't it?' Will grinned at her.

'We're not having an affair,' Kate said primly.

'No, but it feels like it, doesn't it? Sneaking around, thinking up lies, getting caught in the wrong bedroom.'

'Ah, but I don't intend to get caught.'

'Too late.' Will nodded to the garden. Kate had accidentally broken cover while they were talking and Jake had spotted her. He was now waving at her, and Brian had followed his gaze: he was squinting up at her and Will in their various states of undress and didn't look happy.

When she had showered, dressed, plucked her eyebrows and done everything else she could think of to put off the evil moment, Kate went downstairs for breakfast. In the kitchen she found Helen, normally the soul of calm unflappability, in a serious hump, banging pots and slamming cupboard doors.

'Good morning.' Kate flopped down at the table. She was still feeling rather delicate.

'Morning,' Helen said shortly, through pursed lips, and dumped a bowl in front of her.

'Thanks,' Kate croaked and shook corn flakes into it.

Helen returned to pouring flour, sugar, melted butter and milk into a mixing bowl without measuring anything – making muffins, Kate decided.

Jake came in from the garden and leaned his arms on the table.

'Brian thinks Mum's trying to *poison* us!'

'What?'

'Me and Sam. He says the stuff she gives us to eat is poison.'

Kate put her head into her hands. They'd only been here one night and already Brian had managed to piss everyone off – including her.

'That's one of the things he says is poison,' Jake told her, as she poured milk onto her cereal. 'It's not, though, is it?' he asked.

'No, of course not, Jake. Sorry, Helen.' Her sister-in-law was now furiously beating her mixture. It was on the tip of Kate's tongue to say that under-mixing was the key when making muffins, but she thought better of it. 'Where is Brian anyway?'

'He's gone to the village shop to hassle poor Mrs Delaney about soya milk,' Helen said.

'I think you're in trouble with Brian too,' Jake told her.

'Oh? Why?'

Jake put his head on one side, considering. 'Well, I *think* it's because he wanted you to have a sleepover with him and you had one with Will instead.'

'Oh,' Kate said faintly. Out of the corner of her eye, she saw Helen's eyes widen.

'I *told* him you should always share. I said if you let Will have a sleepover tonight you'd definitely let him have the next one.'

'Cheers, Jake. What did he say to that?'

'Brian's greedy,' Jake said disapprovingly. 'I don't think he's good at sharing.'

'He wasn't happy?'

'No. You're in *big* trouble.'

Having dropped his bombshell, Jake skipped back to the garden, leaving Kate studiously trying to avoid Helen's eye.

'Did you push Brian over when he was playing Twister?' Kate asked, desperate to change the subject.

'Well, he was doing a *crab*,' Helen said defensively.

'Oh. Fair enough.'

Helen laughed. 'He seems nice, Kate, really,' she said, bending to put the muffins in to the oven and remove a batch she had already made. 'I'm sure he meant well about the cow's milk. But, Kate . . .' She straightened.

'Yes?'

'Is it true? Did you really have a – you know – *sleepover* with Will?'

'No, of course not. I got shafted into staying for a lock-in at the pub last night – by your bloody nanny. I came home smashed and automatically staggered into bed in my own room, which Will's in. End of story.'

But Helen clearly wasn't going to leave it there. 'Kate, when girls in school told you they'd slept with a boy but nothing happened, you didn't *believe* them, did you?'

'No, of course not! But in this case it happens to be true. Nothing happened.'

'Hmm,' Helen smiled to herself, her good humour restored now that she had a budding romance to think about. She wasn't put off by Kate's insistence that the 'sleepover' had been completely innocent.

'Did you know Lorcan's here?' she asked.

'No! When did he turn up?'

'About half an hour ago. He's in the garden.'

Keen to escape the gleam in Helen's eye, Kate drifted outside. Lorcan was sitting at the table chatting to Grace with Carmen glued to his side, positively glowing with happiness. Will was kicking a ball around with Sam and Jake. He looked up as Kate came out and grinned at her. She blushed and bent down to pick up Sam, who had fallen over.

'You're okay.' Will watched as she set him back on his feet, ruffled his hair, then let him scamper off.

When he had found her in his bed this morning, he had felt disconcertingly happy. He had almost kissed her – had been severely tempted to do a lot more. But, thankfully, common sense had prevailed and he had got out of bed before he succumbed to lust. What Tom had said to him all those years ago still held true: Kate was an O'Neill, and it was way too close to home . . .

'Will!' Jake was yelling, as Sam ran towards the goal.

'Oops, sorry.'

'Lorcan!' Kate put her arms around his neck and hugged him from behind. 'What are you doing here?'

He craned around to look at her, tired and bleary-eyed. 'I was pining,' he said, clasping Carmen's hand adoringly. 'I came to get Carmen and bring her back to New York with me.'

Kate felt an odd pang of jealousy. She couldn't see Brian crossing continents on a whim to be with her – he'd be too worried about his carbon footprint for one thing.

'Wow! So you're going to New York?' she said wistfully to Carmen.

'Why not? It's the holidays, so I have plenty of free time.'

'God, you're so lucky having the whole summer off,' Kate said, sitting down opposite them. 'I wish I'd been a teacher.'

'But you're going to Tuscany with Will and the band,' Grace chipped in. 'That's just as exciting.'

'That sounds like a good gig,' Lorcan said.

'Oh nothing's decided yet.'

'I've rustled you up some breakfast.' Helen had come out to join them and plonked a plate of scrambled eggs, bacon and toast in front of Lorcan.

'You're an angel.' He smiled at her gratefully, then tucked in.

'I made some muffins, too, for anyone who wants them.' She placed a basket in the middle of the table with a pot of strong, fragrant coffee and a jug of Buck's fizz.

'Are you staying for the weekend? Kate asked, grabbing a muffin and eating it in two bites.

'No, we're flying to New York in the morning. Will's giving us a lift to Cork airport later and we're going to Dublin to get Carmen's stuff.'

'Oh, that's a pity,' Helen said. 'We thought we might spend the day on the beach, bring a picnic.'

'Well, you can count Brian and me out,' Kate told her. 'There's some guru he wants to go and see while we're here.'

Hearing this, Will looked over at her. 'You're not going to go to that dynamic bodyshop thing?' he asked.

'Well, I think I *have* to now,' Kate said, accusingly. 'I need the Brownie points after this morning.'

'Well, don't look at *me*. It wasn't *my* fault!'

'But, Kate,' Grace began, 'the whole point of this weekend was for us to get to know Brian. We're all here to spend time with him.'

'I know, Mum, and I'm sorry, but he really wants to go to this thing. We'll still have tomorrow.' Kate secretly thought that she could earn the Brownie points simply by making the offer. She wouldn't have to go to the workshop because Brian wouldn't have the gall to take her up on it. However, she kept this thought to herself, just in case.

Lorcan was looking curiously from Will to Kate. 'What happened this morning?' he asked.

'Oh, nothing.' Kate shrugged. She didn't want Lorcan, of all people, to find out. It would be on the front page of the *New York Times* in the morning.

'Brian caught Kate in bed with Will,' Grace told him matter-of-factly.

'*Mum*!'

'Well, that's right, isn't it?'

'You make it sound like I did it on purpose.'

Lorcan hooted. 'So you're saying you went to bed with Will *by mistake*?'

Good old Will, he thought. He obviously hadn't wasted any time in laying siege to Kate and hadn't let the presence of her boyfriend – or the entire family – put him off his stroke.

'Exactly.'

'Darling, lower your voice,' Grace hissed. 'Will can hear you.'

'So?' Kate asked, exasperated.

'Well, it's not very nice, is it, when you go to bed with someone and the next day they say it was a mistake? I mean, you don't like it when it happens to *you*, do you?'

Kate rolled her eyes. 'This is different. It was – literally – a *mistake*. I got into the wrong bed. How did you find out about it anyway?'

'Jake told me.'

'Jake!' Lorcan laughed. 'I'm glad I came to rescue you from this den of iniquity,' he told Carmen.

Lorcan was disappointed to learn that Will wasn't making the progress he had initially thought. Poor Will. It must be torture for him having to see Kate with Brian when he was clearly besotted with her. He needed to make more of a play for her. After all, what person in their right mind would choose Brian over Will? Lorcan decided it was a good thing he had come home when he had. He wasn't around for long but he might be able to push things along a bit, give Will a bit of encouragement, nudge Kate in the right direction.

Brian returned from the shops to find everyone in the garden guzzling champagne cocktails, with Lorcan holding court – and it was only eleven o'clock in the morning. Really, the sooner he got Kate out of this environment, the better. She was far too influenced by her family. And as for Will! There was no way Brian could let Kate go off to Tuscany with him. He was pissed off that she seemed to want to take the job. But it was nothing compared to the fury he'd felt at seeing her in Will's bedroom that morning. He couldn't quite believe she would be so callous as to carry on with Will right under his nose, yet she looked so guilty whenever he caught her eye – and she'd probably got drunk last night after he'd left the pub . . .

His mood wasn't improved when he discovered that Lorcan had popped over from New York for the day because he was missing his girlfriend. That was exactly the sort of extravagant O'Neill gesture of which he most disapproved. The worst of it was, they all thought it wonderfully spontaneous and romantic, fussing over Lorcan as if he was some kind of conquering hero. Brian hoped Kate would never expect *him* to do anything as idiotic as dashing across the Atlantic on a whim to see her.

He was somewhat mollified when she took him aside and suggested they go to the workshop. 'Oh great, we'd better get off then,' he said, glancing at his watch. 'Do you think someone could give us a lift?'

'Oh!'

'I know it's nearby,' he said, mistaking the reason for her surprise, 'but it starts at eleven-thirty.'

'You know, Brian, that thing with Will – getting into bed with him last night – it was just that I was a bit the worse for wear and he was in my old room . . .'

'And him being your childhood sweetheart had nothing to do with it, I suppose?'

'Brian, I told you, we were *not* childhood sweethearts. I don't know where Mum got that notion.'

'Wishful thinking, I imagine.'

'Look, nothing happened last night. It was just a silly mistake.'

'Some people would say there's no such thing as mistakes,' Brian said. 'I hope you're not thinking of taking that job in Tuscany.'

'Well, yes, of course I am. It'd be really great.'

'And the idea of being with Will has nothing to do with it?'

'No! I *told* you—'

'And my feelings don't come into it? What happened to all that stuff about having to discuss it with me?'

'Of course your feelings come into it. But there's nothing going on between me and Will, if that's what you're worried about. There never has been.'

Brian sighed. 'Well, we don't have time to discuss it now. How about that lift?'

'Oh, um, yes – I'll ask Conor if he'll drive us.'

Kate wandered off, more than a little miffed. It wasn't fair. She had explained and apologised, and, as far as she was concerned, she had made amends by offering to go to the workshop with Brian. But he should have said he wouldn't dream of going when her family had laid on this entire weekend for his benefit. He wasn't supposed to ask someone to drive them there! Sometimes she really despaired of him. Didn't he know *anything*? Still, she reminded herself, Mr Darcy hadn't known how to behave properly until Elizabeth put manners on him. She would just have to be patient.

Conor had agreed to give them a lift, and Lorcan walked out to the car with them. 'Carmen and I will be gone by the time you get back,' he said, putting an arm around Kate's shoulders. 'It's a pity you have to go to this thing – we haven't had a proper chance to talk.'

'I know,' Kate said apologetically, 'but we chat on the phone all the time.'

Brian and Conor got into the car. Kate kissed Lorcan and was about to join them, when he tugged at her hand. 'Go easy on Will,' he whispered urgently. 'I think he's got it bad.' Then he bundled her into the car and slammed the door before she had a chance to ask him what he was talking about.

As they drove away, Kate looked back at her brother, waving to them. She was tempted to jump out and run back to ask him what he'd meant.

'Just let yourself go. Trust your partner to catch you,' crooned Joe, a stern-faced man in an Indian-style pyjamas outfit.

Kate was standing barefoot in a circle of people primed to catch their partners, who formed an inner circle.

'Very good work, Brian,' Joe said softly, as Brian landed, a dead weight, in Kate's arms. She thought it was a bit much that he was getting all the praise when she was the one doing the hard work. It had taken all her strength not to drop him.

Joe paced around the circle as one after another, everyone swooned into their partners' arms.

'Okay. When you've all had a go, switch partners.'

'Just let go,' Brian told Kate encouragingly, as they changed places. 'Don't worry, I'll catch you.'

'Ready?' she asked nervously.

'Yeah, just let yourself fall.'

'Okay, here I go. Ready?' she asked, looking back to check.

'Kate!' Brian said chidingly, as all around her people toppled like ninepins.

'Okay, here goes!' Kate closed her eyes and tried to relax, but she couldn't bring herself to do it. At the last minute, she stepped back woodenly into Brian's waiting arms and let herself go limp. 'Pretend I did it!' she hissed at Brian, flopping in an impressively jelly-like fashion when Joe turned to them.

'Very good.' He beamed at her beatifically, which made her feel even more of a fraud.

'It doesn't *mean* anything,' Kate told Brian, as they settled on the carpet in a big sharing circle. 'It's just a game. You shouldn't take it so seriously. It doesn't mean I don't trust you.'

Everyone sat in the circle, watching Joe, who smiled serenely at them. The silence became unbearable. Kate wished someone would say something. She toyed with the idea of asking if anyone had seen the last episode of Desperate Housewives, to put them all out of their misery, but she didn't think she'd get much of a response from this lot.

'Okay, welcome everyone,' Joe said. The relief in the room was almost palpable. 'That exercise we just did was about trust,' he continued.

Kate wished he'd kept his mouth shut.

'When you really trust someone, you can let yourself go and know that no harm will come to you. You feel completely safe. It's very liberating. I think you all felt that, didn't you?'

Kate nodded eagerly with everyone else but she could feel Brian giving her a dirty look. Oh God, she thought. It's going to be a very long day.

*

With Kate and Brian out of the way, and Will dropping Carmen and Lorcan off at the airport, Rachel took the opportunity to put Helen straight. 'Will and Kate were never childhood sweethearts.'

'Oh, really? Then why did you—'

'It's part of the plan for getting rid of the Tree-hugger,' Grace explained. 'We asked Will to help and I was just trying to give him a nudge.'

'What's Will supposed to do?'

'Just flirt with her, lead her on a bit,' Rachel said. 'It's true that Kate's always had a crush on him – it just wasn't mutual.'

'Are you sure?' Helen smiled thoughtfully. 'Actually, I've always thought Will had a bit of a soft spot for Kate.'

'You're right!' Grace agreed. 'I've always thought so too.'

'*Mum*,' Rachel protested, 'you have *not*!'

'Maybe if she takes this job in Italy and he's thrown together with her, it'll make him realise he fancies her,' Helen said.

'Oh, wouldn't that be wonderful?' Grace pounced on the idea. 'I could have Will for a son-in-law instead of the Tree-hugger.'

'Don't be ridiculous,' Rachel snapped. 'Will is way out of Kate's league.'

'Nonsense, darling.'

'There's no such thing as leagues,' Conor added.

Typical Conor! Rachel thought. He was so gung-ho, he thought you could have anybody you set your mind to. And her mother, sweetly but unrealistically, believed her children were good enough for anyone. Will didn't fancy *her*, for Christ's sake. What hope did Kate have?

But Grace was already fantasising about the wedding and what a perfect son-in-law Will would make. He was practically one of the family already. And she could use the occasion to bring him and Philip together, she thought dreamily. She would be like the American President standing between the Israeli and Palestinian leaders, forcing them to shake hands.

For both their sakes, Grace wished Will would reconcile with his father. Despite his bravado, she knew Will missed Philip. She knew too that Philip profoundly regretted the way he had handled the situation when his first wife died. However harshly Will judged him, it was nothing compared to how harshly he judged himself.

Grace had grown fond of Philip, with whom she had struck up a friendship over the years since Will had come to live with them. They still spoke regularly on the phone, long, entertaining conversations which she faithfully relayed to Will, sometimes even mimicking Philip to give him the full effect. She felt an inordinate sense of victory whenever she made him laugh with something Philip had said. Will was stubborn and implacable, but Grace had proved herself his match in keeping Philip present in his life. Lately she'd thought she'd seen a softening in his attitude towards his father – only a tiny chink in his armour, but it gave her hope. 'Conor's right,' she said now. 'And even if there are leagues, my children are good enough for anyone. But we've got to make sure Kate takes the job in Tuscany so she and Will are thrown together on a more permanent basis. He needs a chance to discover his true feelings for her.'

Rachel groaned. 'Mum, Will told us straight out that he wasn't interested in Kate, remember?'

'He just doesn't realise how he feels about her,' Grace told her. 'Once he starts pretending to be interested, he'll soon discover he has real feelings for her. It's like when you're acting – you wouldn't know about this, darling – and you find yourself becoming the person you're playing.'

'Yes, but when the play ends, you go home and become yourself again,' Rachel argued, knowing from experience that this wasn't necessarily true. Her childhood years had been blighted by her mother's stage success and they had had to live with a succession of tragic heroines from Lady Macbeth to Hedda Gabler. The worst had been a long run of *The Glass Menagerie* when she was a teenager and had had to suffer the humiliation of bringing boys home to be confronted by Amanda Wingfield. Her mother had only just stopped short of referring to the gauche, pimply youths as 'gentlemen callers'.

'You may be right,' Grace conceded, 'but that's all the more reason to get her to Tuscany. You said yourself the best way to separate her from the Tree-hugger is to get her interested in someone else, and, if not Will, then maybe one of the boys in his band will fall for her. That Owen Cassidy, perhaps,' she said dreamily.

'Owen Cassidy!'

'Yes, I know he's a bit wild,' Grace said, misunderstanding

144

Rachel's objection, 'but Kate could calm him down and domesticate him. And the grandchildren would be stunning!'

Rachel couldn't believe her mother thought Kate might actually land Owen Cassidy. Okay, so she couldn't see that Will was out of her league, but surely she must know that Kate was definitely *not* rock-chick material!

'You make me feel so small and helpless,' Brian whimpered at Kate, who was lying on the floor in a foetal position while Brian hurled abuse at her. 'You stop me doing all the things I want to do. You stop me being the person I could be. Why do you make everything so difficult?' he whinged.

Kate buried her face in the carpet and tried to comfort herself with the thought that this would be over soon and she would be at home eating dinner with the family and having a normal conversation.

'I'm sick of you!' Brian was shouting now. 'I just want to be free of you!'

Kate knew it wasn't personal. She was supposed to be embodying Brian's 'fear'. Earlier, she had watched Brian dance around in front of her like some kind of demented Village Person, then fling himself onto the floor in a foetal cringe, a performance she was required to replicate so that he could give his fear a good bollocking. She was glad none of her family was there to witness it – she'd never live it down.

Why can't I have a normal boyfriend who's into football or some-thing? she thought. She wished the ground would open up and swallow her. She imagined herself sinking through the floorboards like Ewan McGregor in *Trainspotting*.

Opening her eyes a slit, she was shocked to see that Brian was almost in tears. Still, she knew how he felt – she was close to weeping herself.

Tina called Will on his mobile as he was driving back from the air-port.

'How's it going over there?' he asked.

'Boring, I've spent all morning sitting around waiting for the light to change. The photographer's a total wanker. And I miss you, darling.'

'Sounds like you're having a ball.'

'Martinique's beautiful, though. We should come here together some time.'

'Maybe we will.'

'Oh, and guess what! I met one of the producers of *Irish Supermodel Search* and she said there may be a vacancy for a new judge on the show next season! She kind of implied the job would be mine, if I wanted it.'

'And *do* you want it?'

'Well, it would be a great introduction to working in TV – and very well paid. But, even better, it would mean I'd be based in Ireland.'

Will didn't say anything.

'That'd be pretty great, wouldn't it?' she said.

'Yes – if that's what you want.'

'Anyway, got to go,' she said. 'Apparently the clouds are lifting.'

She hung up, throwing her mobile onto the sand and gazing out across the beach from beneath a giant umbrella.

'Doesn't look like that lot's going anywhere,' the lighting director called to her, pointing to the sky. 'We might as well call it a day.'

Tina hugged her long legs and rested her chin on her knees. It really was beautiful here, she thought, watching the clouds scud across the sky. She knew it was beautiful, she just wished she could *feel* it.

She picked up a handful of sand and let it trickle through her fingers. She had hoped Will would be more enthusiastic about the idea of her moving to Ireland. He had become distant lately, and she could feel him drifting further and further away from her. But she wasn't someone who let things slip away – not without a fight. She was hardworking and ambitious, personally and professionally, and she wasn't about to give up on Will. She knew they had drifted apart, and they weren't in the heady 'in love' phase any more – but who was? That didn't last for anyone, but it didn't mean you just gave up.

She and Will made sense as a couple. They belonged to the same world and they belonged together. She would show him that. She would take the TV job and move to Ireland, and she would prove it to him.

'Tina, you okay?' one of the crew stopped to talk to her as he left the beach.

'Yeah, I'm fine.' She smiled up at him.

'You seem a bit down in the dumps.'

'Oh, it's nothing a few toots won't cure,' she said, brushing sand off her hands and holding one out for him to pull her up.

'Don't forget we've got a really early start in the morning. You might want to have an early night.

'Oh, fuck that! Where's the party?'

'Oh, Will,' Grace accosted him as soon as he returned to the house, 'you didn't seem to pick up that I was trying to give you an opening earlier to get more flirty with Kate. Maybe I was being too subtle.'

'No, Grace, you weren't.'

'Oh! Then why—'

'Look, I've offered Kate the job in Tuscany, but as for the rest, I can't do it.'

'But, Will, you've met the Tree-hugger—'

'Yes, and I agree Kate deserves better – a lot better. But she doesn't deserve to have me winding her up, toying with her affections.'

'It's only because we care about her.'

'I care about her too, but—'

'You do?' Grace said.

'Yes, of course. I'd like to see her give that smug, self-important git the elbow just as much as you would. He isn't good enough for her.'

'Oh, well, if that's how you feel . . .'

'It is,' Will said firmly.

'Well, let's hope she takes the job in Tuscany, then.'

'Yes, let's hope.' Will couldn't believe she was going to let him off the hook that easily.

Grace smiled to herself as Will walked away. She knew it – he *did* have feelings for Kate. Why else would he be so vehemently opposed to the Tree-hugger? He just needed to spend more time with her to realise how he felt – time they would have in Tuscany. Kate just had to take that job.

This is it, Kate thought, as she stood in the garden at the centre embracing a tree and swatting flies. I'm an official tree-hugger.

'Really engage with your tree,' Joe had exhorted them. 'Really hug it. Feel its energy – let it guide you.'

Then she was supposed to turn to the west and say goodbye to something in her life, and turn to the east and say hello to something she wanted to welcome into her life – or was it the other way around? she wondered. It was hard to think spiritual thoughts when you were being eaten alive by midges.

She tried to centre herself and meditate on the direction of her life, but when she tried to empty her mind of all thoughts, Lorcan's hissed remark about Will popped into it and wouldn't go away. Had Will said something to him, or was it just something he suspected?

Bringing herself back to the matter in hand, she peered through the trees to see what stage everyone else was at. They seemed to have finished the hugging part and were turning to the west, still maintaining contact with their trees. Kate copied them and tried to think of something she wanted to say goodbye to.

'Listen to your heart,' Joe had said. 'Don't try to think of anything consciously – just open your mind and see what comes up.'

But under the circumstances the only thing she wanted to get rid of was the midges, and she didn't think that was the right sort of thing.

Maybe I should ring Lorcan and ask him what he meant, she thought. Surely Will hadn't said something to him. If he had, it couldn't have been today – Lorcan hadn't been at the house for very long and Will hadn't been alone with him at any point.

Oh, forget about Will, she told herself. Maybe she should say goodbye to her ridiculous obsession with him and move forward into her future with Brian. Facing west, she resolved to put Will behind her and solemnly bade him farewell. Feeling calm, purposeful and in control of her destiny, she turned east to greet her future with Brian. As she did so, she saw a car pull into the driveway, the sun glinting off it, and felt the hairs on the back of her neck stand up. It was Will's Jag.

So he wasn't to be dismissed from her life that easily. There must be a word for this, she thought – synergy, serendipity, Fate? Or just plain old Sod's Law? Whatever, it was downright spooky. She watched as he parked and got out. When he spotted her, he waved and strode across the grass towards her.

Kate's heart gave a familiar leap.

'Hi! I came to spring you.' He gestured at the car.

'Hello, Will,' she said, still holding her tree. Right now he was the most welcome sight in the world and she mentally threw her arms around him and welcomed him into her life.

Kate was never so glad to be home. The drive back had been somewhat tense. Brian hadn't taken kindly to being dragged away early, protesting that they'd miss the final 'sharing circle', but Kate had raced to the car and had thrown herself in as if she was being rescued from kidnappers. Will had seemed pleased with himself for having pulled off this coup, and the more pissed off Brian was, the more cheerful he became. Kate had the impression he enjoyed winding Brian up.

She was so glad to be home that she hadn't even protested when they were all herded into the sitting room to watch Tom and Rachel's wedding DVD. After the day she had had, it was a relief to do something so normal and undemanding.

The DVD began with a cringe-making pastiche of Rachel getting ready, while Prince sang 'The Most Beautiful Girl in the World'. Josie let out a hoot of laughter, earning herself a dagger glare from Rachel.

'Who chose the music for this?' she asked Kate under her breath.

'Who do you think?' Kate was glad Lorcan wasn't there – he'd never have been able to keep a straight face.

They watched Rachel getting her nails done, Rachel having her hair put up, Rachel mugging for the camera as she had her make-up applied and, finally, Rachel appearing downstairs in the dress to the gasps and admiration of her family.

'This must have been edited for family viewing,' Conor said. 'They cut out the bit where you had a shower.'

'Oh shut up!' Rachel tutted, unable to tear her eyes from the screen.

Kate thought the DVD wouldn't have been too bad if it was all like this – a sort of montage of the day's highlights set to music, like a pop video. But once they reached the church it was pure fly-on-the-wall documentary and they were forced to sit through the whole wedding ceremony all over again. Jack was snoring loudly by the time Tom and Rachel were taking their vows. Rachel kept making comments like 'Oh, I look quite good there,' and 'My hair turned out well, didn't it?', trying to sound surprised and self-effacing. She even threw others an occasional bone, gushing, 'Oh, doesn't Mum look pretty?' and 'You should wear make-up more often, Kate – it really does wonders for you.'

It could be worse, Kate told herself, I could be back at the workshop.

The reception part proved more entertaining. The cameraman, gay and evidently besotted with Owen Cassidy, zoomed in on him the moment he arrived and kept the camera trained on him throughout almost the entire proceedings, occasionally swinging back dutifully to the wedding party at key moments. So, a hasty shot of Tom and Rachel cutting the cake, Rachel giving her biggest Hollywood smile, was followed by a lingering close-up of Owen scratching his armpit.

Tom and Rachel were seen taking to the floor for the first dance, then abandoned in favour of Owen making a wanking gesture at the choice of music. Even during the speeches the camera cut back to Owen for reaction shots – a waste of time as Owen, clearly paying no attention whatsoever, made no reaction, apart from some raucous whooping and hollering when Will stood up to speak.

Later, as the evening wore on, the camera zoomed through the crowd as the dancing became drunkenly uninhibited and couples snogged or slunk off together.

'This is where I came in,' Brian said – as he could be seen in the background kissing Kate. He stretched and got up. 'I'm going out for a walk. Want to come?' he asked Kate, who shook her head.

There he goes, doing the wrong thing again, she thought, as he made his way out.

But as he was passing Rachel, he murmured, 'It was a beautiful wedding, Rachel. You looked wonderful – so happy.'

'Thank you, Brian.'

For once Kate felt he was a boyfriend she could be proud of.

Everyone went into a daze as the DVD rolled on. Kate saw herself leaving with Will and, shortly afterwards, Carmen and Lorcan were slinking off together. As the camera zoomed in on Owen doing shots with Auntie Iris, Kate noticed the strange girl – Una her name was – who had had her eye on Freddie. She was snogging someone but they were hidden by a pillar. Kate thought how funny it would be if it turned out to be Freddie. Then Una said something and a disembodied hand grasped hers. Kate's blood froze as Brian emerged from behind the pillar and led her out of the ballroom.

Kate felt sick. Hardly able to breathe, she wondered if anyone else had noticed, but there was no indication that they had.

'Auntie Iris is looking well, isn't she?' Conor said, confirming that they were focused on the foreground.

'It's the booze,' Jack said. 'She's preserved in gin.'

Then Kate caught Will's eye and, from the way he was looking at her sympathetically, she knew he had seen Brian too. She couldn't bear it – she was about to burst into tears. She wanted to howl and scream. She had to get out before she lost it.

'Speaking of booze, does anyone want another drink?' she asked, getting up. Rachel and her mother raised their glasses and she collected them, then shot off to the kitchen as fast as her wobbly legs would carry her. She kicked the door closed behind her and turned on the taps full blast, blindly rinsing glasses through a blur of tears.

How could he? How could he? She slumped against the sink. It had been her first day back and he had seemed so pleased to see her. Why did this always happen to her? Why did she never bloody learn? She had really thought Brian was different. She had never imagined he would hurt her in such a crass, banal way. She'd thought he had depth. But despite all his consciousness-raising and third-eye gazing, all the loving-kindness meditation and chakra-balancing, he was still just another bloke who couldn't say no to an available shag.

He had asked her to marry him the next day, for fuck's sake, she thought, kicking the cupboard furiously and stubbing her toe – not a good idea in bare feet. She sucked in her breath as pain shot through her foot. The glass she was holding slipped through her fingers and fell to the floor.

'Shit, shit, shit!' she wailed, tears streaming down her face as she bent to pick up the pieces.

A shard slipped in her hand and sliced painfully into her finger.

'Ouch!' She waved it in the air as blood oozed from the cut.

'Kate, are you okay?'

She jumped at the sound of Will's clipped tones, hastily wiping her eyes on her sleeve.

'I broke a glass,' she sniffed. 'And cut my finger.'

She heard Will cross the kitchen and then he was standing beside her. She bent forward to continue picking up the glass, letting her hair fall over her face to hide it.

'Leave it!'

'I'll just get the big bits,' she said, straightening and making for the bin.

'Don't move,' Will ordered, eyes on her bare feet. 'There's glass all over the place. You'll get cut.'

Kate stood stock still as he took the glass from her hand and threw it into the bin, the crunching under his feet confirming that there were tiny fragments all over the floor. Then he put an arm around her back and bent to pick her up.

'What are you doing?' she shrieked, her body rigid.

'I'm going to carry you over there,' he said, nodding to the other side of the kitchen.

'You'll do your back in!' she protested. She had suffered enough humiliation this evening without having Will crumpling under her weight.

'I'm not as feeble as I look.'

'Still . . .'

'Okay, hop on,' he said, nodding at his feet.

'What?'

'Stand on my feet and I'll walk you over. Come on.' He grabbed her hands.

Standing face to face with Will as he walked her across the room in a strangely intimate dance, Kate thought she should have let him carry her. At least she wouldn't have been eyeballing him. Her heart was skipping so many beats she thought she might pass out. In an effort to appear calm, she fixed her eyes on the broad, tanned column of his throat. She was by no means petite, but Will was so tall that, even standing on his shoes, she could have tucked her head easily under his chin. She had an almost overwhelming urge to lay it on his chest and bawl her eyes out.

God, she thought, Freddie was right. I'm not over you at all – not one little bit. As long as she didn't see him she could tell herself it was just a teenage crush, a first love she'd grown out of. But five minutes in his company and she was right back to square one, sixteen all over again and as much in love with him as ever.

But I was right too, she told herself firmly. What does it matter how crazy I am about you when you don't feel the same way?

When they reached the table, he lifted her onto it as though she weighed no more than a child. 'Let's take a look at this,' he said. Her hand was still bleeding and he picked out a sliver of glass that was embedded in the skin.

'Sorry,' he said as Kate yelped. 'Does it hurt?'

'Just stings a bit.'

He got a cloth and dabbed away the blood. He opened his mouth to speak, but apparently thought better of it. Kate prayed he wouldn't say anything about Brian – she couldn't bear it if he said something sympathetic. She wouldn't be able to stop herself crying, and it was embarrassing enough that he knew.

'I think you'll live. Got any plasters?'

'There should be some in the cupboard over the sink.'

He found the box and fished one out, opening it as he came back to her. Then he took her hand and put it around her finger.

God, this doctor mode is way sexy! Kate thought, beginning to enjoy herself.

'There. All better,' he said and pressed a light kiss to the plaster. Suddenly he looked up and she was knocked sideways by his smile. He really was the most gorgeous man she'd ever seen. 'Remember when Grace used to kiss it better?' he said, still holding her hand.

'Oh, all mothers do that,' Kate said gruffly, blushing crimson and looking away.

'Not when you're twenty-one!' Will said drily.

'True.' Kate laughed.

At that moment, Brian came in from his walk and found Kate sitting on the table holding hands with Will and laughing up into his eyes.

'Oh, Brian!' Kate pulled her hand away when she saw him and jumped down from the table.

'Having fun?' he said, with biting sarcasm.

'Yes, we're playing doctors and nurses,' Will said, smiling impudently but his eyes were cold as ice. 'Or, rather, doctor and patient.'

Without a word, Brian left the room, bootfaced.

'I'd better go after him,' Kate said.

'Go on,' Will said, casting a murderous look after Brian's retreating back. 'I'll clear up in here.'

The next morning, Kate went down to the beach. She needed to clear her head and think things over. She hadn't had much sleep. She had finally got up the nerve to confront Brian with his infidelity, but far from being contrite or penitent, he had been quite *blasé* about it. To her dismay, he didn't understand what she was so upset about. It wasn't as if they were married, he had pointed out – they hadn't even been 'engaged' at that stage. She hated the way he always said 'engaged' in quotation marks, as if it was marvellously ironic. He had also reminded her that they had been on a break. What difference did an hour or two either way make.

Against her better judgement, she had asked him if he had been with Suzanne while she was away – which, of course, he had.

'It's only natural to explore every relationship,' he had said.

'That's just a fancy way of saying you shag all your friends,' Kate had retorted.

'What about you? You've been flirting with Will all weekend.'

'I have *not* been flirting with Will! We're friends, that's all – of course, you wouldn't understand that people can be friends without shagging each other!'

It had turned into a blazing row. They had finally made up after spending almost the entire night talking, but the whole thing had left her feeling wobbly. The trouble was, she didn't feel she was in any position to cast the first stone. It was true that nothing had happened between her and Will, but no thanks to her. Brian could have been with Suzanne if he wanted to, but he didn't: he had chosen to be with her. But if she could be with Will . . . On the other hand, since that was never going to happen, was she supposed to stay single and celibate for the rest of her life? She did love Brian – she just loved Will more.

Kicking off her sandals, she walked along the shoreline, letting the waves wash over her feet. The cold water made her catch her breath, but she soon acclimatised to it.

This whole weekend had been a disaster. Rather than bringing Brian and her family closer together, it had merely emphasised the division between them. She hated to admit it, but it had made her see him in another light. He was different when it was just the two of them, one to one, but too often over the weekend she had found herself being embarrassed by him or apologising for him. Worst of all, she had discovered that she was still head over heels, blind as a bat in love with Will.

She sank down near the water's edge, picking up a twig from the sand. Brian had offered her a fresh start, and that was what they would have, she decided. What they had was real, and they could make it work. It was just that she had been pushed together with Will too much over this weekend, which had brought back her old feelings painfully and vividly. But she would put that behind her. She wouldn't take the job in Tuscany and Will would fade out of her life, resurfacing occasionally on holidays and family occasions.

On a whim, she stood up and wrote, 'I love Will', in large letters on the sand. She watched as the water crept in, slowly encroaching on the words to carry her secret away and erase it for ever. That was the end of it, she told herself.

'Kate?'

She almost jumped out of her skin when she heard him behind her. Her eyes darted back to the sand, and she was relieved to see that the tide had washed away her idiotic doodle.

'Will!' She turned to him.

'I'm just packing up the car – I've got to get back to Dublin early. Do you two want a lift?'

'Oh no, thanks. We'll go later with Mum and Dad.'

'Okay.'

'Will, I've been thinking about the job offer . . .'

'Yes?' He smiled hopefully.

'Um, I'm afraid I'll have to say no,' she said, scuffing the sand with her foot, feeling ungrateful.

'Oh, that's a pity.' He seemed genuinely disappointed.

'Thanks for the offer, though.'

'No problem. Well, I'll see you at the house.'

He started to walk back up the beach. As Kate watched him go, she realised her heart was pounding, though she didn't know why. Suddenly she felt anxious. Hardly knowing what she was doing, but unable to stop herself, she ran after him. 'Will!' she called, when she had almost caught up. 'Can I change my mind?' she panted, shielding her eyes from the sun.

'Sorry?'

'The job in Tuscany – can I change my mind?'

A slow smile spread across his features. 'Of course. That's brilliant!'

Kate smiled back at him and, as the wind whipped through her hair, tying it into knots, she felt as if a great weight had been lifted from her.

'Give me a call when you get to Dublin,' he said, then headed for the house.

As she watched his retreating back, Kate tried not to think too hard about why she felt so happy.

Chapter 7

Two weeks later, on a Friday afternoon in July, Kate arrived at Pisa airport. Emerging into the arrivals hall, she pushed her luggage-laden trolley slowly, eyes scanning the crowd at the barrier. She heard her name called and spotted Louise, Will's assistant, waving to her from among the crowd.

'Hi Kate,' Louise said. 'Did you have a good flight?'

'Oh yes! It was lovely – I'd never flown first class before.'

'Nice, isn't it?' Louise led the way to the exit, helping Kate to manoeuvre the trolley.

Louise was a long-limbed, angular girl, not conventionally pretty but attractive in an offbeat way, with a wide mouth and a long mane of wavy fair hair that reached almost to her waist. Casually dressed in a body-hugging white T-shirt, jeans, trainers and wraparound shades, she was the consummate rock chick.

'I'm glad to see you travelled light,' she commented, eyeing Kate's trolley as they went to the exit.

'I know.' Kate winced. 'I'm sure I don't need half of it but—'

'I wasn't being sarcastic,' Louise hastened to reassure her. 'I'm used to dealing with the likes of Tessa and Tina. They'd bring this much for an overnight stay.'

Normally Kate did travel light, but before coming to Italy her mother had brought her on the promised shopping spree and kitted her out with a whole new wardrobe. Of course Rachel had been roped into the project and the pair of them had been in their element dressing Kate, like two little girls playing with their own life-size doll. But they knew their stuff when it came to shopping and she loved her new clothes so much that she hadn't been able to leave anything behind.

A wall of heat hit them as they emerged from the air-conditioned building into dazzling sunlight. Somehow they managed to stuff all of Kate's cases into Louise's tiny Italian car and were soon on the motorway speeding towards the Tuscan countryside. Louise drove like a native Italian, bombing along with one hand on the wheel, the other arm leaning casually on the open window frame, while she fielded calls on her mobile and chatted to Kate. She nearly missed the exit, slamming on the brakes so hard at the last minute that the car almost went into a 360-degree spin.

'Oops.' She smiled calmly, peeling off across two lanes of traffic amid a riot of honking, shouted Italian expletives and obscene gestures as they zipped past. To Kate's amazement, they left the motorway in one piece, but Louise barely dropped her speed as she drove along narrow, winding roads into the Tuscan hills.

Kate sank back in her seat and gazed out of the window. Fields of terracotta earth, dotted with yellow ochre farmhouses and deep green cypress trees baked in the sun, while up ahead, the red-tiled roofs of hilltop villages shimmered in the heat haze, stone church towers pointing into the azure sky. 'It's so beautiful here,' she breathed.

'Is this your first time in Italy?'

'I've been to Florence and Rome.'

'The villa's amazing. You'll love it,' Louise told her. 'You're the last to arrive. Most of us came out yesterday or the day before. I'm afraid you'll find more people at the house today than you were expecting,' she said apologetically. 'Will got bamboozled into letting the wives and girlfriends come for the weekend.'

'So Tessa Bond's there?' Kate asked, dismayed.

''Fraid so,' Louise smiled sympathetically, 'with her entourage. She decided it'd be the perfect setting to do the photos for her new book so she brought an army of stylists, photographers and assistants with her – her "team" as she calls them – along with Fawn, who's doing the shots with her.'

'Is that *the* Fawn?' Kate asked. *The* Fawn was a stunning Californian model who had risen to fame in the UK as an underwear model and calendar girl. She had dabbled in acting and TV presenting but, like Tessa, was more famous as tabloid fodder than for any of her work.

'Yes. She's a friend of Tessa's, though you'd never know it. They spend most of their time bitching each other up.'

'What's Tessa's new book?'

'It's on yoga,' Louise raised her eyes to heaven.

'I've read that she's really into it.'

'Hmm.' Louise pursed her lips. 'She's been to about five classes and now she reckons she's an expert.'

Kate laughed.

'Anyway,' Louise continued, 'you don't have to cook tonight. I've organised some food from a local restaurant so you'll have a chance to catch your breath and settle in. And they'll all be gone by Monday. Luckily Tessa has commitments back home, so she won't be able to hang around – otherwise, we'd probably never get rid of her. She has to go back to start a new reality-TV series.'

'I hadn't heard about that. What is it?' Kate asked.

'Oh, it's all very hush-hush. It's one of those I'm-a-third-rate-hasbeen-get-me-back-on-the-telly type deals. It's called *Celebrity Cell Block*,' Louise grinned meaningfully at Kate.

'Gosh! Is it what it sounds like?'

'Basically a bunch of so-called celebrities get put in jail. I try not to listen when she starts talking about it,' Louise said. 'Of course, she isn't *supposed* to be talking about it at all. She's not even supposed to tell anyone she's going to be in it. It's meant to be a secret until the "inmates" are revealed when it starts next week.'

'Sounds awful.'

'I'm sure it will be. But it'll keep Tessa out of everyone's hair for a while. Rory could do with a break – she's a real drain on him. So demanding.' She went quiet for a while, apparently lost in her thoughts, but she was soon babbling away again. 'That's one of the reasons Will let everyone come out now. They were supposed to turn up at the end of our stay, but Tessa mightn't be able to come then, depending on how long she lasts in this show – and Rory's life would-n't be worth living if she felt she was missing anything. Anyway, with a bit of luck she'll be banged up all summer once the show starts.'

'Is Tina here?' Kate asked warily. She might as well prepare her-self for the worst.

'No, she's working.'

Kate breathed a private sigh of relief.

'Owen didn't bring anyone either. It's really just Tessa and her travelling circus, and Summer. Have you met her?'

'Only briefly. What's she like?'

'She's cool. She only came because she knew Tessa was going to be here and the guys wouldn't get anything done anyway. She'd never get in the way when they're working. She can seem a bit aloof, but she's lovely once you get to know her, and she takes such good care of Phoenix. She probably saved his life. He was very heavily into drugs when they met, but she straightened him out . . . Rory needs someone like her,' she added.

'Will *you* be staying?' Kate asked, daunted at the thought of all those celebrities. It would be nice to have an ally.

'No. I'm just here to get everyone sorted and settled in. I have some stuff to go over with Will in the next couple of days, but I'll be leaving on Monday too. I have to get back to man the fort,' she said cheerfully, 'but I will be flying out from time to time. Don't worry,' she added, as if she knew how Kate was feeling. 'Like I said, they'll all be gone by Monday, and the guys are really easy – you won't have any problems. I've made some notes for you about likes and dislikes food-wise, but they're not very fussy. Owen and Rory eat pretty much everything. Georgie's borderline anorexic so eats practically nothing. Phoenix is a vegetarian, but I don't suppose that's a problem.'

'Oh, no, I've done a lot of vegetarian cooking. My boyfriend's a vegetarian, actually.'

'Oh, really? Didn't he mind you coming out here for the summer?'

'Well, he wasn't exactly over the moon about it,' Kate confessed, 'but it was such a great opportunity I couldn't pass it up. I couldn't make anything like this kind of money at home. And Will said Brian – my boyfriend – could visit while I'm here.' The prospect of a free holiday had mollified him somewhat.

'Will said that?' Louise said thoughtfully. Kate got the impression that she didn't approve somehow. Maybe she was afraid they would disrupt the calm working atmosphere.

'How's the food shopping here?' she asked, changing the subject.

'There's a great local market twice a week, and some really good shops in the village.' Louise briefed her as they drove, and before long they were turning off the road onto a long avenue lined with ramrod-straight cypress trees towards a huge, apricot-coloured house.

'Wow!' Kate gasped, as they circled an ornate fountain and pulled up.

Louise had called Will when they were turning into the drive, and he came out to meet them. 'Hi, Kate.' He looked tanned, healthy and relaxed.

'Welcome to Tuscany – it's great to see you here.'

Her heart slammed against her ribs as he bent to kiss her cheek.

'I'm glad you survived your drive with Miss Whiplash here,' he said, grinning at Louise.

Louise opened the car boot and Will took out the first couple of bags. 'Leave the rest – I'll have it brought up later,' he said.

They entered a vast tiled hall, wonderfully cool after the heat out-doors.

'Come on, I'll show you your room,' Louise said to Kate.

'Oh, I'll do that,' Will told her, already heading for the stairs.

'Okay.' She seemed a little put out and gave Will a beady look as he led Kate upstairs.

It wasn't lost on Will. He couldn't understand what was up with Louise. She had been reluctant from the start about hiring Kate and, even though they obviously got on well, she still didn't seem sold on the idea.

He led Kate down a long corridor. 'This is it.' He opened a door and ushered her into a big, high-ceilinged room filled with sunlight.

'Oh, it's beautiful,' Kate said. It was almost as big as her entire Dublin flat. A high double bed dominated the main part of the room, and two steps led down to a little sitting area with a sofa and windowseat. There was a vast en-suite bathroom, and shuttered french windows opened onto a little balcony overlooking the garden.

'Glad you like it.'

Sounds of voices, music and splashing water floated up to her from outside. Opening the french windows, Kate stepped onto the balcony. Amid well-kept lawns planted with an abundance of trees and flowers, a huge infinity pool offered spectacular views of the surrounding countryside. The scene below her was a paparazzo's wet dream as major stars and minor celebrities frolicked in the sun. Tessa and a willowy, honey-skinned blonde Kate recognised as Fawn were throwing shapes in their bikinis at the far end of the garden while a photographer snapped them. A couple of topless blondes from Central Casting were cavorting in the pool with Owen.

What had she let herself in for? She couldn't have felt more out of place if she had inadvertently strayed into the *Playboy* mansion.

'I'm sorry about all the extra people,' Will said, joining her at the window and looking down moodily at the scene below. 'Unfortunately everywhere Tessa goes a media circus follows, so our cover is blown. I'm hoping when they all push off, the paparazzi will lose interest and leave us alone. Anyway,' he said, more cheerfully, 'they'll be gone by Monday.'

'Tina wasn't able to come?'

'No.'

'Oh, pity.' Kate tried to sound disappointed for him.

Will tilted his head to one side and regarded her fondly. 'I'm glad you're here,' he said. He seemed genuinely pleased to see her.

'Me too.'

'Well, when you get settled in, come and relax by the pool. Make yourself at home. I'll show you the rest of the place later.'

'Thanks.' Kate smiled as he left the room.

She looked back to the garden. Come out and relax by the pool, Will said, as if it was the simplest thing in the world. The shimmering turquoise water was certainly inviting: she was hot and sticky after the journey and could almost feel it gliding against her skin, like ribbons of silk. But she hadn't counted on wall-to-wall models.

Confident that she would be the only girl at the villa, apart from

Georgie – who, without being bitchy, wasn't exactly a threat – she had got up the nerve to pack the acid-green bikini Rachel had insisted she buy. The bright colour was a perfect foil for her dark hair and olive skin, and Rachel had even said she looked stunning in it. She was glad now that she'd also packed the one-piece with tummy control that Rachel had tried to talk her out of. Pity she hadn't picked up a *burka* while she was at it.

When she had unpacked most of her clothes and put them away, she fished out her swimsuit and changed into it. Models or no models, she couldn't resist the lure of the pool. Tying a sarong around her waist, she slipped her feet into flip-flops and made her way downstairs.

Outside, Will was sitting at the far side of the pool reading a newspaper, his long legs stretched in front of him. Tessa and Fawn were ensconced on sun loungers beside him, evidently taking a break from their photo shoot. Thankfully, Summer was nowhere to be seen, and there was no sign of Owen and his blonde nymphs either, so the pool was empty. At least she didn't have too much of an audience, Kate thought, self-consciously removing her sarong.

Will lowered his paper as Kate emerged from the house and watched her from behind his dark glasses. It was funny – he had suddenly felt really happy upstairs when they were in her room. There was something comforting about her presence; it was like having a little bit of home with him – probably because Kate was the closest thing he had to a sister.

Wow, she's certainly shaped up well, he thought, as she removed her sarong and walked to the edge of the pool. There was nothing brotherly about the way she was making him feel now.

Kate seemed to become aware that she was being watched. Looking up, she blushed as her eyes met his, and suddenly threw herself into the pool in a belly flop.

'Whoa! Surf's up!' Fawn laughed, as Kate hit the water with an enormous splash. 'Shame we didn't bring our boards.'

'D'you think we should put out a tsunami warning?' Tessa joined in, cattily. She caught Will glowering at her. What does he have to be so superior about? she thought. She had seen the way he was looking at the girl before she'd flung herself into the pool like a bloody great whale. She had a good mind to tell Tina.

'Who's that?' Fawn asked, in her Californian drawl, peering into the water, through which Kate was now powering in a graceful crawl. 'Don't tell me Owen brought her? That boy has the weirdest taste in girls.' This observation was largely based on the fact that Owen had failed to make a pass at her.

'Oh, she's not with anyone. She's just the chef,' Tessa said dismissively.

'Oh, they've hired a chef?' Fawn said, perking up. 'Excellent! Maybe we'll get some decent food now.'

'I wouldn't count on it,' Tessa said. 'You could end up with a body like hers.'

'I'll have a word with her later,' Fawn continued, undaunted. 'You know, I've hardly eaten a thing since I got here. I couldn't even get anything on the plane.' Her voice was a querulous whine that made everything she said sound like a complaint – which it usually was.

'Oh, I never eat anything on planes.'

'But the airline made this big thing about how they could cater for people on special diets, so I thought, cool, they're finally getting with the programme. But when I asked the hostess for an Atkins meal, she looked at me like I had ten heads. I tried South Beach – same thing!'

Will was spared having to listen to any more of this nonsense by Tony, the photographer, coming to marshal his troops.

'Okay, I'm ready to finish the shots, girls,' he said, and Tessa and Fawn drifted off in his wake.

Although she hadn't caught what they were saying, Kate had been aware that she was under the critical eyes of Tessa and Fawn and had felt trapped in the pool, reluctant to brave their scrutiny again. She was knackered from swimming up and down and, with the coast clear, took the opportunity to get out. Tessa and Fawn were posing in a gazebo at the far end of the garden and Will had disappeared into the house, so she had the place to herself. She rubbed herself cursorily with a towel, then lay down on a lounger to dry off in the sun, closing her eyes behind her dark glasses as she felt the heat seep into her bones.

'I brought you a drink.'

She opened her eyes to find Will proffering a glass of champagne.

'Oh, how perfect! Thank you.' She took it. 'I feel such a fraud. Shouldn't I be doing something?'

'No,' Will said. 'Just relax and enjoy yourself. You might as well take the chance while you can – you'll have your work cut out for you with this lot tomorrow.'

He went back into the house and Kate picked up a magazine Tessa had left lying around, strategically opened on a gushing interview with her that focused on her new look and her diet and fitness regime.

A combination of sun, champagne and Tessa boring on about her diet must have put Kate to sleep because the next thing she knew her swimsuit was dry and the sun seemed to have gone in. She opened her eyes to find Owen standing over her, blocking it out. She wondered how long he had been standing there.

'Hello.' He grinned down at her. 'I hear you're the chef.'

'Yes. Hi, I'm Kate,' she said, sitting up and holding out her hand.

'We've met before,' Owen said, taking it and flashing that devastating smile. 'You don't remember?'

'Oh yes, I do! I just . . .' She just hadn't expected *him* to remember. He must meet so many people all the time.

'I never forget a beautiful girl,' he said. 'It was at some bint's wedding.'

'That was my sister.'

'Sorry,' Owen grinned unrepentantly.

'It's okay – she's some bint all right.'

Kate shielded her eyes to squint up at him. He was grungy and dishevelled, sporting about three days' worth of stubble and wearing a pair of ridiculously long, baggy yellow shorts, a candy-stripe short-sleeved shirt open over his bare chest and a Rasta hat. Only he could get away with wearing such mismatched, ugly clothes and still manage to look beautiful, she thought.

'Been reading about Tessa?' Owen picked up the magazine. 'Banging on about how she got so skinny, I suppose.'

'Apparently it's down to a combination of her diet – sorry, healthy-eating plan,' Kate corrected herself, 'and her favourite exercise, yoga.'

'Bollocks! You shouldn't believe everything you read. If you ask me, it's down to a combination of liposuction and bulimia. And yoga isn't her favourite form of exercise either,' he added.

'Oh? What is?' Kate asked.

'High-impact star-fucking.'

Kate giggled.

'Really, you should hear her and Rory going at it. Sometimes I think she'll kill him. Mind you, their fights are just as bad. Sometimes it's hard to tell whether they're fighting or fucking.'

Kate nearly jumped out of her skin at a sudden high-pitched shriek.

'Just get the bloody picture!' Tessa yelled at the photographer.

'Let's go and take the piss.' Owen extended a hand to Kate and pulled her up from her lounger. 'I hope your grub's as tasty as you are,' he said, when she was standing beside him. He stared unabashedly into her cleavage as she tied her sarong.

He led her to the gazebo where Tessa was standing on one leg, holding the other out at a ninety-degree angle, trying to keep her balance and maintain a smile that radiated effortless composure. Fawn stood to the side, playing with her hair and adjusting her bikini top, while the blonde clones that Kate had seen in the pool earlier were on the sidelines, wielding cases of cosmetics and hairdressing tools – Tessa's 'team', she supposed.

'Take the fucking picture!' Tessa ground out between clenched teeth. She was wobbling furiously and lost her balance as Tony clicked, landing on her arse with a thud. The blondes darted over, like paramedics rushing to the scene of a car crash, clutching their kitbags.

'Um, maybe we could come back to that one, Tessa,' Tony suggested. 'Why don't we do one of Fawn's and you can have a breather?'

'Okay,' Tessa said sulkily, even more put out as Fawn went into a perfect downward stretch with consummate ease.

'This one is called the Dawg,' Fawn explained to Tony, in her soft drawl, her clear, steady voice evidence of how effortless she found it.

'The Dog?' Owen called, grinning from the sidelines. 'Nice of them to name one after you, Tessa.'

Tessa shot him a filthy look. Fortunately Fawn had her head down and could hide a smile. Tessa was her friend, but she could be a real pain in the ass sometimes.

'That's lovely, Fawn,' Tony said, snapping enthusiastically.

'Lovely,' Owen murmured, admiring Fawn's pert bottom.

Tessa was on the floor now, manoeuvring herself into a complicated knot, legs behind her head, knees at her ears.

'What's this one called? The Slapper?' Owen giggled.

'Or Arse over Tit?' Kate whispered.

Tessa could be heard mumbling crossly, but whatever she said was muffled by her thighs.

'"I find yoga so relaxing,"' Owen intoned mockingly, quoting from the magazine, which he was still holding. '"It really centres me. I feel so calm, positive and at one with the world after my yoga session."'

Tony moved around Tessa, judging the shot from every angle. 'Should I take this from in front or behind?' he asked.

'God, Tessa must be so sick of being asked that,' Owen said to Kate, who collapsed into giggles. 'That's the problem when you have a face like a slapped arse – no one can tell which end should be up.'

'Take it from in front,' Tessa snapped, 'and hurry up before I smother.'

'Um . . . maybe it would look better if you had more clothes on?' Tony suggested.

'Nah, go on,' Owen called to him. 'One for the hand-job brigade!'

'I suppose a few beaver shots never hurt anyone,' Tony mumbled as he snapped.

'Careful Tessa,' Owen called. 'If the wind changes, you could be left like that.'

Tessa unknotted herself, grabbed one of her sandals and shied it at him.

'Fuck off, you fucking ape!' she spat.

Owen dodged the missile, unperturbed. 'Wow, I'd hate to see her *before* she does yoga.'

'Hey, cut it out, you two,' Louise called, coming towards them from the house, like a parent stepping in to referee a fight between five-year-olds.

'He started it,' Tessa pouted.

'Owen, please stop winding Tessa up,' Louise said quietly, when Tessa had gone back to her posing. 'It just makes it harder on everyone having her here.'

'Sorry.' He sounded chastened.

'Rory and Georgie are looking for you,' she told him. 'They're in the studio.' She waved to an outbuilding at the other side of the house. 'Kate, if you like, I can show you around the place now?'

'Sure.'

They walked together to the outbuilding that the band were going to use as a studio. When they opened the door, the air was thick with smoke, and the smell of weed was overpowering. Rory and Georgie were fiddling with the equipment, stopping briefly when Louise introduced Kate. Despite the heat, Georgie was dressed in her trademark tracksuit bottoms and a high-necked T-shirt. The first time they had met, Kate had noticed that eye contact wasn't Georgie's strong point, but now she smiled shyly before her eyes slid away. Rory lifted his chin almost imperceptibly in mute acknowledgement of her, but Kate was struck by the complete transformation that came over him when he looked at Louise. She had seen the way his eyes lit up when she came into the room and he was looking at her now with a smile that softened and smoothed his tough, world-weary features, making him seem immeasurably younger, the wary eyes boyishly vulnerable.

So that's how it is, she thought. Thinking back over things Louise had said in the car, she reckoned the feeling was probably mutual. Which begged the question: if Rory could have Louise, what the hell was he doing with Tessa?

They left Owen in the studio with the others and Louise took Kate on a tour of the main house. There were eight bedrooms on the upper two floors, all with en-suite bathrooms and sumptuous furnishings. A vast living-dining area, with a spectacular arched brick ceiling, took up almost the entire ground floor, and there was an enormous kitchen. Outside there was a built-in barbecue on the pool terrace and, to the side of the house, leading off the kitchen, another terrace with a long table under a pergola. Apart from the studio, there were two more small outbuildings that housed separate apartments, one of which, Louise explained, was occupied by Maria and

Franco, the Italian couple who acted as housekeeper and gardener. Franco had taken Phoenix and Summer into Florence, but Louise brought her to meet Maria, a stereotypical Italian matron straight out of a pasta-sauce advert. Maria greeted Kate warmly in fractured English, kissing her on both cheeks, and saying 'bella' several times. She promised to take Kate into the village on Monday and introduce her to the locals.

The tour finished in the kitchen, where Louise left Kate to explore on her own.

Kate was soon engrossed in making an inventory of the food. Flipping through the notes Louise had given her, she began to feel excited about starting work. This was the sort of job she enjoyed most, real home cooking for a small group, like cooking for one's own family. She enjoyed making people happy with food and liked to see the pleasure it gave.

Taking a notebook and pen, she went back to the terrace to plan menus for the coming week. She was still there when Summer and Phoenix returned from their trip to Florence. 'Hi, Kate, nice to see you again,' Phoenix said, coming out onto the terrace. He was wearing wraparound shades and a baseball cap low over his eyes, probably to give him some measure of anonymity, Kate guessed, so he could walk the streets of Florence unmolested.

He was followed by Summer, laden with shopping bags. 'Hi Kate. Will told us you'd arrived. I've been for some retail therapy,' she said, shaking the shopping bags, which bore designers' names. 'Not Phoenix, though – he spent the afternoon staring at art in churches.' She smiled at him affectionately. 'Well, it's nice to see you again,' she said, and drifted off.

'I still haven't been to the Uffizi,' Phoenix said, sitting beside Kate, as if he was resuming a conversation they had started earlier in the day. He flicked through a big book of Italian art he was holding, opened a page and held it out to her. 'I went to this place today – amazing frescos. These photographs don't do them justice. You must go.'

He patted his pockets, pulling out numerous scraps of paper with scribbling on them, then found a packet of cigarettes. He lit one, took a long draw and exhaled the smoke before offering one to Kate.

'No thanks, I don't smoke.'

'I keep meaning to give up,' he said, waving smoke away from Kate's face. 'Still, could be worse – at least it's not heroin. And when you're an ex-junkie you've got to have something. Have you ever tried heroin, Kate?' he asked conversationally.

'No, I haven't.' Kate said, feeling like a bit of a fuddy-duddy.

'My advice is don't. Such a beautiful thing.' He shook his head sadly. 'You're better off not knowing.' His voice was full of longing, as though he were talking of a lost love. 'Fucking gorgeous.' He sighed wistfully, blowing smoke skywards. 'They have some amazing stuff in the churches here . . .'

It took Kate a moment to realise that he wasn't talking about the quality of the drugs you could score in Florence's churches but had suddenly moved back to Italian art.

Later, Kate helped Louise set the long table under the pergola, opening bottles of wine and water, lighting candles and laying out the food when it arrived from the local restaurant. There were platters of antipasti, a huge tray of cannelloni stuffed with spinach and ricotta in a tomato sauce, another tray of chicken cacciatore, a vast dish of cubed potatoes roasted with rosemary and garlic, a few plates of garlic bread and several pizzas. There was enough to feed an army, she thought, as they laid it on the table.

'I'm afraid I took a bit of a scattergun approach to the ordering,' Louise said.

'I'm a firm believer in over-ordering,' Kate said, popping a cube of roast potato in her mouth. 'I always over-cater as a matter of principle.'

'Well, I was trying to please everyone and account for all tastes, but I'm sure I was wasting my time.'

'I can't imagine anyone finding anything to complain about with all this.'

'Can't you? Just sit back and watch.'

Of course, she was right.

'Oh my God, is this all there is?' Fawn asked in dismay, scanning the table with real alarm on her face as they took their places. 'I don't think there's anything I can eat. It's like a total carb-fest.'

Kate was seated between Louise and Tony with Will and Tessa on the opposite side of the table.

As everyone passed dishes around, Rory held out a plate of garlic bread to Tessa.

'You know I can't eat that,' she snapped. 'I'm allergic to wheat.'

'You can't just *decide* you're allergic to something,' Rory said irritably.

'I'm in tune with my body,' Tessa told him tetchily. 'I know what agrees with me and what doesn't. If I eat wheat I blow up like a balloon.'

'I'd be interested to see that,' Owen muttered to Georgie. 'Maybe if we stuck a pin in her she'd disappear.'

'I can't eat dairy,' Fawn announced to the table at large.

'Oh, me either. I can't eat wheat *or* dairy,' Tessa trumped her. 'I'll just have some of that pasta.'

'But . . .' Kate began, as Tessa scooped one tube of cannelloni onto her plate.

'Say nothing,' Louise murmured. 'She probably thinks pasta's a vegetable.'

To her dismay, Kate noticed that hardly anyone was eating, despite the glorious feast laid out before them. The blonde clones – who had been introduced as Bonnie and Kim, though she still wasn't sure which was which – were just smoking and drinking, intermittently pushing bits of food around their plates. At the far end of the table, Georgie was looking distressed as Summer tried to persuade her to eat.

'Oh, she's just attention-seeking!' Tessa snapped irritably. 'She'll eat if she's hungry.' She knew that bitching up Georgie wasn't going to endear her to anyone, but she couldn't help it.

'Lay off, Tessa,' Rory said quietly.

'Well, it's not helping, the way you all fuss over her and pander to her foibles. You're just feeding into her neuroses.'

'Tessa.' Rory's voice was like thunder now.

Out of the corner of her eye, Kate saw Fawn waving frantically at her, trying to get her attention.

'What's her name?' she asked one of the clones, who shrugged.

'Excuse me, honey! Yes, you,' she said, leaning over to catch

Kate's eye. 'You're the chef, right? Do you think you could make me a whites-only omelette?' She smiled winningly.

'Oh! Okay . . .' Kate said uncertainly, taken aback. She made to get up, but Will put his hand over hers.

'You'll do no such thing,' he said to her. 'Kate isn't starting work until tomorrow,' he told Fawn.

For a second, the doe eyes flickered and Kate was treated to a glimpse of the harridan that lurked below the sweet façade.

'You could eat the chicken,' Tessa told Fawn consolingly.

Fawn regarded it suspiciously, but took a piece and put it on her plate, scraping off the tomato sauce fastidiously.

'I bet it isn't even organic,' she complained.

'So, you're a chef?' Tony said, turning to Kate. A paunchy, per-matanned medallion man, Tony had the sleazy good looks of a play-boy gone to seed. 'I don't think I've seen you on TV, have I?'

'Oh no. I've never been on TV.'

'Really? Not even *Ready Steady Cook*?'

'No.' Kate smiled apologetically, and Tony seemed to lose interest in her.

She noticed that Phoenix was very quiet, talking to Summer and Georgie in hushed tones, occasionally scribbling on his napkin and scraps of paper pulled from his pockets.

Tessa and Fawn, by contrast, were a nightmare, vying for every-one's attention. Kate found it exhausting just to watch them. Tessa kept bringing the conversation back to her new reality show.

'It's not one of those awful things where you have to go to the jun-gle and eat worms, is it?' Fawn asked.

'Oh no. I don't think I could do that, even for charity. I mean, who knows how many calories are in one of those grubs? I'd have to abandon my healthy-eating plan, and it means too much to me. Not that I expect to last too long – I'm sure I'll be the first to get voted off.' She smiled self-deprecatingly, but no one jumped in to contra-dict her.

'Oh well, I'm sure no one *we* know will be watching it anyway,' Fawn said sympathetically.

Gamely, Tessa didn't let the smile slip. 'Actually they're expecting it to be the big hit of the summer. They've got a great line-up of celebs – not that I consider *myself* a celebrity, but that's what they will insist on calling us.'

'So, who else is there?' Fawn asked.

'Well, I'm not supposed to talk about it. It's top secret until the first show.' Tessa was obviously champing at the bit to divulge all and only needed a nudge to do so.

'Oh, I won't tell anyone,' Fawn said airily. 'No one I know watches reality TV.'

'Well, just between ourselves, there's Rosie Grant . . .' Tessa began.

'*Who?*' Fawn interrupted cuttingly, screwing up her face.

'Rosie Grant. She was the star of that TV series *Double Decker*. She was the bus driver.'

'Was it a soap?'

'No, a reality show about a double-decker bus. It followed the bus around for the day and filmed the driver, the passengers, all the funny little incidents that happened on the bus.'

'So, basically, she *is* a bus driver.' Fawn drawled derisively.

'Yes, but a famous one.'

'Who else?'

'James Lewis.'

There was a chorus of 'Who?' from the entire table this time.

'He used to be in that eighties group, The Dog Ate My Homework.'

'Oh yeah,' Rory said. 'They had a number one, didn't they? What was that song they used to sing?'

'"The Dog Ate My Homework",' Tessa said. 'It was the title of the song too.'

'They obviously exhausted their creative talents thinking up the band's name,' Will remarked. 'They were never seen again after that, were they?'

'They had another single,' Tessa said huffily.

'I remember him now,' Louise said. 'He was kind of cool-looking – very flamboyant. He had gorgeous long black hair and wore loads of eyeliner.'

'I think I met him in rehab,' Phoenix chipped in. 'He's an interesting guy.'

'No, not him,' Tessa said crossly. 'You're thinking of the singer. James Lewis was the other one.'

'Oh, I remember!' Will exclaimed. 'The one who stood at the back looking glum, fiddling with a synthesiser?'

'Yes, him,' Tessa said.

'Okay, so far we've got a bus driver and the boring one from some eighties one-hit-wonder group,' Fawn sneered.

'Yeah, that'll have everyone glued to their TV screens,' Owen laughed.

'Well, there's also Vanessa King,' Tessa announced, throwing discretion to the wind.

This name had the desired effect – she had everyone's attention now. Vanessa King was a TV presenter who had had a notorious affair with a Conservative MP. Her kiss-and-tell revelations of kinky sex, misuse of party funds and abuse of political influence had resulted in him being forced to resign. She was currently flavour of the month on talk shows.

'I'm hoping we'll be cellmates,' Tessa went on.

'I was offered a reality show in the States,' Fawn drawled, 'but I turned it down. They're so tacky and make you look so desperate.'

'Well, I would have turned this one down, but it's for charity,' Tessa said sweetly.

'Oh, the one I was offered was for charity too, but my agent said reality TV would be a really bad move for me – I just don't need that kind of exposure.'

Tony was gazing at Fawn's breasts as if he knew exactly the kind of exposure she needed and he'd be happy to help her get it.

'Well, I'm not doing it for the exposure,' Tessa said sanctimoniously. 'I'm doing it for my charity.'

'What charity are you giving it to if you win?' Fawn asked, ready to pounce on whatever it was and tear it to shreds.

'It was hard to decide. There are just so many good causes out there. But I've decided to give it to this group that supports women whose plastic surgery has gone wrong.'

'Oh!' Fawn gasped. 'That's a really good cause,' she breathed, impressed despite herself.

'But is it really a charity?' Summer challenged. 'Will they let you do that with the money if you win?'

'Of course! Why not?'

'Well, any number of reasons – AIDS, famine relief, orphans, refugees, homeless people.'

'Oh yeah, all the so-called "sexy" charities,' Tessa scoffed. 'They get more than their fair share of money and publicity.'

'I agree.' Fawn nodded wisely. 'I mean, don't get me wrong, I have nothing against starving children – obviously – but *please*. That's all you ever hear about, when there are these other charities and most people don't even know they exist.'

'Plus you know where the money's going and that it's not being siphoned off by some corrupt government,' Tessa chimed in.

'Right,' Fawn agreed. 'The starving in Africa must get billions every year in charity money. I mean, how can they *still* be starving, right?' she said.

This was greeted with stunned silence, which Fawn took as evidence of her brilliant incisiveness.

'Well, I hope you win, babes,' she told Tessa supportively. 'You deserve it.'

'Oh thanks.' Tessa attempted a smile that was both modest and saintly.

'No, you really do,' Fawn insisted, even though Tessa hadn't contradicted her. 'Aw, I'm so proud of you, babes, I really am.'

'Her parents weren't kidding when they named *her*, were they?' Kate whispered to Louise.

'You've got terrific boobs, Kate,' Tony said suddenly, looking down her top. 'Let me guess – an F cup?'

'Um, close – E.' Kate blushed crimson as every eye focused on her chest.

'I'm a bit of an expert,' Tony said proudly, winking at her. Glamour photography was Tony's stock-in-trade. Tessa had met him when she had stripped off for a lad magazine. 'They're real too, aren't they?' he said, practically drooling. 'It's not every day you see real ones that size. Ever done any topless work?'

'No.' Kate laughed awkwardly. There's not much call for topless chefs.'

'Pity.' Tony was still peering down her top. 'Still, if you ever want to change direction, I'm sure I could get you work. We could even tie it in with the whole chef thing. You could do a calendar – you know, a recipe for every month with a nice little piccie of you, maybe just wearing a little apron, or lying on a worktop with just a few carefully placed strawberries. Nothing tacky,' he assured her. 'It'd be very tasteful.'

'It sounds it,' Will said, managing to keep a straight face, though his eyes glinted. He found the idea of Kate wearing nothing but an apron or a few strawberries extremely disturbing.

'It'd certainly get men back into the kitchen,' Tony said, with a suggestive leer.

'Yes, but I don't think what they'd be doing there would comply with food-safety standards,' Will drawled, laughing at Kate's discomfiture. She looked so adorable when she went all shy, blushing and squirming like a teenager.

Kate was actually relieved when Tessa started babbling on about her healthy-eating plan, diverting attention from her cleavage.

'You should try it,' she said to Georgie. 'It works for people who need to put on weight too.'

'Really!' Fawn was shocked. 'Why would anyone want to do that?'

'It's about finding the right balance,' Tessa explained. 'I could write you up a diet sheet, if you like,' she said to Georgie.

'No, thanks,' Georgie said, looking uncomfortable.

'Really, it would be no problem. You shouldn't be afraid of food, you know – it's not your enemy.'

'I'm not afraid of food,' Georgie said sullenly.

'Tessa, drop it,' Rory said threateningly.

'I'm just trying to help. If she'd eat properly—'

'Leave her alone. She's all right.'

'But she's *not* all right, is she? She tried to top herself last year, for Christ's sake! I don't call that *all right*.'

There was an appalled silence as all eyes flew to Georgie, who was staring down at her plate.

'So, Tessa,' Kate said wildly, 'tell me – tell me more about this reality show of yours. It sounds fantastic!'

Phoenix sent her a grateful smile from the other end of the table.

'Yeah, will you be getting your kit off?' Owen asked aggressively.

'Well, we do get a bonus if we snog anyone – more for an actual shag. And since I'll be on the women's wing . . .' she giggled, delighted that the conversation had returned to her TV show.

It's impossible to insult her, Kate thought.

'You wouldn't bang a girl, would you?' Fawn asked.

'I'd be doing it for my charity,' Tessa said nobly.

As Fawn and Tessa prattled on, Kate glanced to the other end of the table. Georgie caught her eye and they shared a conspiratorial smile.

The next day, Maria and Franco took Kate to the village and showed her around. She returned to find Georgie and Summer on the terrace surrounded by shopping bags.

'I'm afraid I've been indulging again.' Summer waved her to a seat beside them. 'We've been to a fabulous market, haven't we, Georgie? Lots of really funky clothes and jewellery, and it's cheap too. You two should go some time.'

'I'd like that.'

'I got these fabulous shoes,' Summer was pulling their purchases out of the bags to show Kate, 'and these earrings – they're fun, aren't they? And we got the cutest little dress for Georgie.'

'Summer's always trying to get me to wear dresses,' Georgie told Kate ruefully.

'Well, you should! You're such a pretty girl. I hate to see you hiding away in those ugly sports clothes. You've got great legs.'

'And fantastic arms,' Kate said enviously.

'It's the drumming,' Georgie said.

'Well, I'd better go and pack,' Summer said, stuffing her purchases back into their bags and getting up. 'See you at dinner.'

When she had gone into the house, Georgie and Kate were quiet for a few moments.

'That thing Tessa said yesterday,' Georgie began, 'it's not exactly true.'

'It's okay. You don't have to explain.'

'It was sort of an accident. I didn't mean to—' she broke off. 'I didn't mean to OD,' she began again. 'It was in Paris. My dad had got past security and up to my hotel room. So I was . . . upset. I just sort of started taking those pills and couldn't stop. You know what I mean?'

'I've done that with biscuits.' Kate smiled.

177

'Well, next thing I knew I was having my stomach pumped,' Georgie continued. 'Will managed somehow to keep it out of the papers.'

It couldn't have been easy keeping *that* quiet, Kate thought.

'Phoenix and I took out a restraining order against Dad. If he comes near us again, he gets thrown into jail. He only has to come within ten feet of us.' There was a glint in Georgie's eyes as she said this, as though she wished he would. 'How long have you known Will?' she asked suddenly.

'Oh, ages – he's my brother's best friend.'

'He's great, isn't he?'

'Yes, he's . . . lovely.'

'Do you have a boyfriend, Kate?'

'Yeah.'

'Oh!' Georgie seemed a bit disappointed. 'Will's a great guy, though, isn't he?' she said finally.

'Yes,' Kate said, a bit bemused. 'He is.'

That evening, as Kate began preparing dinner, Fawn breezed into the kitchen. 'Hi, we need to talk,' she said. 'It's Kate, right?' She smiled charmingly.

'Yes.'

'I need to talk to you about the food because the boys are hopeless. I mean, they want us to look like this,' she spread her arms to indicate her perfect figure, 'and then they get pissed off if we won't share pizza and beer with them. I mean, *hello*! It's one or the other, right? *Right*?'

Kate looked at her, saying nothing. 'What do you want?' she asked finally.

'What I'd really love is some plain poached fish and steamed broccoli. Okay?'

Tessa was hot on her heels. 'I can have some carbs today,' she announced to Kate, as she entered the kitchen, waving a copy of her book. She was in a chirpy mood, having found herself featured in a magazine article about stars who were too thin. She presented Kate with the book, showing her what stage of the eating plan she was on and leaving Kate to work out what she could have for dinner.

Tessa's eating plan was a complex colour-coded maze of cycles and zones, but no matter how carefully Kate studied it, poring over the charts and diagrams, she couldn't make head nor tail of it. She was almost in tears of frustration when Will popped his head in.

'Everything okay?' Kate was punching numbers into a calculator.

'Kate, what on earth are you doing?'

'I wish I knew,' she said, miserably.

'What's the problem?'

'This.' Kate held up the book so he could see the cover. *Colour Me Slim*! it shouted, in a fluorescent rainbow, while Tessa grinned from the centre of a colour wheel.

Will was still puzzled.

'It's Tessa's book,' Kate explained. 'I'm trying to work out what she's supposed to eat. She's on day four of the sixth cycle, which means she's in this purple zone here.' She jabbed at a chart. 'Purple means she can have foods from the blue group and the red group – because that's what makes purple. But you have to work out the right percentages, and then there's something about complementary colours. I think you'd need a degree in calculus to get this right – and you know how bad I am at maths.'

Will smiled sympathetically. 'Okay, show me the book.' He held out his hand and Kate plopped it in his palm. He turned a couple of pages, scanning them.

'Okay,' he said decisively.

'You've got it?' Kate asked, awed. She couldn't believe he'd worked it out so quickly – he must think she was the most awful dolt! And, really, if Tessa had come up with it, how difficult could it be?

'Yes. Here's what you do,' he said, shutting the book with one hand and eyeballing Kate to make sure she was paying attention. Then he drew back his arm and flung the book out of the open window.

There was a yelp from the garden as the book clocked Owen and he stood up, rubbing his head.

'Sorry!' Will called, waving through the window.

Owen picked up the missile from the ground. On seeing what had hit him, he gave Will a grinning thumbs-up, then stomped off to find a cow pat in which to bury it.

'Okay,' Will said, rubbing his hands, 'any other problems?'

'Er . . . no. Thanks.' Kate thought it was probably best not to mention that the blender was on the blink. It was a bit wonky, but still usable, and she didn't want it chucked out of the window.

'Kate,' Will said, putting his hands on her shoulders, 'you're here to work for me, not Tessa. You don't have to take orders from her. She's only here on sufferance anyway. Tell her she's welcome to use the kitchen herself if she wants something different.'

'Okay.' Kate was thinking maybe she could retrieve the book when Will wasn't looking and have another bash. She didn't fancy having to tell Tessa to make her own dinner.

'Okay, I'll tell her,' Will had sensed her anxiety at the thought of confronting Tessa. 'Believe me, it'll be a pleasure.'

Kate smiled, relieved.

'I'm beginning to regret letting her come. Still, at least she'll be safely behind bars for the rest of the summer.'

'I wouldn't count on it,' Kate warned. 'She'll probably be the first to get voted off. The public can't stand her.'

'Oh, it won't be up to them if Owen has anything to do with it,' Will said mysteriously, as he left the kitchen.

Chapter 8

The next morning the weekend house guests packed up to leave, amid a great deal of chaos and faffing. Tessa was in a complete panic about what to wear, constantly ripping open her bags to change her outfit and forcing Kim and Bonnie to restyle her hair and retouch her make-up. She was terrified of being caught off guard by paparazzi as she got off the plane and ending up in one of those smug montages of celebs looking like shit.

Fawn, by contrast, was the soul of calm, complacent in the belief that organising her departure was someone else's job. She lounged by the pool, issuing demands and giving orders, even comandeering Tessa's assistants to do her nails while she relaxed in the sun.

Summer had been packed and ready to go since early morning and took the opportunity to escape the mayhem for a quiet cup of coffee in the kitchen with Kate.

'It'll be good for Georgie to have another girl around,' she said.

'She spends too much time surrounded by boys. Sometimes I think they're a bit over-protective, and it's not good for her.'

Raised voices drew their attention to the terrace. Outside, Tessa was now engaged in a heated bilingual shouting match with Maria, each woman babbling away in her own language with no idea of what the other was saying. Not that it mattered: their body language said it all. '*Will!*' Tessa shrieked, calling him in to referee.

'God, if he's any sense he'll hide until she's gone,' Kate said. Over the weekend, she had seen how everyone leaned on Will. She was appalled at the way Fawn and Tessa in particular would turn to him with their trivial problems rather than trying to do anything for themselves. She wondered how they tied their own shoelaces when he wasn't on hand.

'I'm glad you're here for Will's sake too,' Summer said thought-fully. 'I think it's really good for him to have you here.'

'*Me?*' Kate was taken aback.

'Yes, you,' Summer stated. 'I've known Will for quite a long time, but I've never seen him as happy and relaxed as he's been the past couple of days. I can't help feeling that you're what makes the differ-ence.' She stirred her coffee absently. 'Will has such sad eyes, don't you think? He's a beautiful man, but he has the loneliest eyes.' She looked out of the window to where he was on the terrace, trying to calm Tessa. It turned out that she had mislaid her airline ticket and was taking it out on Maria. 'He's a terrific guy. He's so good at what he does, but sometimes, he seems a bit . . . lost. He doesn't seem that way when you're around.'

Kate followed her gaze. Will had instigated a search party for Tessa's ticket and was smoothing Maria's ruffled feathers, speaking to her in fluent Italian.

'Maybe you make him feel . . . safe,' Summer continued.

Kate wrinkled her nose. 'Safe? Not exactly sexy, is it?'

'Don't knock it. After all, most men marry their mothers.'

'I don't think Will's mother ever made him feel very safe,' Kate mused. 'It was more the other way around. He had to look after *her*. He knew she loved him, of course – and he adored her – but I don't think she ever gave him a sense of security.'

'Well, all the more reason why he'd be drawn to someone who does.'

Infuriatingly, Louise chose that moment to round up Summer. 'Nearly ready to roll?' she called, sticking her head around the door.

Kate sighed, frustrated, as Summer went to get her things together. She had been the second person recently to suggest that Will had feelings for her – first there had been Lorcan. Both times, maddeningly, the conversation was cut short.

* * *

'Come on, Kate,' Georgie called. 'It's starting.'

Kate distributed bowls of popcorn on the coffee tables and slid onto the sofa between Georgie and Owen.

It was the Friday after the guests had left, and they were gathered around the TV after dinner to watch the first episode of *Celebrity Cell Block*. There was the usual parade of spurious celebrities, has-beens and wannabes, the laconic male presenter providing much-needed reminders of their claims to fame while making jokes at their expense. Tessa was her usual bright, bubbly self when she rolled up, waving cheerfully to the crowd and beaming for the cameras.

The contestants were issued with prison uniforms, which led to a great deal of complaining from the women. Vanessa King was the most vociferous, disingenuously moaning that she looked ugly in the drab grey overalls.

'She's fucking gorgeous, and she knows it,' Owen said.

'Why do you think she said it?' Georgie murmured. 'Stupid cow.'

Tessa got her wish and was teamed with Vanessa as her cellmate. 'I'm just missing my boyfriend so much,' she whinged, bringing up Rory's name at every possible opportunity.

'God, she's only been in there five minutes,' Owen remarked. 'You've spent more time apart when she's gone to the loo,' he told his brother.

Vanessa set out her stall early on, making a pass at Tessa on the first night. She was notorious for swinging both ways, and rumour had it that she had not only had an affair with the disgraced MP but also with his wife.

On the first day, Tessa made the most of her airtime, leading a yoga class in the exercise yard and offering her fellow inmates unasked-for dietary advice. She had even remained cheerful and upbeat when she was assigned a job in the laundry. But by lock-up it had become too much, and she broke down in tears. 'I feel so alone,' she wailed to Vanessa, who sat beside her on her narrow bed.

'Come on, we'll get through this together,' Vanessa soothed her, putting an opportunistic arm around her. 'Just remember why you're doing this,' she said, stroking Tessa's back.

'I miss my boyfriend so much,' Tessa sobbed. 'My boyfriend Rory.' She must have realised she'd forgotten to mention his name. 'I miss being held and having someone to cuddle.'

'You don't have to miss that,' Vanessa said softly, stroking Tessa's hair, a predatory glint in her eyes. 'Rory Cassidy's loss is my gain.' She kissed Tessa lightly on the lips.

Kate glanced surreptitiously at Rory to see how he was taking this. His eyes were out on stalks. Even Owen was agog. What was it with men and lesbians?

Meanwhile, on screen, Tessa recoiled.

'Sorry,' Vanessa said. 'You're just such a beautiful girl, Tessa – and I've heard some very interesting things about you.'

'All lies,' Rory said. Tessa had always put out stories that made her sex life sound a lot more kinky than it was.

'Well, her publicity-seeking's coming back to bite her on the arse now,' Will said.

'Don't you find me attractive?' Vanessa pouted.

'Oh, yes,' Tessa stammered. 'It's just – it's just that I don't want to be unfaithful to my boyfriend,' she said desperately. Having come up with a plausible excuse for avoiding Vanessa's advances, she was her old self again, playing to the camera for all she was worth. 'You're gorgeous and, believe me, there's nothing I'd like more,' she purred flirtatiously, 'but I couldn't do that to Rory.'

'I bet he'd love to watch.' Vanessa stroked Tessa's hair again. 'We could have a really nice time in here if we let ourselves.'

'Still,' Tessa said, backing away, 'I want to be faithful.'

'Suit yourself.' Vanessa stood up. 'If you change your mind, you know where I am. Believe me, one night with me and you'll forget all about Rory Cassidy – you'll forget about men, full stop.'

With that parting shot, she got into her bed, pulled up the blankets and fell asleep almost instantly. Tessa crawled into bed too but lay there snivelling, obviously expecting Vanessa to jump her the moment she let her guard slip.

Over the next few weeks, life at the villa fell into a quiet, steady rhythm. Free from distractions, the band threw themselves into working on songs for the new album, spending long days in the studio, often without a break. Between intense bouts of work, they took occasional days off, chilling out by the pool, sleeping late, relaxing and generally recharging their batteries. After a few weeks of good food, sunshine and rest, they were all looking considerably less like the living dead. Even Georgie had put on a bit of weight and had some colour in her cheeks.

Kate loved every minute of her new job, from her walk to the shops in the early morning, where she had mimed conversations with the local women, to the quiet, balmy evenings in the garden when they ate together under the pergola, with the cicadas singing. Although she didn't know any Italian apart from food terms, she had become a favourite with the locals, who would help her find what she was looking for, share recipes and cooking tips, and volunteer advice on her love life. All the mothers were keen to introduce her to their sons, waving away her objection that she had a boyfriend at home and talking up their offspring like door-steppers at election time. Resolutely unimpressed by the skinny models who had been frequenting the villa, they approved of Kate's domesticity and fuller figure, deciding that she was a good, traditional girl.

As she became friends with Phoenix, Georgie, Rory and Owen, she no longer felt intimidated by their rock-star status. It was impossible to feel star-struck with people you saw across the breakfast table every morning and ate dinner with every night. But when they played together as a band, they became something else, transforming into the gorgeous glittering creatures she was used to seeing on stage. Behind her drum kit, Georgie's gaucheness fell away and she was a strong, confident girl, cool, sexy and completely in control. Armed with their guitars, Owen and Rory were no longer clownish party animals but assumed an air of authority and gravitas. And Phoenix was pure rock god, charged with a superhuman charisma, his wiry frame pumping with an electric energy as his distinctive voice soared.

It was as if some fairy godmother had waved her wand and, with electric guitars, drums and amplifiers in place of glass slippers, ball gowns and golden coaches, turned them into one graceful, harmonious organism.

Most of all, she loved spending so much time with Will. She loved knowing he would be there every morning at breakfast and that they would have dinner together every night. He usually worked in the morning, shutting himself up in the room he had designated his office to make phone calls and go through the huge bundles of post that regularly arrived by courier. But in the afternoon he was often at her disposal, driving her to the village or into Florence to pick up supplies, hanging out with her by the pool or taking her to visit medieval villages in the hills. Sometimes they took a CD of the new songs with them and drove around playing them full blast on the car stereo. The sound seemed incongruous in this rural idyll, but Kate loved it. She felt as if she was living in a movie and the music was its soundtrack.

Will joined her regularly in the kitchen when he wasn't working, chatting companionably to her while she prepared meals, and even helping her sometimes. She loved the domestic intimacy between them as they worked together and occasionally allowed herself to indulge in a fantasy that they were married and this was their home. Though she spoke to Brian on the phone, she wasn't disappointed when he told her he would be too busy over the summer to visit her in Tuscany. She wasn't missing him as much as she should – or at all, she sometimes thought. But she was enjoying herself too much to worry about it.

As Will sat at his desk, going through the latest parcel of post that Louise had sent out, his eye fell on a small square envelope marked 'Personal', which hadn't been opened at the office. Cutting it open, he pulled out a thick cream invitation card. 'Shit!' The furrow between his brows deepened. There was a note with it and he unfolded it with a sense of dread, glancing over the words hurriedly, as if afraid they would hurt him. Then he put the card and note back in the envelope, pulled open the desk drawer and buried it in there. He would think about it later, he told himself, slamming the drawer closed.

Hearing water splashing, he got up and walked to the window, which looked out over the pool terrace. Kate and Georgie were sitting on the bench at the far end of the pool where the water spilled over the edge, chatting together. It was good to see Georgie happy. It was nice for her to have another girl around, and she and Kate had become friends. In fact, everyone got on well with Kate. He was glad now that he had allowed Grace to bamboozle him into bringing her out here. He himself was glad of her company when the band were holed up in the studio for days on end. He thought that maybe tomorrow he'd take her to San Gimignano – he knew she'd never been there. He knew a restaurant just outside the town, that he was sure Kate would love. Maybe they could stop there for lunch.

Suddenly there was an enormous splash as Owen jumped into the pool with a whoop. He swam up to Georgie and Kate and insinuated himself between them on the bench, his arm resting casually at Kate's back. As Will watched, he turned to Kate, his body curled in towards hers, and Kate roared laughing at something he said. Then he grabbed her hand and pulled her into the water.

'Maybe one of the boys in your band will fall for her:' Grace's words echoed in Will's mind as he watched Kate and Owen circling each other in the pool, splashing and laughing. Was that what was happening? And was Kate falling for Owen? She certainly didn't seem to be missing Brian.

Sighing, he returned to his desk and the post. But his concentration was gone and he couldn't focus. He realised he had been staring into space for several minutes, absently tapping a pen on the desk. Oh, bugger it! he thought, giving up. There was nothing here that wouldn't keep until tomorrow. Maybe he'd take Kate to San Gimignano today, he thought, and headed for the terrace.

In the evenings, everyone gathered in the living room to watch *Celebrity Cell Block*. By now they were hooked on it. Vanessa continued to pursue Tessa, who clearly wasn't as up for it as she liked everyone to think.

Tessa soon managed to piss everyone off and it was no surprise to anyone when her fellow inmates nominated her for 'release' at the first opportunity. The public vote was between her and a clapped-out game-show host, who had made himself hugely unpopular in the prison, by his refusal to take part in the chores, and with the public through his sheer lack of personality.

The day after the nominations, Owen came into the kitchen when Kate was making lunch. 'Kate, have you got your mobile with you?' he asked, looking shiftily to the door.

'Yes.'

'Do me a favour?' he asked, pulling a slip of paper out of his pocket and handing it to her. 'Text "Len" to this number as often as you can – just keep sending it all day.'

Len was the hapless game-show host on *Celebrity Cell Block*, Tessa's rival for release. This was evidently Owen's way of keeping Tessa locked up for the summer.

'Okay, but—'

'Don't worry, we'll take care of your phone bill.' He winked and stalked off, punching numbers into his own mobile as he went.

Later on, sending her umpteenth text of the day, Kate was hoping that Owen would remember his promise and make sure her bill was paid because it was going to be astronomical. She had kept her mobile beside her on the kitchen counter as she worked, stopping every so often to resend the message.

'Hi, Kate!'

She jumped guiltily. She was standing at the sink, washing and hulling strawberries and hadn't heard Rory come in. Glancing at her phone, she was relieved to see that the message was sent and the text had disappeared from the screen. 'Hi, Rory.' She smiled at him, then turned back to the sink.

He took a can of beer out of the fridge and opened it, but instead of going away, he stood where he was, drinking. Kate could feel him stare at her. She turned and looked at him questioningly. 'Why don't *you* do something about Will?' he said suddenly.

'Sorry?' Kate was stalling for time. She had heard him perfectly, and he knew it: he was regarding her with amusement.

'Will,' he repeated quietly. 'You're crazy about him,' he said mat-ter-of-factly. 'Why don't you do something about it?'

Oh, God, was it that obvious? Kate was horrified. She turned back to the sink, busying herself with the strawberries while she considered how to answer him. She could pretend she didn't know what he was talking about. No. Attack was the best form of defence. 'Why don't you do something about Louise?' she asked, facing him. She had spoken on the spur of the moment, but she regretted it as the shutters came down on his already guarded face. For what seemed like minutes he said nothing, just gazed at her through narrowed eyes, like Clint Eastwood sizing up the enemy, leaving Kate feeling like a very unlucky punk.

Then, slowly, a slight smile was playing around his lips. '*Touché*,' he said softly, with grudging respect. Admitting defeat, his smile broadened, the lines around his eyes creasing.

Kate was emboldened. 'No really,' she said, stopping what she was doing and drying her hands on her apron to give him her full attention. 'Why *don't* you do something about it?'

Rory paused. 'I'm just a scumbag to her,' he said, and took a slug of beer.

'I'm sure Louise doesn't think that!' Kate was aghast.

'I don't mean that's what she thinks, so much as . . . Well, she knows I'm just a scumbag,' he said, with affected indifference. But Kate had seen the hurt beneath the gruff exterior – the eyes not able to meet hers, the flinch as he had spoken, as though it pained him even to acknowledge what he felt by saying it out loud. 'I mean, what would a girl like Louise have in common with someone like me? Louise is really smart,' he said, the worshipful expression in his eyes again as he talked about her. 'She's been to college, she's got a degree – actually, she's got two. I didn't even finish school – and most of the time when I was supposed to be there I was bunking off. Her father's a judge, for fuck's sake! If I wasn't in this band, I'd probably be up before him for stealing cars or something.'

'But you *are* in this band, you're not a car thief and you've done something with your life – something really amazing. Anyway, you're a rock star,' Kate continued, when Rory looked unconvinced. 'That trumps class, surely.'

'Maybe.' Rory shrugged. 'Maybe if I met her now . . . But Louise has been with us from the start. She knew me before I was famous.'

'When you were just a scumbag?' Kate joked.

'Exactly.' Rory laughed, relaxing. 'Anyway, you haven't answered my question. I've shown you mine, now you have to show me yours.'

'Will has a girlfriend.'

'Yes – Tina Roche-by-name-roach-by-nature,' Rory mocked. 'You could take her,' he said, sizing up Kate with prize-fighter's eyes.

'And I've got a boyfriend,' she continued, returning to her strawberries, partly to hide her smile. She felt ridiculously pleased that Rory didn't think much of Tina.

'You could dump him.'

Kate sighed. 'The fact is, Will doesn't feel the same way.'

'Could have fooled me.'

'He loves me like a sister,' Kate told him.

Rory regarded her sceptically. 'If I thought that was true, I'd fucking paste him,' he said.

'What?'

'Only fucking hillbillies look at their sisters like that.'

'Like what?'

Rory opened his eyes wide, stuck out his tongue and slavered. Draining the last of his beer, he threw the bottle into the bin and headed out of the door.

'He does not!' Laughing, Kate lobbed a tea towel at his retreating back.

Will gave out the wrong signals, that was all – that was what everyone was seeing. She had fallen for it herself, years ago. He had always been quite flirty with her – she'd thought he might even fancy her a bit. And then that night of the Trinity Ball . . .

It seemed so unreal now that she sometimes doubted it had happened. Now and again when she was out in the car with Will or working with him in the kitchen she looked at his hands, marvelling at the thought that they had once touched her. She tried to imagine those long, slender fingers on her skin, his tongue in her mouth, the weight of his body on hers. If only she could have bottled it, she thought sadly, so she could take it out and experience it all over again.

She couldn't allow herself to start believing he might love her. They were friends, and she had to be content with that. It was better than nothing.

*

The last Friday in July was Will's birthday. Kate had been aware of the date approaching and had planned to make him a special dinner with all his favourite food. Grace had sent his presents to her to give him on the day – and recently another had arrived.

'Just came across this and had to send it to Will,' the covering note read. It looked like a CD, which struck Kate as an odd thing to give Will, but on the morning of his birthday she presented it to him with the other gifts and cards, including one from herself. He seemed pleasantly surprised that she had remembered, and Kate was reminded of how touchingly delighted he had been by the fuss they had made of him on his birthday the year he had lived with them.

Passing the study later, she found him opening his presents. He had just pulled out the CD and was holding it at arm's length, looking at it as though it were a ticking bomb. And no wonder. Peering over his shoulder, Kate saw that it was homemade and recognised her mother's handwriting on the blank case. 'Mum made you a compilation CD?' she asked in amazement. Her mother must be losing her marbles.

'No.' Will laughed uneasily.

'Oh God, it's not a demo from one of her friends' kids, is it?'

'No, it's a DVD – a programme she recorded from the TV for me.' He handed the case to Kate.

'Oh!' she exclaimed, reading her mother's dramatic scrawl. *On the Couch with Sir Philip Sargent.* Below that there was a date, about two weeks previously. Kate was familiar with the programme. *On the Couch* was an acclaimed series of in-depth interviews by Richard Slater, a renowned psychiatrist who also had a distinguished career as a broadcaster. The interviews were probing, intensely personal and often painfully revealing dissections of his subjects.

'She doesn't give up, does she?'

Will took the DVD back from her, continuing to stare at it dubiously.

'Are you going to watch it?' she asked tentatively.

Will looked up at her. 'Yes, I am,' he said.

'Really?' Kate beamed.

'Yes, of course. Actually . . .'

'Yes?'

'Antonia . . .' He said the name carefully, but Kate saw the sad, haunted look in his eyes. 'Antonia's asked me to go to a surprise sixtieth birthday party for my father.'

Antonia Bell was the actress his father had run off with.

'And . . . you're thinking of going?'

'I'm thinking about it, yes,' he said carefully, running his fingers along the edge of his desk. 'It's not for ages yet – not 'til November.' He didn't know why he was telling her this. He hadn't intended to mention it to anyone – certainly not any of the O'Neills. He didn't want to be pressured into anything. But he suddenly found he desperately wanted Kate to think well of him.

'Don't tell Grace,' he said.

'I won't tell a soul,' Kate promised. The last thing Will needed was her mother getting over-excited about it and railroading him into something before he was ready.

'I may not go,' he said. 'I haven't decided yet.'

'I know.' Kate nodded, but she couldn't stop smiling. 'Well, I'll see you later – happy birthday again.'

As she left the room, Will found he couldn't stop smiling either. It felt good to have Kate's approval. If his father was here right now he'd be in danger of making up with him just to please her.

Once Will had closeted himself in the study, Kate got Franco to drive her to Florence to buy food for dinner. Returning home mid-afternoon, she was glad to find that he had gone out. That was a stroke of luck. Hopefully, she'd have time to get everything ready before he returned so it would be a complete surprise. She spent the afternoon cooking and anticipating Will's pleasure at dinner. When she had done as much of the preparation as she could, she started on the *piéce de résistance* – the dense, fudgy, chocolate birthday cake. She had even managed to find candles, and she had bought balloons and ribbons in Florence to decorate the table.

As the afternoon wore on and there was no sign of him, she began to worry that he wouldn't be back in time for dinner. She was folding melted chocolate into whisked egg whites and watching the mixture marble when Owen wandered in. 'What are you making?' he asked.

'Smells great!'

'Chocolate cake,' she told him, licking a finger.

He was standing so close that their bodies touched when she turned, but Owen didn't move. 'You missed a bit,' he said, taking Kate's hand and sucking off the chocolate in a very suggestive way. 'Mmm, gorgeous.' His dark eyes locked with hers, as brown and melting as the chocolate. He was so close she could smell the sun on his skin.

Suddenly Kate felt hot and flustered. 'It's a birthday cake for Will,' she said, returning to the bowl. 'You know it's his birthday today?'

'Oh, haven't you heard?'

'What?' Kate asked, turning back to him.

'I thought you knew,' Owen said, his smile fading. He was looking at her warily now.

'Knew what?'

'Well, it's just that Tina flew in to surprise him and she's taking him out for his birthday dinner. He's gone to meet her in Florence. I think he'll stay overnight.'

'Oh!' Kate struggled to sound normal, but she felt as if she'd been punched in the stomach. And the worst of it was, Owen was looking right at her. He must see how she was feeling. She could feel her face crumpling and there was nothing she could do to stop it.

She turned back to the cake mixture, intent on folding in the rest of the chocolate, furiously blinking away the tears that welled in her eyes. What's there to cry about anyway? she scolded herself, trying to pull herself together, and clutched the spoon so tightly she thought it might snap. It's only a stupid cake, a stupid dinner. When are you ever going to learn? You *know* Will has a girlfriend, you *know* it's not you. Of course he's going out with Tina on his birthday. What could be more normal?

She wanted to say something cheery to Owen to make him go away so she could bawl her eyes out in peace, but the tears were tearing at her throat. Her face caved in and a sob she tried to swallow emerged as a muffled squeak.

'Hey!' Owen said softly, placing warm hands on her shoulders and turning her to face him.

Mortified, Kate couldn't look him in the eye. 'Sorry,' she sobbed brokenly to the floor. 'This is ridiculous.'

'Ssh,' Owen whispered, wiping away the tears with his thumb. He pulled her into his arms, stroking her hair.

His kindness was the last straw and Kate clung to him, burying her face in his neck. He smelled of sunshine and weed, mixed with musky aftershave. His hand stroked her back soothingly.

Eventually the tears subsided and she regained control of herself. 'Sorry,' she said, wiping her eyes with the back of her hand. 'I don't know why I'm crying, really.' She sniffed, trying to smile. 'It's just—' She felt such an idiot, so exposed.

'Hey, it's perfectly understandable. You've gone to all this trouble,' Owen jerked a thumb at the food, 'and the least the stupid sod could have done is let you know he wouldn't be here.'

Kate nodded. She knew he was being kind and that he didn't believe for a moment she was crying over the food, but she was grateful to him for saving her face.

'Hey, I know something that'll cheer us up,' Owen said, grinning down at her. 'Wait here.' He darted out of the kitchen. Kate went to the sink, splashed cold water on her face and dried it with kitchen paper.

Moments later, Owen was back, wielding the biggest bag of weed Kate had ever seen. 'Let's spice up Will's birthday cake,' he said, brandishing it triumphantly. He was already hovering over the mixing bowl, opening the bag and about to tip the contents into the mixture.

'Wait! You can't put it straight in – we need to grind it up first.' She lifted the lid of the food processor.

'How much do you think we need?' Owen asked, tipping in a generous quantity of the buds.

'I don't know. They don't teach you hash cake in cooking school.'

'Hmmm. I don't suppose Delia has a recipe for it either. Still, you seem to know what you're doing.'

'Not really. I've only made hash cakes once in my life, and I had a recipe.'

Kate had ground the buds to fine powder, which she blended now into some melted butter. They both gazed into the pan dubiously, wondering about the amount. Kate knew the principles of hash cooking, but had no idea of the required quantity.

'Stir it in and we'll see how it looks,' Owen instructed. He stood beside her as she did so, watching the process carefully.

'Maybe we should do a bit more, just to be on the safe side,' he said, tipping another large amount into the food processor.

When all the cannabis had dissolved into the butter, she folded the mixture into the chocolate. There probably wasn't much chance of the cake rising now, she thought, as she poured the batter into a tin and put it into the oven – but it would be jolly nice anyway.

'How long will it take?' Owen asked, rubbing his hands eagerly.

'About forty-five minutes.'

'Can't wait.'

That evening, Phoenix, Georgie, Owen and Rory rallied around Kate. They insisted on going ahead with Will's party in his absence. Owen and Georgie blew up the balloons and decorated the table, and they all went out of their way to entertain her. Phoenix was more talkative than she'd ever known him, making her laugh with wildly indiscreet stories about famous fellow musicians and backstage shenanigans.

Everyone was so kind and solicitous that Kate suspected Owen had told them how cut up she had been about Will not turning up for dinner. By now they probably knew about her crush on their manager, but suddenly she found she didn't mind. They were so lovely and sympathetic, making it clear they were on her side and enthusing extravagantly about the food. Even Georgie had second helpings.

'Poor Will,' Rory said. 'He doesn't know what he's missing.' The way he smiled at her made her think he didn't just mean the food.

'Yeah,' Owen said. 'Right now he's probably watching Tina tucking into a salad leaf that cost twenty euro.'

'I bet he wishes he was with us,' Georgie said. 'Tina's such a pain in the arse.'

'She used to be all right,' Phoenix said, 'but she's changed.'

'Too much blow, that's her problem,' Owen said. 'And we all know how Will feels about that.'

Everyone enjoyed Will's birthday dinner, but the hash cake was the hit of the evening. Kate pushed all the candles into it and lit them, almost setting fire to her hair twice. The top of the cake was covered with them and more stuck out at jaunty angles from the sides.

'Jaysus!' Owen exclaimed, when Kate produced it. 'How the fuck old *is* Will?'

'I just thought I might as well use all the candles.'

'We could just sit back and inhale the cake.' Phoenix laughed.

They sang a drunken chorus of 'Happy Birthday' to the absent Will, and all joined in blowing out the candles.

'Dynamite cake, Kate,' Phoenix said, taking a huge bite.

'Well, I can't take all the credit – Owen helped.'

'Wow! It tastes pretty strong,' Rory said, through a mouthful.

Owen fed cake to Kate, breaking pieces off and pushing them into her mouth, his fingers lingering on her lips, gathering crumbs from around her mouth and licking them off.

God, he's sexy, Kate thought.

'Put her down, Owen,' Rory said wearily.

After about an hour, the cake kicked in, which coincided with the evening's episode of *Celebrity Cell Block*. Never had it seemed so hilarious. They booed and hissed when Vanessa King appeared, throwing things at the screen, and screamed with laughter when Tessa turned up in the video-diary room, washed out and haggard after another night on lesbian alert, hissing that she was ready to go home and begging to be voted off the show.

At recreation, Vanessa entertained her fellow inmates by performing fellatio on a bottle of water, deliberately making a show of drinking the water at the end.

'You swallow!' a man exclaimed admiringly.

'Always.' She smiled seductively.

'Does Tessa swallow?' Owen asked Rory.

'No. She doesn't know how many calories there are in it.'

Owen laughed.

'Or whether it counts as protein or carbs,' Rory added.

It was eviction night. As usual, Tessa was up for release and, as usual, she won a reprieve, to the obvious dismay of the presenter. In fact, she didn't stand a chance. Owen's 'texting for Tessa' campaign had continued apace all week. He had got everyone in on the act, and it sounded like a Clangers convention around the pool sometimes, everyone beeping away on their mobiles to keep Tessa incarcerated. When the result was announced, she made a half-hearted effort at jumping for joy.

'Poor Tessa,' Rory said. But Kate had a sneaking suspicion that he had joined in the texting campaign. Or maybe he was just being a supportive boyfriend, trying to help her win, she thought, giving him the benefit of the doubt.

Will wasn't enjoying his birthday. What's the matter with me? he thought, as he toyed with his langoustines. Tina had taken him to a Michelin-starred restaurant, one of the most expensive in Florence. The food was ambrosial, the atmosphere sublime, he was with the most stunning woman in the room, and she had booked a room for them later at one of Florence's top hotels. It was most men's fantasy date. But all he wanted was to be back at the villa eating pizza in the living room with Kate and the others while they laughed themselves silly over *Celebrity Cell Block*.

He knew he was being an ungrateful sod. Tina was incredibly beautiful and desirable, every inch of her skin polished and luminous, her hair a lustrous curtain of silk. But he couldn't help wondering if it was for him or for the paparazzi who would be waiting outside to ambush them. He wished Tina could take him out for his birthday without turning it into a photo opportunity.

Looking at her now across the table, he tried to remember why they had got together in the first place. It hadn't always been like this. There was sexual attraction, of course, but it wasn't just that – they used to have fun. He wondered what had happened to the cool girl who was happy to traipse around the world with him and the band, the party girl who would dance until dawn and DJ into the small hours. He didn't know when she had changed, but somewhere along the way the carefree, hedonistic rock chick he had known had been replaced by a shrewd, controlling businesswoman who believed her own publicity and took herself way too seriously. He wondered when they had drifted so far apart and found himself not caring much about the answer. The fact was that they had.

Nowadays he found her hard-headed, arrogant and aggressive. Most of the time she simply irritated him – like now, he thought, as she raked her hand through her hair yet again with a jangle of bracelets in a gesture he knew was designed to draw attention to its glossy luxuriance as it tumbled around her shoulders. She seemed to imagine the racket the bangles made was charming, but it set Will's teeth on edge and he was fighting the urge to grab her arms and pin them to the table. 'Is everything okay, Will?' she asked, taking his hand across the table. 'You're very quiet.'

He felt like a heel. He wasn't being fair to her. She had surprised him by flying in for his birthday and brought him to this lovely place, and he was being sullen and churlish, acting like a spoilt brat. He hated to admit it, but he had been annoyed when she'd called out of the blue to tell him that she was in Florence and was taking him out for his birthday. He had been looking forward to spending the evening with Kate and the others.

Determined to cheer up, he smiled at her.

'Yes, everything's great. This place is terrific. And I think I'm in there.' He nodded at their waiter, who had been flirting outrageously with him all evening. 'It's nice to know I can still pull.'

Tina just looked cross. 'You should report him to the manager,' she said indignantly. 'He's making you feel uncomfortable.'

'No, he's not. I was joking,' Will said.

'But it's so *rude*!' Tina fumed. 'He can see you're with me. It's not what you expect in a place like this.'

Kate would have laughed, Will thought glumly.

Back at the villa, everyone had drifted out onto the terrace to sit around drinking and smoking over the remains of the dinner.

'Is there any more food?' Rory asked, scraping up the last of the dauphinoise potatoes. 'I'm starving.'

Not satisfied with the hash cake, Owen and Georgie were sharing a gigantic spliff.

'How do you think I'd look with dreadlocks?' Owen mused, exhaling the aromatic smoke.

'Shite,' Rory told him.

'I think you'd look lovely,' Georgie giggled, passing the spliff back to him.

'I'm thinking of becoming a Rastafarian.'

'There's more to it than growing dreadlocks,' Phoenix said.

'I know. There's also the hat – but I've already got that. And smoking *ganja*,' he added, in a Jamaican accent, waving his spliff in the air.

'You can't just get a hat and be a Rastafarian, you twat!' Rory scoffed.

'Why not?' Owen asked. 'Phoenix got a haircut and became a Buddhist.'

'I'm not a Buddhist any more.' Phoenix popped a cold mushroom into his mouth. 'I didn't like their position on sex.'

'Which position was that, then? Missionary?'

'Worse! Basically you're not supposed to have any except to have kids.'

'Christ! Where does that leave you if you're shooting blanks?'

'Exactly. Are there any more potatoes, Kate?'

Kate shook her head. 'We've eaten everything. I'll make more food,' she said, getting up and heading into the kitchen. She had the munchies too. She put a pot of water on to boil and poured herself a bowl of cereal to eat while she waited for the pasta to cook.

'Tina!' shrieked a high-pitched voice beside their table. It was Giovanni Santo, a designer, with Kirstie Long, a very young, very beautiful Hollywood wild child, and her latest squeeze, Peter Hunt, who was just about the biggest actor on the planet at the moment.

'Tina, how fabulous to see you!'

Will was almost suffocated in a waft of expensive perfume as everyone was introduced in a flurry of air kisses. As his heart sank, Tina's face lit up. Soon the newcomers had grabbed chairs and were sitting around their table, trading gossip about mutual friends – who'd got fat, who'd got thin, who'd got married, who'd got whom. Will realised sadly that Tina hadn't been so animated all night.

'Giovanni's going to take us to a really cool club he knows,' Kirstie said brightly. 'Why don't you come with us?'

Tina couldn't hide her eagerness, but she consulted Will. 'Well, I don't know – what do you think?'

The last thing Will felt like doing was going to a club with a bunch of strangers, but he had no great desire to be alone with Tina either. 'Sure, why not?'

'There are paparazzi out front,' Kirstie warned, glancing warily towards the door. 'We're going out the back. You can join us if you like.'

Tina tried to act cool but barely hesitated. 'Oh, we'll go out the front,' she said, affecting recklessness. 'Give the buggers something for their editors.'

If Freddie could see me now, Kate thought woozily, slow-dancing with Phoenix by the pool. She couldn't believe she was swaying in the arms of one of the biggest icons of her generation under a star-studded Tuscan sky. It felt surreal – the effect heightened by the amount of alcohol and cannabis she had ingested over the course of the evening.

Bolstered by copious amounts of cereal, followed by big bowls of the spaghetti with garlic and chilli that Kate had rustled up, they had turned the music up full blast and continued the party on the terrace. Kate was having the time of her life. Owen, Rory and even Phoenix were flirting like mad with her, and being the object of so much male attention made her feel sexy and powerful. Not that she was taking it seriously – no doubt they were missing their partners and, being the only female around who wasn't family, she became the focus of all that stray sexual energy by default. It was harmless fun and it made her feel good.

Owen grabbed her as the music changed to a bouncy pop song, a Motown classic. Giggling, they tried out some ironic sixties dance moves, making swimming motions with their arms and holding their noses to dive underwater. The next track was a cheesy love song, a huge summer hit for a manufactured boyband. 'Whose MP3 is this?' Owen asked disdainfully.

'Um . . . mine,' Kate confessed, cursing herself for having put it on random shuffle rather than selecting a cool playlist.

'Tossers!' Owen said, and Kate remembered that this particular boyband had beaten Walking Wounded's last single to the top of the charts, which made it a lapse in diplomacy as well as taste.

'We'll forgive you this once,' Phoenix called, as he went into the house to skip the track. A few moments later, Kate was relieved to hear a Walking Wounded song pour out of the speakers.

'Glad your taste isn't completely shite.' Owen smiled.

She kicked off her shoes and her dancing became wilder and more abandoned. After a while she became aware that the others had drifted away, and it was just her and Owen. Inhibitions cast aside, she gyrated sensually to the pulsating beat. Weaving perilously close to the pool, she smouldered at Owen. She was a goddess! She was rock and roll! She was sex on legs!

Seconds later, she was sex without legs. Her foot slipped on a wet patch and, with a sick feeling, she windmilled her arms frantically in an effort to save herself, but it was useless. She plunged into the pool, the sudden cold of the water leaving her gasping. Panicking, she flailed about wildly until she came spluttering to the surface. She didn't want to be so rock and roll that she ended face down in the band's swimming pool, her blood pumped full of alcohol and drugs. When she surfaced, Owen was hunkered down at the edge, extending his hand to her. She grabbed it and he pulled her out, coughing, her hair plastered to her head, her dress clinging to her body, snapping back like elastic when she pulled it away from her.

'Better get you out of those wet things.' Owen's eyes gleamed wickedly.

Kate grinned at him and began to undo her zip, turning her back to peel off her dress. Holding it out at arm's length, like a striptease artist, she let it drop into the pool, smiling coyly at him over her shoulder. Privately, she thanked her lucky stars that she had left all her old underwear at home and had only brought the glamorous new stuff she had got on her shopping expedition with her mum and Rachel. She felt exhilaratingly confident standing in front of Owen in just her bra and knickers.

'You'll have to give me your shirt,' she said, grinning mischievously at him over her shoulder.

Owen's eyes lit up and he tore it off, then handed it to her. She took it from him without turning around and shrugged into it, buttoning it as she faced him. Reaching halfway down her thighs, the soft white cotton, still warm and smelling of him, was already damp and transparent in places where it stuck to her wet body.

'That's better,' she said, pulling her hair free of the collar and shaking it loose. 'I needed to get into something warm and dry.'

'I need to get into something warm and wet.' His eyes darkened as he pulled her to him, toying with tendrils of her hair, which was already curling into snaky ringlets.

A shock of white-hot lust shot through her as those dark eyes locked with hers. This was the best night ever!

This is the worst birthday ever, Will thought, looking at his watch for the umpteenth time. It was three a.m., but there was no prospect of leaving any time soon. Seated alone at a table, surveying the scene with bored detachment, the heavy throb of the music pounding in his ears, he was desperate to escape. The glitzy throng, packed into the hot, overcrowded VIP room of the club Giovanni had brought them to, exuded wealth and privilege. Everywhere he looked he saw acres of pampered, toned flesh, polished hair, designer clothes and sparkling jewellery.

On the opposite side of the room a young hip-hop mob swarmed around a group of tables along the wall. The men resembled a motley crew of successful pimps and wealthy sports players, flashy furs and chunky diamonds mingling with football shirts, baseball caps and fat, gleaming white sneakers. The women all had endless legs emphasised by spiky heels, their luminescent flesh spilling voluptuously out of spangly micro-dresses that barely contained their generous curves. Everything about them seemed to glow, from their dewy skin, in various shades of honey and caramel, to their glossy black hair and dazzling gems.

The dance floor was a sea of writhing bodies, fuelled by cocaine and Cristal. Tina was among them, having abandoned him almost immediately on arrival to schmooze the A-list celebrities. At least she was happy, he thought. She had pulled off a great coup in arriving with Kirstie and Peter, the hottest couple in the world, and she was making the most of it. This was the sort of thing she really cared about, he thought. He felt he hardly knew her any more. He didn't know if he or she had changed – perhaps they both had.

Watching her partying, he felt resentful and a bit sorry for himself. After all, it was his birthday. She was supposed to have planned this evening as a surprise for him, but she wasn't giving a thought to what he wanted. She didn't even seem to realise that he wasn't enjoying himself.

As he watched, the homies across the room parted and he glimpsed 2Tone, a globally famous rapper, sitting in the centre of the group, a still, calm figure amid all the swagger and bravado. 2Tone – Tony to his friends – had supported Walking Wounded on an early tour. Will remembered him as a quiet, almost shy boy with old-fashioned American manners and a friendly, easy going disposition completely at odds with his aggressive public persona.

Spotting Will, Tony gave him a broad grin and ambled over to join him. Will was glad of the company. He liked Tony. His career had gone supernova since he had toured with Walking Wounded, but he was still the same unexpectedly quiet, unassuming character, with none of the flashiness of the strutting peacocks that surrounded him. He was good company, entertaining, droll and witty, and as they chatted, Will found himself laughing for the first time that evening.

'Are you here on your own?' Tony asked after a while.

'I'm with Tina.' Will nodded to her on the dance floor.

'She know that?' Tony smiled sardonically.

She does now, Will thought. She had spotted him with Tony and was weaving her way back to him. At the same time, Tony's friends, jealous of his company and curious about anyone he would cross a room to speak to, were gravitating to where he was sitting with Will and reassembling around his table. With Tina now happily ensconced among Tony's crowd, Will took the opportunity to make his escape. Pleading that he had work to do in the morning and needed some sleep, he asked if she would mind if he left. He might have been hurt by her readiness to let him go if he hadn't been so relieved.

'I'll be in town again in a few weeks for my birthday,' she said, kissing him. 'I'll make it up to you then.'

Stepping out into the Florentine night, Will took a deep breath. Fresh air had never felt so good. He must be getting old, he thought. He wanted nothing more than to sleep in his own bed, wake up at the villa and have breakfast with Kate in the morning.

Somehow, Kate had ended up alone in the studio with Owen. She wasn't too sure how she had got there, but she had a vague recollection of professing a lifelong desire to be in a band. Owen had grabbed her hand and they had run here together, leaving Phoenix, Georgie and Rory raiding the kitchen again. Now he was plugging an electric guitar into an amp and placing it over her head, spending an inordinate amount of time adjusting the strap across her breasts.

Trying out a chord, Kate was thrilled at the power of the sound she produced with the merest touch of her fingers. She thrashed the strings, dancing around in what she felt was a very rock-goddess kind of way.

'It sounds shite,' Owen roared, above the din, 'but you look totally brilliant.'

Getting up from his position on the floor, he put his hand over hers, stilling her fingers.

'That's enough of that,' he said softly, his eyes boring into hers and turning her legs to jelly. He lifted the guitar over her head and put it down. Then he placed his hands on her shoulders and pushed her gently against the wall.

Will found the villa in a shambles, lights blazing, doors thrown open and music blaring. His first thought was that the place had been ransacked. All sorts of scenarios flashed across his mind – kidnappers, crazed fans, enraged fathers whose daughters Owen had ravished. But it didn't take him long to recognise the signs of a party and to realise that it was just business as usual. The kitchen looked as if it had been raided by a family of rampaging bears. Cereal boxes were torn open, spewing their contents onto the work surfaces, which were covered in dishes of half-eaten spaghetti. In the living room the floor was scattered with popcorn, cake crumbs and bottles, and the TV was still fizzing away in the corner, competing with the speakers from the sound system.

He turned off the TV and the stereo and began to pick things up. When he bent to collect an empty beer bottle from the floor, he glimpsed something out of the corner of his eye that made his blood run cold and his heart pound. Straightening, breathless with dread, he looked out through the open doors to the terrace. His heart leaped into his mouth – something red was bobbing around in the swimming-pool. It was Kate – he recognised the dress immediately.

And she seemed to be floating lifelessly, drifting to and fro with the lap of the water against the filters.

Barely able to breathe, he forced himself to move towards the pool on leaden legs, heart hammering. It must only have been seconds before he reached the edge, but it felt like a lifetime. Then, looking down, he gave an almost hysterical shout of laughter when he saw that Kate's dress was unoccupied by its owner. Weak from shock, he exhaled and sank to his knees. He rubbed his face with shaking hands, trying to dispel the horrific images that were still flashing through his mind.

He fished the dress out of the water, automatically wrung it out and spread it out on a nearby sun-lounger to dry. Weariness overcame him as the adrenalin abated, and he stayed where he was, smoothing the material absently with his fingers. He remembered how gorgeous Kate had looked in it the other night – and wondered why she had taken it off out here and thrown it into the pool.

Once he had grasped the fact that Kate hadn't drowned, relief was followed by anger. If Kate was there now he would have been torn between the desire to kiss her senseless and the impulse to throttle her.

In the studio, Owen had Kate pinned against the wall. 'You're so sexy, Kate,' he muttered, stroking her mouth seductively.

'So are you!' Kate breathed, laying a hand on his taut, tanned chest and feeling his heart jump against her palm.

He bent his head towards her, sooty lashes closing over those melting brown eyes. Then he was kissing her, his tongue darting in and out of her mouth while his hands stroked her body, brushing the sides of her breasts, his thumbs grazing her nipples, which leaped into life.

I'm kissing Owen Cassidy, Kate told herself, trying to feel the appropriate level of excitement. He really was an amazing kisser – all that practice had certainly paid off.

She gasped as she felt his warm hand against her thigh. The other was sliding inside the open V of the shirt, and Kate's head rolled back as his fingers found her breast.

Lifting his head, Owen fished in his pocket and held out his palm with two little white pills in it. 'Have you ever made love on E?'

Kate shook her head.

'Really?' Owen seemed amazed. 'You've got to try it,' he said, putting a pill into her hand. 'It's incredible.' He popped the other into his mouth.

Kate looked at it uncertainly. She didn't want him to think she was a prude, but she was a wimp where drugs were concerned. She was always afraid she would be the one person in a million who would keel over and die from a heart-attack the first time she tried something.

'Go on,' Owen urged. 'You'll love it. Nothing bad will happen to you, I promise.' He was kissing her face again, his thumb stroking her ear erotically.

Suddenly the room was flooded with light. 'What the fuck is going on here?' a harsh voice rasped.

Kate opened her eyes groggily to see Will in the doorway, like an avenging demon. She felt as if a bucket of cold water had been thrown over her.

His eyes darted to the pill in her hand.

'*What* did you give her?' he rounded on Owen, eyes flinty.

'Nothing.'

'What did you give her?' Will demanded, his tone menacing.

'It's just an E,' Owen admitted.

'Christ, Owen!' Will snatched the pill from Kate's hand and hurled it across the room. 'What the hell are you doing?' he raged at Owen. Kate had never seen him so furious.

'I was doing quite well until you turned up.' Owen tried to make light of the situation.

But Will was not amused. 'Jesus, I leave you alone for *one fucking day* and all hell breaks loose! The kitchen looks like a bomb hit it!' he roared at Kate. 'And you're supposed to be here to work,' he yelled at Owen, 'not to get high and get laid! You could do that at home, for fuck's sake! I've got the record company on my back about the new album. I'm buying you time every day so you don't have to put out a piece of shit. I bring you here so you can concentrate on it, and all you can do is fuck around!'

'Hey, chill, man!' Owen smiled nervously. He had never seen Will so wound up – not even when he'd got stoned at the Brit Awards, danced bullock-naked on the table and asked the head of their record company to give him a blow job.

'That's not fair! Owen's been working bloody hard,' Kate protested, emboldened by the weed and booze she'd had earlier.

But she only succeeded in drawing his wrath on herself. 'And *you*,' he said, turning to her, '*you're* supposed to be here to work not to – to get your tits out for the lads,' he spat, his lip curling contemptuously.

Kate was speechless. She had never seen Will like this, and it was terrifying. He was incandescent with rage. She couldn't believe he was speaking to her like this.

He seized the advantage. 'Christ, Kate,' he was looking at her as though she was something unpleasant he had stepped in, 'I never took *you* for a star-fucker!'

'What?' Kate gasped.

He was looking at her with malice in his eyes, clearly taking spiteful pleasure in the shock and hurt that registered in her face. Struggling not to cry, she took a deep breath and looked him in the eye.

'Fuck you!' she said quietly, keeping her voice steady with a tremendous effort of will. 'I quit.' With all the dignity she could muster, she brushed past him and stalked out of the room.

This brought Will to his senses. He blinked hard, as if he was waking up from a dream. 'Kate, wait,' he called after her, but it was too late.

'Jesus, what have I done?' He sank onto a bench and buried his head in his hands.

Owen sat down beside him and lit a spliff.

'Sorry, Owen. I had no right to speak to you like that,' Will said quietly, his shoulders slumped. As his fury abated, the realisation of what he had said in the heat of the moment dawned on him. 'I don't know what got into me.'

'You should have told me she was spoken for, man,' Owen said softly. 'I'd have steered clear.'

'Since when did that ever stop *you*?' Will said. 'Anyway, you know Kate's spoken for – she has a boyfriend at home.'

'Oh, I don't mean that twat,' Owen said airily. 'But I'd have stepped aside for you.'

'For me?' Will looked askance at him. 'I don't know what you're talking about.'

'Whatever you say.' Owen grinned. 'If it's any consolation, Kate was upset because you didn't turn up for dinner. I was just trying to cheer her up.'

'Really?' Will said, brightening. 'She was really upset?' He knew he shouldn't find the idea so cheering but he couldn't help it.

'Yeah, she'd made you this special birthday dinner. She was gutted when I told her you weren't coming back.'

'God, what did I say to her?' Will chewed his thumbnail.

'You called her a star-fucker,' Owen reminded him brutally.

'Oh God.' He tugged at his hair. 'She's going to leave, isn't she?'

'I'd say she's packing her bags as we speak.' Owen held out the spliff to him and, to his surprise, Will took it, had a long, slow drag, then handed it back to him.

'What am I going to do?' Will asked, helplessly.

'If I were you, I'd apologise.'

They walked back into the house together. In the kitchen, Will took off the jacket of his beautifully cut Italian suit jacket, rolled up the sleeves of his shirt and started to clear up.

'What are you doing?' Owen asked.

'I'm not leaving this mess for Maria,' Will told him, loading plates into the dishwasher. 'It's not fair on her.'

'Oh, okay.' Owen began to collect glasses.

'What happened here anyway?' Every pot, glass and piece of cutlery seemed to have been used.

'Like I said, Kate made you this special birthday dinner.'

'*This* was my birthday dinner?' Will eyed the leftover pasta. 'I'm glad I missed it.'

'Oh no, your dinner was gorgeous, and there was a chocolate hash cake. We scoffed the lot, and then we all got the munchies, big-time.'

'So that's when you ate the entire contents of the kitchen.'

'Yes,' Owen smiled sheepishly.

'I can't *believe* Kate made me a hash cake.'

'The hash bit was my idea – I told you, she needed cheering up.'

Will felt chastened. He was appalled at the things he had said to Kate, wincing anew as they flashed across his mind, remembering the wounded look in her luminous green eyes with a fresh stab of guilt. He really didn't know what had got into him. Tina had been getting on his nerves. The record company was on his back about the album. Then he had arrived home, exhausted to find this place trashed. But, deep down, he knew it wasn't any of that. Something had snapped inside him when he had seen Owen and Kate kissing. He had been disappointed – *devastated*. And it had been a shock to realise he felt that way. He ought to have been relieved – after all, he had only asked Kate to come as a favour to Grace, and Owen would suit Grace's purposes just as well as himself.

He had been jealous. It was as simple as that – as simple and ridiculous and pathetic as that. In that moment he had known how he felt about Kate. As he had been belting down the motorway, he had subconsciously been coming home to her. When he had longed for home earlier, it wasn't his house in Dublin he had been thinking of, but this house, these people . . . Kate. But this wasn't his home and Kate wasn't his family. The home he longed for didn't exist.

When they had finished clearing up, Will put his jacket back on. That had been the easy part. Clearing things up with Kate was going to be more difficult. He went outside and picked a flower from the garden – a beautiful big orange thing whose name he didn't know. As he rounded the corner of the house by the pergola, he saw the table, covered with ribbons and streamers, empty wine bottles and some now-flaccid balloons. Once more he was filled with remorse for the things he had said – and childish disappointment at having missed his party.

'Good luck!' Owen called after him, as he went through the kitchen and headed for the stairs. 'Oh, and by the way . . .'

'Yes?' Will turned in the doorway.

'Happy birthday!'

Kate had been stewing in her room since she'd stormed out of the studio. She had thrown herself onto the bed and burst into tears of rage.

How dare Will speak to her like that? How *could* he call her a star-fucker? Her mind was spinning with images of him towering over her, yelling at her. She kept thinking about the things he had said, the stinging contempt in his beautiful eyes. She tried to maintain right-eous indignation – Will had been totally in the wrong, flying off the handle for no reason. She and Owen were both single adults. Well, she *was* engaged to Brian, but Will didn't know that. As far as he was concerned, they had a perfect right to snog each other if they wanted to. But – much as she hated to admit it – she was more hurt than enraged. She couldn't bear Will to think badly of her. She had always felt he liked and respected her, but tonight he had looked at her as though he hated her.

She had pulled her suitcase from under the bed and started fling-ing clothes into it haphazardly. But halfway through she faltered. It was all very well making a grand gesture, but how could she leave without Will's help? She longed to sweep down the stairs with her bags and storm out with her head in the air while Will ran after her, begging her to stay, but where would she go? She couldn't wake Franco at this hour and ask him for a lift. Besides, what if he said no? Will was his employer, after all.

She was sitting on the bed feeling thoroughly hacked off and deflated when there was a tentative knock. 'Kate?' Will called and knocked again.

'Go away!' she shouted.

'Kate, please open the door.'

Sighing heavily, Kate got up, opened the door a chink and peered out at him warily.

'Kate, I am so, *so* sorry,' he said, seeming genuinely remorseful. 'I don't know what came over me.' He held out a flower to her.

'You had no cause to speak to me like that,' she said.

'I know, I know.' He nodded helplessly. 'There's no excuse for it. I'm really sorry.'

'But you called me—'

'Please don't remind me.' Will put up a hand to stop her. 'I'm truly sorry.'

She took the flower.

'Please don't leave,' he said, his eyes on the half-packed suitcase.

Kate followed his gaze to the mess on her bed. She was stalling for time, feeling she ought to make him work harder but knowing she was about to cave in. As she turned back to him, the world seemed to tilt on its axis and she felt as if the floor was rushing up to meet her. Staggering, she grabbed the door for support.

'Kate! Are you okay?' Will grasped her arms to steady her.

'I just feel a bit . . . dizzy,' she said faintly, clinging to him.

Without a word, Will sat her on the bed and pushed her head between her knees. 'Better?' he asked a moment later when she sat up. He was looking anxiously into her face. He's really tired, she thought and nodded, not trusting herself to speak.

'Did you take anything?' he asked urgently.

'No,' Kate croaked. 'I just had too much wine and hash cake.' Tears were making her eyes smart and she bent her head again. She felt so ashamed that she couldn't look him in the eye. He had been right to shout at her, she thought miserably. She was supposed to be helping, making his life easier, but she was just another blithering idiot he had to babysit.

'I'll get you a glass of water,' he said, going into her bathroom.

When he was gone, Kate flopped back on the bed and closed her eyes. Suddenly realising how exhausted she was, she curled up, snuggling into the pillows. If she passed out, at least she wouldn't have to face Will again.

When Will came back, he found Kate conked out on the bed, amid a jumble of clothes, her hair tumbling around her shoulders, her face flushed. He bent over her to listen to her breathing, which sounded reassuringly normal. He pulled a sheet over her and sank down into a chair beside the bed. He sat there for a long time listening to her breathe, watching the soft rise and fall of her chest, trying to come to terms with what he was feeling.

The minute he had seen Kate kissing Owen he had known that he wanted her for himself. He wanted her now. He wanted her with him always. He wanted to share everything with her. He wanted her in his home and he wanted her travelling with him. He wanted to make love to her and sleep with her and wake up with her in the morning. He didn't think he'd ever wanted anything or anyone so much in his life. Somehow, somewhere, he had fallen in love with Kate. It was painful and bloody inconvenient – but he would get over it.

Chapter 9

Kate woke the next morning with a bad case of drunkard's remorse, cringing as flashbacks of last night's drunken antics flooded back: her ridiculous striptease by the pool; her woeful thrashing of Owen's guitar; worst of all, Will bursting in to catch her and Owen snogging. Except that *wasn't* the worst part. She groaned aloud at the memory of almost passing out in Will's arms. She remembered how tired he had looked, anxiously quizzing her about what she had taken – no doubt wondering if he'd have to round off his birthday by carting her off to hospital to have her stomach pumped. Dammit, why couldn't she have been one of those people who just blacked out and remembered nothing the next day?

Eyeing her half-packed suitcase, the idea of a flit had never seemed more appealing. Still, it was too late now, she told herself. She couldn't cower here for ever. She would just have to get up and brazen it out.

In the kitchen she found Maria humming softly to herself as she prepared lunch. Kate had forgotten about Maria and felt a fresh stab of guilt as she remembered the state they'd left the place in last night.

'Kate!' Maria turned, smiling at her sympathetically. 'You okay?' She frowned. 'Will say you no feel so good.'

'Oh no, I'm fine, thanks.' Kate blushed, feeling even worse as she looked around the gleaming kitchen. Poor Maria, it must have taken her hours to clear the place up. 'I'm sorry, I slept it out. Let me do that.'

'No, no, ees fine,' Maria waved her away. 'Will say you have day off. I cook. I make you breakfast – what you like?' She smiled kindly.

'Oh, just some toast.' She didn't want to be a bother, but she wished she could have the kitchen to herself to fry up the entire contents of the fridge – if there was any food left after last night.

Despite her protestations, Maria insisted that Kate sit down while she made her coffee and toast. As she watched the older woman bustle around, it occurred to her that maybe she had been replaced. Perhaps Will was waiting for her to surface so that he could give her her marching orders. She was eating her breakfast and wondering disconsolately if she should go upstairs and finish packing when the door swung open and he came in.

'Oh Kate, you're up.' His eyes were wary. 'Feeling okay?'

'Yes, thanks.' She smiled at him shakily. She wished everyone wouldn't be so solicitous towards her – it made her feel even guiltier. After all, it had been completely self-inflicted.

'Good. Come and see my birthday present from the guys.'

Grateful for the diversion, Kate followed him out to the front of the house. Sitting in the drive was a gleaming red Ferrari with a big silver bow on the bonnet.

'Wow!' Kate wasn't really a car person, but there was no denying the beauty of this thing, all sleek, elegant curves and gleaming bodywork. With its suggestion of barely constrained power, it was sex on wheels. 'It's beautiful!'

'Isn't it?' Will put an arm around her shoulders and gazed at it adoringly. He loved cars. 'It's just been delivered.'

'It's amazing,' Kate said, awed. Privately, she decided it was a good thing Will hadn't turned up for dinner last night – the car made her offering of dinner and a birthday cake seem rather pathetic.

Pulling the bow off the bonnet, he said, 'Come for a spin with me. I can't wait to try it out.'

'But what about lunch? I've already slept through breakfast – if I still work here, that is,' she added tentatively. She couldn't bear the suspense any longer – she had to know where she stood, for better or worse.

'What do you mean?' Will looked perplexed. 'Of course you still work here.'

'Well, I seem to remember quitting last night,' she said to her shoes. 'I didn't mean it.'

'Good . . . Kate, I'm sorry about last night,' he said awkwardly.

'I was going to say the same thing.'

'You? What do you have to be sorry about?'

'Well,' she mumbled, 'like you said, I came here to work, not to—' She broke off, seeing his eyes widen with horror as he thought she was going to repeat what he had said to her last night. 'Not, you know . . . to have fun,' she finished lamely.

'God, Kate, I didn't mean anything I said last night either. I don't know what got into me. I want you to have today off. Maria's already agreed to take over. Come on – I'll buy you a big lunch. If you're up to lunch, that is?'

'Oh God, yes,' Kate breathed, almost tearful with relief. 'The bigger the better.'

'Good. We'll see if we can find somewhere that does pasta by the bucket.' He opened the passenger door for her.

Ecstatic that she seemed to have been forgiven, Kate jumped in. Will sat into the driver's seat and spent a few minutes familiarising himself with the controls. Then he gunned the engine and they roared off down the drive.

Will was thrilled with his new car and was enjoying driving it so much that Kate began to wonder if they would ever stop for lunch. Her spirits lifted every time they came to another town, only to sink again as they roared straight through and out the other side. He was like a kid with a new toy, enthusing about the car's acceleration, handling and hi-tech gadgets, apparently oblivious to Kate's wistful backward glances as they whizzed past quaint roadside inns and zoomed past pavement cafes basking in the sunshine.

'It's an amazing present.' She was glad to see him so happy. 'Did you have a nice birthday?'

'Not especially.' Will smiled at her ruefully. 'I think you all enjoyed it more than I did. I'm sorry I missed my party.'

Last night, in her intoxicated state, it hadn't occurred to her that Will should have been shagging Tina in some plush hotel in Florence instead of coming back to the villa in the small hours to bawl her out. It made her rather glad of the bollocking. 'I thought you were going to stay in Florence.'

'I changed my mind. I wanted to get—' Will stopped. 'I wanted to get back,' he finished.

Kate smiled to herself. She knew she shouldn't be pleased that Will hadn't enjoyed his birthday, but she couldn't help it. She was so glad he hadn't stayed with Tina in Florence. He couldn't be crazy about her – they hadn't seen each other in ages, and he'd had no reason to be back at the villa today.

'Oh, I love this song,' she said suddenly, cranking up the volume to drown the spectacular rumbling of her stomach. She was sorely tempted to ask Will if brakes were included among the Ferrari's amazing features.

Eventually they stopped at a restaurant in an old mill on the out-skirts of a tiny hilltop town. A handful of tables stood in a pretty, shaded courtyard, presided over by an Italian mama whose ample girth augured well for the food. The menu promised exactly the sort of hearty, rustic fare that Kate needed to quell her hangover.

'Hungry?' Will asked, as they perused the menu.

'Starving!' Kate's stomach backed her up with a long, low growl.

'God, sorry.' Will laughed. 'We should have stopped earlier. Well, now we're here, let's have all the courses. We've got plenty of time.'

Taking him at his word, Kate ordered bruschetta, followed by pasta, then lamb with potatoes and spinach. Unable to face wine, she decided to stick to mineral water, to the obvious disapproval of the matronly proprietor, who did a lot of tutting and chuntering when they both eschewed the wine list, seeming to take it as a personal affront as well as a slur on Italian wine. In an attempt to appease her, Kate tried to mime a hangover, at which point Will stepped in. He said something to the woman in rapid Italian, which had a magical effect.

A beatific smile spread across her face and she nodded as she cast a knowing glance at Kate.

'What did you say to her?' she asked Will once the woman was out of earshot.

'I told her you're pregnant.' Will looked very pleased with himself.

'What?' Kate gasped, laughing. 'Why on earth did you tell her *that*?'

'It explains why you're not drinking any wine. And it gives you the perfect excuse to eat for two.'

'Are you the father?' Kate asked.

'Of course.'

'Well, I don't think she approves of you not marrying me. I caught her checking out my ring finger.'

'She'll probably frogmarch us to the nearest church and make me do the decent thing.' Will laughed.

I wouldn't mind, Kate thought longingly. 'Anyway, what's *your* story? Why aren't *you* drinking wine? Are you a recovering alcoholic?'

'Ah, I couldn't drink wine in front of you when you can't have any – wouldn't be fair.'

'That's very nice of you.'

'I thought so. So did she, actually.'

When the proprietor came back with their antipasti, she chatted some more to Will.

'What did she say?' Kate asked Will, when she had bustled off again.

'She asked whether I was hoping for a boy or a girl.'

'And what did you say?'

'I said I don't mind as long as it's healthy,' Will said, reciting the stock reply as if by rote.

'Good answer,' Kate said, grudgingly. 'Standard, but good.'

'Ah, but I also said I'd secretly like a little girl who'd look exactly like her beautiful mother.'

'*Very* good answer.' Kate grinned.

'I can't help it – I'm just crazy about you,' Will said.

God, I wish you weren't joking, Kate thought.

Christ, I wish I was joking, Will thought, aware that he was in

217

serious trouble. He had never felt like this about anyone before in his life, never experienced this bizarre, heady cocktail of emotions that left him feeling scarily off-balance, at once happy and terrified. He had no idea how it had happened or when it had started – he had been right in the middle of it before he knew what had hit him. One thing he was sure of: he didn't *want* to feel this way about Kate. He wanted to go back to thinking of her as Lorcan's little sister, someone he loved as a friend, but nothing more. For starters he could stop this ridiculous flirting every time he was with her.

'So, you and Owen!' he exclaimed heartily – too heartily, he thought. He was trying desperately to sound casual – pleased, even. After all, that was the normal reaction to two people you liked getting together, wasn't it? But it came out way too 'hail fellow well met'.

'Do you like him?' he asked hesitantly. God, he thought disgustedly, I sound like a bloody teenager. Besides, what did it matter to him if she liked Owen or not? Even though he was in love with her, it wasn't as if he intended to do anything about it. He was being ridiculous. What did he expect? That she would always be there waiting for him if he should ever change his mind, ready to resume her teenage crush on him as soon as he clicked his fingers? He would just have to get used to the idea of Kate being with someone else. Why not Owen? At least he was better than that creep Brian. Grace would be pleased. And it couldn't possibly matter to him, he told himself firmly. Still, he found himself waiting with bated breath for her answer.

'Well, yes, of course I like him,' Kate began. 'He's lovely, isn't he?'

'It's just – I mean Owen can be a bit . . .'

God, he's trying to warn me off, Kate thought, horrified. What happened to the light-hearted banter? A moment ago, Will had been flirting with her and now he looked all serious and awkward. Had he brought her here to give her a talking-to about Owen, like she was some troublesome groupie?

'I mean he's great,' Will continued awkwardly, 'but with girls he's not exactly . . .' He trailed off uneasily. 'I just don't want you to get hurt.'

'Oh, don't worry. It's nothing serious, if that's what you mean. I'm not expecting a proposal or anything,' Kate joked.

'I'm sorry, it's none of my business.'

'Last night was just the heat of the moment,' Kate continued. 'We'd both had too much to drink and got a bit carried away. It didn't mean anything.'

It occurred to her that she could almost have been talking about her and Will . . . except that *had* meant something – at least, it had to her.

'Honestly, you don't have to explain yourself to me. I'm sorry if the way I carried on last night gave you the impression that you did. I don't know what got into me,' he said, for the umpteenth time.

'I'm afraid I can't say the same.' Kate smiled wryly. 'I know exactly what got into me – a shedload of alcohol.'

'And the rest,' Will said drily.

'Well, yes, there was the hash cake too,' Kate admitted, 'but I wasn't going to take that ecstasy.'

'I'm glad to hear it – especially in your condition.'

'Who needs ecstasy?' Kate smiled wryly. 'I'm a girl – I pretty much imagine I'm in love with anyone I have sex with as it is.' Suddenly remembering that she had had sex with *him*, Kate blushed. 'Well, not everyone, obviously,' she babbled, back-pedalling furiously. 'Sometimes you have a one-night stand and that's all it is – just fun. I can have meaningless sex as easily as the next girl,' she said, tossing her head airily in her best devil-may-care fashion.

They were both relieved when their conversation was interrupted by the arrival of the next course. Kate seized on the opportunity to change the subject. 'So,' she said, rather wildly, determined to get in before Will could say anything, 'have you thought any more about going to your father's birthday party?'

The moment the words were out of her mouth, she could have bitten out her tongue.

Will's face registered surprise, but he didn't seem angry.

'Yes, I've thought about it,' he said cautiously, forking Parmesan through his pasta. 'I just haven't decided yet.' He opened his mouth as if to say something else, but stopped.

Kate had always tended to dismiss as wishful thinking her mother's belief that Will longed to be reconciled with his father. It would be typical of Grace to decide that was how Will felt because that was how she thought he ought to feel. But now she wasn't so sure. 'What's holding you back?' she probed gently.

He cast her a wary look and seemed to be deciding whether to answer or not. 'I don't want him to think—' He broke off.

'What?' Kate coaxed. 'You can tell me.'

'I don't want him to think I forgive him,' he said, 'because I don't.'

She said nothing.

'Aren't you going to tell me it was all a long time ago?'

'No. What has that got to do with anything?'

'Most people seem to think there's a statute of limitations on these things. Maybe they're right.' He sighed. 'I suppose it's not very attractive to bear a grudge for so long.'

'You can't help how you feel.'

'I could say the words. I could *say* I forgive him, but the fact is, I don't. I can't. It would be like saying it's okay – what he did . . . what happened to mum. And it's not okay. It wasn't okay then, and it hasn't become okay just because time has passed.'

Will sat back. 'And it would seem like such a betrayal,' he added.

'Of your mother,' Kate said softly.

'Yes.'

Kate noticed that Will's eyes held that haunted look again. She wished she could soothe it away for ever. 'But he's your father, Will, and he's a very clever man. I'm sure he'd understand all that. I think he'd just be happy to see you – on any terms.'

'Maybe.' Will was tired of being angry with his father and of keeping up the wall between them. He might not be able to forgive him for the past, but he could stop punishing him for it, which was exhausting and futile, only serving to make him feel more lost and alone. And he was tired of feeling alone. He wished Kate could be there with him when he went to see his father. Pathetically, he wanted her to be there to hold his hand. He wanted her gentle, soothing presence, her calm reassurance, her unconditional support and understanding. Perhaps childishly, he felt that it would be easy if she was there – that she could somehow make everything okay.

By the time they got to dessert, it was late in the day and customers were drifting in for early dinner. The food was delicious and Kate was thoroughly enjoying herself, delighted that Will wasn't put off by her greed. It was so much more fun than listening to Brian's neurotic analysis of every morsel he put into his mouth and his nagging about what she put into hers.

Will enjoyed watching Kate eat with such gusto. It made a welcome change from sitting opposite Tina while she shifted food around on her plate, expertly rearranging it so that it looked like she'd eaten something. For some reason he had never been able to fathom, she liked to perpetuate the myth that she had the appetite of a horse and was given to pigging out regularly on junk food. Apparently there was no kudos is being thin because you starved yourself.

'I hope Maria didn't mind doing the cooking,' Kate said. She was still feeling a bit guilty about being out with Will, especially after last night.

'No, she doesn't. She's very fond of you, you know. Anyway, you deserve a break. You haven't had any time off since you've been here. I didn't mean to be such a slave-driver. I just wasn't thinking.'

'Honestly, I don't need a day off. The job is bliss. I'm enjoying myself so much it's more like a holiday than work. I just wish there were more jobs like it.'

'Any idea what you'll do next?'

'Not really. Of course, Conor thinks I should become a celebrity chef – get on TV and hit the big time.'

'Of course,' Will said. 'He gave me a bollocking about the first single we released off the last album – said it was completely the wrong one.'

Kate laughed. 'That's Conor!'

'Trouble is, he was right.'

'That's the annoying thing – he usually is.'

'So maybe you *should* be a TV chef?'

'No,' Kate shook her head. 'I couldn't bear to be on television. Besides, I hate that whole cooking-as-pornography thing – people sitting at home watching other people doing it on TV instead of doing it themselves. Drooling over food magazines and cookbooks, but never setting foot in their kitchens.'

'I never thought of it in that way.' Will laughed. 'Any other ideas?'

'Well, Brian wants me to be the cook in a retreat centre he wants to open.'

What a waste, Will thought.

'Mum thinks I should get married to someone very important and cook fabulous dinner parties for his important friends and colleagues. Rachel thinks I should cook fabulous dinner parties for *her* husband's important friends and colleagues, which she'll then pretend she did herself.'

'And what do *you* want to do?'

It was nice for a change to be asked what she wanted instead of being told what she should do by her bossy family. Everyone seemed to think they knew what was best for her. 'What I would really love,' she said, 'is to have my own restaurant.'

'Really?' Will was surprised. 'I thought you hated working in restaurants.'

'Ah, but it would be different if it was my own.'

'What sort of place would it be?'

'Much like this, really,' Kate waved her spoon to encompass their surroundings. 'Laid back, unpretentious, with good home style cooking.'

'Sounds great. Tell me more.'

'You'll be sorry you asked. I warn you, I could talk for Ireland about this.'

'No, I'd really like to know.'

Kate didn't need any more encouragement. She had spent so much time fantasising about her own restaurant, it was as if she was describing somewhere that already existed, down to the tiniest detail.

'You obviously haven't given it much thought, then,' Will teased her, when she had finished.

'Oh well, it costs nothing to daydream. The reality is I'll probably wind up cooking macrobiotic smorgasbords for an endless parade of Brian's lost souls.'

'Why don't you do it – the restaurant?'

'I don't have the money, though I have saved a lot since I've been here,' she added, not wanting to appear ungrateful. She had hardly spent a cent since she'd arrived and, true to his word, Will was paying her an outlandish sum, well over the odds. However, she had an awful feeling that Brian would expect her to sink her funds into his growth-centre venture.

'You could borrow,' Will suggested.

'I'm not a very good credit prospect.' Kate smiled regretfully. 'Like I say, most of my jobs don't pay this much.'

'It's not as if you haven't earned it. I don't imagine most of your jobs are so full-on. You haven't had a night off since you got here.'

'What would I do with one? I don't know anyone here except you guys.'

'Well, why don't I take you out for dinner one night – just the two of us?'

'You don't have to do that.'

'But I'd like to – as an apology for my behaviour last night.'

It was on the tip of Kate's tongue to insist once again that she didn't need a night off, but then she realised she was about to turn down the chance to go on the date she'd wanted to be on since she was thirteen. Don't be a chump, she told herself. 'Okay. I'd really like that.'

On the drive back to the villa, Kate noticed that Will was particularly quiet. She hoped she hadn't upset him by bringing up the subject of his father. But he hadn't seemed offended – he was probably just engrossed in his new car.

In fact, Will was mentally cursing himself for whatever impulse had driven him to suggest he take Kate out to dinner. What the hell had he been thinking? He had been fighting a burning desire for her from the moment she had sat into the car beside him. Even now he was uncomfortably aware of her. As she shifted in her seat, he had to battle the compulsion to reach out and touch her smooth brown thigh, revealed when her dress had hitched up a little. The inn where they had had lunch had a few rooms, and he had been fantasising all afternoon about taking Kate to one and spending the rest of the evening discovering if she had the same earthy, enthusiastic approach to sex as she had to food. What had made it almost unbearable was the feeling he had that Kate felt the same – that if he made the slightest move towards her she would more than meet him halfway.

But if something happened today, it would change everything. Neither of them had been drinking so they couldn't plead temporary insanity and brush it off as a drunken aberration. They would have crossed a line. It had been almost impossible, but somehow he had escaped without doing anything irrevocable. He had got himself off the hook – only to put himself in the way of further temptation and set himself up for a night of agony.

Well, there was no going back on it now. He would just have to behave like a bloody Boy Scout on their 'date'. He would be friendly and affectionate in a brotherly way, and he would keep his hands off her. They would have dinner, talk, and then he would drive her home. And that, he told himself firmly, would be that.

At least Tina was due in a couple of weeks. She would take his mind off Kate. He knew it wasn't working between them and he had to break up with her, but now was not the time. She had planned a big birthday bash for herself in Florence at the end of the month, and half of the British Isles were coming over for it, including May Kennedy, her gossip-columnist friend, who would loyally write it up as the party of the year. She had also invited *Wow!* magazine to cover it. He knew that, as far as Tina and everyone else was concerned, he was part of the package, and he was willing to play the loyal boyfriend for another month or so. After all, it wasn't as if he wanted to be free to be with Kate – quite the opposite: he wanted Tina as camouflage, to convince himself and everyone else that she was the sole object of his desire. For once he would be happy to play his half of the golden couple. He hadn't been looking forward to her visit, with the attendant media circus, but now he couldn't wait for her to arrive.

It turned out, he didn't have to. As Will pulled up in front of the villa, the door opened to reveal Tina, looking every inch the goddess in a red silk shift dress that showed off the perfection of her figure, her long brown hair falling in soft curls around her shoulders. When he got out of the car, she ran up to him, throwing her arms around his neck.

'Tina! I thought you weren't coming for another couple of weeks.' More relieved than pleased to see her, he kissed her enthusiastically with all the pent-up desire Kate had aroused.

'This is a nice surprise,' he murmured. 'You've come early.'

No, Tina thought, eyeing Kate suspiciously over his shoulder as she jumped out of the passenger seat, I think I've come just in time.

She had woken up alone that morning in the vast double bed of the penthouse suite in one of Florence's plushest hotels. Not that she hadn't had plenty of offers – with Will out of the way, she could have shared that bed with any one of about ten guys. But that wasn't what she wanted. Sitting up in the middle of that huge bed, her cocaine-fuelled confidence of the night before descending into jittery paranoia, she realised she had made a big mistake in letting Will leave. Last night she had been too high to notice or care, but in the cold light of day, sober, she saw that Will had been all too anxious to get away. She couldn't understand why. She sat in an anxious huddle in the sheets and went over everything he had said, searching for clues. And then, gradually, it dawned on her that Kate O'Neill's name had come up rather too often. At first she dismissed the idea as her imagination playing tricks on her. But the more she thought about it, the more convinced she became that – incomprehensible though it was – Will had developed a crush on that bovine lump of a girl.

Gripped by a paralysing anxiety that was almost overwhelming, Tina toyed with the idea of riding it out, just letting the insecurity and neurosis wash over her – she wouldn't even have to get up. The idea was strangely appealing, but she only indulged it briefly. She might have been more inclined to give in to apathy if it weren't for the little packet she had picked up in the club last night and which she knew was in her bag. There was no need to languish in bed feeling sorry for herself when help was so close at hand. There were things she wanted in life and she wasn't going to get them cowering in a hotel room, letting fear overwhelm her. Damn it, she'd put in a lot of spadework on Will, and she wasn't about to let Kate O'Neill swoop in and make off with him.

Tina's friends were all getting married, settling down and having babies, and she wanted to do the same. She was tired of modelling, tired of the travelling, the gypsy existence, the pressure to be always 'on'. She was tired of only eating fish and vegetables. Most of all, she was tired of the constant sense of anticlimax, waking up alone in anonymous hotel rooms after glittering nights filled with flirtatious, admiring crowds. Too often she had indulged her hedonistic side at her own expense, sacrificing long-term comfort for short-term pleasure. Well, no more. It was time to wise up, she told herself sternly.

With a huge effort of will, she got out of bed, grabbed her bag and went into the bathroom. Rifling through the jumble of make-up, she became increasingly panicky when she failed to find what she was looking for, tipping everything out onto the marble surface beside the basin and searching through it with shaking fingers, almost on the verge of tears.

'Get a grip,' she told herself. She took a deep breath and began to search more methodically, looking through her wallet and opening her diary upside down, in case the packet had fallen between the pages. Almost despairing, she had a final feel around inside the empty bag and felt a tear in the lining. She fumbled inside the hole and finally – alleluia! – seized on the little cellophane packet. She tore it open, took a credit card from her wallet and chopped out two fat lines. Slowly now, savouring the moment, she took a note, rolled it and bent to snort them. Lifting her head, she smiled at herself in the mirror as she felt the almost visceral surge of confidence and exhilaration course through her veins. God, how could she ever give up something so delicious?

'The rehab starts tomorrow,' she told her reflection jauntily – a favourite catchphrase among her crowd.

She would have to sort herself out once she was married to Will anyway, she thought complacently. Of course he knew that she had the odd toot when she was out – he wasn't completely naive – but he had no idea how much she counted on it just to keep going and to combat boredom. It wasn't that she felt she had anything to be ashamed of – it wasn't as if she had a serious problem – but she knew Will was capable of making her feel like a complete skank even for the pathetic amount she used. He was such an old woman about drugs. She often marvelled at how he managed to survive in the music business with an attitude like that.

If he knew how much she used, Will would make it into a big deal, and it wasn't a big deal. It was precisely because it wasn't a problem that she could keep doing it. Coke was the only thing she did regularly – and only the very best stuff. It went with the life she led. When she gave up the life, she would give up the coke. Easy.

When she had showered and changed, she made a quick call to her agent and cancelled her engagements for the week. Eleanor was clearly pissed off, but that was her problem, Tina thought haughtily – let her earn her percentage for once. She spent a long time styling her hair and making up her face, using every trick she knew to eradicate the ravages of too much alcohol and cocaine, and too many late nights. When she was finished, she stood back and surveyed the results with a satisfied smile. She was stunning – glowing, youthful and radiant. She smirked at herself in the mirror.

Kate O'Neill is toast, she thought.

Tina was essentially a pack animal, and over the next few days various members of her inner circle turned up at the house.

'Don't worry, it won't mean extra work for you,' Will told Kate, as more and more people appeared. 'They're all models – they don't eat.'

Kate was shocked but relieved to discover he wasn't exaggerating. Tina and her cronies survived on a diet of alcohol, cigarettes and coffee – combined, of course, with plenty of the 'supplements' that you couldn't pick up in Boots.

Kate detested having Tina around. She felt like a particularly clumsy elephant in her presence, and Will no longer had time to hang out with her. He was at Tina's beck and call, dancing attendance on her and her friends, and she missed him so acutely that it shocked her.

But, she told herself sternly, it was just the reality check she needed. How could she have thought that Will might be interested in her when he had someone so impossibly glamorous and beautiful and . . . thin? Okay, so Tina was possibly the most boring woman on the planet and had virtually no sense of humour, but that sort of thing never seemed to bother men. Kate felt like Jane Eyre after Blanche Ingram turned up to stay at Thornfield, forcing herself to face up to reality, however painful it was. She tried to ignore the little voice in her head that kept reminding her Jane was the one Mr Rochester had really loved all along.

Kate wasn't the only one who was less than happy with the new arrivals at the villa. Will had thought that having Tina around would take his mind off Kate, but instead he found himself resenting the intrusion, and Tina's petulant diva behaviour only made him yearn more for Kate. He wanted everything to go back to the way it was. He wanted to have dinner with Kate and the band in the evenings, instead of being whisked off to some fashionable club or restaurant in Florence to party with the 'beautiful people'.

He was increasingly irritated by Tina's moodiness and neurosis. He didn't like the people she surrounded herself with, or the influence they had on her. She hadn't always been so superficial and mercenary, but her friends brought out the worst in her, and he didn't like the person she had become. He detested her constant publicity-seeking, and he loathed her drug-taking – she seemed to think he had no idea she did it and he hated that. How could she take him for such an idiot?

If Tina stopped to think about it, she would realise she wasn't happy with him either. But she didn't: image was everything, and they looked too good on paper for her to admit that the reality was less than idyllic. For his part, he found keeping up the pretence exhausting, and it would be a huge relief to put an end to it. But there was the charade of her birthday to get through first. He owed her that.

By the end of the week, he was so fed up that he jumped at the chance to fly to Rome to meet some Italian record-company executives rather than spend time with her. Tellingly, she seemed quite happy to see him go, once he'd promised he'd be back in time on Saturday to accompany her and her friends to the 2Tone concert at the Mandela Forum. He didn't flatter himself that it was his company she craved: she wanted the access-all-areas privileges he brought and the opportunity for backstage schmoozing. If he had cared about her more, he might have felt hurt.

Will had left his new car at the airport, and when he arrived back the following morning, he went for a long, leisurely drive, relishing the solitude, finally arriving back at the villa at around five. Turning into the long driveway, he noticed a crowd of people in the grounds, close to the door. As he drew closer, he realised, with a sinking feeling, that it was a gaggle of reporters and photographers, tooled up with microphones, cameras and recording equipment. They had been waiting somewhat desultorily but on spying Will's car, they roused themselves and got ready to spring into action, primed to ambush him as soon as he got out.

'Bugger!' Will cursed. What had Owen been up to now? he wondered, slowing down as he approached the house to buy himself time. It must be pretty serious, he thought, as he scanned the cluster of reporters, recognising some faces – hacks from English and Irish tabloids. There were some unfamiliar ones too and, worryingly, some more weighty journalists. A couple were even shouldering TV cameras. These weren't just paparazzi hoping to get a shot of Tina having a bad-hair day or looking too bony in a bikini. Obviously some story had broken at home and, whatever it was, it must be big.

Why the hell hadn't he been warned? Where the fuck was Louise? Where was Martina or Karen or Anne-Marie – or any of the army of publicists, press agents and PR people to whom they paid a small fortune to keep on top of things like this? He couldn't believe someone hadn't called to give him a heads-up.

Angrily, he pulled his mobile out of his jacket pocket and saw it was switched off. '*Fuck*!' He was angry with himself now. He'd forgotten to switch it on again after getting off the plane.

Stalling for time, he turned it on while he made a meal of parking the car. He waited what seemed like an age for it to register and the display to light up. As soon as it did, it started beeping message alerts. Will's heart sank as the incoming texts and voicemail messages racked up. People had been trying to reach him all day, which added to his sense of foreboding. There were countless messages from Louise, Tina, Phoenix – even Grace and Lorcan. What the hell was going on?

Reluctant to face the mob without some clue as to what it was all about, he looked at a couple of text messages from Louise, but they just asked him to get in contact as soon as possible. Feeling guilty now that he had been tooling around the Tuscan countryside, leaving everyone to deal with God knew what, he just wanted to get into the house and make sure that everyone was all right. But first he had to run the press gauntlet.

The journalists were beginning to crowd around the car. Knowing he didn't have much time, he listened to the most recent voice message. It was Louise, sounding uncharacteristically panicked: 'Will, I've been trying to reach you all day. Tina can't get you either. Please call me as soon as you get this message, or ring someone at the house.' There was a pause, as if she had been about to say something else but had decided against it. 'Well, ring me back as soon as you can,' she continued. Again she hesitated. 'I'll probably fly out this evening. Okay, 'bye,' she said, sounding worried, and was gone.

'Shit!' Will cursed, throwing the phone onto the passenger seat. He'd just have to wing it with the press – pretend he knew what this was about and 'no comment' his way to the door, get inside and find out what the hell had happened. Then he would get down to the serious business of throttling Owen. No doubt it was something to do with him.

Bracing himself, he assumed a calm, deadpan expression and opened the door. As soon as he stepped out, journalists were swarming around him, shoving microphones in his face. Photographers called his name and reporters shouted questions.

'I have nothing to say,' he said stoically, not even listening to the barrage of questions. Trying to look all-knowing but resolutely tight-lipped, he moved towards the house, his progress impeded by the throng. Amid the cacophony of shouted questions, it was difficult to make out what anyone was saying, but he became aware that their questions had nothing to do with Owen or any of the band. They were asking him about his father. What had the old goat been up to now?

'When did you last speak to your father, Will?'

'Had you seen Sir Philip recently?'

'Is it true you hadn't spoken to him in more than ten years?'

'Had there been any reconciliation between you?'

'No comment,' he repeated, moving forward doggedly. He was almost there.

'Will,' a voice called from behind him, 'had you spoken to your father before he died?'

Will froze, unable to move or speak. His legs felt as if they were going to give way. Then he spun around in the direction of the voice, his mouth dry. He found himself confronting a middle-aged man with thinning, greasy hair and watery, reptilian eyes.

'*What?*' His mouth formed the word, but no sound came out. He tried again. 'What?' he breathed, his voice a barely audible whisper.

'Had you spoken to your father before he died?' the man repeated, in a London accent.

'Died?' Will croaked, blinking uncomprehendingly.

'Yes, had there been any reconciliation—' On seeing Will's face, the man stopped short. His face changed, realisation dawning. 'You didn't know?' he asked, unable to conceal the gleam of triumph in his eyes at the shock in Will's face.

Will just looked at him blankly while cameras whirred and clicked.

'Sir Philip passed away last night,' the reporter said piously. 'It was a heart-attack, very sudden.' His reverential tone was belied by the excitement in his face. 'I'm sorry to be the one to tell you.'

No you're not, Will thought, longing to smash his smug face in. You're not sorry at all. You're fucking delighted. He had to clench his fists to stop himself lashing out.

'He was a great man, Sir Philip,' the reporter said solemnly. 'A great loss to us all.'

As if you knew him. As if anything he did meant fuck to you. Name one of his plays, you fucking Neanderthal!

The rest of the gaggle of reporters, who had fallen silent during this exchange, sprang into action once more, all shouting questions at once. Had Will really not known about his father's death until this moment? Was he in touch with Antonia Bell? Had he spoken to Sir Philip before he died? How did he feel? How did he feel? How did he feel?

Somehow Will turned on his heel and walked purposefully towards the house, the newsmen tripping over each other as they struggled to keep up with his long stride. Head down, shoulders hunched, his mouth shut in a grim line, Will ignored the questions, refusing to look into the cameras thrust in his face. He just had to hold it together until he got inside. He wouldn't give them the satisfaction of breaking down in front of them. When he got to the other side of the door, he could howl and scream and go to pieces. He just had to keep it together for another couple of steps.

Chapter 10

Kate arrived back at the house a couple of hours later. Since everyone else was going to the 2Tone concert tonight, she didn't have to cook dinner, so she had taken advantage of the opportunity to do some sightseeing and treat herself to a little retail therapy – or a lot, as it turned out. She had set off with the noble intention of spending the afternoon doing the rounds of Florence's art treasures, after a quick trawl of the shops to pick up some presents for people back home. But once she hit the streets, Michelangelo and Botticelli were side-lined in favour of Prada and Versace. Seduced by Florence's wonder-ful shops and markets, she had walked her feet off, pounding the hot pavements, enjoying the rare luxury of having plenty of money to spend. One shop led to another and another, and before she knew it, the hours she had meant to spend gazing at art in churches and gal-leries had telescoped into a quick flit around some frescos, which she dutifully squeezed in before falling into a cab.

Though Will and the band had done their best to persuade her to go to the concert with them, she had refused, opting instead to have a quiet night in by herself. If Tina wasn't around she'd have jumped at the chance to join them, but the thought of spending an entire evening in her company was more than Kate could bear. She couldn't relax around Tina, who seemed to go out of her way to make her feel like a fifth wheel, a terminally uncool hanger-on. Besides, she was looking forward to a deliciously self-indulgent evening. She would play with her purchases, take a long, luxurious bath, eat supper on her lap in front of the TV and have a long-overdue early night. It was lovely being able to watch trashy TV like Celebrity Cell Block without Brian making faces.

Thinking of Brian, she realised that a phone call to him was also long overdue. She'd ring him tonight. It was a good thing she'd managed to take in the frescos, even if it was an afterthought – at least it would give her something cultural to tell him and he wouldn't think she was a complete philistine – or, worse, that she had become a slave to Mammon. She could talk up the frescoes and play down the shopping. Unfortunately, he was too high-minded to want to listen to scurrilous gossip about celebrities, which was a pity because she had loads to tell. Besides, she was dying for a bitch and, with everyone out of the house, it would have been the perfect opportunity to let off steam about Tina and her friends. Maybe she'd ring Freddie first . . .

She arrived home at about seven. Expecting to find the house empty, she sailed into the living room, prepared to drop her bags, kick off her shoes and flop onto one of the couches. She was taken aback to find Tina draped sulkily on one of them, flanked by two of her friends, bitching about something. They were all stunningly beautiful and dressed to the nines, but Kate was reminded of the three witches in *Macbeth*.

Tina looked up as Kate came in, then resumed her conversation as if she wasn't there.

'I'm not being selfish, am I?' she was saying in a low voice to Julie, a blonde, baby-faced waif.

'No, of course not,' Julie purred soothingly. 'You've been looking forward to this for ages. Naturally you're disappointed.'

'If anything, he's the one who's being selfish,' Gwen, an angular redhead with endless legs and cheekbones that could have cut diamonds, chimed in supportively. 'He knows how much this means to you.'

'It's just my luck,' Tina huffed. 'Why do these things always happen to *me*?'

'Why do bad things ever happen to good people?' Gwen asked philosophically.

Kate's first instinct was to make for the kitchen but, as they had seen her come in, she felt that would be rude. So she decided to tough it out and determinedly threw herself onto the couch opposite, greeting them with a cheery 'hi.'

Tina looked at her as if the cat had spoken. Kate's spirits sank. Faced with the clannish hostility of Tina and her mates, she felt suddenly lonely for a friend. If only Freddie was here for a post-shopping show-and-tell and an evening of giggly gossip and bitching over a bottle of wine.

'You've been shopping?' Julie enquired, nodding to Kate's bags.

'Yes. I got a bit carried away.' Kate smiled ruefully.

'Oh, the shops here are just to die for, aren't they?' Julie wrinkled her nose conspiratorially. 'I love that place – their stuff's amazing,' she said, pointing to a bag from a trendy designer shop.

'Let's see what you got,' Gwen said brightly, with a pop-eyed expression of enthusiasm and an inane smile. She might have been speaking to a three-year-old.

Reluctantly, Kate obeyed, pulling out a beautiful silk dress in a bold, richly coloured print.

'Oh, that's *gorgeous*,' Gwen gushed, fingering the material.

'It's really sweet, isn't it?' Julie consulted Tina.

Tina eyed the dress sceptically. 'I didn't know they did plus sizes,' she said.

'Oh, you're not a plus size, are you, Kate?' Julie said kindly. 'It's only – what? – a twelve?'

'A fourteen,' Kate blushed.

'Well, fourteen isn't a plus size, is it?' Julie cooed. 'Except in modeling, of course.' She rolled her eyes. 'Size twelve's a plus size for us, isn't it?' she said to Tina and Gwen. 'Which is completely ridiculous.

A friend of mine – remember Carla?' she asked Gwen, 'she's a size 12 now and she can only get outsize work.'

'But she looks amazing!' Gwen enthused.

'Oh yes,' Julie hastened to assure Kate. 'Fantastic.'

'I wish I had a figure like that,' Gwen said.

'No you don't,' Tina said witheringly.

'Well, no,' Gwen admitted, with a laugh, 'but that's just because I'd be out of a job.'

Kate couldn't decide which was worse: Tina's open hostility or her friends' being-kind-to-lesser-mortals condescension.

'When are you all off to the concert?' she asked, hoping she didn't sound too eager. 'I thought you'd be gone by now.'

'We should be,' Gwen said gloomily. 'The guys left ages ago. Except Rory – he's waiting for us.'

'So, what's the matter?' Kate asked, against her better judgement.

'Will won't take us,' Julie explained, glancing warily at Tina. 'We're waiting for him to arrange a car for us.'

'It's ridiculous,' Tina spat sulkily. 'I don't see why he won't let me drive his. Just because he's not going, there's no reason why I can't enjoy myself.'

'Well, he probably knows you'll want to have a drink,' Gwen suggested diplomatically.

'Will isn't going?' Kate asked, surprised. 'Why not?'

'Because his father died,' Tina snapped waspishly, as if Kate ought to have known.

'What?' Kate gasped in shock. 'His *father*? But – but he can't have,' she stammered.

'Well, no one told him that apparently,' Tina drawled, clearly relishing the impact of her words. 'Because he did.'

'He's *dead*?' Kate couldn't take it in.

'Yes,' Julie nodded. 'It was very sudden, apparently.'

'A heart attack,' Gwen added solemnly.

'Oh my God!' She surveyed the three of them. Through the doors to the terrace she saw Rory sitting by the pool listening to his MP3 player, eyes closed, face upturned to the fading evening sun. 'Where's Will?' she asked.

'Up in his room, having a hissy fit.' Tina raised her eyes to heaven.

'Isn't anybody with him?'

'No, and if you're planning on offering tea and sympathy, I wouldn't, if I were you,' Tina said. 'I tried to talk to him and he threw a vase at me.'

Kate was astonished, but Tina appeared unscathed.

'He missed,' she said grudgingly. 'But it was a huge bloody thing and it smashed to pieces against the wall. He could have done serious damage.'

'He could have taken your eye out.' Gwen shook her head reprovingly.

'It could have been the end of my career.'

'You were really lucky,' Julie murmured.

'*He* was lucky!'

Kate didn't wait to hear any more. She left Tina wallowing in her grievances and made for the stairs.

'You could have him for assault!' she heard Julie say.

'I've a good mind to. And all I said was—'

Kate was at the foot of the stairs but turned back and marched up to Tina. '*What* did you say?' she demanded, forgetting to be intimidated by her.

Tina regarded her coldly. 'I just said I didn't see why he was making such a fuss. Will hated his father when he was alive. He's just being a hypocrite, playing the drama queen now that he's dead.'

'You *said* that to him?'

'Oh come on, it's the truth – you know it as well as I do. He wouldn't give the man the time of day when he was alive so it's a bit late to be playing the dutiful son now, don't you think?'

'I'm not surprised he threw a vase at you.'

'He lost it because he knows it's true,' Tina snapped. 'Everyone knows he hated his father.'

'God, you're so stupid!' Kate said scornfully, turned on her heel and made for the stairs.

As she approached the door of Will's room, Kate started to lose her nerve. She wasn't any good at this sort of thing – she never knew what to say or if it was better to say nothing. She wished Lorcan was there. Still, worrying about feeling shy and awkward at a time like this was selfish. She should think of Will and what he must be going through.

She knocked timidly on the door of his room. When there was no reply, she pushed it open tentatively.

'Who is it?' Will was sitting on the bed.

'Just me,' she said apologetically.

At the sound of her voice, Will's body relaxed and his features softened. She took in the lines of strain in his face.

'Kate.' He stood up, plunging his hands deep into his pockets. 'What can I do for you?' he asked. It broke Kate's heart that he even mustered a weak smile.

'Nothing!' She was appalled that he thought she was coming to him with some problem.

He was looking at her expectantly.

She took a deep breath. 'Will, I'm so sorry about your father,' she said softly. 'I've just heard.'

Will pressed a fist to his mouth and swallowed hard. His face crumpled and a muscle twitched in his cheek.

'Come in.' He frowned when he had regained his composure as Kate hovered in the doorway. 'Don't worry, I won't throw any vases at you.'

As she moved into the room, Kate's eye was caught by the huge blue vase that lay shattered in the corner.

'I could have hit her if I'd wanted to,' Will said, following her gaze. 'I didn't throw it anywhere near her.'

'I'm surprised you *didn't* want to. I heard what she said.'

'I suppose she's making the most of it?'

'Yes,' Kate said. 'She's downstairs telling her coven what a brute you are.'

'Probably wondering how best to spin it to the papers. I think she'd be happier if I hadn't missed – it would have made a better story.'

'Mmm. I did get the impression she was a bit miffed not to have any scars.'

'Well, the night is young,' Will said grimly.

Kate had never seen him like this before. He seemed dangerously on edge, pacing agitatedly around the room like a caged tiger. In this mood, it was easy to see how Tina had come a cropper by saying the wrong thing.

'Um, can I get you anything?' Kate asked nervously. God, that sounded so trite – especially with Tina's tea-and-sympathy jibe ringing in her ears.

'No thanks.' Will shook his head. He seemed hardly to notice her presence now and she wondered if she should go. But she didn't want to leave him in this state.

'When's the funeral?' she asked softly.

Will stopped pacing and looked at her, stunned. 'I don't know,' he said.

'Haven't you spoken to Antonia?'

'I couldn't – I couldn't call her,' he said abjectly. 'I'm probably the last person she wants to hear from right now.'

Kate felt hopelessly inadequate in the face of his despair.

'She may not even want me at the funeral,' he continued.

'Of course she'll want you there.'

'I wouldn't blame her if she didn't.' Will resumed pacing.

'Have you spoken to Mum?'

'I haven't spoken to anyone except Tina. And look how that worked out,' he said, gesturing at the smashed vase.

Suddenly all the fight seemed to go out of him and he sank down onto the bed. 'I shouldn't have taken it out on Tina,' he said dully, rubbing his forehead. 'She only said what everyone must be thinking.'

'No,' Kate whispered emphatically. 'We don't all think that.' Tears stung her eyes. She couldn't bear to see him so distraught.

Will saw the tears glinting in Kate's eyes, and something in him snapped. Until now anger had kept him going – anger with the journalists, anger with Tina, anger with himself – even anger with his father for pulling the rug out from under him one last time. But in the face of Kate's sympathy, he broke down.

'I thought . . .' he drew a ragged breath. '. . . I thought there was *time*! I thought I had time to be pissed off with him. It wasn't meant to be for ever,' he cried.

'I know, I know,' Kate soothed, forgetting about herself in her concern for Will. She rushed over to sit beside him on the bed and put an arm around his shaking shoulders.

'And now it's too late,' he sobbed brokenly. 'He's dead and he never knew—' He wiped away tears roughly with the back of his hand. 'He died thinking I hated him,' he said bleakly.

'Oh God, don't.' Kate pulled him closer. 'He didn't think you hated him,' she said, holding him tight as he turned into her arms. He was crying in earnest now, great shuddering sobs, and she felt the wet of his tears as he buried his head in her neck. 'How could I have been so stupid?' he railed. 'All those times I refused to talk to him and wouldn't see him. Now I'd give anything if I could just see him one more time.'

'I know.' Kate stroked his hair as he clung to her. His hot breath on her neck sent little ripples of pleasure through her, which was inappropriate, to say the least. She was supposed to be comforting Will, not taking advantage of the situation to get a pervy thrill.

'I'm sure he knew you loved him,' she said.

'How could he?' he said, lifting his head to look at her, blinking away tears from his eyes.

Kate's eyes welled. 'Mum always knew you loved him, didn't she?' she reasoned. 'Even *I* knew that. He was your *father*, Will. If we knew, he must have known.'

'Do you really think so?' he asked hopefully, like a child seeking reassurance.

'Absolutely.' Kate nodded. 'Besides,' she added, smiling wryly as a thought occurred to her, 'I'm sure Mum will have told him.'

Will's expression brightened. 'She would, wouldn't she?' He sniffed.

'Only every time she spoke to him, I imagine.' She was glad she'd somehow hit on the right thing to say. She brushed his hair off his forehead and wiped away a stray tear that rolled down his cheek.

Will mirrored the action, tracing a tear down her cheek with his thumb, his eyes following its course until it reached her mouth. She tasted the salt before Will brushed it away. His gaze lingered on her lips, his thumb tracing their outline. Kate tried not to squirm with pleasure.

Suddenly their eyes met. Kate knew he was going to kiss her, and then his hands pushed into her hair pulling her face towards his, and she felt his lips on hers, tasting the salt of their mingled tears as he kissed her, tentatively at first, then more urgently. His hand stroked the side of her face coaxingly, urging her lips to stay locked to his. Kate didn't need any coaxing. She kissed him back enthusiastically, her fingers stroking the short hair at the nape of his neck.

Will broke the kiss and pulled back a little, his eyes on hers. Kate whimpered, leaning into him, and he pulled her into his arms, his mouth opening hungrily over hers. Kate shivered with excitement as she felt his tongue in her mouth, her fingers tensing on his broad shoulders. The world melted away until nothing existed but Will's mouth, the clean, citrus smell of his skin, the taste of him, the pounding of his heart against her chest.

A soft knock on the door made them jump, and they sprang apart. Will stood up. 'Come in,' he called hoarsely.

Kate got up as the door opened, hoping she didn't look as guilty as she felt. She was amazed when Louise came in.

'Hi Kate.' She smiled. 'Will, I came as soon as I could,' she said, rushing across the room and throwing her arms around him. 'I'm so sorry about your dad.'

'Thanks.' He dropped a kiss on her forehead. 'And thanks for coming.'

'We were so worried about you,' she said. 'We were trying to contact you all day and no one could reach you. Grace was frantic – calling me every five minutes to see if I'd managed to get hold of you. When no one could find you, we were afraid . . . Well, we didn't know if you'd heard the news or not.'

'Sorry – I forgot to turn my mobile on when I got off the plane. I hadn't heard the news – not until I got back here.'

'So Tina told you?' Louise said, sounding relieved.

'No, it was some, um' – Will gulped – 'some bloke outside.' He waved in the general direction of the drive. 'A reporter,' he said tightly. 'I didn't get his name.'

'A reporter!' Louise gasped. 'Christ, I'm so sorry, Will.'

This was the first Kate had heard of that, and her heart went out to him. No wonder he had been so wired and had lashed out at Tina. She longed to put her arms around him again. Her eyes met the yearning in his own. 'Well, I'll leave you to it,' she said awkwardly. 'You're sure there's nothing I can get you?'

*

Kate was in the kitchen when Louise came downstairs, a set of car keys in one hand and her ever-present mobile phone in the other. 'I'm going to take this lot to the concert,' she told Kate, jerking a thumb towards the living room.

'I can't believe Tina's still going,' Kate said.

'I know. Still,' Louise sighed, 'it's probably as well to get her out of Will's way. I'd happily tell her to get stuffed, only I think he wants her and her posse off the premises.'

'I suppose you're right. She's not exactly helping things.'

'No, she's made things a whole lot worse. It's her bloody fault all these reporters are crawling around here in the first place.'

'I didn't notice anyone around when I got back.' Kate frowned.

'No, apparently they cut their losses and followed the guys to the concert when there was nothing doing here.'

'Poor Will. I wish he hadn't heard it that way.'

'He's in a terrible state.' Louise said. 'I got him to ring your mum – he's talking to her now. I think that'll help.'

'Good. Everyone's being so unsympathetic. I'm surprised they buggered off to the concert,' she said, somewhat accusingly. 'All except Rory, but he's just sitting out there.' She pointed to the terrace where Rory still sat, his leg jumping to the beat of whatever was playing in his earphones. 'Nobody was with Will when I came home.'

Louise looked out at him. 'They just don't get it,' she said sadly. 'You mustn't blame them.'

Louise knew Rory cared about Will – they all did – but none of them would understand what he was going through. Leery of fathers as a species, Louise knew that Will carrying on a feud with his was one of the things that had endeared the band members to him in the first place. It was about the only thing they had in common.

But Will's feelings about his father were complicated, whereas theirs were brutally simple. Rory and Owen's father had disappeared when they were children, hadn't been seen since, and that was the way they liked it. They were primed and ready to beat him to a pulp if he should ever raise his head above the parapet. Phoenix and Georgie hadn't been so lucky. Their fame and wealth had brought their father crawling out of the woodwork and he had taken to turning up at their hotels and trying to see them. A lump-sum payment and a restraining order had kept him at a safe distance so far – along with enthusiastic threats of violence from the Cassidy brothers. His death would signify nothing more than the assurance that he would never darken their door again.

'Do you know yet when the funeral is?' Kate asked.

Louise nodded. 'It's on Monday, but Will's flying back to England tomorrow. I'll be staying here to take care of things while he's gone.'

'Isn't anyone going to the funeral with him?'

'Oh, I expect Madam will rouse herself for that – there might be photographers,' Louise said drily. 'Your mum'll be there, of course,' she added, more brightly, 'and Lorcan's flying over from New York.'

Kate noticed how drained Louise looked. She had obviously had a wearing day, with all the worry over Will, then a last-minute flight.

'Are you coming back when you've dropped them at the gig?' she asked. 'Do you want me to make you something to eat later?'

'No thanks,' Louise said. 'I'll stick around with them and try to keep them out of mischief – and keep Tina away from journos,' she added. 'You'll be here, though, won't you?'

Kate nodded.

'Good. I think he'll be better off with just you. I know you'll look after him.'

Rory sat on the terrace, twitchily tapping along to his MP3 player and cursing his luck. Tina had been creating such a fuss about Will not taking her to the concert that he and the other band members had decided one of them should stay behind and go with her to get her off Will's back. Although they were bewildered by Will's grief, they weren't unsympathetic, and it was the only way they could think of helping. He had drawn the short straw. The others would be there by now, partying backstage with Tony and his crew, getting high and catching up with old friends. It seemed incredibly unfair that when he had Tessa out of the way for once and could really enjoy himself, he should get lumbered with Will's harpy girlfriend. He pulled out his mobile phone and idly sent another text to vote Tessa's latest rival off *Celebrity Cell Block*.

A tap on his shoulder startled him. Louise was standing beside him, rattling car keys. 'Hi, Rory.'

A grin spread slowly across his face. He didn't know where she had appeared from, but it seemed somehow natural and completely in character that she should materialise like an angel when someone was in trouble. 'I'm taking you guys to Tony's gig,' she explained, smiling down at him. 'Ready?'

Rory beamed up at her. Suddenly that straw wasn't looking so short.

When everyone had gone, the house seemed eerily quiet, and Kate realised she hadn't been alone here since the moment she'd arrived. But instead of enjoying the peace and solitude, she felt nervy and on edge, moving restlessly from room to room, unable to settle to anything. She turned on the TV in the living room and sat down to watch *Celebrity Cell Block* but couldn't concentrate. In the first ad break she realised she had been staring blankly at the screen for fifteen minutes without having taken in a second of it. She decided to cook something and found herself standing in the middle of the kitchen, staring indecisively at the cupboards. She didn't know whether she should go and check on Will or if he would rather be left alone, and headed for the stairs half a dozen times, only to change her mind and turn back.

All she could think about was that kiss and how fantastic it had been. She wondered what would have happened if Louise hadn't arrived when she did. How much longer would he have gone on kissing her? She didn't know whether to be glad or sorry that they had been interrupted, but she couldn't help smiling to herself every time she thought of it, hugging it to herself like a delicious secret – although rationally she knew Will had been reaching out for comfort and she had just happened to be there. Still, she was hyper-aware that they were now alone in the house together. She couldn't control the images that kept flashing through her mind: Will coming downstairs and kissing her again . . . Will tearing her clothes off and ravishing her by the pool . . . Will bending her over the kitchen table . . .

God, she had to do something to take her mind off it. What kind of person was she? Will was devastated because his father was dead and all she could think of was screwing his brains out. Not sure if he would want to eat, she decided to make a shepherd's pie, which wouldn't be spoiled by hanging around. She took her time, working slowly and methodically, finding she had to make a huge effort to focus even on this familiar task. Eventually the steady routine of chopping, slicing and stirring calmed her down somewhat and soothed her frazzled nerves. When she had the pie in the oven, she poured herself a glass of wine and went to sit on the terrace, not sure what to do next. All that nervous energy had left her exhausted, but unable to relax.

It was a beautiful balmy night, the sky a deep inky blue, and Kate sank back in her chair, listening to the chirping of the cicadas, making a conscious effort to relax. But as soon as she closed her eyes, the porno channel in her brain started playing again.

Wham! Will was slamming her against the patio door, pulling her dress up over her head. She could taste his hot breath in her mouth as his tongue crashed against her teeth. His hand was delving into her knickers and now his fingers were inside her, describing little circles against her clitoris . . .

Shifting restlessly in her seat, she decided to try some relaxation techniques she had picked up from Brian. She tried to empty her mind and focus on counting as she breathed in slowly, paused for a second, then counting again as she breathed out. In . . . one . . . two . . . three . . . four . . .

Now Will was lying on top of her on the grass. She could feel the cool night air on her skin as his tongue flicked across her hardened nipples. His cock was like an iron bar against her stomach as he licked, sucked and stroked, turning her insides to liquid. Rolling over so she was on top of him, she unzipped his fly and straddled him . . .

This was no bloody use! Sighing impatiently, Kate gave up trying to focus on her breathing. Instead, she'd try the one about the waves on a beach.

Okay, I'm the waves on a beach – or am I the beach? she thought confusedly. Anyway, doesn't matter. The waves are rolling *slooowly* in . . . stopping for a second or two . . . rolling *slooowly* back out.

She shimmied down in the sun lounger and exhaled deeply, trying to convince herself that this was working.

Okay, concentrate. Rolling slowly in . . . stopping . . . rolling *slooowly* back out ... *slooowly* in ...

Will's head was between her legs and his tongue was inside her, gently rolling in ... rolling back out ... rolling in. A huge tidal wave was building inside her and was about to crash—

'Has everyone gone?'

Kate came back to earth with a bang. Will was standing in the doorway, looking at her. She wondered how long he had been there and hoped she didn't look as flustered as she felt. She was surprised by how normal he seemed – but then, of course, he didn't know they had just been having wild sex. 'Yes.' She smiled. 'The coast is clear.' She tried to appear calm, but her heart was racing and she felt incredibly shy, as if they'd really just been writhing about naked on the grass.

Will breathed a sigh of relief and sank into a chair opposite her. 'I was going to put on that DVD Grace sent me,' he said. 'Dad's *On the Couch*. Watch it with me?' he asked, boyishly anxious.

'Of course, if you want me to.'

Kate followed him into the living room. He put the DVD in the machine and sat down next to her, their thighs almost touching. He pressed a button on the remote control and the screen sprang into life. Kate was filled with anxiety as the familiar theme tune struck up, worried that the programme would be too harrowing in the circumstances and upset him even more.

'My guest this evening is the distinguished playwright Sir Philip Sargent,' Richard Slater was saying. The camera pulled back to reveal Philip sitting opposite his interviewer in an identical brown leather armchair. It must be a shock for Will to see his father still alive, Kate thought and was struck by how attractive Philip still was. A devastatingly handsome man in his youth, years of partying too late and drinking too hard had left their mark, etching deep lines on either side of his mouth and around his soulful, penetrating eyes – which were the same intense blue as Will's. But the lines and furrows added interest and character to his refined features, and the silver-grey of his still thick hair gave him a distinguished air.

Philip was immensely charismatic, funny and charming, and Kate found herself wishing she had had the chance to meet him. She could see why her mother had become so fond of him over the years.

After trawling through Philip's childhood and hell-raising early adulthood, the conversation became more serious as he talked about his difficult marriage to Helen Kilgannon, Will's mother. He spoke movingly of his ultimately futile attempts to cope with her manic depression. He was ruthlessly self-critical, not sparing himself as he explored his ineptitude in dealing with his wife's disintegration, his shortcomings as a husband and father, and his ultimate failure as both with the breakdown of his marriage and the abandonment of his child.

'Looking back,' Philip said, 'I can't believe how crass I was. I mean, I was a grown man – pretty resilient, I liked to think – and *I* couldn't cope with Helen's illness. *I* couldn't live in that house any longer. *I* had to leave to save my sanity. So I walked out and left my teenage son to deal with it alone. He was only a boy.'

The camera lingered mercilessly on his face, registering every flicker of emotion. The sadness and regret in his eyes made him seem older.

'So you feel you were wrong to leave when you did?' Richard's hushed voice came from off-camera.

'Yes, absolutely,' Philip said matter-of-factly.

'How did you feel about it at the time?'

'Well, guilty, of course – but not enough to stop me doing exactly what I wanted.' He smiled self-mockingly. 'I thought I had a right to be happy.'

'And didn't you?'

'Not at my son's expense,' he said shortly. 'But I come from a generation that scoffed at the notion of staying together for the sake of the children, or working at marriage – the whole idea of self-sacrifice. We believed that personal happiness was paramount.'

'You don't believe that any more?'

'Well, it's utter nonsense, isn't it? It's what you tell yourself because you don't want to admit the truth – that you're too lazy or selfish to do anything remotely difficult or unpleasant. We're led to believe that life should tickle *all the time*. When it doesn't tickle any more, you simply move on. It's an infantile view of the world.'

'Getting back to your first son, what's your relationship like with him now?' Richard probed gently.

'Non-existent,' Philip said laconically. 'He doesn't speak to me – won't have anything to do with me. I don't blame him.'

'What caused the breakdown in that relationship?'

'When Helen died, he blamed me.' Philip paused. 'And then, instead of helping him deal with it, I packed him off to boarding school. In that awful American phrase,' he smiled witheringly, 'I wasn't there for him when his mother died.'

There was a long pause.

'It wasn't entirely selfish,' Philip said eventually. 'I thought it would be good for him – toughen him up. I was afraid he'd turn out like his mother – too sensitive for the world. But I underestimated him. He was well able to take care of himself – stand up to me. I think he takes after me more than his mother.'

'Have you tried to reconcile with him?'

'Yes, of course – I'm trying all the time. But, as I say, he's like me – stubborn, implacable and convinced he's right, which, of course, in this case he is.'

'So he's right not to forgive you?'

'Yes,' Philip said, only the tensing of his jaw betraying any emotion. 'Why?'

'Because it was unforgivable,' Philip said, with devastating simplicity, looking his questioner square in the eyes.

The camera lingered relentlessly on Philip's face in the silence that followed. He blinked rapidly, starting to chew his lip as the silence stretched painfully. He was so exposed, so defenceless, it was almost unbearable to watch.

'You really believe that?'

'Yes, I do. I think he's right not to forgive me. I respect him for it.'

'You respect him for being implacable . . . resentful?'

'I respect him for knowing what's right and not accepting anything less – for having the courage of his convictions.'

'Even if it means that he's cut you out of his life?' Richard probed.

'Particularly if it means that. It's not the easy thing to do. The easy thing would be to pretend everything's fine, to compromise yourself – to say, "You're my dad and I love you, so anything you do is okay."'

'But can you hope for reconciliation if there's no forgiveness?'

'I think so,' Philip said quietly. 'I hope so. I don't need him to forgive me. I just want to see him again,' he said bleakly. 'Quite apart from the fact that he's my son, he seems like someone who would be worth knowing. And besides—' His voice broke, and he looked at his hands, overcome with emotion.

'Yes?' Richard prompted.

Philip cleared his throat, struggling visibly to regain his composure. 'He's the only connection I have to Helen.'

Kate swallowed hard, tears springing to her eyes. She had been almost afraid to look at Will throughout the interview, but she glanced at him now and saw that tears were streaming silently down his face. She wanted to take him in her arms and comfort him, but he might have thought she was expecting him to kiss her again. She wiped her eyes as the programme ended and the credits rolled.

She stood and switched off the TV. 'Do you want something to eat?' she asked. 'I made shepherd's pie.' She winced inwardly. Brian was always accusing her of thinking food as the solution to everything. Perhaps he was right.

'Yes please,' Will said, brushing away the tears. 'Actually, I'm starving.'

Perhaps Brian wasn't right, after all, she thought. Will didn't seem to find the idea of food incongruous. Maybe what people needed at times like this were the basic comforts. Food. Sex. The thought came unbidden. At least watching the programme had taken her mind off sex for an hour or so, but now it was over, it was at the front of her brain again.

They decided to eat in the kitchen as there were only the two of them. Kate felt like a nervy horse, so aware of Will it was ridiculous. She felt him behind her and practically leapt ten feet in the air when he put his hand on her bare shoulder as he reached over her to take glasses from an overhead cupboard. If she leaned back just a centimetre their bodies would be touching. If she turned, she would practically be in his arms.

'Calm down,' she told herself crossly. 'He's just setting the table. It's not foreplay.'

But the air seemed charged with electricity and Kate felt ready to burst into flames at his slightest touch. She wondered if it was just her or if he felt it too. Without the usual crowd of people, it seemed incredibly intimate, just the two of them sitting down to eat at the kitchen table. It was a big table, but they sat close together at right angles to each other. The lightest, most casual touch seemed charged with eroticism. When she passed him a serving spoon and their fingers brushed, she felt as if she'd received an electric shock, the ripples reverberating somewhere in her groin.

'This is really good,' Will said, forking shepherd's pie into his mouth.

'You spoke to Mum?' she asked quietly.

'Yes. She'll be at the funeral.'

'And you're off to England tomorrow?'

Will nodded. 'Louise has me on a flight in the morning. Antonia wants me to stay with her.'

'That's good.' Kate nodded encouragingly, hoping he intended to accept the offer. She couldn't bear the thought of him being alone at such a time.

'It's very kind of her,' Will added. 'It'll be strange, though. I don't know her – and I've never even met Paul, my half-brother.'

'How old is he now?'

'About sixteen,' he answered, without hesitation.

Of course – he had been a new baby when Will's mother died.

'It's a horrible age to lose your father,' he said.

'Yes. But there's no good age, is there?' Kate said softly.

Will felt an overwhelming surge of love. He wanted to ask Kate to go to the funeral with him. He had always wanted her there when he went to see his father – he just hadn't expected to be going to see him in his coffin. That made him want her there all the more.

He ate mechanically. He couldn't concentrate on the food – couldn't concentrate on anything, if the truth be told. All he could think of was their kiss upstairs – the way Kate had kissed him back, the soft crush of her breasts against his chest, how wonderful it had felt to hold her in his arms. It was inappropriate to say the least – his father was dead and all he could think about was how much he wanted to take Kate to bed. But he couldn't forget her warmth, the passion of her kiss. When he had come downstairs and found her sitting on the patio, all he had wanted to do was drag her off to bed and lose himself inside her. It was still all he wanted. Even setting the table together had seemed like an erotic tango, and it had taken gargantuan self-control not to grab her right there. Standing behind her at the counter, he had longed to touch his lips to the soft skin at the nape of her neck. There had been only a quarter of a centimetre between them and he had yearned to wrap his arms around her and pull her into him . . . to undo the tie on the halterneck dress she was wearing and let the top fall to her waist . . . to cup those amazing breasts in his hands . . . he could almost feel their soft weight in his palms . . .

'Will? Are you okay?' Was it her imagination or was he staring at her breasts?

'What? Oh, yes,' he said absently.

He was probably in a daze, not focusing on anything, and her chest had just happened to be in his line of vision. Pity. She wished he was interested in her breasts. She imagined him undressing her, how marvellous his cool lips would feel on her nipples . . . She shivered at the thought.

'Are you cold?' Will's voice was husky.

'Mmm? No.' Kate shook her head.

Will looked at her mouth, longing to kiss her again. He wondered what her face looked like when she came. He imagined himself making her come, making her scream and moan and writhe beneath him . . . or on top . . . standing up against the wall ...

'Tired?' Kate asked. His eyes were dark and heavy-lidded. He must be worn out, she thought.

'No, I'm fine,' he said throatily. 'It's just a bit hot in here.' He shifted restlessly in his seat.

'It is, isn't it?' Kate felt as though she was on fire. 'Why don't we have coffee in the living room?' she suggested, jumping up to clear the plates. 'It's cooler in there.' In a frenzy of lust, she needed to move around to stop herself pouncing on him. 'You go on through.'

When she brought in the coffee, she didn't sit next to Will, instead choosing the couch opposite his, with the coffee table as a buffer between them. When they both reached for the milk jug and their hands touched, she pulled hers away as if it had been burned. They drank their coffee in silence. Will seemed on edge again, drumming his long, slender fingers on the arm of the sofa. Kate watched them, imagining them in her hair, stroking her skin, exploring the curves and crevices of her body . . .

'So, um, what time is your flight in the morning?' she asked.

'Ten o'clock.'

'Right. You'll have to be up early. Is there anything I can do for you?'

Take off your dress. Kiss me. Wrap your legs around me. Let me inside you. Will could think of a million things. 'No thanks,' he said, draining his coffee.

'Well . . .' She stood, awkwardly smoothing her dress. 'It's getting late and you've got an early start. I think I'll go to bed.'

Suddenly Will shot to his feet. 'Take me with you,' he said urgently, his eyes burning into hers, his breathing ragged.

Kate stared at him, terrified she had misheard, or misunderstood. But before she had a chance to speak, he had crossed the distance between them and was kissing her with a desperate hunger. 'Take me to bed with you,' he breathed into her mouth.

'Yours or mine?' Kate kissed his throat, tugging at his T-shirt until Will raised his arms for her to take it off over his head. Her hands ran feverishly over the warm skin of his chest, while she kissed his mouth, his stubbly chin.

'Whichever is nearest.' Will shuddered as she grazed a nipple with her teeth.

But they knew they weren't going anywhere. They exploded against each other, lips, teeth and tongues clashing, hands tearing at each other's clothes. Kate felt the cool air against her skin as Will unhooked her bra, followed by his warm, caressing hands on her breasts. She felt his body clench as she unzipped his jeans and took his cock in her hand. But even as his kisses became more urgent, his hands less gentle, she felt the tension in his body and sensed his restraint.

Kissing her way down his chest, she dropped to her knees in front of him. He shivered as she kissed his taut stomach, his fingers digging into her shoulders as she curled her tongue into his belly button. He groaned jerkily as she took him into her mouth.

'Kate . . .' he breathed, stroking the side of her face. She heard a world of tenderness in that one word.

As she flicked her tongue around the head of his cock, circling it slowly, the quiet was shattered by a piercing, high-pitched shriek.

The next thing she knew, Will had given her an almighty shove and she was sprawled half-naked on the floor, with Tina glaring down at her, looking like the wrath of God. He had his back to her and was zipping up his jeans. Kate covered her breasts with an arm, scrabbling frantically on the floor for her bra. Before she could get to her feet, Tina flew at her. 'You fucking bitch!' she snarled, claws out.

Will spun around in time to block her, grabbed her flailing arms and held her off. Tina struggled ineffectually to escape his grip, whimpering with rage.

'Christ, sorry Kate. Are you okay?' Suddenly realising he had knocked her flying, he reached down to help her up. But as soon as he loosened his grasp on Tina, she broke free of him and hit out blindly, scratching his face and pummelling his chest and head.

'Jesus!' Will swore, holding an arm in front of his face. He managed to grab both her arms and held them behind her back. 'What are you doing here anyway?' he said, almost accusingly.

'You bastard!' she screamed, straining to break free of him. 'I came back because I was worried about *you*! I thought you were upset about your father. But instead I find you here getting your jollies with this ... this *blimp*!' she spat, her eyes sparking fury as Kate scrabbled on the floor for her clothes. 'What happened?' she yelled. 'Did you run out of food to stuff your face with so you had to gobble my boyfriend the minute my back was turned?'

With a supreme effort, she wrenched herself free of Will and lunged at Kate, grabbing a handful of her hair and jerking her head back so hard that Kate felt her neck would snap. She gasped in agony. 'Can't you last a second without shoving something in your fucking mouth?' Tina screamed.

'Let go,' Will said, taking Tina's wrist and squeezing it until she cried out in pain.

'You shit!' she spat, eyes blurred now with tears.

Kate seized her opportunity. With Will occupied in holding Tina off, she abandoned the search for her bra, scrambled to her feet and, clutching the top of her dress to her chest, and shot out of the room.

'Kate!' Will shouted after her, but she kept going.

She took the stairs two at a time. As she reached the top, she heard the front door open.

'Kate?' Louise called after her, but she didn't look back.

She ran along the corridor and into her room. Slamming the door behind her, she collapsed against it while heaving sobs racked her.

'Oh fuck, oh fuck, oh fuck,' she whispered to herself. She had never been so humiliated. To be caught by Tina was bad enough, but what tortured her was Will shoving her away the moment Tina had shown up. If Kate had ever been in any doubt as to how he felt about her, that had said it all. He was happy enough to use her for a quick comfort shag when he was feeling down but to cast her aside like an old shoe when his bitch of a girlfriend turned up – as if she was nothing. He had practically hurled her across the room in his panic at getting caught. She had actually fooled herself into thinking it was her he wanted, not just somebody – *anybody*.

What made it even worse was the knowledge that she was in the wrong. However much she disliked Tina, Will *was* her boyfriend, and she was entitled to be furious to find Kate giving him a blow job. In fairness, she acknowledged that Tina had every right to beat her to a pulp in the circumstances – which made it all the more humiliating.

Kate didn't know how long she lay slumped inside the door, crying her eyes out. Finally, she picked herself up and sat on the bed. Starting to shiver, she pulled on a jumper over her dress and contemplated her dilemma. She knew she had to get away. She couldn't face Will tomorrow. She couldn't bear to see the cagey morning-after look on his face, and she'd die if she had to have the last-night-was-a-mistake conversation with him. Besides, Tina would claw her eyes out if she got another chance. She *had* to find a way. As she sat there, she heard Louise go into her room along the corridor and perked up a little. Help was at hand. Kate might not be able to arrange a quick getaway but she knew a woman who could.

Louise's room was a couple of doors down from hers. Kate tiptoed down the corridor and knocked softly.

'Kate!' Louise's welcoming smile faded as she took in Kate's stricken, tear-streaked face.

'I need to go home!' Kate said urgently, her voice trembling. 'Can you get me out of here?'

'Well, sure . . .' Louise said hesitantly, giving her a puzzled look.

'*Now?*' Kate said emphatically. '*Tonight?*'

Louise didn't hesitate. 'Yes,' she said simply.

Tears of gratitude sprang to Kate's eyes.

'Come on, I'll help you pack,' Louise said briskly, and bustled Kate back along the corridor to her room.

Kate was glad of the help. Her hands were shaking so much, she couldn't fold anything. She threw clothes willy-nilly into her suitcase, which Louise took out again and folded neatly before repacking them. Her tour-manager muscle kicked in and she moved through the room like a tornado, quickly stripping it of Kate's belongings and packing them into the two cases she had brought with her. Instinctively picking up on Kate's need for secrecy, she bundled her out through the kitchen so they wouldn't have to pass the open living-room door where Tina was still screaming and throwing things at Will.

Once Louise took over, it all happened so fast that Kate felt dizzy. Though it would strike her as peculiar later, she was grateful to Louise for not asking any questions. She didn't try to talk her out of it or tell her to sleep on it. She didn't try to persuade her that things would seem better in the morning – Kate knew they wouldn't. She simply accepted that she wanted to leave and set about making it happen.

Fifteen minutes later, they were racing towards the airport, Louise occupied on her mobile for most of the drive, making arrangements.

'There's a flight in two hours,' she told Kate. 'We should be able to get you on that if we hurry.'

Overwhelmed with relief, Kate found she couldn't stop crying. She turned her face to the window and watched the tears rolling down her face, while Louise babbled on the phone, periodically passing her tissues.

Though she was bursting with curiosity, Louise refrained from asking Kate what had happened. She could make an educated guess anyway: she had arrived to find Kate disappearing upstairs half-naked and Tina screaming at Will like a fish wife while trying to break the entire furnishings of the house on his head.

When they got into the airport building, she left Kate queuing at the check-in line, while she went to the ticket desk. Moments later she shoved a ticket into Kate's hand. When Kate had checked in her bags, Louise walked her to the gate.

'I must pay you for the ticket,' Kate said, fishing around in her bag.

'No you won't,' Louise said brusquely. 'A return airfare was part of the deal, remember?'

'Well, yes, but—'

'No buts,' Louise said firmly. 'There'll be a car to meet you in Dublin. The guy will have a card with your name on it, so look out for him. His name's Dave.'

'Oh, there was no need for that,' Kate said, tears springing to her eyes again at Louise's thoughtfulness. 'I could have got a taxi.'

'Don't be silly. You're in no state to deal with a taxi driver.'

There was just time for a quick hug before Kate had to run for her plane.

'Take care,' Louise said.

'Thanks for everything.'

'You'd better run.' Louise let her go. 'And call me,' she shouted after her. 'You have my number?'

Kate nodded, waving as she disappeared.

Chapter 11

Kate sat on the sofa wrapped in a duvet, watching dawn break over Dublin while she let the events of last night sink in. It had all happened so fast. It was hard to believe that only last night Will had pulled her into his arms and asked her to take him to bed. She could still feel his mouth on hers, his heart jumping beneath her hand, in the same way that she could still feel the motion of the plane. The taste of him was still on her tongue, the impression of his hands on her body. She felt like an amputee – as though Will was a physical part of her that had been lopped off by a cack-handed surgeon. Tears fell down her cheeks again and she dabbed at them gingerly with a sodden tissue. They were already raw from crying and gritty from lack of sleep.

She heard Freddie's bedroom door open and he padded softly into the living room behind her.

'Hello, Miss Thing!' he gasped. 'What are *you* doing here? Got tired of the rock-chick lifestyle and decided to slum it with us plebs

for a while? You should have told me you were coming, I'd have—'
He stopped short as he took in Kate's puffy, red eyes and the confetti
of crumpled tissues that surrounded her. 'Oh my God! What happened, sweetie?' He plonked down on the sofa and put an arm
around her.

Kate had managed to stop crying, but Freddie's sympathy
brought a new lump to her throat.

'Will's father died,' she said shakily, not knowing where to start.

'Yeah, I saw it on the news.' Freddie nodded. 'You didn't know
him, though, did you?' he asked.

'No,' Kate shook her head, 'it's not that. But Will was really
upset, and . . . well, one thing led to another . . .' She trailed off.

'Oh my God, you shagged him!' Freddie's eyes were nearly popping out of his head.

'No . . . Well, yes . . . more or less,' Kate hedged. 'And then Tina
walked in.'

'And she caught you shagging?'

'Yes.' Kate nodded miserably. 'Well, not exactly shagging.' She
was plucking threads from a cushion absently.

'*What* exactly?'

'Well, I was sort of . . . I mean, I kind of . . . um, you know . . .'

'Jesus! You're starting to sound like Hugh Grant!'

Kate took a deep breath. 'Okay. I was giving him a blow job,' she
said quickly.

'*What?*' Freddie's voice cut like ice.

'Well, his father had just died,' Kate said defensively.

'Right, okay.' Freddie had apparently accepted this. But he could-
n't contain himself for long. 'And you didn't think maybe a nice cup
of tea?' he exploded.

'I know, I know.' Kate groaned, hugging the cushion to herself
and burying her face in it. 'God, how could I have been so stupid? I
can't *believe* I did that. He's going to think I'm some kind of nut who
goes around giving out blow jobs to the recently bereaved.'

'Jesus!' Freddie laughed. 'I've heard of a sympathy fuck before,
but this has got to be the first condolence blow job!'

Kate smiled weakly, peeping up from the cushion. 'It's not funny,'
she said, punching Freddie's arm.

'I beg to differ,' he said archly. 'But hang on – what are you doing here? I mean, I don't think it was your best idea ever, but you're not going to tell me he didn't *enjoy* it. He's a bloke. It was a blow job. Can't go wrong, basically.'

'He was enjoying it well enough until Tina turned up.' Kate sniffed. 'It was so awful, Freddie! The minute she appeared, he just pushed me away. He couldn't get rid of me fast enough.'

Just then Freddie's bedroom door opened again and Ken shuffled in, yawning, wearing nothing but a pair of boxer shorts. His eyes half closed, he looked as if he was sleepwalking.

'Kate!' he said groggily. 'This is a nice surprise. I didn't know you were here.' He flopped onto the sofa beside her, put his feet on the coffee table and laid his head on her shoulder, snuggling into her neck with a contented sigh. 'What are we talking about?' he asked, closing his eyes against the sun streaming through the window.

'Previously on *Desperate Flatmates*,' Freddie said, doing his best American voiceover impression.

Kate shook her head almost imperceptibly at him, but Freddie ignored her. 'Will's girlfriend caught Kate giving him a blow job last night,' he said before Kate could stop him.

That woke Ken up. He lifted his head from Kate's shoulder and dropped a kiss on the top of her head. 'Poor you! Do you want me to go?' he asked, jerking a thumb in the direction of the door. 'Leave you alone with Freddie?'

'Oh no, you have to stay,' Freddie told him. 'Ken is great at this sort of thing,' he informed Kate.

'What do you mean, "this sort of thing"? Just how many cases of *fellatio interruptus* has he had to deal with?'

'You'd be surprised,' Ken said drily. 'But, seriously, I'd be happy to help. So – take it from the top,' he said, leaning forward with his elbows on his knees, hands clasped, businesslike.

Another Mr Fix-It from the same stable as Conor, Kate thought, her heart sinking. Trust Helen to have ferreted him out. 'Well,' she began reluctantly, 'Will had just found out that his father had died, and he was really upset . . .'

'So you thought a blow job would be just the thing to cheer him up,' Ken finished.

'Well, not exactly. I mean, it's not as if I said, "Sorry for your loss," and dropped to my knees right away.'

'Because *that* would have been inappropriate,' Freddie said.

'It just sort of happened,' Kate continued, ignoring him. 'It was more . . . organic. It just seemed . . . right somehow.'

'*Really?*' Freddie screwed up his face in disbelief.

'Well, I didn't want him, you know, worrying about me . . . you know, about . . .' Kate struggled to explain. 'It's like risotto,' she said finally.

'*Risotto?*' It was Ken's turn to look bewildered. 'Why risotto?'

'It's the ultimate comfort food. Think about it. It's totally effortless to eat, the cook does all the work – you hardly even have to chew. It's practically pre-digested, for Christ's sake.'

'Oh right.' Ken nodded. 'So you're saying a blow job is the risotto of sex?'

'Well . . . yes.'

'Okay, so there you were, feeding Will his organic risotto. What happened then?'

'Tina appeared and started screaming her head off. Will shoved me away, and the next thing I knew I was on my arse on the floor and Tina was going for me bald-headed.'

'You were bitch-slapped by Tina?' Freddie said excitedly. 'God, I wish I'd been there.'

'Hang on a sec.' Ken made a halting gesture with his hands. 'Back up. Where *exactly* were you when Tina came in?'

'I was in the middle of . . . I was sort of, um . . .' Kate faltered. Why did Ken have to have all the gory details anyway? she thought crossly. She tried again. 'I was kind of . . .'

'In prayer position?' Freddie supplied.

'Yes.' She blushed.

'Worshipping at the Altar of Dong?' he elaborated gleefully.

'Yes,' Kate mumbled.

'Okay, Freddie, I think we get the picture,' Ken broke in. 'So you were in the act when Tina came in screaming her head off?'

'Yes. I heard her before I saw her. For a second I thought it was Will, you know . . . um, having a good time.'

'Kate, Kate, Kate.' Ken laughed, shaking his head. '*Of course* he pushed you away.'

'Yes, but it was the way he did it. It was so . . . instinctive.'

'Bet your arse it was! It's called the survival instinct.'

'What do you mean?'

'Kate, you had his dick in your mouth and you got a fright. The poor guy was probably afraid you were going to give him an oral castration.'

'Oh!' Kate breathed. 'Do you really think that could have been it?'

'Of course it was, you idiot!' Freddie ruffled her hair affectionately. 'I told you Ken was good at this sort of thing.'

'Just promise me one thing, Kate,' Ken said.

'What's that?'

'That you'll never go in for bereavement counselling.'

'Yeah,' Freddie said, 'and when you go to greet the mourners at the end of a funeral, you *shake their hand.*'

'Ha Ha, very funny.' But she was so happy with this new slant on things that she didn't mind them taking the piss.

Ken stood up, stretching extravagantly. 'Look, I don't know about anyone else, but I need some breakfast. I'll go out for the croissants and you guys get the coffee on. Then we'll put our heads together and figure out your next move,' he said to Kate.

'Okay,' Kate jumped up, 'and I'm going to make muffins. I'm starving.'

Later, the coffee table laden with warm, freshly baked muffins, flaky croissants, several kinds of jam, a jug of orange juice and a pot of strong, fragrant coffee, Kate felt a lot brighter.

'What's your next move?' Ken asked, licking jammy croissant crumbs off his thumb.

'Well,' Kate said consideringly, 'I might eat my own weight in chocolate.'

'That's no good.' Ken shook his head. 'You've got to get back in there and consolidate your advantage.'

'What advantage? I jumped Will when he was at a low ebb and got bitch-slapped by his girlfriend for my trouble. How do I improve on that?'

'Don't be so negative,' Freddie said. 'Ken's right. You've got to get back in the game – let Will know there's plenty more where that blow job came from.'

'But what if he doesn't want more?'

'Why wouldn't he?' Ken asked. 'Are you, like . . . not so hot at the old sword-swallowing?'

'Please! It's my best thing,' Kate said indignantly.

Ken bit into a muffin. 'God, Kate, *these* are your best thing. I take it all back. Stay here with us and cook our breakfast every morning.'

Kate smiled. 'All I mean is, what if it was just the heat of the moment and he doesn't really fancy me in the cold light of day?'

'You didn't give the poor guy a chance. You just pegged it out the door before he even had a chance to reholster his weapon, from what I can gather,' Ken said.

'And what about Tina? She'll tear me to pieces if she ever sees me again.'

'I'm sure you've got a few moves of your own.'

'You've got to stop being so spineless,' Freddie said, trying to sound stern. 'Ooh, this is so cool,' he squealed excitedly, spoiling the effect. 'I feel like the head nun in *The Sound of Music*, telling Maria to get back and nail the Captain before the Baroness gets her mitts on him.'

'I don't think that's *quite* what the Mother Superior was advocating,' Ken said.

Freddie ignored him. 'I could gaze out of the window and sing "Climb Every Mountain", if you think it would help,' he said eagerly.

'I don't.'

'On the contrary.' Ken smiled. 'It would be just the thing to send you haring back to Italy as fast as your legs would carry you.'

Kate smiled grudgingly. 'Anyway, it's hardly the same situation.'

'True,' Freddie allowed. 'Maria was afraid she'd given her feelings away because she got a bit hot and bothered when the Captain was giving her a twirl in his *Lederhosen*.'

Despite herself, Kate giggled.

'And who'd blame her?' Freddie continued. '*You*, on the other hand, came right out and swallowed his ceremonial sword. I think it's safe to say *your* cover is well and truly blown.'

'Much as Will was,' Ken said.

'Oh, I don't know why I'm laughing,' Kate moaned. 'It's not funny. And you two could try not enjoying it so much either.'

'Well, we could *try*,' Freddie said, 'but I doubt we'd get very far.'

'The point is, you've shown your hand already, so what have you got to lose?'

'Certainly not any dignity,' Freddie said chirpily. 'That ship has sailed.'

She knew they meant well, but Kate was feeling seriously ganged up on. As if he had sensed this, Ken's tone changed. 'I know it's not an easy thing to do,' he said gently, 'but this is Will we're talking about – the love of your life. I mean, he *is*, isn't he?'

'Yes.' Kate sighed defeatedly. 'I wish he wasn't, but he is.'

'Well, that's that, then,' Ken said, with an air of finality, grabbing the fat Sunday paper he had brought back from the shops and shaking it open.

He was right. If she had any chance of being with Will, she had to go for it. At least then if it didn't work out, she would have nothing to reproach herself with. But she had to do something else first.

'I've got to break up with Brian,' she said. She might never have Will, but she couldn't use Brian as a safety net – it wasn't fair on him.

It occurred to her that she had never had to dump anyone before – she was usually the one dumped – and she didn't have a clue how to go about it. She knew all too well how painful it was to be dumped, and she dreaded having to do that to Brian. It was a lot easier to be the dumpee.

Suddenly Ken sat up with a jolt, almost choking on his coffee.

'What is it?' Kate and Freddie asked in unison.

'Oh, nothing,' he spluttered, folding the paper he'd been reading while Freddie slapped him on the back.

'*What?*' Without waiting for an answer, Freddie picked up the paper and opened it to the page Ken had been reading.

'Oh my God!' He darted a panic-stricken glance at Kate.

Kate looked at the paper in his hands. 'Oh God – May Kennedy,' she said faintly. It was the paper in which Tina's journalist friend had her social column – though 'column' was something of a euphemism since it took up the entire back page.

'Look,' Ken said brightly, 'it's going to be a beautiful day. Let's do something!'

'Like what?' Freddie asked, eyes still on the paper.

'We could go to the zoo,' Ken said.

'The *zoo?*' Freddie looked askance at him.

'Now you're really scaring me,' Kate said.

'It's not that bad,' Freddie said.

'Just give me the highlights.'

'It's quite short,' Freddie said, and proceeded to read the whole thing. '"Friends of Ireland's favourite celebrity couple, Will Sargent and Tina Roche (and yours truly counts herself as one of their closest friends and most devoted fans)" – smarmy cow! – "will be saddened to hear that all is not well, with rumours rife of a split after Tina fled the house in Tuscany where the couple were staying just weeks before her birthday. Friends were already starting to descend on Florence for what promised to be the party of the year. Earlier in the week Tina had joined Will at the beautiful villa in the Tuscan countryside, to which he had decamped for the summer with Walking Wounded, but she made a hurried departure from the house in the early hours of this morning in an obvious state of distress and it appears she will not be joining Will in England for his father's funeral.

'"News of Sir Philip's death came as a great shock . . ." blah, blah, blah. She goes on about Philip Sargent for a while.'

'It's not that bad,' Kate said tentatively.

'Wait, there's more at the end,' Freddie said, his eye scanning down the page.

'"Meanwhile, Tina is remaining tight-lipped about the alleged split, but her exit from the villa came just hours after the hasty departure of one Kate O'Neill—"'

'Oh no!' Kate groaned in anguish. 'She actually mentioned my name?'

'"—one Kate O'Neill,"' Freddie nodded, resuming, '"sparking rumours that a third party was involved. Kate, the youngest daughter of the actress Grace O'Neill, had been working as a cook at the house. Personally, I feel that this is just a temporary blip, and that this gorgeous couple will soon be as loved up as they ever were. I'm sure I'm not alone in wishing them well – the Irish social scene would be a far drearier place without them. The phrase "made for each other" is over-used, but in this case, it just happens to be true."'

'Well, she would say that, the stupid cow,' Freddie went on.

'She's just miffed at being done out of a party,' Ken added.

'Still . . .' Kate said despondently. She knew that May had been instrumental in promoting Will and Tina as Ireland's premier celebrity couple, largely at Tina's instigation. Naturally she would talk up the fairytale she had helped to create. Besides, she was Tina's friend. But she couldn't shake off a niggling doubt that maybe May knew what she was talking about – after all, she must have spent plenty of time with them as a couple.

'It's not that bad,' Freddie said consolingly, 'apart from the naming and shaming bit. I mean, it could have been a lot worse, couldn't it?'

'It's not that bad *in itself,*' Ken said. 'I mean, as far as it goes . . .' He left the thought hanging in the air.

Kate knew what he was getting at. 'It's the fact that it's out there,' she said.

It had put the whole thing in the public domain, fuelling speculation and spiking interest, and Kate had an awful feeling that this was only the beginning.

Waking early the following morning, after a fitful night's sleep, Kate found Ken and Freddie already up, sitting side by side at the breakfast bar eating toast and marmalade. Freddie was wearing boxers and an old Walking Wounded tour T-shirt that he often used as a sort of dressing gown, but Ken was dressed for work in a sharp suit, crisp white shirt and red tie. The bar was covered with newspapers and, when Kate came in, Ken hastily shuffled one to the bottom of the pile.

'Morning, Kate!' he said cheerily – too cheerily, Kate thought.

She eyed the pile of newspapers. 'You got them all?'

Freddie looked up from the tabloid he was reading. 'Ken went out first thing.'

'And?' she asked warily.

'You want the good news or the bad news?' Ken asked.

'There's good news?'

'Well, there's nothing in *The Irish Times,*' he joked feebly.

'Ha ha.' She looked at Freddie, who was once more engrossed. 'How bad is it?' she asked him.

'It's bad . . .' he said slowly. His eyes widened as he read on. 'It's *very* bad.'

'Define very bad.'

'They've got details.'

'Details!' Kate shrieked. 'You don't mean—'

'Yep – the whole story. Blow job and all.'

'I thought Tina was remaining tight-lipped,' Kate said shakily.

'According to this, it comes from "sources close to the couple" or "close friends of Tina's".'

Gwen and Julie, Kate thought. No doubt Tina had given them the okay to blab so that she could feed her side of the story to the papers while appearing to maintain a dignified silence.

'Well, I might as well know the worst,' she said, with more conviction than she felt. Steeling herself, she climbed onto a stool at the opposite side of the counter. Freddie handed her a paper open at the relevant page.

'"Tina's love rival" – love rival! – "has been revealed as curvy cook, Kate O'Neill (32) . . Thirty-two!' she squealed. 'They can't even get my age right!'

'You're thirty-one in this one,' Freddie said, waving his tabloid.

'I've got thirty,' Ken added.

'And they call me curvy – that's a euphemism for fat.'

'So does this one,' Freddie said. 'Listen to this. "Curvaceous Kate (31) is the daughter of Grace O'Neill, one of our most cherished actresses."'

'Mum will like that.'

'She gets a mention in this one too,' Ken said. 'It says, "*The buxom brunette*—"'

'Buxom!' Kate screeched in outrage.

'"The buxom brunette,"' Ken continued, '"is the daughter of Grace O'Neill (56), one of Ireland's finest actresses."'

'Fifty-six!' Kate gasped. 'Mum won't like that!'

'Why? How old is she?' Ken asked.

'Fifty-six.'

'Then she definitely won't like it,' Freddie said.

'God, how many ways are there of saying plump?' Kate huffed. Meanwhile, Tina was described as 'willowy', 'stunning', 'leggy' and 'super-fit'. The contrast was obvious and deliberately bitchy.

While her age and the euphemisms for 'plump' varied from paper to paper, the story was almost identical in them all. They said that Tina and Will had had a blazing row on the day his father died, several hinting that Tina's attendance at a 2Tone concert was the cause of the quarrel. The tone of some of the articles was slyly censorious on this point. One noted that 'Just hours after Will learned of his father's death, Tina was spotted partying with the Cassidy brothers at a 2Tone concert in Florence's Mandela Forum', while another commented that she had 'left Will to grieve alone in the €6 million Tuscan mansion', insinuating that it was her fault he had turned elsewhere for consolation.

But the sly digs at Tina didn't make Kate feel any better about her part in the affair – especially not when it came to the bit where Tina had returned early from the concert to find Kate giving him a blow job.

'Oh God, I can never go out again!' she wailed, as she waded through one paper after another. Whether it was just a slow news day or because Tina was such a favourite with the gutter press, the story had been prominently splashed in every one of the tabloids.

'Look on the bright side,' Freddie said. 'At least now you won't have to break the news to Brian.'

'Unfortunately, it's not even good for that. Brian lives in a bubble as far as this sort of thing is concerned. Wait – I haven't seen that one.' She pointed to the paper Ken had pushed to the bottom of the pile.

'I'm afraid you made its front page.' Ken said, and reluctantly handed it over.

Kate gasped. Under the headline there was a large picture of a distraught Tina driving away from the villa and a smaller inset of Kate, which she recognised as having been taken a couple of years ago at one of Lorcan's opening nights. 'Oh *no*!' she wailed.

The article was by far the most damning piece, portraying Kate as a conniving sexual predator, just waiting to pounce as soon as Tina's back was turned. Kate knew that Tina was the darling of this particular paper, having a close relationship with the Editor, so it was hardly surprising, but that didn't make it any easier to take. 'Well, so much for keeping a low profile,' she said, on the verge of tears.

'It's just a load of old rubbish,' Ken said. 'Don't pay any attention.'

That was easier said than done. It wasn't long before the phone was ringing. Her mother was the first. 'I've just seen the papers, darling. Marvellous news about you and Will!' she trilled.

'Well, I wouldn't exactly call it marvellous, Mum.'

'Your father and I are just off to England for Philip's funeral,' Grace continued, 'but I couldn't go without ringing to tell you how delighted I am.'

Kate could hardly believe her ears. 'Have you actually *read* the papers?'

'Of course,' Grace said breezily. 'Like I said, it's great news. I really couldn't be happier for you.' There was a momentary pause. 'I suppose this means it's off with the Tree-hugger?' her mother asked tentatively. 'You know, I didn't like to say anything before, but I never thought he was right for you, sweetheart.'

'You hid that well, Mum.'

'And I never thought Tina was good enough for Will either,' Grace rushed on.

Kate was torn between extreme irritation and gratitude. Her mother was infuriating, but she couldn't help feeling touched that she didn't automatically take it as read that Will was out of her league, as she knew many would – Rachel, for instance.

'Well, I'll be seeing Will later on. I'll give him your love, shall I?'

'*Please* don't say anything, Mum.'

'Better yet, why don't you come with us?'

'I don't think that's a good idea.'

'Well, I suppose you're right – it would probably be best to wait until all this blows over.'

'Mum, have you actually *seen* what they wrote about me?' she asked in exasperation.

'You mean the way they keep getting your age wrong? I know it's annoying, darling, and it's a shame they printed that awful picture of you before you'd lost all the weight.'

'No, I don't mean that. I mean the things they said about me. They made me sound like a conniving bitch.'

'Or a man-eating slut,' Grace conceded.

'I can't ever go out in public again!' Kate whined.

'Oh, don't be silly, darling,' Grace said. 'It'll be forgotten in no time. Besides, you know what they say – there's no such thing as bad publicity.'

'Mum!' Kate groaned in exasperation. 'That may be true for people who *want* publicity in the first place. I *don't*.'

'Nonsense, darling! Everyone wants publicity nowadays. It's the latest thing.'

'Well, *I* don't. What would I do with it?'

Of course, Conor had the answer to that one. 'The public aren't all going to be on Tina's side by any means,' he told her. 'Everyone loves to see someone like her get her comeuppance – especially other women. There'll be a backlash and you can use it to your advantage, if you play it right.'

'But I don't *want* to be on a reality-TV show.'

'It doesn't have to be that.'

'Or do a kiss and tell,' she said flatly, 'or endorse a range of kinky underwear for fat girls, or write a sex column or have my own cookery show on TV.'

'Well, there are plenty of other things you can do,' Conor continued, undaunted. 'You really should get a publicist . . .'

Kate sighed, hardly listening any more. At least she didn't have to worry about her family feeling she'd shamed them, she thought wryly. They seemed to regard it as the next best thing to winning the lottery.

Later in the day, she was surprised to get a phone call from Louise. 'Kate, I'm sorry about all this hassle you've been getting in the press,' she said. 'I know how miserable it must be for you.'

Kate was momentarily taken aback by Louise's apparent omniscience, but then she realised that of course she would be aware of anything in the media concerning Will.

'I wish I could say it'll get better, but I don't think it'll go away for a while yet, not with Tina involved. She's sure to milk it for all it's worth. You know she's a client of Dev Tennant?'

'Yes, I know,' Kate sighed.

Dev Tennant was the most powerful publicist in Britain, revered and reviled in equal measure for his Machiavellian ability to manipulate the media and public opinion.

'We haven't made Will aware of any of this stuff yet,' Louise was telling her. 'Obviously it's not such a big story in England, so he's not likely to see it. And even if any of the English tabloids pick it up, I'm sure Antonia Bell would never get them.'

'No, I don't imagine she would.'

'Anyway, look, if you want any help with the media, I can put you in touch with our PR.'

'I don't want to do anything to add fuel to the fire. I just want it all to go away.'

But Louise was right – it got worse. The story continued to run over the next couple of days, fuelled by Tina's friends popping up to have their say. Every member of her coterie who had stayed at the villa was tracked down to comment on the story. Their impressions of Kate were far from flattering, dismissing her as someone they had barely noticed and expressing astonishment that Will had even been aware of her. They put down his lapse to derangement caused by grief over his father's death and characterised Kate as a big, awkward girl, hopelessly out of her depth in the glamorous world at the villa where she had been surrounded by celebrities.

Just when it looked as if the story was fizzling out, Tina rekindled it by breaking her silence, 'speaking of her heartache for the first time' in an 'exclusive' interview in her pet tabloid, which was promptly picked up by all the others. Hell hath no fury like a woman scorned, and Tina had more fury than most. She played her wronged-woman role to the hilt. But what really tore Kate apart was what she said about Will. She told the interviewer how later that night, after Kate had left, Will had stayed up for hours telling her he still loved her and pleading with her to give him a second chance. Tina said she had believed him when he said that his dalliance with Kate had meant nothing, but she didn't know if she could forgive him, and she needed time apart to think things over.

The next few days were a feeding frenzy for the press, and Kate couldn't go outside the door without being snapped by paparazzi and hounded by reporters. Will rang her mobile several times, but she didn't pick up. Reading how he felt in the papers was bad enough. She didn't need to hear him spell it out to her. It was no consolation that the backlash against Tina had started, as Conor predicted. Rival tabloids took sides, one even conducting a poll, which came out sixty-forty in favour of Kate. Columnists used the story to fuel a debate about 'curvy' girls versus 'stick insects', holding up Kate as a kind of heroine to 'real' women. They ran pictures of Kate and Tina side by side, inviting their readers to decide whose figure was preferable.

Tina's favourite tabloid retaliated with a dazzlingly beautiful picture of Tina juxtaposed with one of Kate looking like a sleep-deprived, mentally subnormal bag lady while she bawled out a photographer who had been chasing her the previous day. Beside her, Tina was a creature from a different species, ethereally beautiful, cool and elegant. The implication was clear: no man worthy of the name would choose Kate when they could have *this*.

Nonetheless, she had her admirers and all sorts of offers flooded in – everything from modelling lingerie for 'bigger' girls to taking part in the inevitable reality-TV show. She even received a couple of marriage proposals from lonely men who had seen her picture in the paper and liked the look of her. Every day brought a new batch of offers, from the mundane to the truly bizarre. She refused them all, despite Conor's protests. 'There's a lot of goodwill towards you at the moment,' he advised. 'You should use it to your advantage.'

'I don't *want* to be some kind of plump-girl icon.'

'It won't last for ever, you know,' he admonished.

'Promise?'

Chapter 12

Will returned to Tuscany at the end of the week, physically and emotionally exhausted from the strain of his father's funeral and its aftermath. Eager to mend fences and for him and his half-brother, Paul, to get to know each other, Antonia had insisted he stay with them after the funeral. She couldn't have been kinder, and Paul had been sweet, taking Will under his wing as though *he* were the elder brother, going out of his way to make him feel comfortable and at home and to share memories of their father. But Will struggled to recognise the father he had known in the indulgent, supportive parent Paul described, and no matter how hard he stared at the pictures of Philip, trying to conjure some feeling of connection, a stranger gazed back at him. He couldn't share Antonia and Paul's desolating sense of loss and felt like an impostor.

He was glad to have had the chance to get to know Paul, but on further acquaintance, he found Antonia brittle and imperious. It irritated him that she felt she had a claim on his sympathy; it angered him that she appropriated the entire bereavement to herself, as though Paul hadn't lost Philip too – and kind and welcoming though she was now, he couldn't forget that when it had counted she hadn't wanted him around. Not wishing to be cruel, but fast losing patience with her, he decided it was time to leave.

He was also anxious to get back to the villa and see Kate. He had tried phoning her while he was away but she had never answered, which worried him. But perhaps it was just as well – it would be easier to talk to her in person.

He was just settling in on the flight back to Italy when the stewardess inexplicably flung his paper at him, shooting him a filthy look.

'What's *her* problem?' he muttered conspiratorially to the woman beside him, an elderly Irish matron.

'Should have brained you with it,' she growled, eyeing him coldly from beneath forbidding eyebrows.

'*What?*' Will was baffled – he had never seen either woman before in his life.

'You're no better than you should be.' The woman buried her nose in *Wow!* magazine.

Mystified, Will kept his head down for the rest of the flight, not wanting to attract any more abuse but more anxious than ever to get back to Italy and find out what they had been saying about him in the press.

Returning to the villa in the early afternoon, he found Louise in the study, going through the mail. 'Hi!' he said.

'You're back!' She smiled up at him as Will collapsed into the chair opposite her.

'How was it?' she asked.

'Oh, you know.' Will shrugged expressively. 'Sad. Horrible. Antonia wants to be friends.'

'I don't imagine she's the easiest person to get on with.' Louise said sympathetically.

'Very high maintenance.' Will grimaced. 'Paul's great, though.'

'Your brother? I'd love to meet him.'

'You will. He's going to come and stay with me some time. He's a huge fan of the band,' Will smiled fondly.

They fell silent, and Will sank into a reverie. He was glad to be back with the people who really knew him, enjoying the fact that he could sit with Louise in companionable silence and neither of them felt the need to say anything.

A feeling of immense calm descended on him, and it came to him that everything was all right and as it should be. He had made his peace with his father – too late, perhaps, but he no longer felt the need to rewrite the past. He had his own life now, a life that he had made for himself, with work, a home, even a family of sorts. He had been happy – whether because of his father or in spite of him hardly seemed to matter any more.

Finally rousing himself, he got up and went to the door. 'Where's Kate?' he asked casually.

Louise hesitated, and Will came back into the room.

'She's gone,' Louise said shiftily, peeping up at him from under her lashes but not quite meeting his eyes. She made a show of getting back to work, standing up and shuffling papers around on the desk.

'Gone? Gone where?'

'Home – to Ireland.'

'Oh!' Will was surprised. 'When's she coming back?'

'She's not. She's left – for good.'

'What? When did she go?'

'The night before you left for England. The night Tina caught the two of you together.'

'You know about that?'

'Oh come on, Will,' Louise snapped. 'The whole world knows about that. You didn't think Tina would keep the gory details to herself, did you?'

Registering the anger in her eyes and her accusing tone, Will suddenly became very still. He moved closer to Louise, his eyes flinty. 'Tell me you didn't have anything to do with her going,' he said menacingly.

'Only in that I drove her to the airport, booked her ticket and paid for it with the company credit card,' Louise told him.

Will was momentarily lost for words. Then he said, 'You're fucking fired.'

'I fucking quit!' Louise flung back.

'What?' He blinked at her uncomprehendingly, completely taken aback.

Louise was taken aback too. Oh my God, did I really say that? she thought, panicking. She loved her job. She loved the band. Leaving them would be like abandoning her children. And how could she leave Rory? But she couldn't work for someone who treated people as Will had treated Kate, she told herself staunchly, resolving to stand her ground. She would never have believed him capable of such callousness.

They stood staring at each other, stunned into silence, both fuming.

Finally Will spoke. 'You can't quit,' he said arrogantly – and irrationally, Louise thought, considering he had just fired her. 'Just get Kate back here.'

'No,' Louise said, standing her ground though Will was towering over her intimidatingly.

'What is your problem with her?' he raged.

'I have no problem with Kate!'

Will raked a hand through his hair distractedly. 'Oh, come on, it was obvious you were against her being here from the start. But I thought you were getting on well.'

'We were! I really like her.'

'So why did you take the opportunity to get rid of her the minute my back was turned?'

'I didn't "get rid" of her! She *wanted* to leave.'

'Well, she was on a contract,' Will said, clutching at straws. 'She can't just waltz off whenever she feels like it. And why were you in such a bloody hurry to help her go?'

'Because I like her and I didn't want to see her get hurt. So when she came to my room that night crying her eyes out and desperate to get away, I was more than happy to help. I knew what was going on, Will.'

'You know nothing about what happened between me and Kate,' Will interrupted angrily, eyes blazing. 'Christ, Louise, you of all people should know better than to believe everything you read in the fucking papers!'

'I'm not talking about what I read in the papers,' Louise stormed. 'I'm talking about what I've seen with my own eyes.'

'I don't know what you think you've seen—'

'I *know* what you're doing, Will. I know all about your little *mission*,' she spat.

'What *mission*?'

Louise sighed. 'I know why you asked Kate to come here. I know you're pretending to be interested in her because her mother asked you to. I couldn't *believe* you'd agree to do it. I never thought you could be so cruel.'

Will was stunned into silence. Eventually he said, 'You heard that?'

Louise nodded. 'I know Grace asked you to flirt with Kate to push her into breaking up with her boyfriend. I just can't believe you're doing it.'

'I'm not,' Will said dazedly. All the fight seemed suddenly to have gone out of him.

'Oh come on, Will, you've been flirting with her since the moment she got here. The poor girl doesn't know which way is up.'

'But I'm not doing it for Grace.'

'Why are you doing it then? Just to amuse yourself?'

'No!' Will protested vehemently, but a look of intense vulnerability flashed across his face.

'Oh!' Louise stopped dead in her tracks. 'Oh, I see,' she said dropping into a chair.

Will's face was shuttered.

'You weren't pretending,' Louise stated.

'No.'

'Sorry,' Louise mumbled. 'But what was I supposed to think? I heard that, and the next thing I know Kate's on the payroll and you're all over her like a rash.'

'You might have given me the benefit of the doubt.'

'Okay, I'm sorry – but don't worry, I'll sort it out,' Louise said, jumping up. 'I'll get Kate back here right away.'

'She won't come,' Will said bleakly.

'I'll tell her the contract is binding and she has to. I'll tell her she'll never work again if she lets us down.'

Will sighed. 'No,' he said, rubbing his temples wearily, as if to stave off a headache. 'Don't do anything.'

'But—'

'Don't do anything,' he repeated, his shoulders slumped. 'It's probably for the best.'

Louise looked at him, aghast. 'How can you say that when—'

'Louise – drop it.' His voice was as cold as ice.

'Okay. But just for the record, I think you're making a big mistake.'

'Just for the record,' Will said, 'you're probably right.'

'What have you been saying to Louise?' Rory demanded, marching into the kitchen. Will was sitting at the table, soothing his frazzled nerves with a soft drink. Evidently Rory was next in line to take a pop at him, he thought. Some days he felt he ought to go back to drinking.

'Nothing. We just had a bit of an argument, that's all.'

'She seems really upset. And I heard her saying she quit.'

'She hasn't,' Will said. 'Don't worry, Mummy and Daddy love each other really.'

'Glad to hear it.' Rory grinned. 'One broken home is enough.'

He went to the fridge, got a beer, cracked it open and sat down opposite Will. 'What were you fighting about?' he asked conversationally.

'Kate.'

Rory raised his eyebrows.

'Louise is upset that I don't plan to go haring off to bring Kate back,' he said.

'You don't?'

'No.' He had hoped his tone would put an end to the discussion. But Rory didn't leave it there. 'That's mad!' he said. 'Why not?'

'We won't be here that much longer, and Maria can cope with the cooking for the last few weeks.'

'I'm not talking about the fucking food, and you know it.'

'Really? What are you talking about then?'

'I'm talking about you and Kate.' Rory gave him a long, hard look. 'You've got to go for it, man. Life's too fucking short. Your old man dying should tell you that.'

'It's not that simple,' Will said irritably.

277

'Why not?'

Will sighed. 'Because it's *Kate*,' he said wretchedly. 'Her family's practically my family.'

'Well, happy days!' Rory said.

'But what if it didn't work out? What if it ended badly?'

'You can't live your life by what-ifs. Have some balls!'

'Look who's talking!' Will scoffed.

'What's that supposed to mean?'

'It means you're in no position to preach to me. How long have you been in love with Louise and done nothing about it?'

Rory looked cornered, and Will instantly regretted having said anything.

'Sorry.' He felt like a shit.

'Different situation,' Rory said finally. 'It's not mutual.'

Will thought otherwise, and it was on the tip of his tongue to say so, but Rory was obviously so uncomfortable talking about it that he didn't have the heart to push it.

'Kate feels the same about you,' Rory said. 'I know she does. You've got to go for it. What have you got to lose?'

Everything, Will thought. 'If it didn't work out, if it did end badly,' he said hesitantly, 'I wouldn't just lose Kate. I'd lose everyone.'

'You'd still have us.' Rory grinned appealingly.

Will smiled at him. 'Don't think I don't appreciate it. But what would I – I mean, where would I—' He spluttered. 'Where would . . .' He didn't know how to say what he meant without sounding childish and idiotic.

'Where would you spend Christmas?' Rory finished Will's sentence for him.

'Well . . . yes,' Will admitted. 'Metaphorically speaking.'

'Have you thought about where you'll spend Christmas if you *don't* go for it?' Rory fingered his beer bottle thoughtfully, scooping up drips of condensation.

'What do you mean?'

'You'd be with Kate and her family, right?'

'I suppose so.' Will shrugged. 'Same as usual.'

'Do you really think you could hack that, year after year?'

'Why not?' Will said, puzzled.

278

'Spending Christmas with Kate and her family – and whatever tosser she ends up marrying? And her children who aren't *your* children?'

Will gulped. He hadn't thought about it like that. He was thinking about it as if they were all going to stand still in time. But of course Kate would end up marrying someone else, having children with him. He found the thought horrifying.

'Maybe she'll marry that boyfriend of hers,' Rory mused, twisting the knife. 'What's his name again?'

'Brian,' Will gritted, through clenched teeth. God, maybe she *would* marry him – she was still engaged to him, after all. But even if it wasn't him it would be someone else.

Rory smiled sympathetically at the horror spreading across Will's face. Obviously the picture he had painted had had the desired effect. Pulling a scrap of paper from the pocket of his jeans, he grabbed a pen from the table and scribbled something on it. 'Look, go for it with Kate, and if it doesn't work out, I'll make good on that,' he said, handing the paper to Will.

Will looked at it. In Rory's crabbed, spidery scrawl it read, 'IOU a family Christmas'. 'If that's not an incentive to go for it, I don't know what is,' Rory added gruffly.

'I could do a lot worse,' Will said, touched.

'You haven't seen Owen stuff the turkey.' Rory got up and picked up his bottle.

'Seriously – thanks.' Will smiled at him.

'Don't worry, it'll work out. You're one of the good guys, Will.' He raised his bottle in salute.

Outside the door, Rory bumped into Louise. His heart lurched as he wondered how long she had been standing there. She couldn't have heard, could she? She was looking at him questioningly, but he avoided her eyes and, with a casual 'Hi, Louise', brushed past her and went out onto the terrace.

Sitting on a low bench by the wall, he lit a cigarette, his movements slow and deliberate, but his fingers were shaking.

'Rory?' Louise had followed him. She walked slowly across the terrace and came to sit beside him on the bench. He looked straight ahead, not meeting her eyes.

'Rory,' she began hesitantly, 'I heard what Will said.'

Fuck! Here it comes – the big blow-off! 'Yeah?' He half turned to her as he took a long drag on his cigarette. Christ, he wasn't going to make this easy.

'He said – he said you were in love with me,' she said bluntly.

'Oh, *that*.' He looked at her cagily, his shoulder hunched defensively, like a child caught out in a lie – or a terrible guilty truth. Looking away, he exhaled on a long, deep sigh.

'Is it true?'

'Yeah, it's true,' he said quietly, meeting her eyes now, almost defiantly. He looked down, flicking an imaginary speck of ash off his jeans. 'I love you,' he said, his gaze direct and unflinching again. 'I'm in love with you – have been for ages,' he said, with a crooked smile, as though he was telling her something funny.

'Since when?' Louise asked.

'D'you remember that day coming up to Christmas when we all met at Will's house? It was bucketing down outside. You had this red bandana-type thing over your hair and you were wearing those red suede boots.' He remembered how dazzled he had been by the gorgeous sparkly eyed, long-limbed girl, and how many light years out of his reach she had seemed. 'You bought me some cigarettes,' he said softly, smiling at her. 'Remember that?'

She was surprised Rory remembered the cigarettes. While they had been talking she had noticed him reach into his pocket for a cigarette only to find the packet empty. When she had told him there was a shop on the corner if he wanted to get more, he had said it was too wet out and he wouldn't bother; but Louise had seen the resignation in his eyes and had guessed that he didn't have any money and was too proud to say so. Pretending she used to smoke the same brand and might have some left, she had gone out on the pretext of looking for them in her car, and had then snuck to the shops and bought some, removing the cellophane and even taking out a couple for extra authenticity.

'You knew?' she said softly. 'You knew I bought them?'

Rory smiled affectionately at her, the lines around his eyes crinkling. 'Yeah, I knew. I think that was what did it for me.' He took a last drag on his cigarette, tilting his head to blow the smoke skywards, then stubbed it out on the edge of the bench, taking his time, his movements careful.

'But that was . . .' Louise faltered. '. . . that was the first day I met you.'

It was the first day she had met all of the band. Still in the process of trying to lure her away from a well-paid job in marketing to go and work for him, Will had taken her to see them play a small gig the night before in an attempt at convincing her. And she had been convinced. The gig wasn't well attended, and the band were unpolished, raw and awkward, with more passion than accomplishment. But they had an energy and charisma that were breathtaking, and from that night on, she understood Will's enthusiasm for his pet project and knew she wanted to be a part of it.

She hadn't hung around after the gig because she'd had a date – funny, she thought, she couldn't remember now who with. The next day she had met the band at Will's house and they had embarked on the great adventure that was Walking Wounded. It had been the day that her life, as she now knew it, had begun.

She remembered Rory that first day, and how moved she had been by him. She was instantly drawn to his air of quiet authority, his stoicism and dependability. He had been so calm and still, in contrast to Phoenix's wired ramblings, Georgie's nervy fidgeting and Owen's hopped-up garrulity. She had noticed how Georgie stayed close to him, clinging to his sleeve like a comfort blanket, how the others deferred to him as the grown-up among them, though he had been little more than a teenager at the time.

'Jesus, Rory! All that time and you never said anything.'

'Doesn't matter.'

'Of course it *matters*.'

'I can't help it,' he said. 'But don't worry, I'm not going to jump you or anything.' He sounded slightly annoyed. 'Just forget it. It's okay, I'm used to it. And we've been good mates, haven't we?'

'Yes, we've been good mates,' Louise said. 'But Rory, I never wanted to be "good mates" with you – not for one minute.'

Rory looked at her steadily, saying nothing.

'Didn't it ever occur to you that I might feel the same way?'

'No,' he said flatly. 'And I wouldn't expect you to,' he added. 'You deserve better.'

'Rory, there *isn't* anyone better than you. Not for me.'

She took his hand, which felt strong and warm, his fingers hard and calloused from guitar strings. 'I love you,' she said. 'I've loved you since that day too.'

With his free hand, he outlined the contours of her face, lightly, tracing her cheek, the corners of her eyes, the outline of her mouth.

'Jesus!' he murmured.

Then his eyes dropped to her lips, and there was that glorious moment of recognition when she knew he was going to kiss her.

Will found Phoenix sitting on the terrace, scribbling lyrics on an A4 pad. 'Hi.' He sat down in the chair beside him.

'Hi.' Phoenix's eyes were cold.

'Where's everyone else? In the studio?'

'Yeah.' Phoenix bent his head to his notepad again. 'But I'd stay out of their way, if I were you.'

'Sorry?' What the hell was wrong with everyone today?

'They're not your biggest fans at the moment – neither am I, to be honest. We all really liked Kate.'

'Oh, so you're back!' They looked up to see Owen storming across the terrace towards them. Georgie followed him, darting anxious looks between him and Will.

'You can get right off your high horse,' Will snapped, his anger rising.

'Oh, I can, can I? Would you like to take this outside?' Owen's eyes blazed.

'*What*? Oh, for fuck's sake! We're already outside, Owen.'

'Okay, then, bring it on.' Owen beckoned Will towards him.

'I'm not going to hit you, Owen, tempting though it is.'

'Come on – you know you want to.' Owen raised his fists threateningly.

'I don't have time for this,' Will said, scraping his chair back and getting up. 'I've got a plane to catch.' He turned and went to the french windows.

'Where are you going?' Owen asked.

Will turned in the doorway. 'Not that it's any of your business,' he said coldly, 'but I'm going to Ireland – to get Kate.'

'Oh!' Owen dropped his fists. 'That's all right, then.'

'Love Rat Will Returns to Italy.' Will read the headline from one of yesterday's tabloids. Louise had given him a bundle of cuttings to read on the flight to Dublin to bring him up to speed with what the press were saying about him and Kate. As he thumbed through them with mounting dread, he was glad he hadn't opened them until he'd got on the plane. If he'd known how bad it was he might not have had the nerve to show his face in Dublin.

Bloody Tina! He'd always known that when they broke up she'd turn it into a career move, but he was outraged by the blatant lies she was telling. What appalled him most was the treatment meted out to Kate. The amount of sheer vitriol aimed at her was astonishing. The ones who championed her were almost worse, he thought, disgusted – celebrating her as some kind of saucy sex kitten, salivating over her lush body and inviting her to 'get her kit off' for their readers' delectation. He wanted to punch their lights out, every last one of them.

One picture of her was particularly heartbreaking. Eyes down, jacket pulled closed, she was shielding her face from the camera with one hand, but you could tell she was close to tears. Will lingered over the picture, absently tracing the outline of her beautiful full lips, and felt a lump come to his throat. He wished he had been there to protect her.

By the end of the week, Tina had cut her losses and let it trickle out that she couldn't forgive Will his infidelity and had decided to end their relationship. She called off her long-planned lavish birthday party and set about lobbying for martyred sainthood. In the current issue of *Wow!* she was pictured cavorting on a Cambodian beach with a horde of smiling orphans. Somehow she had got a gig as ambassador for a children's charity, and eight pages of the magazine were devoted to a gushing interview, amply illustrated with pictures of her looking stunningly beautiful and caring as she carried out her new role 'with her trademark grace and style', cuddling and playing games with the children, chatting with local charity workers.

You had to hand it to Dev Tennant, Will thought, he was good. He certainly worked fast. It was amazing. In a week, Tina had transformed herself into a shining angel of mercy, smiling valiantly through her tears, her eyes attractively dewy and luminous as she held a sick baby in her arms.

'She's lovely, that Tina Roche, isn't she?' the woman beside him said, peering over his shoulder. 'So caring.'

'Mmm.'

'Some of those big so-called stars could learn a lot from her. All they ever think about is their fancy haircuts and designer clothes. And she's gorgeous too, isn't she?'

'Beautiful.'

'That fella of hers wants his head examined, if you ask me, doing the dirt on a beautiful woman like that. Must be mad.'

'Tonto!' Will agreed.

He went back to the interview with Tina.

'"Seeing the plight of these children puts your own problems into perspective," says Roche, looking impossibly glamorous in Cambodian traditional dress, surrounded by children. "I've been hurt in the past," she adds obliquely. "I've been betrayed by those I love. But when I see the bright, happy smiles on the faces of these children, it just puts my troubles in the shade. These children have been hurt – they've been betrayed by the people closest to them in many cases. But they're still smiling, they're still trusting, they still have hope for the future. If they can do it, so can I."'

'Excuse me,' he said to the woman beside him, 'will you be using your sick bag, do you think?'

'Er – no.' She eyed the one in front of his own seat.

'Would you mind?' he nodded to hers. 'It's just that I feel this article may be a two-bag job.'

By the time he got off the plane, Will felt depressed. He hadn't had a lot of sleep in the past week, and the reading he had done on the plane had left him feeling guilty and dejected. Though he was desperate to see Kate and put things right, he was also anxious about facing her after all he had put her through. And he had deep misgivings about his welcome at the O'Neills'. So he was amazed and touched when he came into the arrivals hall and saw Lorcan in the throng at the barrier. At least Lorcan still had faith in him, he thought, smiling at him as he made his way towards him. It didn't even register at first that Lorcan wasn't smiling back, but as he got closer, he noticed that his friend's mouth was set in a grim line and his eyes were spitting fire. Still, he was here, Will thought – at least he was giving him the benefit of the doubt. 'Lorcan, it's so—'

Wham! The next thing Will knew, he was lying on the floor, his face throbbing. He would have said he didn't know what had hit him, but he had seen Lorcan's arm move and had at first expected him to throw it around his shoulder. Instead, he had landed a ferocious punch on Will's nose. By the time he sat up and opened his eyes, all he saw was his friend's rapidly retreating back as he stalked out of the airport, shoulders hunched.

Still dazed, Will had just picked himself up and was brushing himself off in front of an audience of open-mouthed onlookers when a flash went off in his face.

'Will! Will!' the eager photographer called, but he was lurching towards the doors. His nose stung and his eyes were pumping water.

By the time he got outside, Lorcan had disappeared, but he soon found Dave, his driver.

'Home, Will?' Dave enquired, looking at him curiously as he tossed his bag into the boot.

'No, drop me at Lorcan's, then take the luggage home.'

Realising for the first time that his nose was bleeding profusely, he took a handkerchief from his pocket and pressed it to his face.

Catching sight of himself in the driver's mirror, he was shocked by his appearance. He looked totally dishevelled and washed out. His clothes were bloodstained and grubby, his face deathly pale. He looked like a kid who had been beaten up in the playground – and by his best friend, he thought, feeling thoroughly sorry for himself.

'You all right?' Dave asked, making eye contact with him in the mirror.

'I'm okay, thanks,' Will answered. 'Just stings a bit,' he said, in an attempt to explain away the tears that, to his mortification, were welling in his eyes. He was shaking uncontrollably, and he knew it had less to do with the physical trauma than with the shock that Lorcan could have done such a thing. On top of everything else he had been through in the past week, it was the last straw. He longed to crawl under a duvet and cry his eyes out.

Carmen answered the door on the third ring.

'Hi Carmen.'

'Hello Will.' She didn't ask him in. 'Lorcan doesn't want to see you,' she said apologetically.

'Please, Carmen, I have to talk to him.'

She thought for a second, then nodded wordlessly, standing back to let him in and waving him towards the living room.

'He's in there.' She stood on tiptoe to kiss his cheek, then slipped quietly out of the house.

Lorcan was pacing twitchily around the living room. When he saw Will in the doorway, he came to an abrupt halt. His eyes widened in surprise and his face froze, his mouth set in a furious line. 'Did Carmen let you in?' he asked, his eyes as hard as Will had ever seen them.

'Yes.'

'Well, you can let yourself out again,' he said coldly. 'I don't have anything to say to you.'

Will was momentarily rendered speechless by Lorcan's bitterness. 'Lorcan,' he began, 'please, just let me explain.'

'What's there to explain?' Lorcan raged, eyes blazing. 'Did you or did you not shove your dick in my sister's mouth?'

'It's not like they say in the papers.'

'Oh, which bit did they get wrong? The bit where you screwed her and ditched her? Or the bit where you whined to your precious girlfriend that it didn't mean a thing and you couldn't live without her?'

'Where did you get that? *Wow!* magazine?' Will snarled, his anger rising now to meet Lorcan's. He noticed a bundle of tabloids on the coffee table – they weren't Lorcan's normal reading.

'They make it sound so sordid and . . . commonplace,' he said.

Lorcan hooted derisively. 'Whereas this was one of those magical blow jobs that only comes along once in a lifetime?'

'Exactly,' Will countered defiantly. 'God, I shouldn't even be discussing this with you,' he said, tugging at his hair distractedly.

'Fine by me. You know where the door is.'

'I need to see Kate.'

'You stay away from her,' Lorcan said. 'I think you've done enough, don't you?'

'I cannot *believe* you feel you occupy some sort of moral high ground here,' Will fumed.

'*Me?*' Lorcan howled. 'Why? What have *I* done?'

'Don't play the innocent. You were practically pimping your sister to me—'

'*Pimping?*' Lorcan was beside himself.

'You know what I'm talking about. I couldn't believe you'd go along with it – but you said it was a fantastic idea!'

Lorcan seemed genuinely bewildered. 'You mean when you asked me what I thought about you and Kate?'

'Yes, and you said if I could lure her away from Brian, I'd be doing you all a huge favour. You couldn't have been more enthusiastic!'

'Well, I didn't realise quite what you had in mind!' Lorcan spluttered.

'What did you *think* was going to happen?'

'I certainly didn't think you were talking about a quick knee-trembler! Call me a romantic fool, but I thought you were in love with my bloody sister!'

'I *am* in love with your bloody sister!' Will shouted back.

'You are?'

Will sighed. 'Yes, I am,' he said, looking Lorcan squarely in the eye.

As his fury abated, Will realised that something didn't quite add up. Why had Lorcan imagined he was in love with Kate back then? What had he thought he was asking him? Bloody Rachel. He could cheerfully strangle her. She had set him up. He realised now that Lorcan knew nothing about the family's sordid little scheme to break up Kate's engagement. He should have trusted his instinct that Lorcan would never have gone along with it. He decided not to enlighten him now. 'Look, things have gone a bit pear-shaped, but I've got to see Kate.'

'You'll have to get past Freddie first,' Lorcan said, with rather too much relish, still not quite prepared to forgive Will. 'He's very protective of her, you know.'

'Any tips for getting around him?' Will asked hopefully, sensing that Lorcan was softening and loath to leave until they were friends again.

'You could try sticking your tongue down his throat – I think he'd like that.'

Will narrowed his eyes at Lorcan.

'Well, you are a handsome devil,' Lorcan said bitchily.

Will waited, but nothing more was forthcoming. 'Wouldn't be the first time,' he said finally, leaving the words hanging in the air.

As he had hoped, Lorcan's insatiable curiosity wouldn't allow him to ignore that. 'What, *you've* snogged a bloke?' he asked disbelievingly.

'I went to public school, remember.'

'For about five minutes,' Lorcan scoffed.

'I'm a quick learner.'

Despite himself, Lorcan smiled.

'Well, you're full of surprises, aren't you?'

'I do my best,' he smiled.

Lorcan shook his head ruefully.

'So – any advice for handling the formidable Freddie?'

'Tell him that story and he'll love you for ever.'

Giving up, Will turned to go.

'Be nice to his cats,' Lorcan said to his back.

'Freddie? Hi, it's Will.'

'Oh my God! It's Will,' Freddie mouthed to Ken, pressing the intercom handset to his chest.

Ken raised his eyebrows. 'Buzz him in,' he said, when Freddie appeared immobilised by panic.

'Come up,' Freddie said, and pressed the button.

At least he had a few minutes to compose himself while Will climbed the four flights of stairs. When the knock came, he opened the door, determined to be steely and cold. 'Oh my God!' he gasped. 'What happened to you?'

'Lorcan – he met me at the airport.'

'Ouch!' Freddie said sympathetically. 'Well, you'd better come in,' he said, pursing his lips, stiffening his resolve to be forbidding.

'Thanks.' Will strode into the room, cast his eyes around and spied a fat black and white cat curled up on the sofa.

'Oh, you've got a cat! I love cats,' he said, throwing himself down beside Didi and picking him up.

Apparently cats liked him too. To Freddie's amazement, Didi didn't protest at being disturbed, and within seconds he was squirming with pleasure on Will's lap, legs sprawled, purring like a tractor while Will knuckled his belly.

Freddie positioned himself opposite them, perched on the edge of a hard chair, ready to do battle. He was feeling more hostile towards Will now, resenting the way he made the apartment feel instantly smaller and how Didi had rolled over for him.

'She's lovely,' Will said, smiling down indulgently at Didi. 'It is a she, isn't it?'

'You'd think, wouldn't you?' Freddie said drily, as Didi tumbled and writhed ecstatically under Will's lazily stroking fingers. 'We think he's gay.' *Slut!* he thought and shot Didi a filthy look.

'Well, Mister, what have you got to say for yourself? I take it you didn't just come here to mooch the cat?'

'No. I came to see Kate.'

'She isn't here.'

'Oh.'

Just then, Ken appeared from the kitchen. 'This is my boyfriend, Ken,' Freddie told Will. 'He's a solicitor,' he added threateningly.

'Hello, nice to meet you,' Will stood and shook Ken's hand then sank back abjectly into the sofa.

'What happened?' Ken nodded to Will's face.

'Lorcan,' Freddie explained.

'Look, I know what you probably think,' Will said, 'but that stuff in the papers is all bollocks.'

'Really?' Freddie said cautiously.

'It's a pack of lies. Tina and I broke up that night. Kate ran off before I got a chance to say anything to her, and then I had to go to England for my father's funeral. I thought she was still at the villa until I got back there yesterday.'

'So you're not in love with Tina?' Freddie said, brightening.

'No. I'm in love with Kate. I've got to see her.'

'She's really not here, though,' Freddie said, quite sympathetically now.

'Well, can I wait until she comes back?'

'Yes, of course, but I don't know how long she'll be.'

'Where is she?'

Freddie looked warily at Ken. 'She's gone to see Brian.'

'Oh!' Will looked utterly defeated.

'Don't worry,' Freddie said. 'She's gone to break up with him. Only he's doing some weekend-workshop thing and she had to go to Wicklow, so it could be quite late when she gets back.'

'I don't mind.'

'You've nothing to worry about,' Freddie said consolingly – Will looked very glum. 'Kate's crazy about you. Besides, you're every woman's dream now – a rich orphan. Sorry about your father, by the way.'

'Thanks.'

Freddie sighed, evidently satisfied. 'I suppose we'd better give him some peas,' he said to Ken, who nodded and went back into the kitchen.

'Oh, no thanks, I'm not hungry,' Will said hastily.

Freddie laughed. 'They're not to eat, silly,' he said, rolling his eyes indulgently. 'They're for your eye.'

Ken returned and handed Freddie a bag of frozen *petits pois* and Freddie leaped onto the sofa beside Will, pressing it to Will's nose.

'Thanks.' Will reached up to hold the bag for himself, but Freddie slapped his hand away.

'Come on, let me do it. I'll probably never get another opportunity – there's not much chance of any boyfriend of mine getting into a fight.' He threw a fondly disparaging look at Ken.

'I hope I'm not interrupting anything?' Will said.

'Oh no. We were just having a girls' night in. We've got a DVD – one of those movies where the geeky girl gets to go to the prom with the coolest boy in the school. I love those movies about the prom, don't you?' he said cosily.

'I live for them,' Will said drily.

'And we've got another for later – *Fist of Glory*.'

'Oh, a boxing movie?' Will asked, surprised. He hadn't thought that would be Freddie's type of thing.

'Um, no, not exactly,' Freddie grinned.

'Oh! Oh, right.'

'You're welcome to stay for dinner,' Freddie said. 'I don't know what we're going to have yet.'

'I think it's obvious,' Ken said, grinning. 'Will looks to me like a man in dire need of a good risotto.'

For some reason that Will couldn't fathom, Freddie seemed to find this hilarious.

'Actually I'm not that fond of risotto,' he said.

To his bewilderment, they both cracked up. It must be a gay thing, he thought, bemused.

In the end, they had pasta and garlic bread. Freddie and Ken drank lots of red wine and kept up a steady stream of light-hearted chatter, trying to distract Will from the fact that Kate still hadn't come home. Afterwards they watched the high-school-prom movie, which Will found surprisingly moving. Freddie sobbed openly, plucking fistfuls of tissues from a box. As the credits rolled, he had a text message from Kate to say she wouldn't be coming home. He showed it to Will: 'Staying here 2nite. 2 long 2 explain. CU 2moro. KateX'

Freddie tried to ring her back, but her phone was switched off. 'I'm sure it's nothing,' he said consolingly to Will, who looked really dejected.

'I'd better get off.' Will got up to leave.

'Oh no, stay here with us.' Freddie said.

'Oh, I couldn't—'

'Of course you can – you can have Kate's room, since she won't be home. You don't want to spend the night on your own in that big empty house of yours.'

Thinking about it, Will realised Freddie was right – he didn't want to go home alone. 'Thank you, you're very kind,' he said, sinking back into the sofa.

'Besides,' Freddie said, giving his knee an affectionate squeeze, 'you don't want to miss *Fist of Glory*.'

'Well, that was . . . educational,' Will said, yawning, an hour and a half later.

'Oh, you're absolutely knackered,' Freddie said. 'You should have just gone to bed. Come on and I'll show you where everything is.'

291

Left alone in Kate's room, Will sat on the bed and drank in her presence. He liked being among her things, taking in the pictures on the walls, the jumble of clothes spilling out of her wardrobe, the piles of shoes, the suitcases and storage boxes slung on top of the cupboards, the Manhattan skyline of cosmetics on the dressing table. It was as if by concentrating hard on the things she had touched he could somehow conjure her presence.

Why hadn't she come home? he fretted, getting up and fingering the jumble on her dressing-table, picking up necklaces, opening bottles of perfume and breathing in the fragrance. He picked up a photograph that was propped against a jewellery box, smiling at the picture of Kate and Freddie mugging drunkenly for the camera at a New Year's Eve party. As he was putting it back, another, slotted into the mirror frame, caught his eye – a picture of her and Brian holding hands and beaming at each other. Where the hell was she? he thought, scowling at it.

He sat down on the bed again, flopping back against the pillows, drawing comfort from the thought that Kate had lain there too and wishing she was with him now. Then, too exhausted even to think any more, he undressed and crawled under the duvet.

When Freddie looked in on his way to bed, Will was out cold.

'Oh, look,' he said dotingly, beckoning Ken to the open doorway.

'So peaceful, isn't he?' he whispered as Ken came to stand with him, putting an arm around his shoulders.

'Poor bloke! He's really been through the mill.'

They stood for a moment, watching Will sleep.

'This must be what it's like having a child,' Freddie muttered. 'Maybe we should adopt.'

'Maybe we should.' Ken squeezed his shoulder. 'You'd make a great parent.'

'Do you really think so?' Freddie's face lit up.

'Absolutely. You were terrific with him tonight.'

Freddie sighed happily and turned back to Will.

'Freddie?' Ken murmured, when he showed no sign of moving.

'Mmm?' Freddie said distractedly.

'You do know we can't adopt him?'

'I guess so.' Freddie sighed regretfully. 'Though he is an orphan now,' he pointed out hopefully.

'Too old.'

'It's so unfair! Everyone wants babies – the older orphans always get left.'

'Come on, Freddie. Let's go to bed.'

While Will slept in her bed, Kate lay awake in a narrow single bed at the Shanti Centre. Her mind was racing and every muscle in her body twitched.

She had arrived at the centre in the lush Wicklow countryside earlier in the day by taxi. As she pushed open the unlocked front door, the familiar smell of incense assaulted her nostrils. She had made her way straight to the reception area to ask for Brian.

'Are you here for the Relationship Detox Weekend?' the moon-faced girl behind the desk had asked. She spoke so quietly and smiled so inanely, like some kind of airhead Stepford woman, that Kate had wanted to slap her.

'No, I just need to see Brian. I'm a . . . friend of his.'

'Well, he's in a session at the moment so I can't disturb him. They'll be taking a break at twelve. You could talk to him then.'

She was ushered to a comfy sitting room and kicked her heels for almost an hour. Finally, at twelve, she heard a door open, and the house was filled with hushed chatter. Across the hall, people streamed out of a room in socks or bare feet, whispering to each other as they donned shoes and spilled out into the sunshine. Through the window she saw Brian surrounded by a group of admirers. She wasn't surprised to see that Suzanne, Brian's most die-hard fan, was among them. Going outside, she caught his eye. He looked surprised to see her – more than surprised, actually. Almost . . . panicked? He muttered something to the group around him, then darted to Kate and pulled her behind a tree.

'Kate! This is a nice surprise!'

'Is it?' she asked.

'Of course!'

He did look pleased to see her now – though she couldn't help wondering why they were behind a tree. 'I need to talk to you, Brian.'

'Well, this isn't a good time. I'm working.'

'What time do you finish?'

'It's not exactly a nine-to-five thing,' he said pompously. 'It's a bit more full-on than that. Look, why don't you stay?'

'Oh, I don't think—'

'We're going to have a sweat lodge tonight,' he said persuasively.

'You know they aren't really my thing.'

'Oh, it'll be good for you. Besides, you've come all this way, you might as well make the most of it. You never know, you might enjoy it.'

Kate knew she wouldn't. Dehydrating in a home-made tepee with a bunch of hippies was never going to be her idea of a good time. 'I need to talk to you in private. Couldn't you get away for an hour?'

'Sorry.' Brian looked anything but. 'I'm the facilitator. I need to be available to these people for the whole weekend. They've invested a lot in coming here.'

Kate discovered just how much they had invested in being there when Brian, refusing to take no for an answer, frogmarched her to Reception and announced to the moon-faced girl that Kate would be staying for the weekend and needed a room. Then he drifted off, leaving them to make the arrangements. The girl consulted her computer. 'I've only got a dorm room left,' she said, smiling ethereally. 'You'll be sharing with three others.'

'Okay,' Kate felt trapped and resentful.

'It's a beautiful room,' the girl said cheerfully, 'right at the front of the house. It has a lovely energy. In the morning, the sun pours in.'

'Lovely.' Kate dredged up a smile, feeling churlish.

Moon-Face tapped away at her computer again. 'That will be three hundred euro,' she said, favouring Kate with a particularly beatific smile.

'What? Um . . . you do know I'm only staying the one night?'

'That includes all your meals and the workshop,' the girl explained. 'I know you missed this morning, but I'm afraid I can't give you a discount.'

'Oh no, I'm just visiting,' Kate explained, relieved that there had been a mistake. 'I'm not doing the workshop.'

'I'm sorry,' Moon-Face said kindly, 'but we don't allow visitors during a workshop. We feel it's not fair to the participants.'

'Oh! I won't bother them, I promise. You won't even know I'm here. And I won't listen in and try to pick up free tips or anything.'

Moon-Face seemed a little put out but managed to maintain the holier-than-thou smile – just.

'Problems?' Brian asked, coming back.

'She says I can't stay unless I do the workshop,' Kate whispered.

'That's right,' Brian said. 'No spectators, right, Sheila?'

'Right, Brian!' she said matily.

Kate wanted to hit them both.

'So, that will be three hundred euro,' Sheila said smugly.

She didn't seem so otherworldly when she zapped Kate's credit card.

'I know it's expensive, but I'm worth it,' Brian said, giving Kate's shoulder a squeeze. 'I'll see you later, okay?'

She nodded.

'He is worth it,' Sheila said admiringly. 'Have you been with Brian before?'

'Um . . . yes,' Kate replied.

'Marvellous, isn't he?'

'Brilliant.' Kate was sorry now that she hadn't broken up with him behind the tree. It would certainly have been cheaper.

'You have a group session with Brian at four. Dinner is usually at six, but we're fasting tonight in preparation.'

Kate had to bite her lip to refrain from asking acidly if tonight's non-existent dinner was one of the meals included in the three-hundred euro.

'We're going to do a sweat lodge tonight!' Sheila squealed.

Kate wanted to cry.

In the free time that was normally taken up by dinner, Brian pulled her aside. 'I'm sorry we can't share a room,' he said.

'Oh that's fine!' Kate was relieved she wouldn't have to spend the night fending him off and trying to find excuses for why she didn't want sex.

'Listen, could you not let anyone know we're together?' Brian asked, looking a bit shifty.

'Okay,' Kate said dubiously.

'It's just that I feel it wouldn't be fair to the group. It's my responsibility to be one hundred per cent available to them, and if they knew we were in a relationship, they might feel that wasn't the case.'

'Fine, no problem,' Kate said. What a load of bollocks, she thought. Still, at least maybe it explained why he had dragged her behind a tree earlier to talk.

'Great! I'm glad you decided to stay and give it a go,' he said, patronisingly. 'I'm sure you'll get something out of it.'

He thinks I'm buying into all this. He doesn't know me at all, Kate thought.

'And I have lots to tell you tomorrow. I've finally become macro-biotic!' he announced.

'Oh!'

'I've been meaning to do it for ages, and with you away, not trying to lure me out for pizzas and the like, it seemed like a good time to do it. I feel so much better already.'

'Fantastic!'

Glimpsing her life as it would be if she married Brian – cutting his vegetables into *yin* and *yang* shapes, trying not to transmit seething resentment into the food she cooked and contaminate it with ill will – Kate knew she had made the right decision.

The sweat lodge was a nightmare. The group were really psyched up about it and kept asking Kate if she had ever been in a sweat lodge before. When Suzanne asked if she had ever 'experienced a sweat', she replied disingenuously that there was a sauna at her gym. Suzanne smiled at her pityingly, which Kate supposed was as close as she ever came to rolling her eyes.

At dusk, they trooped out into the grounds to the fetid little tepee, fashioned from branches and twigs, and covered with grungy blankets. After cleansing their auras by smudging themselves with burning sage, the group crawled into the tiny tent and sat cross-legged around a pit in the centre. Brian was the master of ceremonies, heaping hot rocks into the pit, leading incantations and chanting. He was in his element, in full-on shaman mode, like some wannabe Sitting Bull.

Come off it! Kate screamed at him in her head. You're not a fuck-ing Red Indian. Your father's a chartered accountant. You grew up in a semi-d in Terenure.

The group seemed to be entering into the spirit of the thing, willing themselves to have a spiritual experience. All Kate was expe-riencing was extreme discomfort. The intense heat left her gasping for breath, and the ceiling was so low that she had to hunch her head and shoulders so that her neck ached as the ceremony dragged on. She was almost dizzy with hunger, having barely eaten all day. She wondered irritably how on earth this was supposed to improve your relationships – she was ready to kill someone.

Tired, hungry and irritated, she longed for bed.

But now that she was in bed, she couldn't sleep. She was too wound up. Her three roommates were snoring their heads off, which at least had given her the opportunity to send Freddie a furtive text message from under the blankets, letting him know she wouldn't be home. Earlier, when she had whipped out her mobile in Reception, Moon-Face had acted as if she'd produced a hand grenade and was intent on blowing them all into oblivion. Brian had joined in, telling her that mobiles were strictly forbidden.

Giving up on sleep, she decided to go downstairs and read for a while. She crept out of the room, pulling the door closed softly so as not to wake the others. As she stepped out onto the landing, she heard two voices, one male, one female, on the landing above. They were speaking in a low murmur.

'I wish you could make everyone else go away,' the girl whispered. There was something distinctly intimate in her tone.

'You know I can't do that.'

Recognising Brian's voice, Kate froze.

'I just want to be with you.' The girl sighed.

'I want to be with you too.'

There were silences between their exchanges that Kate knew instinctively were filled with kisses. She could picture how Brian would be holding the mystery girl, stroking her face, gazing into her eyes. There was a long silence, punctuated by a lot of heavy breathing.

'I want you so much!' Brian groaned.

'I could come to your room,' the girl said urgently.

'I don't want anyone else in the group to know we're together. It wouldn't be fair on them.'

'Don't worry. I'll leave before morning. I'm just buzzing and I know I can't sleep. I guess I'm still on a high from the sweat lodge. I had such an amazing experience in there.'

'I can tell. You have an incredible energy right now.'

'And I want to share it with *you*!' the girl squeaked.

This was followed by more panting and groaning.

'Okay, let's go to my room,' Brian said breathily.

Hearing them move, Kate darted back into her room and stood behind the closed door like a burglar fearing discovery. She was in shock, her legs wobbly, her heart pounding. She couldn't believe what she had heard. And yet, in a way, deep down, she felt she had known this about Brian all along. It wasn't even as if it was the first time she had caught him: there had been that girl at Tom and Rachel's wedding.

She stood at the door for what seemed like an age. Finally rousing herself, she crept back to bed. She knew that in the circumstances it was irrational to feel betrayed, but she did. After all, Brian didn't know that she intended to break up with him. As far as he was concerned, they were engaged – which meant he should be faithful to her. She felt ridiculously hurt, and furious with him – not only for cheating, but for cutting the rug from under her. She knew now, as certainly as if he had told her, that he'd never been faithful. She remembered the adoring faces of the girls in the sweat lodge tonight and it suddenly hit her that he had slept with every one of them.

Bastard! She longed to run out and confront him now. She had been too taken aback to react immediately, and now it was too late – he'd be plugged into the 'incredible energy' of his latest conquest. Twitchier than ever, she waited for morning.

Chapter 13

At breakfast, Kate managed to identify the girl she had heard with Brian last night. She recognised her lilting Cork accent and noticed the significant eye-meet they exchanged when they thought no one was looking. Poor sap! she thought, noting the girl's flushed, eager face as she chatted to him. Her name was Liz – a petite, bony wisp of a thing, with pale, freckled skin and masses of uncontrollable frizzy auburn hair. She was quite attractive in an offbeat way, Kate mused, dispassionately. Strangely, she felt no animosity towards her. If she felt anything, it was pity as another victim of Brian's hollow charm.

Armed with the evidence of his infidelity, she tried to confront him after breakfast, but without success. He was bombarded by members of the group, vying for his attention, and fobbed her off again. 'Kate, I know you want to talk, but I can't give you my full attention right now.'

'Well, you wouldn't want anyone here to think you weren't *available* to them,' she said waspishly. But her sarcasm was lost on him.

'Just wait until this weekend is over and I'll be able to focus on what you have to say,' he continued. 'In the meantime, try to be in the now. If you engage in this process, you'll get a lot out of it.'

'Fine,' she said, fuming at his unmitigated gall.

'Don't sulk.' He smiled. Then, pulling her aside, he said in a low voice, 'I've missed you so much this summer. Believe me, there's nothing I'd like more than to make all these people disappear and be alone with you.' Touching her cheek lightly with a finger, he shot her an intimate, seductive look.

Kate marvelled at what a good liar he was. He still looked at her as if he adored her. He had always made her feel special, but she knew now that it was nothing to do with her. It was just a trick, and the next moment he would be using it on someone else.

Left with no choice, she joined the rest of the group for the morning session. There was a hushed atmosphere as they removed their shoes outside the door, padded into the room barefoot and sat cross-legged in a circle on the carpet. Kate felt certain that her flash of insight yesterday had been right: somehow she knew that Brian had slept with practically every female in the room. And she didn't care anymore.

Brian kicked off by asking them how they had felt about last night, which prompted several of them to 'share' their sweat-lodge experience.

'I felt like the veil was lifted and I suddenly saw everything as it really is,' Suzanne gushed. 'It was only for a moment – just a glimpse – but it was really special.' She gave a smile of spiritual rapture.

'Great.' Brian nodded encouragingly at her. 'How about you, Kate?' he asked quietly. 'How did you feel about last night?'

'Yep, pretty much the same,' she nodded at Suzanne. 'Veil lifting, seeing things as they really are. Last night was a bit of a revelation for me.'

'Really?' Brian said, obviously surprised that she was opening up to all this.

'Oh yes, it was very enlightening. I had a bit of an epiphany, actually,' she said meaningfully, eyeballing him.

'Good, good.' He was clearly oblivious to her mood. 'Thank you for sharing. How about you, Liz?'

Kate seethed as he turned to the frizzy-haired girl with the same caring, encouraging smile.

When the sharing circle was finished, Brian explained how they were going to spend the morning. 'You've come here because you're in relationships that you feel are destructive or unhealthy. Perhaps you have people in your lives who undermine your confidence, your self-esteem, your ability to fulfil your potential, people who block your energy and stop you becoming the person you could be. You're here today because you're ready to confront the reality about these toxic relationships. It may mean coming to a new understanding with that person. It may mean letting them go. Either way, it's not easy. Even if a relationship is harmful to us, it can be difficult to let it go, and I know it's taken a lot of courage for you all to take that first step.'

Several members of the group exchanged a smug smile.

'Today we're going to confront those people. We're going to tell them how they make us feel, how their behaviour affects us, and they're going to listen. Because that's the one thing that never happens in a toxic relationship. We're never listened to,' he said.

You could almost hear the group sigh admiringly *en masse*, Kate thought, as they devoured Brian's pearls of wisdom.

'While you talk, the rest of us,' Brian indicated the circle with a sweeping gesture, 'will listen. We will represent the person you want to confront. We won't respond or argue, just accept what you have to say. There's no judgement. This is a safe space.

So,' he said, 'who'd like to start?'

First up was a man called Terry, whose 'toxic' person was his wife. Everyone listened supportively as he launched into a tirade against her. 'You don't support me in the spiritual journey I'm on,' he said querulously. 'You don't want to grow as a person, and you try to stop me growing too.'

'Oh, grow *up*!' Kate snapped, unable to stop herself.

'Is she allowed to say that?' Terry appealed to Brian.

'We're just listening, Kate,' Brian admonished her.

'But he's saying his wife doesn't understand him!' Kate protested, as if she was appealing to a referee. 'Surely you can do better than that old chestnut,' she said to Terry.

'Please, Kate,' Brian said, 'we're not here to judge, remember.'

'Except Terry's wife – we're judging her! It's not fair when she's not here to defend herself.'

Brian sighed patiently. 'This isn't about Terry's wife *at all*, Kate. It's about Terry's *experience* of the relationship – how his wife's behaviour makes him feel.' He looked as if he was regretting having asked her to stay. She wondered if anyone had ever been thrown out of a sharing circle for being disruptive.

'Okay, carry on, Terry,' Brian said.

Thrown by the interruption, Terry took a deep breath to gather his thoughts. He was soon in his stride again. 'You take the children to McDonalds',' he whined. 'You buy them toys you know I don't approve of. You undermine the values I'm trying to instil in our children.'

'When?' Kate exploded.

'Sorry?' Terry looked confused.

'*When* do you try to give your children these values?'

'Kate—' Brian began.

'No, it's okay, Brian. I'm interested in hearing what Kate has to say.' Terry turned to Kate. 'What do you mean, Kate?' he asked earnestly.

'Well, today is Sunday and instead of being with your kids instilling your values in them, you're here slagging off your wife to a bunch of strangers who won't answer back. And you have the nerve to call *her* unsupportive!'

'Well, yes, I suppose you do have a point.' Terry deflated like a punctured balloon.

'They're probably at McDonald's as we speak! I'm sure your wife would be delighted if you offered to do something else with them for the day.'

'Kate, please!' Brian threw Terry an apologetic look. 'You have a right to your feelings, Terry,' he said. 'You don't have to apologise for them.'

'No, it's okay, Brian,' Terry said. 'I value Kate's input.'

'Well, carry on,' Brian said softly. 'What else would you like to say to your wife?'

Terry cleared his throat. 'Well, I realise I've been a bit selfish,' he said, shamefaced. 'I've left you to cope with the kids on your own far too often lately and I don't appreciate how difficult your role is. I complain that you don't listen to me, but I see now that I haven't listened to you either, when you've tried to tell me what you need. But I'm going to be more supportive from now on, and I'm going to try to be a better father. So, basically, I want to say sorry – sorry for not being there, sorry for not listening, sorry for not understanding. Just – sorry,' he finished quietly.

There was a stunned silence followed by muted applause as Terry rejoined the circle, sheepishly.

'Okay!' Brian said. 'Who'd like to go next?'

'Me!' Kate volunteered, jumping to her feet.

'Kate! Okay. Who would you like to confront?'

'My boyfriend,' she said innocently.

If this is the way you want to play it, fine, she thought. If you won't talk to me in private, we'll just have to do it in public.

Brian struggled to look neutral. 'Your boyfriend, okay. Please, go ahead.'

Standing in the middle of the circle, all eyes on her, Kate took a deep breath. 'I want to break up with you. I know you've been unfaithful to me all along. There was that girl at Rachel's wedding, but I know now that that wasn't the only—'

'We don't mention specifics,' Suzanne interrupted helpfully, prompting her in a stage whisper.

'Suzanne's right,' Brian quavered. 'We don't need to know the circumstances. It's about your experience of the relationship. Just stick to talking about your feelings – how your boyfriend's behaviour makes you *feel*.'

'Oh – okay.' Kate was quite enjoying herself now. 'Well, last night when I heard you making out with Liz on the landing, it made me *feel* very angry.'

Suzanne's face crumpled, and she looked accusingly at Liz, who had blushed to the roots of her hair.

'When I heard you arranging to go to her room to spend the night with her, it made me *feel* very stupid for ever believing you. I felt such an idiot for not realising what you were like all along. And I really resented you for making me feel that way.'

Brian's caring smile was slipping, and the group were shifting and mumbling among themselves, casting suspicious glances at each other.

'I guess deep down I suspected it all along,' she continued, 'but I thought now that we're engaged—'

'You're engaged!' Suzanne gasped, staring accusingly at Brian. She couldn't have been more horrified if Kate had announced that he was a paedophile.

'Well, not any more.' Kate beamed at her. 'He's all yours. And yours.' She turned to Liz. 'And probably every other woman in the room's, for all I know.'

'I thought you didn't believe in marriage,' Liz was saying to him in a shocked whisper.

'I was going to break it off with you anyway,' Kate continued airily. 'I'm in love with someone else. Probably nothing will come of it, but I might as well tell you. It's Will, since you'll probably find out anyway. It's been in all the papers. His girlfriend caught us together and tried to beat me up.'

At this the whole group erupted. Brian sat stony-faced as the session descended into chaos. Suzanne and Liz ran from the room in tears, and several other girls were throwing wounded glances in Brian's direction. Terry stood up and pumped Kate's hand enthusiastically.

'Thanks for your help, Kate. I'm off home to give my wife a hand with the kids.'

'Oh good,' she smiled. 'Sorry if I was a bit—'

'No, you were great,' he said. 'Good luck with that bloke of yours.'

'You're not going back to Dublin by any chance? Only I could do with a lift.'

'Sure, no problem. I'll see you out front in ten minutes.'

Kate grinned triumphantly at Brian.

'You were right,' she told him. 'It was very empowering.' And with that she walked out of the room and out of his life.

Letting herself into the flat, Kate was immediately accosted by Freddie. 'At last!' he said accusingly.

'Well, it's official, my life is crap,' Kate said, moving past him into the living room and throwing her keys on the table.

'What happened?' Freddie asked. 'And why did you stay out last night? You did break up with Brian, didn't you?' he asked, his eyes narrowed suspiciously.

'Yes.' Kate sighed wearily. 'I did. But you wouldn't believe what I had to go through to do it – sweat lodges, sharing circles, role-playing – *and* it cost me three hundred euro!'

'Bit of a bargain, if you ask me,' Freddie muttered. 'Well, never mind. It's over now, and you can get on with your life.'

'What life? I don't *have* a life any more. I have no job, no boyfriend—'

'Don't speak too soon, Baby Bear.' Freddie smiled enigmatically, barely able to contain his excitement.

'Baby Bear?' Kate screwed up her face. 'What are you on about?'

In answer, Freddie put an arm around her and steered her across the apartment.

'Someone's been sleeping in *your* bed,' he said, pausing outside the door of Kate's room. 'And he's *still there!*' he said theatrically, opening the door with a dramatic flourish.

Kate couldn't believe her eyes because there, fast asleep, was Will, flanked by Didi and Gogo, nestled into his body on either side, purring in time with his rhythmic breathing, eyes tightly closed and expressions of transcendental bliss on their faces. Will's ridiculously long black eyelashes rested on his cheeks, and she saw that he was sporting a livid bruise under one eye. For a moment she was too stunned to speak.

'Poor thing, he must have been exhausted,' Freddie cooed. 'He's been sleeping for almost twelve hours.'

'But how did he get here? When—'

'He came here last night, looking for you.'

'And you let him stay?' Kate couldn't help feeling a little betrayed.

'Not until I'd given him a really hard time. I'm not a total pushover, you know, not even for a face as pretty as that. I really put him through the wringer.'

Kate couldn't imagine Freddie putting anyone through the wringer.

'You can ask Ken!' Freddie said, reading her expression.

'Oh my God,' Kate gasped, 'you didn't do *that*, did you?'

She indicated Will's bruised face.

'No, of course not. That's Lorcan's handiwork.'

'*Lorcan*? What on earth got into him?'

'He was doing the protective-brother bit, defending your honour – "Unhand my sister, you blackguard." Very Anna Karenina.' He sighed admiringly.

'Oh God!' Kate groaned. She found the thought of Lorcan and Will falling out deeply upsetting – especially if it was over her.

'Oh, don't worry, I gather they've made it up now,' Freddie assured her.

'Oh really?' Kate said, needled. 'What about my honour?' She knew she was being irrational, but she couldn't help it. 'Will seems to have got around everyone,' she said peevishly.

'Even Didi and Gogo are devoted to him,' Freddie said fondly, 'and you know how standoffish they can be.'

'But what's he doing here – apart from schmoozing the cats?' she asked petulantly.

'What do you think?'

Kate hardly dared to believe what he was implying. 'Really?'

'Why do you think I let him stay? You know I love you, Kate, but you can be awfully dense sometimes.'

They jumped as Will stirred, his eyelids fluttering.

'Oh, he's waking up!' Freddie hissed and hurriedly pushed Kate into the room while he ducked out, shutting the door after him as if to stop her escaping.

Will's eyes fluttered open. 'Hello,' he said groggily, sitting up in bed and rubbing his eyes.

'Hello,' Kate said, feeling incredibly shy.

'What time is it?'

'Almost one.'

'Christ! I can't believe I slept so long.' His voice was thick. As he sat up higher in the bed, Didi and Gogo miaowed in protest at being disturbed and jumped off to stalk away moodily.

Will pushed a hand through his hair and blinked rapidly, then smiled up at her. Kate couldn't help thinking how good he looked in her bed, stripped and ready for action – her favourite fantasy come to life. 'What are you doing here?' she asked.

'Oh, Freddie said it would be okay – since you weren't coming back last night.'

'I meant here in Ireland.'

'I came to get you.'

'You did?' Kate perched on the end of the bed. 'But I thought you'd gone straight back to Tuscany.'

'I had. But I thought you were still at the villa until I got back there and discovered you'd left.'

'I'm sorry I ran off like that.' She plucked nervously at the duvet, her eyes downcast.

'Christ, I'm sorry about the whole thing, Kate. It should never have happened. If I'd known—'

Kate leapt off the bed as if she'd been scalded and scuttled over to the window. She couldn't bear it – he was going to give her the what-happened-between-us-was-a-mistake speech. 'Don't worry about it,' she said, affecting all the nonchalance she could muster. 'No permanent damage done.'

Will squinted at her. 'But that night, it wasn't—'

Whatever he was about to say, she didn't want to hear it.

'Look, I'll leave you to get dressed,' she said and dashed from the room before he could say another word.

Freddie was sitting at the kitchen table, drinking a cup of coffee and flicking through a glossy magazine when Kate came in.

'Well, when's the wedding?' he asked casually. 'You'd better be making me bridesmaid.'

'What wedding?' Kate snapped. 'You got it all wrong. He just came here to say that what happened was a mistake and to get me to go back to work.'

Freddie was aghast. 'Bloody heteros! You couldn't organise a shagfest in a brothel!'

Leaping to his feet, he grabbed Kate's hand and dragged her back to her bedroom door.

'He loves you, you love him,' he hissed. 'Now, get back in there and don't come out until I've got a hen night to arrange and a wedding dress to design.' He opened the door and gave Kate an almighty shove in the back, sending her staggering into the room.

'You're back!'

'Freddie thought I should listen to what you have to say,' she mumbled.

'Remind me to lobby the Church for his canonisation.'

'So?' Kate prompted. 'What were you saying?'

Will sighed. 'Just that I'm really sorry about everything. I had no idea about all the flak you'd been getting in the papers.'

'Oh!'

'If I'd known, I'd have come back sooner. I wouldn't have hung you out to dry like that.'

'It doesn't matter,' Kate told him. 'It was my own fault, really. I shouldn't have run off like that.'

'No, you bloody shouldn't. I sacked Louise when I discovered her part in it.'

'You didn't!' Kate gasped, her eyes huge.

'Don't worry,' Will laughed, 'she told me to fuck off. But you have to come back to Tuscany with me. I'll be lynched if I go back without you! They're all threatening to go on hunger strike.'

'But what about Tina?' Kate asked, bracing herself.

'She's always on hunger strike.'

'You know what I mean. I'm sure she wouldn't want me there.'

'I don't see what it's got to do with her,' Will shrugged casually. 'As far as I know, she's busy reinventing herself as the Mother Teresa of Cambodia. Good luck to her!'

'Don't you mind?' Kate asked. It was like picking a scab. She knew no good could come of asking, but she had to know.

'Mind! Why should I mind?' Will looked puzzled.

'But I thought – I mean, aren't you . . .'

'No, I'm not *heartbroken*. No, I didn't beg her to take me back.'

'You didn't?' Kate asked, edging closer and sitting on the bed.

'No. We had a huge row after you'd gone. I told her she and I were through. I'm afraid she chose to spin that as a declaration of undying love.'

'So, you're not still in love with her?' Kate asked, feeling as if the sun was rising after the longest, darkest night.

'No.' Will shook his head, gazing at her intently. 'I never said all those things Tina claims I did. She made it all up. I'd have thought you'd know that.'

'Me?'

'You.' He looked at her for a long time. 'I love you,' he said eventually. 'I came here to tell you that.'

Kate could hardly breathe, her heart was pounding so wildly. 'You do?'

'Yes, I do. I thought I'd made that pretty obvious. Am I too late?' he asked.

'Too late? What do you mean?'

'Freddie said you'd gone to see Brian yesterday.'

'Yes, I did – to break up with him.'

'But you didn't come home last night,' Will said, his eyes dropping to the duvet. 'What happened? Did he talk you out of it?'

When he looked up again his expression was impassive, but the tightening of the muscles along his jaw betrayed his anxiety.

Kate realised that he actually felt unsure of her. 'No, he didn't talk me out of it.'

'So you did break up with him?'

'Oh yes. Very publicly and spectacularly.'

'Good.' Will seemed more sure of himself. 'Why?'

'Oh, lots of reasons. I caught him cheating on me, for one thing, but mainly because I'm head over heels in love with someone else.'

'Anyone I know?'

'You,' she said, not wanting to tease any more. 'I love you.' It was such bliss to be able to say it out loud and to know he felt the same way.

'Well, thank God for that.' Relief lit his face. 'I'd hate to have sat through *Fist of Glory* for nothing.'

'Oh God, did Freddie make you watch gay porn?' Kate giggled. 'Sorry! And I'm sorry Lorcan hit you,' she said, touching the bruise under his eye. 'Does it hurt?'

'A bit.'

She touched her lips lightly to the bruise. 'There! All better.'

'Now I wish he'd beaten me up more. Come here.' He put a hand on the back of her neck, pulling her face to his, and then his mouth was opening against hers, his stubble rough on her skin. 'I love you,' he breathed into her mouth, his hands tangling in her hair as they kissed on and on.

Kate clung to his broad shoulders, feeling the warmth of his skin beneath her fingers. She was aware that he was probably naked under the duvet. She wanted to rip off her own clothes and feel his bare skin against hers.

Seemingly he was aware of it too. 'I feel at a bit of a disadvantage here.' He slid a warm hand inside the back of her T-shirt, while his tongue darted in and out of her mouth.

The kissing was fantastic, and his hands were driving her crazy, but Kate was very aware that she was still wearing yesterday's clothes, and she suspected that there were bits of twig and leaf from the sweat lodge in her crevices. When Will popped open the top button of her jeans and the warm hand on her stomach strayed downwards, she leaped away.

Will looked wounded.

'Sorry,' she smiled regretfully, 'it's just that I stink. I didn't have any clean clothes, and these have been through a sweat-lodge ceremony.'

'If it's just your clothes that stink, we could always take them off.' Will reached for her again.

'I'm too knackered to take advantage of you, anyway,' Kate said, flopping onto the pillow beside him and burrowing into his neck. 'I didn't get a wink of sleep last night.' She noticed the rather peeved expression that flitted across Will's face. 'Not because I was bonking Brian.' She grinned. 'I didn't sleep with him last night, if that's what you're thinking.'

Relief passed across his face like a wave, smoothing and softening his features.

'No. Actually, I slept in a dorm with three other women who'd been on a steady diet of beans all weekend – probably all their lives, actually.'

'Were they not fragrant?' Will grinned.

'I was afraid to go to sleep in case I was carried off by carbon-monoxide poisoning.'

'Serves you right for not coming home,' Will said, stroking her hair. 'You could have been here with me.'

'I still wouldn't have got any sleep, would I?'

'Absolutely none.' He kissed her again.

The magic was shattered by Kate's stomach, which growled long and low.

'Sorry!' she mumbled, embarrassed. 'I'm also weak with hunger. I haven't eaten since breakfast.'

'No wonder you dumped Brian. Come on. Will sat up. I'll take you out to lunch. I'm not going to make the mistake of forgetting to feed you.'

In a daze of love, Kate didn't think about where they were going as they walked hand in hand through the winding, cobbled streets. However, she came to an abrupt awakening when Will stopped outside Paradise, an exclusive Michelin-starred restaurant. 'We can't go in there.' She tugged at Will's hand as he pulled open the door.

'Why not? You're hungry, aren't you?'

'Yes, but I'm not dressed.'

'What do you call this?' he said, pinching her top between his fingers.

'You know what I mean! I'm not dressed for this place – and neither are you. I mean, look at us!' She spread her arms to indicate their general dishevelment.

Though she had changed her clothes, she was still bleary-eyed from lack of sleep and feeling seedy. Will's clothes looked as if he'd slept in them and, with his rapidly developing black eye, he resembled a low-life thug. 'You look adorable,' he said, bending to kiss her.

'Besides, we don't have a reservation,' Kate protested. 'I'm sure we'll never get a table.'

'It's okay, they know me here,' Will said, and pulled open the door before Kate could stop him. 'Come on, the food here is fantastic.'

The tall, glamorous hostess greeted Will by name with a warm smile. Appearing not to notice his black eye or the walking haystack on his arm, she whisked them to a secluded table in an alcove. Kate pulled out the chair opposite Will's, but he grabbed her hand and pulled her into the plush banquette beside him, their thighs touching.

Bubbling over with happiness, Kate thought how much she liked Will's world. The tables were covered with thick white linen, the crystal glasses sparkled, the waiters bustled around noiselessly, catering to their every need – and the food was sublime.

'Oh my God, this is amazing!' Kate groaned, as she ate the best lobster ravioli she had ever tasted. 'To think I began today eating quinoa porridge.'

'Sssh, keep your voice down,' Will said. 'You don't want to get us thrown out.'

She and Will sat practically entwined as they ate, barely able to keep their hands off each other. She made him laugh, telling him about how she had dumped Brian in the middle of his own sharing circle. Then Will filled her in on events in Tuscany.

'Rory and Louise finally put us out of our misery,' he said, 'not to mention themselves.'

'You mean . . . ?

'Yes, they got together. Not before time.'

'Oh, that's great!' Kate was delighted. 'They're so obviously nuts about each other.'

'Owen's called off the campaign to keep Tessa in the celebrity jail. I think Rory wants her out now, so he can dump her. Louise isn't happy about sneaking around behind her back.'

'Oh, I can't wait to see them! When are we going back to Tuscany?'

'There's no rush. Why don't we have a few days here first, just the two of us?' A few days in bed, his eyes were saying.

'Sounds great!'

'Come home with me,' Will said, taking her hand. 'Pack your bags and come to stay at my place. We can go back in a couple of days.'

'Okay. But I'm seriously in need of some kip first.' Already exhausted, the wine was making her even droopier and she could hardly keep her eyes open.

'You can kip at my house.' Will's index finger dug into her palm, sending shivers up her spine.

'I don't know . . .'

'Don't you trust me to keep my hands off you?'

'I'm just not sure *I'd* be able to keep my hands off *you.*'

Will gave a low growl. 'You shouldn't say things like that to me in a crowded restaurant,' he said, leaning in to kiss her, his lips clinging to hers as if they wanted never to let go.

Kate didn't want to let go either. Maybe she wasn't so tired after all, she thought, her senses pinging to life as the kiss deepened.

Finally Will pulled away. 'Okay, have it your way,' he said huskily.

'You go home and sleep and come over to my place later. I'll cook.'

'You'll cook?'

'Don't look so surprised. I had lessons from this fantastic chef I know.'

After another protracted snogging session outside her building, Kate didn't fancy her chances of getting any sleep, so she was amazed to wake up just after six o'clock and discover she had slept for almost four hours. She felt marvellous, still dizzy with happiness as the events of the past few hours flooded back to her.

She had always scoffed at those magazine articles that told you how to spend several hours – sometimes even days – getting ready for a date. Now, as she skipped to the bathroom armed with enough products to stock a small branch of Boots, she knew where they were coming from.

'I see you didn't manage to wipe that smile off your face,' Freddie said, when she finally emerged into the living room.

'Can't be done,' she said gaily. 'Not if I spent a whole week in the bathroom.'

'You almost did – I had to go next door to pee. I'd hate to see what you'd be like if you were going to the Oscars.'

'This is better than the Oscars,' Kate said blissfully. 'I know my name's in the envelope.'

By the time she rolled up in a taxi at Will's, she felt as buffed up and glamorous as a Hollywood starlet strutting the red carpet.

'Hi!' Will opened the door, barefoot, wearing jeans and a black T-shirt, looking heart-stoppingly beautiful and gratifyingly excited to see her. He seemed a lot brighter than he had earlier, his black eye only adding to his sexiness, giving him an edgy, rakish air.

'Wow, you look amazing.' His eyes devoured her hungrily, and he smelt divine as he bent to kiss her.

'Thanks,' she said shyly, moving past him into the large hall. Her heart was pounding already. 'So do you.'

She removed her jacket and he came up behind her, taking it from her.

'I can't believe you're here,' he said, stroking the back of his hand down her bare arm.

Kate shivered excitedly. 'I've been here before,' she said shakily, 'loads of times.'

'Not like this,' Will said, dropping a kiss on her neck.

'No, not like this,' Kate gasped as he nuzzled her neck and shoulder. His arms came around her and he pulled her into him, lifting her hair to trail kisses along the nape of her neck and up to her ear. Moaning low in his throat, he turned her in his arms, and their lips met, his mouth opening against hers.

'So, did you cook?' she asked breathlessly, rather hoping the answer would be no.

Will nodded as though he had been woken from a dream. 'Yes,' he said absently.

Taking her hand, he led her into the kitchen. The table was set for two and a delicious smell was coming from the oven.

'Would you like a glass of wine?' A bottle of red stood open on the table.

'Yes, please.'

Will handed her a glass and she took a big slug, wondering how on earth she was going to make it through dinner. All she wanted was Will – right here, right now.

'What did you make?' she asked, taking another swig. It was strong and heady – as if she didn't feel light-headed enough already.

'Lamb,' Will said, as if he was answering a totally different question, his eyes burning into hers.

'Sorry?' She was in such a frenzy of lust, she couldn't concentrate on anything.

'Lamb,' Will repeated, never taking his eyes from hers. 'Are you hungry?' There was a predatory glint in his eyes as they locked with hers that took Kate's breath away.

'No, not really,' she said breathily.

'Good. Me neither.'

In one fluid movement he took Kate's glass from her and set it on the worktop. His hard, muscular body slammed against hers, his fingers tangling in her hair as he opened her mouth with his.

'What about the lamb?' Kate rubbed her cheek against the rough stubble of his jaw.

'It'll keep.' He tugged her dress off one shoulder, dropping his lips to the bare skin.

'I hope you didn't go to too much trouble.' Kate slid her hands up inside his T-shirt.

'No trouble at all.' He raised his arms and she pulled it off over his head.

'Do you think maybe we should turn it off?' Kate asked between kisses.

'Turn what off?' Will was sliding down the zipper of her dress.

'The lamb.'

'Fuck the lamb.' Will's hand pushed inside her bra.

Kate gasped as his thumb brushed her nipple. 'No,' she whimpered. 'Fuck *me!*'

Kate woke the next morning to find the sun streaming through the muslin curtains and Will gone. Stretching languorously in the vast bed, she discovered she had little aches all over her body, as if she had done a really good workout – which, in a way, she had, she thought, though it had been a hell of a lot more fun than the gym. Sitting up, she glanced at the clock on the bedside table. It was only eight forty-five. Hearing noises downstairs, she got up and put on a dressing gown, then went in search of Will.

She found him in the living room, already dressed, his hair still wet from the shower. He was sitting cross-legged on the sofa in front of the television, eating a peach. He smiled as she came in, turned down the sound, tossed the peach onto a plate beside him and stretched out an arm to her. Kate leapt onto the sofa and snuggled up to him. Peach juice trickled down his chin and she licked it as she kissed his dimple.

'Good morning.' He kissed her mouth. He tasted wonderfully fresh and summery.

'What are you doing up so early? I thought we were having a holiday,' she said, breathing in his fresh, citrus smell.

'Something came up, there's some business I have to take care of. Sorry.' He grimaced apologetically.

'Couldn't it wait?' she asked, disappointed.

'Not really. It's a new, um, project I'm working on. I need to get it up and running before we go back to Italy.'

Kate couldn't help feeling a bit miffed that instead of being disappointed not to spend the morning in bed with her, he seemed pretty pleased with himself.

'Something's happening at the celebrity jail,' he said, waving to the TV.

Kate looked at the screen. He was watching *Celebrity Cell Block*, and a crisis was unfolding. Instead of the usual live coverage of the inmates, the presenter was standing outside the prison, speaking straight to the camera. From time to time, it cut to Tessa, who was wearing civvies instead of the regulation uniform.

'What's going on?' Kate asked.

'Tessa seems to be leaving,' Will said, turning up the sound again.

Just then, a breaking news update ran across the bottom of the screen, stating that Tessa was quitting the celebrity jail later today. The picture showed her packing her stuff and giving her cellmate an enthusiastic hug, then being led out of her cell by the 'warder'.

'Wow! Owen calling off the campaign worked fast.'

'She hasn't been voted off.' Will shook his head. 'It's something else, but they're being very cloak and dagger about it.'

As they watched, the camera returned to the presenter standing outside. Her hushed tone imbued the event with all the seriousness of a military coup. She said she could confirm that Tessa would be leaving later today, but at the moment, they couldn't reveal why. All she could say was that Tessa had to go for 'health reasons', then added paradoxically that she could assure Tessa's family, friends and legions of fans that she wasn't ill and there was nothing to worry about. 'What we *can* tell you is that Tessa requested an item from the pharmacy yesterday. We haven't been told what it was, but subsequent to that, she had discussions with the producers and it was decided that she should leave immediately.'

'Oh my God, she's pregnant!' Kate's hands flew to her face.

'Shit!' Will's eyes were wide with shock. 'Do you think that's it?'

'An item from the pharmacy – it must have been a pregnancy-testing kit. And she's not ill, but she has to leave for health reasons. What else could it be?'

'Oh Christ! Poor Louise.'

'You don't think Rory's just going to dump her, do you?'

'That's exactly what he'll do.'

'But he can't! He's nuts about her! And, besides, they've only just got together.'

Will looked at her squarely. 'Have you ever *heard* Rory on the subject of fathers who bail on their kids?'

Kate looked at him in silence as the truth of his words sank in.

'Oh my God, you're right!' Kate knew exactly what Rory thought of men who abandoned their children.

'Poor Louise.'

'Poor Rory.'

In Tuscany, Louise was sitting in front of the TV with Rory, watching the same programme, having been tipped off that something was happening with Tessa at the jail.

'She's pregnant!' she whispered.

Rory stared at the screen in numb disbelief. How could this have happened? They had always been so careful. But accidents happened. He didn't say a word, but his mind railed against the dawning reality.

Maybe Tessa wasn't pregnant, he thought hopefully. Maybe everyone was jumping to conclusions. No one had actually *said* she was pregnant. There was still hope, he told himself. But he didn't voice it out loud: deep down, he knew he was clutching at straws because he didn't want it to be true. In his heart, he knew Tessa was pregnant, and it was like a death sentence.

He cursed himself for being so careless and stupid. He thought of all those wasted years when he could have been with Louise, regret gnawing at him. If only he had had the courage to follow his heart. If only he had realised years ago that Louise felt the same way. If only he had never been with Tessa. If only, if only, if only . . .

They both stared determinedly at the screen, afraid to look at each other. Rory reached for Louise's hand and gripped it as their world fell apart before their eyes. When his phone rang, they jumped. He let go of Louise's hand, stood up and moved away to take the call. When he had disconnected, he came back. 'Tessa wants me to be there when she comes out.'

Louise nodded silently, blinking hard to stop the tears.

'Louise, I—'

'I know,' she interrupted. She couldn't bear to hear him say it. 'You have to go. It's okay.'

She had known it would happen. The moment she realised Tessa was pregnant, she had known she would lose Rory. No one who knew him as she did could have doubted it. She couldn't resent him for it or even wish it was otherwise. She understood that he had to go. He wouldn't have been the man she loved if he didn't. It was just horribly ironic and unfair that the very qualities she loved in him were taking him away from her now – his inherent decency, his dependability, the way he looked after people, his gritty determination to shoulder his responsibilities.

Wordlessly, they got up and began to make preparations, Louise helping Rory to pack. They moved about like automatons, studiously avoiding touching. Louise was terrified that if he touched her now she would end up begging him to stay, and she didn't want to make it any harder for him than it already was.

Rory knew that if he held her now he would never be able to let her go. Only when he was about to leave did he take her in his arms, holding her so tightly she could hardly breathe. He didn't say anything, but he didn't need to. His eyes said it all: I'm sorry, I love you. Then he kissed her with a fierce passion, and their lips clung together as if for the last time – which they both knew it was.

'I love you,' she whispered. 'I'll always love you.'

'I love you too,' he said grimly. And then he was gone. She watched his car drive away. Only when it was out of sight did she allow the floodgates to open and sank to the gravel in a heap, sobbing hysterically. Which was where Owen found her some time later. 'Louise! What the fuck?' He knelt down beside her and took her in his arms. 'What the fuck's the matter? Where's Rory?'

'He's gone,' she sobbed brokenly, clinging to him. 'Rory's gone.'

Kate had just got out of the shower when her mobile rang. 'Hello?'

'Kate! Where are you?' Rachel demanded sharply.

'At Will's.' Wrapped up in her own little world, it hadn't occurred to her that everyone didn't know the wonderful events of the last twenty-four hours.

'At Will's?'

Rachel's sharp tone brought her down to earth with a bang. She wished she hadn't answered the call – she didn't want to have to explain her and Will to anyone just yet.

'What are you doing at Will's?' Rachel asked.

'I'm – well, I'm . . .' Kate faltered. *I'm shagging his brains out every chance I get.* 'We're together now, Will and I.'

'*Together?*'

'Yes, together,' Kate said, stung. Rachel couldn't have sounded more incredulous if she'd said she'd hooked up with the Dalai Lama.

'You don't mean—'

Kate sighed. 'Yes,' she said defiantly. 'We're together. What's so unbelievable about that?' Of course, it *was* unbelievable, but Rachel had no right to think so.

'Nothing, it's just— What about Tina?'

'Oh, all that stuff in the papers was rubbish. Tina and he are finished.'

'Oh!' Rachel was silent for a moment. 'Anyway,' she continued breezily, 'the reason I called: I was wondering if you could do a dinner party for me, as you're out of a job again. Tom wants me to throw one for some of his yawn-a-minute legal cronies.'

'Can't, sorry,' Kate chirped, feeling anything but. 'I'm going back to Tuscany with Will.'

'Oh, okay,' Rachel said smoothly. To Kate's amazement, she didn't even sound put out. 'Well, let me know if your plans change. We want to do it Saturday week. I was thinking we could start with those crab tarts you make, they're always so popular . . .'

Kate hardly listened as Rachel proceeded to outline the menu to her as if she had said yes. Why is she telling me this, she thought, infuriated. What part of 'can't' did she not understand?

'Yes, but I won't be doing it,' she cut in, as Rachel pondered the relative merits of tiramisu versus lemon tart.

'Well, you never know, a lot can change in a couple of weeks. You might decide not to go back to Italy after all. Anyway, keep it in mind, just in case.'

Kate disconnected and threw her mobile on to the bed in exasperation.

When Will had gone, she spent the day chilling out at his house, sunbathing in the garden and waiting for him to return, missing him intensely. Later, she went into the village to buy groceries, planning to make a beautiful dinner for when he came home. Returning laden with bags, her heart leapt when she saw his car in the drive and she skipped up the steps, letting herself in with the key he had given her. She was about to go into the kitchen when she heard him on the phone and stopped in the doorway. He had his back to her and obviously hadn't heard her come in.

'I don't want her here!' he was saying into the phone. 'Get rid of her!' He sounded livid.

Kate hesitated in the doorway, feeling a chill go up her spine.

'No, *you* can tell her!' he roared. '*You* created this situation, *you* can bloody well sort it out.' He slammed down the receiver angrily.

'Problems?' Kate asked shakily.

He spun around, clearly startled to see her, the fury in his face replaced by surprise . . . and something else that Kate couldn't put her finger on. He looked at her blankly, struggling to shake off the phone call, his eyes still flashing angrily.

'Just staff problems,' he said, raking a hand through his hair.

'Oh!' Kate said, feeling sorry for the hapless employee on the other end of the phone. 'I'm going to make dinner.' She plonked her bags on the table and started to unpack them.

'Looks great.' He bent to kiss her. 'I'll just go and have a shower. By the way, Freddie rang. He wants you to call him back. He said he couldn't get through on your mobile.'

Kate fished in her bag for her phone, wondering why she hadn't heard it ringing. She pulled it out. 'Oh, shit! It's dead,' she said as Will left the room. 'I'll call him from the landline.'

When she picked up the phone to call Freddie, Kate was dismayed to hear other voices on the line. Whoever Will had been talking to hadn't switched off their mobile properly. She was about to hang up, when she recognised the voices as those of her mother and Rachel. That meant Will had been talking to one of them just now – so why had he lied about it? Her blood ran cold.

'. . . very grateful to him for helping us out with Kate and the whole Tree-hugger business,' Rachel was saying. 'But I told him we're not going to let him lose Tina over it.' Kate froze, hardly daring to breathe. 'He did a brilliant job of luring Kate away from the Tree-hugger,' Rachel continued, 'but we can't expect him to fall on his sword and end up stuck with her for the rest of his life. I mean, she's there right now – she's practically moved in!' Rachel sounded indignant. 'I was talking to her this morning. She thinks they're *together* now.'

Kate felt rooted to the spot, her blood turning to ice in her veins.

'But, darling, don't you think—'

'Look, Mum, I know you like the idea of Will and Kate together, but it's not real, and the sooner she realises it, the better.'

'I'm sure Will would never—'

'Oh, come on, Mum,' Rachel interrupted impatiently. 'We put him up to it, remember? Though he did exceed his brief. I specifically told him we didn't expect him to go so far as to sleep with her. Still, I suppose he thought he might as well get some fun out of it.'

'Rachel!' her mother protested. 'Why can't you believe that Will's in love with Kate?'

'Mum, you were *there*. He told us straight out that he wasn't interested in Kate in that way. He couldn't have made it clearer. We had to twist his arm to get him to agree to take her to Tuscany if you remember.'

Oh God, oh God, oh God! Kate clutched the table for support. She felt as if she was falling very fast into a deep, deep pit. She couldn't listen to any more. Her hand was shaking as she replaced the receiver, and for minutes she stood paralysed, leaning weakly against the table as the world crashed down around her.

I don't want her here! Get rid of her! Will's words reverberated around in her head, taunting her. How could she have been so stupid? The past couple of days had felt like a fantasy, and now it turned out that that was exactly what they had been – a fantasy dreamed up by her mother and Rachel and dutifully played out by Will. In an agony of humiliation, she wanted to crawl into a corner and hide and never have to face anyone ever again.

She thought of how Will had looked at her so lovingly last night, his passionate touch, his tender words. It had all seemed so real. She was shaking, too shocked even to cry.

Hearing Will moving around upstairs shook her out of her trance. She took her mobile out of her bag and called a taxi. Numbly, as if in a dream, she went upstairs to Will's bedroom, where they had thrown her case last night, and repacked it. It didn't take long. Passing the bathroom door, she heard Will still in the shower and fervently hoped she would be gone by the time he came out. She dragged her bag downstairs and went into the kitchen to wait for the taxi, pacing up and down restlessly, watching for it out the window, at the same time listening for Will.

The bathroom door opened, and Kate's pacing quickened. Almost simultaneously the bell rang. As she opened the door, Will came downstairs to investigate, a towel wrapped around his waist.

'Taxi?'

Kate nodded, and the driver went back to his car. But as Kate made to follow him, Will ran down the last few steps, bounded across the hall and stood in front of her, blocking her way. He was still wet from the shower, little rivulets of water running down his face.

'Kate, what's going on?' he asked, eyes darkening with concern as he took in her stricken face. 'What's the matter?'

'Nothing,' she said tightly, making to pass him.

But he wouldn't move, putting a wet hand on her shoulder while the other held onto the towel.

'You're upset.' He frowned. 'What is it? Did Freddie have bad news?'

'I wasn't talking to Freddie,' she said, shrugging off his hand.

'Where are you going?' He looked down at her case.

'Home.'

He reached out and touched her cheek, and she flinched. The wounded look on his face was the last straw and something snapped inside her. 'You can cut that out!' she snapped, taking advantage of his surprise to duck away from him.

When he grabbed her arm to stop her, she shook him off. 'Oh relax!' she snarled. 'The engagement's off!'

'What are you talking about?'

She turned to him. 'I know, okay? I know you were doing all this to get me to dump Brian. Well, I *have* dumped him. Your work is done!'

'What?' He was clearly shocked, but the guilt etched on his features was unmistakeable. 'That's ridiculous!' he protested, when he had recovered a little. 'I love you, Kate. I'm crazy about you.'

'Oh, stop it! You've achieved what you set out to do. You don't have to pretend to . . . to like me any more.'

'You can't honestly believe that! Christ, what do you think last night was all about?'

'I don't know. Maybe you decided to make the best of a bad job. "Overstepping your brief" was how Rachel put it,' she said bitterly.

'Rachel? What's she said to you?'

'Nothing. I heard her and Mum talking – I know they put you up to it.'

'Kate, come back inside and we can talk about this – please!'

'There's nothing to talk about.'

'You don't know what you're saying,' he said dully. The look of hurt on his face made Kate want to scream. 'Kate, I love you. I've never felt like this about anyone before in my life. And you love me too,' he said.

'Yeah, well, that was the general idea, wasn't it?' she said bitterly.

'I can't believe you think I'd do that to you.'

Just then the taxi driver got out of his car. 'You coming or not, love?' he shouted impatiently at Kate. 'I can't wait all day.'

'Good – fuck off!' Will bellowed at him savagely.

'No, I'm coming.' Kate turned and ran before Will could stop her.

'Kate, this is insane,' Will called after her. 'Wait—'

She sprang into the taxi, and slammed the door. 'Go!' she hissed at the driver, as Will hopped down the gravel drive after them, his shouts fading as they drove away.

'Looks like you had a lucky escape there, love.' The driver chuckled. 'I Claudius there looks like a right nutter.'

And just in time, Kate thought, as another taxi turned into the driveway and she glimpsed Tina in the passenger seat. Jesus, no wonder Will had been so anxious to get rid of her this morning. Thank God she'd found out in time and hadn't hung around to be thrown out by Tina.

'So, where are we going?' The driver looked at her in the mirror. 'Airport?'

'Oh no, just . . .' Kate stopped short. Why not? she thought. She still had her passport in her bag, she was packed and had plenty of money in her bank account. And there was no one she wanted to face right now.

'Yes, the airport, please,' she said, sinking back against the seat.

'Where are you going? Anywhere nice?'

'Mmm, anywhere nice,' she murmured.

Rory sat in a limousine outside the celebrity jail on the outskirts of London, waiting for Tessa to emerge. He felt as if he was going to his execution, dreading the moment when the gates would open to disgorge Tessa – and his life would be over. At the same time, he was racked with guilt for thinking like that – after all, there was the baby to consider. It wasn't the poor little thing's fault that he had screwed everything up, and he promised himself he would never make it suffer for his mistakes. He would make sure that his child never felt unloved or unwanted. He would just have to devote himself to being a good father, and be content with that.

He looked out through the darkened windows at the press and the *Celebrity Cell Block* cameras. Finally, the huge gates swung open and Tessa emerged, small and vulnerable, one hand resting protectively on her stomach. The assembled paparazzi snapped and yelled, and the *Celebrity Cell Block* cameras followed her the few short steps from the gate until she was bundled into the car by a member of the production team. The second the door was closed, they drove slowly up the hill and away.

'Oh, I'm so glad you're here, baby,' she smiled tearfully, throwing herself into Rory's arms. 'It was awful in there.'

Rory wondered what he had ever seen in her.

'And I was so bloody popular with the public I thought I'd never get out. Well, thank God it's over!' she said emphatically, flopping against the upholstery with an exaggerated sigh. Then she rooted in her bag and pulled out her cigarettes.

Rory couldn't believe his eyes as she lit up and sucked deeply, exhaling on a long, contented sigh. 'What the fuck do you think you're doing?' he said angrily, snatching the cigarette and stubbing it out.

'Hey!' Tessa protested. 'What the fuck do you think you're doing?'

'You can't smoke.'

'No one can see,' Tessa said crossly, indicating the darkened windows.

'I don't give a fuck! What about the baby? Look,' he said, trying to be reasonable, 'I know it was hard in there, but—'

'*Baby?*' Tessa's lip curled contemptuously. 'There's no *baby*.'

'What?'

'There's no baby, silly. God, I'm not *that* stupid!'

'Then why—'

'Because if I'd had to spend another second in that hellhole with that stupid dyke trying to jump me every night I'd have gone fucking insane!'

'So you pretended you were pregnant?' Rory said faintly. He knew he should be furious with her – part of him was – but he couldn't stop the smile that was spreading across his face.

'Yes.' Tessa smiled back at him, looking very pleased with herself. 'And, *voilà*, here I am, a free woman! Aren't I clever? Dev will be so proud of me.'

'You pretended you were pregnant to get off the show?'

'Yes – and now we can spend the rest of the summer together.' She threw her arms around him and kissed him.

'Aren't you in breach of contract?' Rory asked, pushing her away firmly.

'I never *said* I was pregnant,' she said airily. 'It's not my fault if people jumped to that conclusion.'

'And what happens when it becomes obvious you're not?'

'I've thought of that,' she smiled smugly. 'In a couple of months I'll take to wearing dark glasses and going around looking glum for a while. Everyone will assume I've had a miscarriage.'

'There's really no baby?' He was grinning from ear to ear.

'No.' Tessa said, surprised that Rory was so pleased. She'd suspected that he would be a bit soppy about kids. 'Well, obviously this is good news. I guess you don't want kids any more than I do.'

'Not with you, you mercenary bitch.'

'*What?*' His grin was so at odds with his words that it took her a while to grasp what he had said.

'Not with you,' he repeated. He rapped on the glass partition between them and the driver. 'Stop the car!' he ordered the man when the partition slid back.

'What are you doing?' Tessa asked as the car slid to a halt.

Ignoring her, Rory got out and strode back down the road to the prison gates where the photographers and cameramen were packing up. Seeing him approach, the *Celebrity Cell Block* crew started filming again. He marched straight up to one of the cameramen. 'Can I say something?' he said, nodding to the camera. 'Is this live?'

'Go ahead.'

Rory looked straight into the lens. 'Louise, if you're watching, Tessa's not pregnant,' he said. 'She just pretended she was to get off the show. I love you.' He beamed. 'I'm coming back, sweetheart. I'll see you soon.'

The assembled press went wild, snapping pictures and yelling questions at Rory. Never before had anyone heard him say so much. Several of the women remarked to each other how attractive he was and wondered why they had never noticed it before.

Rory ignored their questions and calls for pictures.

'Thanks, man,' he said quietly to the cameraman and gripped his hand briefly.

By this time, Tessa had tottered down the hill to investigate what was going on and reached Rory as he turned to go back to the car. 'Tessa will answer all your questions,' he said, pushing her into the crowd of journalists and cameras.

Tessa yelped when she saw that Rory intended to abandon her to the wolves, but it was too late as they mobbed her. 'Rory!' she yelled furiously, to his retreating back. 'Rory!'

He ignored her and got back in the car.

Could you take me to the airport,' he asked.

The driver looked at him in his mirror. 'Sorry, sir, but my job is to drive Miss Bond home.'

'I'll give you a thousand pounds if you take me to the airport

326

now.' Rory didn't usually throw his weight around, but this was urgent.

The driver considered it. 'Sorry,' he said finally. 'Can't do it. More than my job's worth, mate.'

'Look, what's your name?'

'Winston.'

'Okay, Winston. Do you know who I am?' Rory winced inwardly – he had never said that before.

'Sure – you're Rory Cassidy, out of Walking Wounded. I've got all your albums.'

'Well, how would you like to come and work for us?' He pulled a piece of paper out of his pocket and scribbled Louise's number on it. 'Just call this number – I'll arrange it.'

Winston peered at the piece of paper, then at Rory.

'What about Miss Bond?'

Rory looked down the hill. Tessa was still swamped by media, trying to fight them off. 'Leave her. I think she'll be busy for a while. And I'll still give you that grand if you take me to the airport right now.'

Winston didn't hesitate any longer. He turned back to the wheel, gunned the engine and did a U-turn. Then they roared back down the hill. Rory glimpsed Tessa's livid face as they swept past, leaving her in a cloud of dust.

Chapter 14

On the second Thursday in December, Kate made her way through the throng of late-night shoppers on Grafton Street. A canopy of Christmas lights twinkled overhead, and every few yards carol singers were belting out old favourites, 'Jingle Bells' mingling with 'Silent Night', accompanied by the jangle of collection tins. Shop windows sparkled in the darkness, decked out in sumptuous colours and rich fabrics, shining like beacons of warmth and luxury in the bitter cold. Already laden with bags and chilled to the bone, Kate longed to go home, put on her Christmas pyjamas and curl up on the sofa, but she forced herself to press on. She was way behind with her Christmas shopping, having only returned from her impromptu travels the previous week.

Determined to get one more present before she gave up, she took refuge in the warm, comforting cocoon of Brown Thomas. She wandered aimlessly around the brightly lit opulence of the cosmetics hall, bewildered by the dizzying abundance of products spread out across the counters and the brightly wrapped gift boxes piled high on display stands. Lingering by the Jo Malone counter, she tried out one perfume after another. Recognising the scent Will used, she couldn't resist spraying some onto her wrist and breathing in the citrus fragrance, which sent shivers of longing up her spine.

'Are you looking for a gift?' The sales assistant shook her out of her reverie.

'Oh – yes.'

'That one is gorgeous for men.' She indicated the bottle Kate had just tried. 'I always buy it for my boyfriend. It's so sexy.' She giggled conspiratorially.

'Yes, it is.'

'Is it for a boyfriend?'

'Oh no.' She was shocked to find herself fighting back tears. When was it going to stop feeling so raw? 'Actually, I want something for my mum.'

'Oh, well, this one is lovely and very popular . . .'

She only half listened as the girl went into her sales spiel. She normally loved Christmas, but now she understood why some people dreaded it. Everything about it seemed calculated to make her miss Will more intensely. All the things she usually adored were robbed of their magic and sparkle, rendered futile because she wasn't sharing them with him. It was as if she had lost the sense of taste and her favourite foods were flavourless in her mouth.

Having paid for her purchases, she decided to call it a day and was on her way out the door when her mobile rang. It was Lorcan. 'Hi, Kate. You doing anything tonight?'

'No,' she said warily, thinking longingly of the sofa.

'Well, get your glad rags on and come over to the Shelbourne. We're celebrating.'

'Celebrating what?'

'Carmen and I are getting married!'

'What?' She felt winded and leaned against the store window for support.

'Well, don't sound so enthusiastic,' Lorcan laughed.

'Sorry,' she said. 'It's great news, really, just a surprise. You haven't known each other long.'

'*Et tu, Brute,*' Lorcan sighed tragically.

'I'm not criticising, honestly – you know how much I like Carmen. Congratulations, I'm so pleased for you,' she said, trying to inject a smile into her voice, but her face was anaesthetised. Thank God he couldn't see her.

'Thanks.'

She really *was* happy for him – so why did she feel like bursting into tears?

'Come over whenever you're ready. We'll be in the Horseshoe Bar. And bring Freddie.'

As she walked home, weighed down with parcels and a heavy heart, Kate was still wrestling with the tears. What the hell was wrong with her? Why did she feel so gutted by Lorcan's news? Why couldn't she just be happy for him? Deep down, she knew. It was because she was jealous – jealous that it wasn't her. It was just one more thing that conspired with the rest to make her feel lonely and left out.

Oh, snap out of it, she told herself crossly. It's not as if it's you or them. There's plenty to go around. She was tired of feeling sad and hurt, and she didn't want to become a bitter, dried-up old maid, envious and resentful of other people's happiness. As she passed Meetinghouse Square, a movie was playing on the big screen and she wandered in to have a look. It was *Meet Me in St Louis*, and Judy Garland was singing 'Have Yourself a Merry Little Christmas', her glorious voice as warm as toast in the chill night air. There were seats dotted around the square in front of the screen, but not many people had braved the cold. A few little groups of twos or threes were huddled together in the darkness, some sharing blankets. Kate sank into a chair and dropped her bags, grateful for the rest. There was something so comforting about the cosy familiarity of a film she had seen many times before, and she watched, entranced, as Judy Garland tried to persuade Margaret O'Brien, as fat tears poured from her luminous eyes, that next year all their troubles would be miles away.

You're not even convincing yourself, Judy, Kate thought, wiping away the tears that were now trickling down her own cheeks. In the anonymity of the dark square, she allowed herself to sob to her heart's content, deciding it would be cathartic. If she indulged herself now and had a good howl, she might be able to act like something resembling a normal person at Lorcan's celebration.

'Looks like you did well,' Freddie said, when she came in, indicating her shopping bags.

'Not bad,' Kate said, divesting herself of coat, scarf and gloves. 'I'm still not half finished, though.'

'You okay?' he asked, as she sat on the sofa beside him.

'Fine. God, it's freezing out there,' she said, blowing on her hands to warm them.

'You look like you've been crying.' Freddie eyed her suspiciously.

'Oh, they were showing *Meet Me in St Louis* in the square and I stopped to watch. Gets me every time.'

'Oh, me too. Why don't you get into your jim-jams and we'll veg out in front of the TV? Dinner will be mini crab tarts, devils on horseback, goujons of sole and mini quiches,' Freddie announced, getting up. 'I hereby declare canapé season well and truly open.'

Broke from buying presents and partying in the run-up to Christmas, Kate and Freddie traditionally survived on leftovers from Kate's catering jobs, supplemented by ligging at as many drinks parties as they could get into.

'We can't do canapé night tonight,' Kate said regretfully.

'Oh, are you going out?'

'Yes, and so are you. Lorcan wants us to go down to the Shelbourne for drinks and dinner.' She paused, schooling her features. 'He's getting married,' she said.

'*Married*!' Freddie sank onto the sofa again.

'Mmm. He told me just now.'

'You don't seem very happy about it.'

'Oh no, I am. It was just a surprise.'

Freddie was gazing at her sceptically.

'I think it's great,' she protested. 'Honestly. I'm happy for them.'

'But?' Freddie nudged.

'But I'm sick of being happy for other people,' she said. 'I want to be happy for *myself* for a change. I want other people to be happy for *me*,' she wailed.

'I know,' Freddie said, pulling her head onto his shoulder and ruffling her hair.

She smiled, grateful to him for not making her feel more ashamed of herself than she already was. 'It just dredges up all those always-the-bridesmaid feelings. And there's the wedding to freak out about, of course.'

'What do you mean?'

'Well, you know who'll be best man.'

'Oh Christ, of course! Shit!' He thought for a moment. 'Will he be there tonight?'

'No. He's still away on tour with Walking Wounded.'

'Thank God for that. So, when are Lorcan and Carmen sashaying down the aisle?'

'I was so stunned I didn't think to ask.'

'Well, look on the bright side. Carmen hasn't said that she wants you to be bridesmaid.'

'True,' she said. 'I shouldn't be feeling sorry for myself.'

'No – if anyone should be feeling sorry for themselves, it's me. Never the bridesmaid, never the bride!' Freddie sighed tragically.

'You know you'll be bridesmaid at my wedding.'

'Really?' Freddie perked up.

'Of course. But I wouldn't get too excited about it, if I were you. At this rate, even *you'll* be married before I am.'

The Horseshoe Bar was heaving when Kate and Freddie arrived. Lorcan waved at them and they fought their way to him through the crowds.

Everyone was there: Tom and Rachel, Conor and Helen, Grace and Jack, all surrounding the happy couple. They seemed in high spirits, but Kate couldn't help noticing that, with the exception of Lorcan and Carmen, they seemed rather uncomfortable when she joined them, their eyes sliding away after over-bright hellos. Even Rachel looked ashamed.

Oblivious of the atmosphere, Lorcan jumped up to greet her and Freddie.

'Congratulations!' Kate threw her arms around him.

'Thanks.' He grinned down at her, so happy that all Kate's gloom melted away.

As he passed on to Freddie, she turned to Carmen, who looked lit from within. 'Congratulations!' She hugged her. 'I'm really pleased for you.'

She and Freddie sat on the seats Lorcan had somehow managed to save, and he poured some champagne from one of the bottles that nestled in an ice bucket beside him.

'So, when's the wedding?' she asked Lorcan, as Freddie cooed over Carmen's ring.

'New Year's Eve.' Lorcan grinned.

'Oh my God!' Kate gasped. 'So soon!'

'Not soon enough,' he said, glancing adoringly at Carmen. 'I don't know how I'm going to wait that long.'

'But don't you have to give notice?'

'All done. Actually, we started planning ages ago. We just decided not to make it public until the last minute. We didn't want people telling us we were crazy because it was so soon. You know how people can interfere.'

'Yes.' Kate sighed. 'I do.'

He cleared his throat, suddenly awkward. 'Will's going to be best man,' he said, warily.

Kate nodded silently, dredging up what she hoped was a reassuringly placid smile.

'Unless there's any reason he shouldn't be.'

'No, of course not.'

'Look, I don't know what happened between you two . . .' He left the words hanging in the air.

'No, you don't,' Kate said flatly.

'. . . but Will was pretty gutted when you went off like that,' Lorcan continued, almost accusingly.

'Really?' Kate said coldly.

'Okay, none of my business,' Lorcan said, seeing her set face.

'Did it escape your notice that Tina was there when I "went off like that"?' she said sharply, annoyed that she had been goaded into defending herself. 'Or did Will forget to mention that little detail?'

'*Tina?*' To Kate's astonishment, Lorcan had the nerve to guffaw at this. 'Don't tell me that's why you hared off?'

'Well, it's a good enough reason, don't you think? His girlfriend was moving in. What was I supposed to do? Hang around and help with her stuff?'

'But that wasn't Will's idea,' Lorcan said. 'He was as surprised as you were when she turned up. He thought she was safely on the other side of the world, tormenting Cambodian orphans. He didn't want her there at all.'

I don't want her here. Get rid of her. Will's words had reverberated around in her head for the past three months. Could he have been talking about Tina? And what could Tina coming back have to do with her mother and Rachel?

'Apparently it was some hare-brained matchmaking scheme of Rachel's, believe it or not,' Lorcan said, as if in answer to her unspoken question. 'I guess she must have believed all that guff in the papers about Will wanting Tina back. For some reason, she took it upon herself to try to reunite them.'

'*Rachel* did?'

'I know – most unlike her! Anyway, she got it hopelessly wrong. Will sent Tina packing straight away. I don't think she even got out of the car.' Lorcan laughed. 'It just did a U-turn in the drive.'

'God, poor Tina!'

'Serves her right for believing her own publicity.' He snorted. 'I mean, she'd made up those stories in the papers and then somehow persuaded herself they were true.'

Or Rachel had persuaded her, Kate thought. *You created this situation, you sort it out*, she had heard Will bawl into the phone. He had been telling Rachel to get rid of Tina, not her. It didn't alter the fact that he had been faking it with her, but at least he hadn't been talking about her in the awful, dismissive way that had haunted her ever since.

'Poor Rachel got it from both sides.' Lorcan chuckled. 'Tina and Will were both furious with her for interfering. Will really put the wind up her – not easy with Rachel, as you know. Thankfully, I think the whole episode has cured her of matchmaking. There never was a stupider Cupid.'

She wondered how long Will would have let it go on before he dumped her, if things hadn't come to a head. Maybe he felt he had painted himself into a corner and was trapped into keeping up the pretence, at least for a while. Maybe, like Tina, he had even started to believe his own bullshit.

'So, if it's because of Tina that you left—' Lorcan was saying hopefully.

'It wasn't just that.' Kate smiled sadly. 'But there are no hard feelings. I don't want anyone avoiding Will on my account. Or beating him up.'

'Okay.' Lorcan was clearly not satisfied, but was willing to drop it.

Kate had noticed her mother darting apprehensive glances at her while she was talking to Lorcan. Rachel's eyes flicked warily in Kate's direction too, as though she was a wild animal that might attack at any moment. 'Is Will coming to us for Christmas?' she asked Lorcan.

'No, he's going to Antonia's. She invited him, and I don't think he felt able to refuse – not this year, at least. He'll be back for New Year, though.'

'Gosh, yes. Aren't Walking Wounded playing the O2 on New Year's Eve? That'll clash a bit with your wedding, won't it?'

'Not really. He'll be there for the important bits.'

'So, how were your travels, Kate?' Helen asked brightly.

'Oh great,' Kate said, and tried to inject some enthusiasm into her voice as she told Helen about her trip. The truth was that there had been something depressingly half-hearted about her aimless wanderings – as if she was just going through the motions. It had unnerved her to feel so numb about something she usually found exhilarating, but her heart hadn't been in it. It seemed to be AWOL a lot, these days.

When everyone moved off to the restaurant for dinner, Grace and Rachel cornered Kate.

'Don't worry, I'm not going to tell Lorcan about your plot,' she said wearily.

'Darling, you don't have to make it sound so underhand,' Grace quibbled.

'Well, what would *you* call it? If you think it was above board and hunky-dory, why are you so worried about Lorcan finding out?'

'You know Lorcan,' Grace said fussily. 'He'd overreact and make a big drama out of it. I don't want him to fall out with Will.'

'Well, neither do I, so you can rest easy,' Kate said, needled that Will seemed to be the person her mother was most concerned about in all this.

'Have you heard from Will lately?' Grace asked.

'No – at least I haven't spoken to him.' He had bombarded her with phone calls while she was away, but she had never answered them. It had been a relief to discover that there were still some places in the world where mobile coverage didn't extend and you could be truly out of reach. It had added to the already abundant charms of Vietnam.

'Well, you'll see him at Lorcan's wedding,' her mother said consolingly. 'You can patch things up between you then.'

'There's nothing to patch up, Mum. There was nothing there in the first place, remember?'

'Oh, that's not true, Kate,' Grace said briskly. 'The poor boy has been heartbroken since you left, hasn't he, Rachel? Moping around the place like a stray puppy.'

Kate looked up at her from under her eyelashes but said nothing. Grace sighed helplessly, which Kate found unsettling: her mother was rarely so timorous.

'We just wanted you to be happy, darling,' she pleaded. 'I knew it would be disastrous for you to marry the Tree-hugger.'

'Yes, it would – but I would have found that out for myself, Mum. And what's *your* excuse?' she asked Rachel.

'She was only thinking of you, weren't you, darling?' Grace answered hastily, clearly not trusting Rachel to speak for herself.

'I was thinking of the whole family,' Rachel said sullenly. 'None of us wanted you marrying that knobhead. And none of this would have happened if you hadn't got engaged to him in the first place.' Rachel was a firm believer in attack as the best form of defence.

'Oh, so it's all my fault?'

'Well, poor Mum was desperate,' Rachel said, ignoring Grace's signals to shut up. 'I was only trying to help.'

'Anyway, it's all turned out for the best in the end, hasn't it?' Grace said hopefully to Kate.

'No, Mum, it hasn't. How on earth can you think that?'

'Oh, don't be so coy,' Rachel snapped. 'You always fancied Will and now you've got him – thanks largely to me. You might be more grateful.'

'*Grateful?*'

'Yes, grateful.'

'Will really does love you, Kate,' Grace said.

'As you'd know if you'd stuck around for five minutes,' Rachel said, still smarting from the bollocking Will had given her. It was enough to put you off good deeds for life. She had only been trying to do something nice for Will and Tina, and in return, she had been lambasted by them both. She had never seen anyone as angry as Will was that day – at least, not until Tina turned up. Well, it was the last time she would try to do *him* a favour. Infuriatingly, when she had said as much to him, he had asked if he could have that in writing. Sarcastic bastard!

'If you'd seen how unhappy Will was—' her mother began.

'I really don't want to discuss it any more,' Kate said tightly. 'We should go in to dinner. Lorcan will be wondering where we are.'

'But, Kate—'

'*Please* Mum.' She felt that one more word would tip her over the edge. 'Look, I know you meant well, okay? Let's just leave it at that.'

Her mother had convinced herself that Will had fallen in love for real – but, then, she had an uncanny knack for believing what she wanted to believe. Kate wished she had that talent. Because, try as she might, she couldn't block out Rachel's words on the phone that day: *He told us straight out that he wasn't interested in Kate . . . we really had to twist his arm.*

'I hate to see you so unhappy, sweetheart,' her mother said sadly. 'I just think—'

Thankfully, Kate was spared any further torture by Lorcan and Freddie coming in search of them.

'What are you three plotting?' Lorcan grinned at them, unaware of any undercurrents.

'Oh, just discussing what to wear to your wedding,' Grace said, the consummate actress.

'Come on,' Freddie said, pulling Kate to her feet. 'You don't want to miss the chance to eat dinner with a knife and fork!'

*

'I'm getting a strong sense of *déjà vu* about this wedding,' Kate said to Freddie two days later, as they sat kicking their heels between takes on the set of *Northsiders*. 'Yet another family wedding with no boyfriend when I want to be looking amazing with a fabulous bloke to make Will jealous. Plus all my bloody aunts looking at asking me pityingly if I've "met anyone nice".'

'You can borrow Ken if you like.'

'Oh I couldn't,' Kate was touched. 'Thanks for the offer, but I wouldn't do you out of the chance to show off your boyfriend. Besides, Will knows him.'

'True. Well, at least you'll look fabulous.'

'No, I won't. It's so close, I have no time to find something fabulous to wear – and in the middle of the Christmas rush too, when I have so much work, and any time I *do* get to the shops I have to concentrate on buying presents.'

Freddie considered. 'Don't worry, I'll make you something.'

'Oh, please don't bother. I'll find something.'

'No bother,' he said, giving her shoulder a squeeze. 'Consider it an early Christmas present.'

Kate was enjoying a rare night home alone, wrapping her Christmas presents in front of the television, when she heard Freddie's key in the door. 'Hi, honey, I'm home!' he called, coming into the flat followed by a tall, flaxen-haired hunk. 'Kate.' Freddie led the hunk to the sofa. 'This is Jonathan.' He seemed very pleased with himself.

Kate hoped he wasn't two-timing Ken. 'Hi, nice to meet you.' She stood up to shake Jonathan's hand.

'Jonathan's going to be your date for the wedding.'

'Oh! Really?'

Jonathan grinned down at her from his lofty height. 'Sure,' he shrugged amiably, 'if you like.'

He was unfeasibly good-looking, like an underwear model, with shoulder-length golden hair, piercing blue eyes that would have given Brad Pitt's a run for their money, and the ridiculously square jaw of a comic-book hero. Even though he was wearing a leather jacket over a thick sweatshirt, you could tell he had a six-pack.

'Um, that's really nice of you,' Kate smiled uncertainly at him. 'Would you like some tea or something? Coffee? Wine?'

'Coffee, please.' He smiled lazily, revealing perfect Hollywood teeth.

'Okay, have a seat – I won't be a sec. Freddie, could I have a quick word with you in the kitchen?'

Freddie followed her in and she shut the door after them. She put the coffee machine on and waited for it to start hissing before she spoke. 'What's this all about?'

'Just something to complete your outfit, sweetie – a little arm candy,' he said, taking mugs out of the cupboard.

Is he an escort? Do I have to pay him?'

'Oh no,' Freddie said. 'Don't worry, he's not a gigolo or anything – he's *much* lower down the food chain than that.'

Kate looked at him enquiringly.

'He's a model 'slash' actor – and you know what *that* means.' Freddie raised his eyebrows.

Kate had no idea what that meant.

'Will work for food!' Freddie hissed, as if stating the blindingly obvious. 'Seriously, just feed him some soup and crackers and he's all yours.'

'But where would I even meet someone like him?' Kate fretted. 'If everyone knows I've just hired some random bloke for the day, I'll look sadder than ever.'

'You've just been away for three months, haven't you? You can meet all sorts travelling around the world. Jonathan could easily be a backpacker – he has that kind of slacker look, don't you think? And he's already got a tan,' Freddie said dreamily, as Kate made the coffee and loaded a tray with mugs, sugar and milk.

'We need biscuits,' he said and flung open the cupboards. He found a packet of shortbread, emptied it onto a plate and then picked up the tray. 'Come on, we'll get to work on your cover story.'

'So, how do you know Freddie?' Kate asked, as they sat on the sofa drinking coffee and Jonathan laid into the biscuits.

'I used to go out with his friend Matthew.'

Kate froze. 'You *what?*' she gasped. 'Oh my God, you're . . . you're—'

'Gay? Yeah, is that a problem?' Jonathan looked at her innocently.

'Yes! I mean no,' she faltered. 'I mean, no offence but, well, you're supposed to be coming to this wedding as my boyfriend. This isn't going to work,' she said, in a panicky voice.

'No one will know,' Freddie said calmly. '*You* didn't know until he told you. He can totally pass. Besides, he's an *actor*.'

'Yeah, I can play it straight.' Jonathan smiled nonchalantly. 'It'll be good experience for me, playing the romantic lead. Got any more of these?' he asked, as he polished off the last biscuit.

'Are you sure?' Kate asked apprehensively.

'Oh yeah, I work out a lot – and I have a really fast metabolism.'

'I don't mean about the biscuits. I mean are you sure about playing my boyfriend?'

'No problem,' he said affably. 'I'll even snog you, if you like.'

Kate felt trapped.

'So, what's the dinner going to be at this wedding?' Jonathan asked.

Freddie shot her a told-you-so look. 'I'll get some more biscuits,' he said. 'You two can start on your back story.'

'Where are we going to say we met?' Jonathan asked.

'Well, I've just been away for three months, travelling, so perhaps we ran into each other somewhere then.'

'Okay,' Jonathan nodded, 'sounds good.'

'I was in India, Thailand, Vietnam, Cambodia – have you ever been to any of those places?' she asked hopefully.

'No,' Jonathan said.

'Laos? Sri Lanka?' Kate asked desperately.

'Sorry – I've been to Benidorm,' he said, 'and I spent a weekend in Ibiza once, but I don't remember any of it.'

'Right. It's not really the same thing.'

'Okay,' he said, pushing his hair back from his face, suddenly business like. 'Let's say we met in Thailand.'

'Thailand?'

'Yeah. I've never been there, but I love Thai food. And I've done lots of drugs,' he added helpfully. 'Oh, and I went through a Buddhist phase for a while.'

'Great! You're practically a native!' God help me, she thought. This is going to be a disaster.

* * *

'. . . dying of food poisoning, so I threw myself into this tuk-tuk, practically at death's door, and asked the driver to take me to a doctor. Next thing, he's unloading me into his uncle's silk shop and insisting I can see a doctor there, and to have a browse while I'm waiting . . .'

God, he's good, Kate thought, as everyone laughed at another of Jonathan's stories about his travels in Thailand. He had more stories about Thailand than *she* had, and she had actually been there.

She was glad she had brought him to the wedding. He had been really sweet and solicitous towards her, seeming to sense how wobbly she felt around Will, putting a protective arm around her shoulders or clasping her hand whenever he came near. So far it was going swimmingly. She had managed to avoid Will most of the time, apart from the briefest peck on the cheek when they had arrived at the church and she introduced Jonathan. Now he was safely tucked away at the top table, though she was uncomfortably aware of his eyes on her all the time. She and Jonathan were sharing a table with Helen and Conor, Ken and Freddie.

'So, where did you meet Kate, Jonathan?' Helen was asking.

'At a food stall in Chiang Mai,' he answered readily, smiling fondly at Kate. 'She was cooking the most amazing *pad thai* I've ever tasted in my life.'

'You were cooking at a food stall?' Helen asked.

'Yeah, I'd got chatting to the woman who ran it and she was giving me an impromptu lesson in Thai cooking.'

She wished she didn't feel so self-conscious. That had really happened – apart, of course, from the bit about Jonathan being there. At least they weren't sitting with Rachel. She had seemed sceptical when Kate had introduced her to Jonathan and was still watching them beadily. Her mother looked as if there were a million questions she wanted to ask, but she was swallowing every one.

'What do you do, Jonathan?' Conor asked.

'I'm an actor.'

'Are you?' Conor said, interested. 'Would I have seen you in anything?'

Oh God, she hadn't reckoned on Conor bullying Jonathan about his career.

'I doubt it. I've done a bit of modelling, and some showcases attached to my acting classes, but that's about it.'

'Are you any good?' Conor asked, with typical bluntness.

'Yeah, actually, I am.'

He was giving a bravura performance right now, Kate thought.

'You should come and see me – I might be able to help you.'

'Oh, they're starting the speeches,' Kate said, grateful for the diversion as Will stood and introduced Carmen's beaming father, who made a short, incomprehensible speech in heavily accented English before passing the microphone to Lorcan.

Finally, it was Will's turn and Kate was able to gaze at him quite blatantly. He was so heartbreakingly beautiful.

I'm still so in love with him, she thought despairingly.

Promising to be brief, he was true to his word. 'I'm not normally given to quoting poetry,' he said, 'but everything I feel about Lorcan – and about his family – can be summed up in a couple of lines of Yeats:

"Think where man's glory most begins and ends
And say my glory was I had such friends."

I'm sure Lorcan and Carmen will be very happy together.'

He turned to Carmen, almost as an afterthought.

'None of us has known Carmen very long, but she seems wonderful and I'm sure she'll make Lorcan very happy. She'll have me to answer to if she doesn't,' he finished, fixing Carmen with a mock-steely gaze.

This was greeted with nervous laughter, no one quite sure how to react, but on seeing Carmen laughing up at Will, everyone's anxious titters dissolved into rapturous applause as he sat down again.

As soon as dinner was over and everyone was circulating, Freddie sought out Will. 'Brilliant speech!' he enthused. 'It had just the right balance of sentimentality and menace. Threatening the bride with mayhem was an inspired touch.'

'Glad you enjoyed it.' Will glanced furtively at Kate. 'So, how's Kate?' he asked ultra-casually.

Freddie wondered how long he'd been practising that. It was a good job he'd never pursued a career in acting. 'She's fine,' he replied. 'You know – okay.' He tried to sound ambivalent. Will was clearly miserable, so he didn't have the heart to rub it in and talk up how happy she was with her new boyfriend, as he was supposed to.

'Where did she—' Will gulped. 'Where did she meet this new guy?'

'In Thailand. They bonded over dysentery or something.' He was beginning to regret having come up with the idea of Jonathan. 'It probably won't last,' he found himself saying.

'Do you think so?' Will asked, gazing longingly across at Kate, who was being pulled into Jonathan's arms on the dance floor. He had braced himself for this. Lorcan had warned him that Kate was bringing a man to the wedding, but nothing could have prepared him for the torture of seeing her with someone else.

'Holiday romance,' Freddie said dismissively. 'They never do.'

'Now would be a good time for that snog,' Jonathan whispered, as they swayed on the dance floor. 'Your bloke's watching.'

'Oh, you don't have to do that.'

'No problem.' He put a hand on the back of her neck as his lips met hers. 'All part of the service.'

He was a good kisser, and he certainly gave it his all, bending her back over his arm and kissing her on and on as they came to a standstill, apparently so wrapped up in each other that they were oblivious of their surroundings. But all the time Kate could feel Will's eyes burning into her back.

However, as they came off the dance floor, she saw that he wasn't watching her any more at all. He was engrossed in conversation with Freddie and didn't even seem to notice her as she passed.

Suddenly weary and depressed, Kate decided to go home. The party was in full swing and she was sure she could slip away unnoticed. She told Jonathan that she was leaving, then got her coat and left the hotel. It had been freezing all day and now it was snowing. She stood at the edge of the pavement trying to hail a cab, but with no success. She had forgotten it was New Year's Eve and that getting one would be nigh impossible.

'I hope you're not leaving because of me,' a deep voice said at her shoulder.

She spun around to find Will behind her, his breath a white cloud in the icy air.

'If you are, you can relax,' he said. 'I'm leaving now, so you can go back in and enjoy the party.'

As if by magic, a car appeared at the kerb at that moment, and Kate recognised Dave, the driver who had met her at the airport.

'Oh no, I wasn't.' Why did he make her feel so damn guilty? 'I think I will go back in, though. There's no chance of getting a cab anyway.'

'Wait!' As she turned to go, Will grabbed her wrist. 'We need to talk.'

'No, we don't.' She pulled her hand away. 'I have to go. My – um – my boyfriend wouldn't like me being out here with you.'

'Jealous type, is he?'

'Yes, as a matter of fact, he is.'

'Ditch him!' Will said, his eyes glinting.

'What?'

'Ditch him and come home with me.'

'And why on earth would I do that?'

'Because you don't love him – you love me,' he said.

Kate felt utterly defeated and exposed. She wasn't fooling anyone – he knew damn well she hadn't moved on.

'And I love you,' he said. He leaned almost imperceptibly closer, and for an awful, heart-stopping moment she thought he was going to kiss her.

Kate looked away, breaking the spell. 'Don't you have a concert to go to?' She eyed the car hovering in the background.

Will glanced distractedly at it, then back to her. 'Come with me,' he said urgently, grabbing her hand.

She shook her head, not trusting herself to speak.

'Come on, everyone would love to see you, and we could talk properly.'

'There's nothing to talk about,' she said tightly.

'I love you,' he pleaded despairingly. 'Why can't you believe that?'

Kate sighed. 'How long have we known each other, Will?' she asked rhetorically. 'And in all that time you've never looked twice at me – not in that way. Not until my mother and Rachel put the idea in your head.'

'Haven't I?' he said.

'No.' Surely he wouldn't have the gall to admit now that he remembered that night of the Trinity Ball, after all those years of pretending it had never happened.

'Are you sure about that?' he persisted. 'That night of the Trinity Ball?'

'Okay, maybe you did once,' she said. 'But you were out of your head – you didn't know what you were doing.'

'*In vino veritas*,' he said. 'They say you don't do anything drunk that you wouldn't do sober.'

'Then how do you explain karaoke?'

Will laughed. 'No one can explain karaoke.'

The snow was falling thicker and faster now, great chunks settling on Will's hair and shoulders. It melted on Kate's eyelashes and into her hair.

'Hadn't you better go?' She nodded to the car.

Will glanced at his watch. 'Come with me,' he pleaded.

'No.' She felt frozen to her core, and it had nothing to do with the snow.

'But I love you!'

'Do you?' She examined his face, longing to believe him. 'I don't know,' she said defeatedly. 'I guess I'd always be wondering if it was real. Maybe you would too.'

'Christ, nothing has ever felt more real in my entire life! What do I have to do to convince you?'

Kate looked at him yearningly, almost willing him to say something that would.

'I don't think you can,' she said sadly.

Will was on the verge of tears, she saw, or was it just the biting cold that made his eyes sparkle? He glanced at his car and waved to the driver.

Still he didn't move. 'I never got a chance to give you this,' he said, reaching into his coat pocket and pulling out a shiny red envelope.

'It's your Christmas present.'

Kate looked at it. 'I didn't get you anything,' she said, feeling mean. 'I didn't think—'

'Doesn't matter. I got it ages ago. Take it.' He thrust it at her.

Kate shook her head. 'Maybe you should give it to someone else.'

'It's not *for* someone else, it's for *you*. It wouldn't suit anyone else.'

'Thanks,' Kate said, in a small voice, reluctantly taking it from him.

'Aren't you going to open it?' Will asked.

'Later,' Kate said, putting it in her pocket. 'It's freezing.' She shivered. 'I'm going back inside.'

Just then, a miracle happened. A taxi with its light on turned into the street. Kate dashed to the edge of the pavement, waving frantically, and it stopped.

'Kate!' Will called, as she got in and slammed the door.

Heaving a sigh of relief as the taxi pulled away, Kate looked at the envelope in her hand, tempted to throw it away from her, as if it were a ticking bomb. Vouchers, she thought, turning it over in her fingers – what else would fit inside an envelope? Still, she couldn't help wondering why, if it was vouchers, he felt it wouldn't do for anyone else. Maybe they were for some boutique that only stocked 'outsize' clothing – like anything above a size ten, she thought wryly. Curious despite herself, she opened it.

Inside, there was just a card with an address written inside it and a key taped underneath. She stared at it, wondering what it meant. Suddenly she had goosebumps all over, which had nothing to do with the cold.

'Could we go to this address instead, please?' she asked the taxi driver, showing him the card.

She could hardly sit still as they made their way slowly through the city-centre traffic. Eventually, they pulled up outside a darkened building.

'That's it there, love,' the driver said, pointing. 'Are you sure you have the right address?'

'Yes,' she said shakily. 'I think so. Can you wait, please?' she asked, getting out, her legs so wobbly she wasn't sure they'd hold her up.

Her fingers were trembling as she turned the key in the lock. The door swung open, and she stepped into a dark room, fumbling around for a light switch. She found it – and felt as though she had walked into a dream. She was standing in a restaurant she had never been in before, yet she recognised it. It was *her* restaurant, exactly as she had always pictured it, down to the minutest detail – exactly as she had described it to Will that day in Tuscany. She walked into the kitchen, examining everything, laughing in amazed delight at every little touch.

'Hello?' a voice called, and she went back into the dining room. The taxi driver had followed her. 'I just wanted to make sure you were all right.'

'Oh yes, I'm fine, thanks,' Kate assured him, eyes bright with tears. Spotting a staircase in a corner of the room, she said, 'I just want to check something.'

She bounded up the stairs two at a time, pushed open the door at the top and stepped out onto the roof. She turned on a light switch by the door to discover she was in the prettiest little roof garden, with tables and chairs set among planters of shrubs. Big gas heaters were dotted around while fairy lights and coloured lanterns hung in the trees.

Kate stood, gazing in wonder, as the snow covered the tables like white linen.

'This is something else, isn't it?'

She hadn't been aware that the taxi driver had followed her up.

'So, it's going to be a restaurant. Is it yours?'

'Yes.'

'What are you going to call it?'

Kate swallowed the lump in her throat. There was only one explanation for all this. 'It's the Taj Mahal,' she said. She remembered standing at the Taj Mahal, admiring its breathtaking beauty, and someone beside her saying, 'Just think, this was all built for love.'

'Going to be an Indian restaurant, then, is it?'

'Oh no.' Kate laughed. 'Sorry – a private joke.'

'Well, maybe you'd better think of another name. Might be a bit misleading.'

Kate and the taxi driver went back downstairs, where she switched off the lights and locked the door.

'So, home now?' he asked, rubbing his hands as they got back into the cab.

'No, I've changed my mind. I want to go to the O2.'

'The Walking Wounded concert?' He glanced at her in his mirror as he pulled out into the traffic. 'Have you got a ticket?'

'No.'

The driver sucked his breath in through his teeth. 'I wouldn't bother going there if you haven't, love,' he said, sagely. 'They were like gold dust – sold out in about half an hour.'

'Oh, it's okay. I know the band.'

She hadn't even thought about the logistics of getting in. She just knew she needed to see Will. Her doubts about him had melted away as she stood on that roof terrace and she couldn't wait to tell him. She remembered the excitement in his face that morning when he had told her he was working on a new 'project'. This must have been it. And she remembered how bleak he had seemed tonight, that sad, haunted look back in his eyes. She wondered now how she could ever have doubted him.

Of course, the taxi driver was right. She couldn't get into the auditorium without a ticket, and her attempts to get through the stage door were met with a solid wall of resistance in the shape of two very burly and extremely conscientious security men. Her pleas that she knew the band were met with heard-it-all-before indifference.

'I'm a friend of Will Sargent's,' she pleaded, trying a new tack.

'Course you are, love,' one said patronisingly.

Of course, it wasn't very plausible. After all, any Walking Wounded fan would know Will's name – and if she really was a friend of his, why wasn't she on the guest list? No doubt they *had* heard it all before from crazed fans desperate to get backstage and into Owen's jocks.

'Can you *please* just let him know I'm here?' she begged. 'He'll want to see me.'

'Sorry.' He shook his head implacably.

'Look, love,' the other one was regarding her almost pityingly, 'it's New Year's Eve. You must have somewhere better to be than standing here arguing with us.'

348

'Yeah, you're not getting in, so why don't you go home?' the first one said, not unkindly.

Kate was aware of how pathetic she must look, shivering in the snow, all tricked out in her wedding finery like some weird groupie well past her use-by date. But she didn't care.

'What about Louise?' she persisted. 'Could you tell *her* I need to see her?'

'Louise?' The security men perked up at the mention of Louise – that wasn't a name with which the average fan would be familiar.

'I'm Kate O'Neill,' she said eagerly. 'Please just tell Louise I'm here. If she doesn't want to see me, I'll go away, I promise.'

The two men exchanged a look, then seemed to come to a decision, one nodding to the other. While one drew away to talk into a mobile, the other continued to block the door. Kate waited anxiously, but moments later, to her intense relief, Louise appeared. 'Kate!' She beamed, and the security guards stepped aside. 'It's really good to see you.' She hugged her, pulling her inside.

'Louise, I have to see Will,' Kate babbled.

'Good. I was hoping that was why you were here.' Louise smiled. 'Come on.' She began to lead Kate towards the backstage area. 'No, hang on a minute.' She came to an abrupt halt. 'I've got a better idea . . .'

Backstage, Will's mobile rang. Checking the display, he was surprised to see that it was Tina. 'Hi!'

'Don't sound so scared,' she said.

Will gave a wry laugh. 'I'm just . . . surprised, that's all.'

'I bet. Guess where I am!'

'I don't know – Cambodia?'

'No. Rehab!' she announced brightly.

'*Rehab*?'

'Oh come on, you're not that surprised, are you? Turns out the only person I was fooling was myself.'

'Well, I'm glad you're getting it sorted out. So, how's it going?'

'It's okay, actually,' she said, sounding surprised. There was a moment's silence. 'Anyway,' she began again, slightly awkward, 'one of the things they've been getting us to do here is to apologise to people we've hurt in the past and . . . well, I figured I owed you a call.'

For a moment Will was stunned into silence. Then he said, 'You don't owe me anything, Tina.'

'Really? I know I was a bit of a nightmare the past year or so.'

'I was no picnic myself.'

'I could say it was the coke but, well, I'm trying to accept responsibility for my behaviour these days,' she said ruefully. 'So, I'm sorry for being such a pain in the arse.'

'If anyone's apologising, it should be me. I'm sorry about the way things ended.'

'Oh, you weren't entirely to blame. I guess we both knew we were flogging a dead horse. It was my fault we hadn't called time on it long before. But you know me, letting go was never my strong point.'

'No,' Will laughed, 'it wasn't.'

'Let's say we're quits.'

'Okay – quits.'

Tina took a deep breath. 'So, how's old whatserface?' she said jauntily.

'*Kate* is fine – I think. I mean, she seems fine. I saw her earlier at Lorcan's wedding.'

'Oh! You're not—'

'We're not together, no. It . . . didn't work out.'

'Oh . . .' There was a long silence.

'This is where I should say I'm sorry to hear that,' Tina said eventually, 'but—'

'That's okay.'

'This forgiveness thing, well, it's kind of a learning curve.'

'You're doing great.'

Tina sighed. 'Well, I'd better go. I think there's a group hug or something at midnight. I'm not sure I can stand the excitement!'

Will laughed. 'It's good to hear from you, Tina,' he said, and meant it. 'You sound more like your old self.'

'Well, I'm getting there. Happy New Year, Will.'

'Happy New Year.'

The minute Kate entered the auditorium, the heavy thump of bass blasting from the amplifiers hit her like a punch to the gut. The atmosphere was electric. A vast sea of bodies writhed in ecstasy as

Owen and Rory wove around the stage and Phoenix's strong, spell-binding voice soared over the heads of the crowd. The beautiful, sexy creature that was Walking Wounded live was at its most thrillingly seductive.

A huge roar went up from the crowd as Owen played the opening chords of one of their most anthemic songs, and several thousand hands were raised to punch the air in unison. Kate was lowered carefully into the mosh pit by two of the security team – to howls of outrage from some of the throng, who stared at her with a mixture of curiosity and indignation. She smiled at them apologetically, feeling self-conscious. She was ludicrously overdressed for a rock-gig and was regretting having let Louise talk her into this. She should have gone backstage and met up there with Will, she thought, growing increasingly anxious as midnight approached. There seemed to be so much that could go wrong. Damn Louise and her sense of the dramatic.

Suddenly a clock replaced the faces of the band being projected on to the big screens and the countdown to midnight started, the crowd shouting 'TEN, NINE, EIGHT . . .'

Backstage, Will heard the countdown begin with a heavy heart. The start of another whole year without Kate, he thought. What was there to celebrate about that? She had looked so gorgeous today at the wedding – so gorgeous and so unhappy . . .

'THREE, TWO, ONE,' the crowd thundered. 'HAPPY NEW YEAR!'

The auditorium exploded in a riot of cheers as stardust and balloons floated down from the ceiling, showering everyone with coloured glitter. The band broke into a souped-up version of 'Auld Lang Syne', and everyone grabbed each other for New Year kisses. The audience cheered as Summer appeared from one side of the stage, shyly kissing Phoenix, and Louise appeared from the other, to receive a very enthusiastic embrace from Rory. Georgie hopped down from her drum riser and threw her arms around Owen, who gave her a brotherly kiss on the cheek.

'Okay,' Owen said into the microphone, holding up his hand for attention, 'there's one more member of the band who should be with us tonight. Without this guy, none of us would be here. So, please, give it up for Will Sargent!' he shouted, and the crowd cheered and whooped like mad.

'What's this?' Will said irritably to their tour manager, Roy, who was backstage with him. 'We didn't plan it.'

'I guess they want you to join them onstage.'

Will sighed. He wasn't in the mood for this. But Owen had the crowd chanting his name now, a rhythmic mantra, urging him onstage.

'Will! Will! Will!' they chanted in unison, led by Owen.

Bowing to the inevitable, Will plastered a professional smile on his face and marched on stage. The crowd erupted as he appeared, blinking in the spotlights. Though he had removed his jacket and bow tie, he was still rather over dressed in his wedding attire, and there were several wolf whistles, which he received with a self-deprecating smile.

'Oh, isn't he gorgeous?' the girl next to Kate squealed to her friend.

Owen threw his arm around Will, holding him in a firm grip as they stood facing the audience, preventing his escape.

'Ladies and gentlemen,' Owen said, into the microphone, 'everyone should have someone to kiss on New Year's Eve. We've all had a New Year kiss,' he indicated the band, to a roar of approval. 'You've all had a New Year kiss,' he waved at the audience, who hollered their assent. 'But poor Will here hasn't.'

'Awwww!'

'So, girls and boys, we're looking for a volunteer from the audience.'

The crowd went wild at this, hundreds of girls throwing their hands into the air, shrieking excitedly.

'For fuck's sake, Owen,' Will growled through clenched teeth, 'we're not doing panto!'

'Who'd like to give Will a New Year kiss?' Owen continued, blithely ignoring his protests.

Will struggled to maintain a good-humoured smile as Rory was despatched to pick someone out of the audience to kiss him. He'd paste Owen for this later – and anyone else who'd been involved in it, he thought, noticing the eager excitement on Louise's face.

Gosh, Will's really popular, Kate thought, dismayed as the girls around her jumped up and down excitedly. 'Me, me, me,' they squealed, stamping on her feet and elbowing her in the ribs as a beefy bouncer, guided by Rory, scanned her section of the mosh pit. Panicking that he wouldn't spot her among the ocean of bodies, Kate hopped up and down too, waving frantically at Rory. Then his eyes met hers, and he smiled. 'Her,' he said, pointing her out to the bouncer, whose thick, muscle-bound arm plunged into the throng. Kate reached out to him, but in the fray it was impossible for him to determine which flailing arm was attached to which girl and, to her horror, his big hand closed around the arm of the girl beside her, who grabbed him with a triumphant yelp.

'Hey!' Kate yelled in outrage. 'Hands off, he's mine.'

Fuelled by a huge surge of adrenalin, Kate whacked the other girl's arm until she was forced to let go, and she grabbed the bouncer's. Then, as if by magic, she was being lifted into the air, floating over the sea of bodies and landing on the stage beside Rory.

'Hi.' He grinned at her, eyes crinkling at the corners. 'I thought we'd lost you there for a minute. Lucky you've got such a mean left hook.'

'Oh God, I hope I didn't hurt that girl.' She glanced back into the mosh pit. She couldn't believe she'd lashed out like that.

'I'm sure she'll live. Now, go get him.'

Meanwhile, Will couldn't see what was going on at the other side of the stage, his view blocked by the clutch of security men involved in hauling the volunteer out of the mosh pit.

Better get it over with, he thought, bracing himself to give a polite peck on the cheek to whoever Rory had pulled out of the audience – probably some groupie who wanted to be onstage with Owen.

Then the bouncers dispersed, and he couldn't believe his eyes, because there, walking shyly across the stage towards him, was Kate. She ran the last few steps and threw herself into his arms.

He looked down at her, almost floored by the love in her eyes, which sparkled with pure happiness.

'I love you,' he said.

'I know. I'm sorry I didn't believe you.'

Then their lips met, and the crowd whooped as they kissed passionately while fireworks crashed around them.

'Oh my God! That was nearly me,' the girl the bouncer had grabbed initially moaned to her friend, rubbing her arm as she watched enviously.

'Don't be stupid!' her friend snapped. 'She was a total plant.'

'It's okay, boys and girls, I think they know each other already,' Owen was saying, as Will and Kate kissed, oblivious of the thousands watching.

Only when the band started playing the gorgeous, swirling guitar intro to a romantic ballad did they come up for air and realise that everyone else had left the stage and the gig was resuming.

'We've got work to do.' Rory grinned. 'Scram!'

Taking a playful bow to huge applause, they hurried offstage hand in hand.

'I love my Christmas present,' Kate said, as she stood in Will's arms at the side of the stage. 'I'm sorry I didn't get you anything.'

'I can think of a few ways you can make it up to me,' he said, kissing her again.

'Anything in particular you have in mind?'

'Actually, there is *one* thing – it's a lot to ask, though.'

'Is it very perverse?' Kate smiled mischievously.

'*Very.*'

'Have you ever done it before?'

'Never.'

'Couldn't find a girl willing to do it?'

'Never found a girl I wanted to do it with.'

'Do you think I'd like it?'

'I hope so. It'd mean a lot to me if you'd do it.'

'Okay then.' Kate shrugged.

'You don't even know what it is,' Will teased.

'So tell me.'

'Okay – but don't forget you've already said yes.'

'I won't back out.'

Will bent and whispered in her ear, and Kate gasped.

'That *is* perverse,' she said.

Just then her mobile rang. It was Freddie.

'Happy New Year, sweetie!'

'Happy New Year, Freddie!'

'Where the hell did you get to? I've been searching everywhere for you.'

'Actually, I'm onstage at the Walking Wounded gig.'

'Oh my God, you're with Will!' Freddie squealed. 'Thank Christ for that!'

'And, Freddie, I've got news for you. Are you sitting down?'

'I'm positively horizontal.'

'You're going to be a bridesmaid!'

Acknowledgements

I would like to thank the following people who helped in the writing and publication of this book.

My sisters, Trish and Emer, and my mother, who read the book in draft as a painfully slow serial. Their enthusiasm kept me going, and but for their constant nagging for the next instalment, I may never have got to The End.

My fellow writer and fairy godsister, Claire Allan, for waving her magic wand and telling me my book could go to the ball. Without her extraordinary generosity, it might still be locked in the cellar.

My wonderful agent, Ger Nichol, for loving it so much, and for always making me feel like a star.

My editor, Ciara Doorley, for seeing the wood for the trees, and for all her patience, hard work and commitment in toning up the manuscript.

Everyone at WriteWords for invaluable advice, support, encouragement and friendship.